THE CHRISTMAS
BABY BONUS

BY
YVONNE LINDSAY

MILLS &
BOON

HarperCollins
PUBLISHERS

First Published in Great Britain 2017
By Mills & Boon, an imprint of HarperCollins*Publishers*
1 London Bridge Street, London, SE1 9GF

© 2017 Dolce Vita Trust

ISBN: 978-0-263-92846-4

51-1217

Printed and bound in Spain
by CPI, Barcelona

A typical Piscean, *USA TODAY* bestselling author **Yvonne Lindsay** has always preferred her imagination to the real world. Married to her blind-date hero and with two adult children, she spends her days crafting the stories of her heart, and in her spare time she can be found with her nose in a book reliving the power of love, or knitting socks and daydreaming. Contact her via her website, www.yvonnelindsay.com.

To my wonderful friends,
who often know me better than I know myself.
In particular to Nalini, Nicky and Peta for
prompting (aka pestering) me to write this book
while I stared with loathing (yes, I'm a Grinch)
at a Christmas tree, and to Shar,
who couldn't make it that night
but who would have been pestering, ahem,
prompting me right along with them.

One

There, let that be the last tartan bow to be tied, Faye begged silently as she stood back and eyed the turned-wood balustrade that led to the upstairs gallery of the lodge. Swags of Christmas ribbon looped up the stairs, with a large tartan bow at each peak.

Not for the first time, she cursed the bad luck that had seen her boss's usual decorator fall off a ladder and dislocate her shoulder a week before Piers was due to arrive at his holiday home here in Wyoming for his annual Christmas retreat and weeklong house party.

Faye had suggested he go with a minimalistic look for the festive season this year, but, no, he'd been adamant. Tradition, he'd called it. A pain in the butt, she'd called it. Either way, she'd been forced out of her warm sunny home in Santa Monica and onto an airplane, only to arrive in Jackson Hole to discover weather better suited to a polar bear than a person. So, here she was. Six days away from Christmas, decorating a house for a bunch of people who probably wouldn't appreciate it. Except for her boss, of course. He loved this time of year with a childlike passion, right down to the snow.

She hated snow, but not as much as she hated Christmas.

She turned slowly and surveyed the main hall of the lodge. Even her late mother would have been proud, Faye thought with a sharp pang in her chest, before she pushed that thought very firmly away. The entire house looked disgustingly festive. It was enough to make a sane person want to hurl, she told herself firmly, clinging to her hatred of the season of goodwill. There was no reason to be sad about being alone for the holidays when she hated the holidays with a passion, right?

At least her task was over and she could head back to the sun, where she could hide in her perfectly climate-controlled apartment and lose herself in her annual tradition of binge-watching every *Predator* movie made, followed by every *Alien* DVD in her collection, followed by any other sci-fi horror flick that was as disassociated from Christmas as it was from reality.

She moved toward the front door where her compact carry-on bag was already packed and waiting for her retreat to normality and a world without decorations or Christmas carols or—

The front door swung open and swirl of frigid air preceded the arrival of her boss, Piers Luckman. Lucky by name and luckier by nature, they said. Only she knew what a hard worker he was beneath that handsome playboy exterior. She'd worked for him for the past three years and had the utmost respect for him as a businessman. And as a man...? A tiny curl of something unfurled deep inside her. Something forbidden. Something that in another person could resemble a hint of longing, of desire. Something she clamped down on with her usual resolute ferocity. No. She didn't go there.

Piers stomped the snow off his feet on the porch outside then stepped into the lobby and unslung his battered leather computer satchel from one shoulder.

"Good flight?" she asked, knowing he'd probably piloted the company jet himself for the journey from LA to Jackson Hole.

He had no luggage because he always kept a full wardrobe at each of his homes peppered around the world.

"Merry Christmas!" Piers greeted her as he saw her standing there and unzipped his down-filled puffer jacket.

Oh, dear mother of God, what on earth was he wearing underneath it?

"Weren't you supposed arrive on Saturday, the day before your party? You're four days early," she commented, ignoring his festive greeting. "And what, by all that's holy, is *that*?"

She pointed at the gaudy hand-knitted sweater he wore. The reindeer's eyes were lopsided, his antlers crooked and…his nose? Well, suffice to say the red woolen pom-pom was very…bright.

A breathtaking grin spread across Piers's face.

Faye focused her gaze slightly off center so she wouldn't be tempted to stare or smile in return. The man was far too good-looking, and she only remained immune to his charms because of her personal vow to remain single and childless. That aside, she loved her job and getting a crush on her boss would be a surefire way to the unemployment office.

After all, wasn't that what had happened to a long line

of her predecessors? It wasn't like he could help it if personal assistants, who had an excuse to spend so much time with him, often found him incredibly appealing. He was charming, intelligent, handsome and, even though he'd been born with a silver spoon lodged very firmly in that beautiful mouth, he wasn't averse to working hard, overseeing his empire with confidence and charisma. The only time Faye had ever seen him shaken had been last January, when his twin brother had died in a sky-diving accident. Since then he'd been somewhat quieter, more reflective than usual.

While Faye had often felt Piers had been a little on the cavalier side in his treatment of others—particularly his revolving door of girlfriends—he'd become more considerate over this past year. As if Quin's death had reminded him just how fleeting life could be. Even Lydia, his latest girlfriend, had been on the scene far longer than was usual. Faye had even begun to wonder if Piers was contemplating making the relationship a permanent one, but then she'd received the memo to send his usual parting gift of an exquisite piece of jewelry in a signature pale blue box along with his handwritten card.

It was purely for reasons of self-preservation that she didn't find him irresistible, and she was nothing if not good at self-preservation. Besides, if you didn't have ridiculous dreams of happy-ever-after then you didn't see them dashed, and you didn't get hurt—and without all of that, you existed quite nicely, thank you.

"This?" he said, stroking a hand across the breadth of his chest and down over what she knew, from working with him at his place on the Côte D'Azur where swimwear replaced office wear, was a tautly ripped abdomen. "It's my great-aunt Florence's gift to me this year. I have a collection of them. Like it?"

"It's hideous," she said firmly. "Now you're here, I can go. Is there anything else you need me to attend to when I get back to LA?"

Piers looked at his erstwhile PA. He'd never met anyone like Faye Darby, which was exactly why he kept her around. She intrigued him, and in his jaded world there weren't many who still had that ability. Plus, she was ruthlessly capable, in a way he couldn't help but admire. It might have been cruel to have sent her to decorate the house for him for the holidays—especially knowing she had such a deep dislike of the festive season—but it needed doing and, quite frankly, he didn't trust anyone else to do it for him.

And as to the sweater, although his late great-aunt Florence had knitted him several equally jaw-droppingly hideous garments in the past, the truth was that he'd seen this one in the window of the thrift store during his morning run and he'd fallen in love with it instantly, knowing exactly how much Faye would hate it. The donation he'd made to the store in exchange for the sweater was well worth the look on Faye's face when he'd revealed the masterpiece.

But now she was standing there, having asked him a question, and waiting for a response.

"I can't think of anything at the moment. Did you send the thank-you gift to Lydia?" he asked.

Another thing he probably should have dealt with himself, but why not delegate when the person you delegated to was so incredibly competent? Besides, extricating himself from liaisons that showed every sign of getting complicated was something best left to an expert. And, goodness knew, Faye had gained more than sufficient experience in fare-welling his lady friends on his behalf.

To his delight, Faye rolled her eyes. Ah, she was so easy to tease—so very serious. Which only made him work that much harder to get a reaction out of her one way or another.

"Of course I did," Faye responded icily. "She returned it, by the way. Do you want to know what she said?"

Piers had no doubt his latest love interest—make that ex-love interest—had been less than impressed to be dusted off with diamonds and had sent the bracelet and matching earrings back to the office with a very tersely worded note. Lydia had a knack for telling people exactly what she thought of them with very few words, and he would put money on her having told him exactly where he could put said items of jewelry.

He also had every belief that Faye agreed with Lydia's stance. The two women had gotten on well. Perhaps a little too well. He cringed at the thought of the two of them ganging up on him. He wouldn't have stood a chance. Either way, he would stick firm to his decision to cut her out of his life, although he'd had the sneaking suspicion that Lydia would not give up as easily as those who'd gone before her.

"No, it's okay, I can guess," he answered with a slight grimace.

"She isn't going to give up," Faye continued as though he hadn't spoken. "She said she understands you'd be getting cold feet, given how much you mean to one another and your inability to commit."

"My what?"

"She also said you can give the jewelry to her in person and suggested dinner at her favorite restaurant in the New Year. I've put it in your calendar."

Piers groaned. "Fine, I'll tell her to her face."

"Good. Now, if there's nothing else, I'll be on my way."

She was in an all-fired hurry to leave, wasn't she? He'd told her she was welcome to stay for his annual holiday house party, but Faye had looked at him as if she'd rather gargle with shards of glass.

"No, nothing else. Take care on the road. The forecasted storm looks as if it's blowing in early. It's pretty gnarly out there. Will you be okay to drive?"

"Of course," she said with an air of supreme confidence.

Beneath it, though, he got the impression that her attitude was one of bravado rather than self-assurance. He'd gotten to understand Faye's little nuances pretty well in the time she'd worked for him. He wondered if she knew she had those little "tells."

Faye continued, "The rental company assured me I have snow tires on the car and that it will handle the weather. They even supplied me with chains for the tires, which I fitted this morning."

"You know how to fit chains?" he asked and then mentally rolled his eyes. Of course she knew how to fit chains. She pretty much could do everything, couldn't she?

"You don't need to worry about me."

While she didn't ever seem to think *anyone* should worry about her, Piers was pretty certain he was the only person looking out for her. She had nobody else. Her background check had revealed her to be an orphan from the age of fifteen. Not even any extended family hidden in the nooks and crannies of the world.

What would it be like to be so completely alone? he wondered. Even though his twin brother had died suddenly last January, both his parents were still living and he had aunts and uncles and cousins too numerous to count—even if they weren't the kinds of people he wanted to necessarily be around. He couldn't imagine what it would be like to be so completely on your own.

She reached for her coat and Piers moved behind her to help her shrug it on, then Faye bent to lift her overnight case at the same time he did.

"I'll take it," she said firmly. "No point in you having to go back out in the cold."

Her words made sense but grated on his sense of chivalry. In his world, no woman should ever have to lift a finger let alone her own case. But then again, Faye wasn't of his world, was she? And she went to great pains to remind him of that. "Thanks for stepping into the breach and doing the house for me," he said as they hesitated by the door.

Faye gave one last look at the fully decorated great hall—her eyes lingered on the stockings for Piers's expected guests pinned over the fireplace, at the tree glittering with softly glowing lights and spun-glass ornaments—and actually shuddered.

"I'll leave you to it, then," she said with obvious relief.

It was patently clear she couldn't wait to get out of there.

"Thanks, Faye. I do appreciate it."

"You'd better," she warned direly. "I've directed the payroll office to give me a large bonus for this one."

"Double it, you're worth it," he countered with another one of his grins that usually turned women to putty in his hands no matter their age—women except for his PA, that was.

"Thank you," Faye said tightly as she zipped up the front of her coat and pulled up her hood.

He watched as she lifted her overnight case and hoisted the strap of her purse higher on her shoulder.

Piers held the door open for her. "Take care on the

driveway and watch out for the drop-off on the side. I know the surface has been graded recently but you can't be too careful in this weather."

"Trust me, careful is my middle name."

"Why is that, Faye?"

She pretended she didn't hear the question the same way he'd noticed she ignored all his questions that veered into personal territory.

"Enjoy yourself, see you next year," she said and headed for the main stairs.

Piers watched her trudge down the stairs and across the driveway toward the garage, and closed the front door against the bitter-cold air that swirled around him. He turned and faced the interior of the house. Soon it would be filled with people—friends he'd invited for the holidays. But right now, with Faye gone, the place felt echoingly empty.

The wind had picked up outside in the past couple of hours and Faye bent over a little as she made her way toward the converted stables where she'd parked her rental SUV. Piers hadn't seen fit to garage the Range Rover she'd had waiting for him at the airport, she noted with a frown, but had left the vehicle at the bottom of the stairs to the front door. *Serve him right if he has to dig it out come morning*, she thought.

It would especially serve him right for delivering that blasted megawatt smile in her direction not once but twice in a short space of time. She knew he used it like the weapon it truly was. No, it didn't make her heart sing and, no, it didn't do strange things to her downstairs, either. But it could, if she let it.

Faye blinked firmly, as if to rid herself of the mental image of him standing there looking far more tempting

than any man should in such a truly awful sweater—
good grief, was one sleeve really longer than the other?

Well, none of that mattered now. She was on her way
to the airport and then to normality. A flurry of snow
whipped against her, sticking wetly to any exposed
patches of skin. Had she mentioned how much she hated
snow? Faye gritted her teeth and pressed the remote in
her pocket that opened the garage door. She scurried
into the building that, despite being renovated into a six-
stall garage, was still redolent with the lingering scents
of hay and horses and a time when things around here
were vastly different.

Across the garage she thought she saw a movement
and stared into the dark recesses of the far bay before dis-
missing the notion as a figment of her imagination. Faye
opened the trunk of the SUV and hefted her overnight
bag into the voluminous space. A bit of a sad analogy
for her life when she thought about it—a small, compact,
cram-filled object inside an echoing, empty void. But she
didn't think about it. Well, hardly ever. Except at this time
of year. Which was exactly why she hated it so much.
No matter where she turned she couldn't escape the pain
she kept so conscientiously at bay the rest of the year.

An odd sound from inside the SUV made her stop in
her tracks. The hair on the back of her neck prickled and
Faye looked around carefully. She could see nothing out
of order. No mass murderers loitering in the shadows. No
extraterrestrial creatures poised to hunt her down and rip
her spine out. Nothing. Correction, nothing but the sudden howl of a massive squall of wind and snow. She really needed to get going before the weather got too rough
for her to reach the airport and the subsequent sanity her
flight home promised.

Stepping around the SUV to the driver's door, Faye

realized something was perched on her seat. Strange. She didn't remember leaving anything there when she'd pulled in two days ago, nor had she noticed anything amiss this morning when she'd come out to fit the chains on the tires in readiness to leave. Was this Piers's idea of a joke? His joy in the festive season saw him insist every year on giving her a gift, which every year she refused to open.

She moved a little closer and realized there were, in fact, two objects. One on her passenger seat, which looked like a large tote of some kind, the other a blanket-covered something-or-other shaped suspiciously like a baby's car seat. A trickle of foreboding sent a shiver down Faye's spine.

At the end of the garage, a door to the outside opened and then slammed shut, making her jump. What was going on? Then, from the back of the building, she heard a vehicle start up and drive away. Fast. She raced to the doorway in time to see a flicker of taillights as a small hatchback gunned it down the driveway. What? Who?

From her SUV she heard another sound. One she had no difficulty recognizing. If there was anything that made her more antsy than the festive season, it was miniature people. The sound came again, this time louder and with a great deal more distress.

Even though she'd seen the hatchback leaving, she still looked around, waiting for whomever it was who'd thought it funny to leave a child here to spring out and yell, "Surprise!" But she, and the baby, were alone. "This isn't funny anymore," she muttered.

It wasn't funny to start with, she reminded herself. The blanket covering the car seat began to move as if tiny fists and feet were waving beneath it. A slip of paper pinned to the blanket crackled with the movement. With her heart hammering in her chest, Faye gently tugged the blanket down.

The baby—a boy, she guessed by the blue knitted-woolen hat he wore and the tiny, puffy blue jacket that enveloped him—looked at her with startled eyes. He was completely silent for the length of about a split second before his little face scrunched up and he let loose a giant wail.

Nausea threatened to swamp her. No, no, no! This couldn't be happening. Every natural instinct in her body urged her to comfort the child, but fear held her back. The very thought of holding that small body to hers, of cupping that small head with the palm of her hand, of inhaling that sweet baby scent—no, she couldn't do that again.

Faye thought quickly. She had to get the baby inside where it was warm. Babysitting might not be the holiday break Piers had been looking forward to, but he would just have to cope with it. She reached out to jiggle the car seat, hoping the movement might calm the baby down, but he wasn't having it.

"Sorry, little man," she said, flipping the blanket back over him to protect him from the elements outside. "But you're going to have to go undercover until I can get you to the house."

The paper on the blanket rustled and Faye took a second to rip it free and shove it in her pocket. She could read it later. Right now she had to get the baby where the temperature was not approaching subzero.

Again she wondered who had left the baby there. What kind of homicidal idiot did something like that? In these temperatures, he'd have died all too quickly. Another futile loss in a world full of losses, she thought bleakly. Whoever it was had waited until she'd showed, though, hadn't they? What would they have done if she'd chosen to stay an extra night? Leave the child at the door and ring the doorbell before hightailing it down the driveway? Who would do something like that?

Whoever it was didn't matter right now, she reminded herself. She had to get the baby to the house.

Swallowing back the queasiness that assailed her, Faye hooked the tote bag over one shoulder and then hugged the car seat close to her body, her arms wrapped firmly around the edges of the blanket so it wouldn't fly away in the wind. She scurried across to the house, slipping a little on the driveway in shoes that were better suited to strolling the Santa Monica pier than battling winter in Wyoming, and staggered up the front stairs.

The baby didn't let up his screaming for one darn second. She didn't blame him. By the time she reached the front door, she felt like weeping herself. She dropped the tote at her feet and hammered on the thick wooden surface, relieved when the door swung open almost immediately.

"Car trouble?" Piers asked, filling the doorway before stepping aside and gesturing for her to enter.

"No," she answered. "Baby trouble."

Two

"Baby trouble?" he repeated, looked stunned.

"That's what I said. Someone left this in the garage. Here, take it."

Faye thrust the car seat into his arms and pulled the door closed behind them. Damn his eyes, he'd already started the Christmas carols collection. One thousand, two hundred and forty-seven versions of every carol known to modern man and in six different languages. She knew because she'd had the torturous task of creating the compilation for him. Seriously, could her day get any worse?

Piers looked in horror at the screaming object in his arms. "What is it?"

Faye sighed and rolled her eyes. "I told you. A baby. A boy, I'd guess."

She reached over and flipped down the blanket, exposing the baby's red, unhappy face.

Piers looked from the baby to her in bewilderment. "But who…? What…?"

"My thoughts exactly," Faye replied. "I don't know who, or what, left him behind. Although I suspect it was possibly the person I caught a glimpse of speeding away in a car down the driveway. For the record, no, I did not get the license plate number. Look, I have to leave him with you, I'm running late. Oh, by the way, he came with a note." She reached into her jacket pocket, pulled out the crumpled paper and squinted at the handwriting before putting the note on top of the blanket. "Looks like it's addressed to you. Have fun," she said firmly and turned to leave.

"You can't leave me with this," Piers protested.

"I can and I will. I'm off the clock, remember. Seriously, if you can't cope, just call up someone from Jackson Hole. I'm sure there'll be any number of people willing to assist you. I can't miss my flight. I have to go."

"I'll double your salary. Triple it!"

Faye shook her head and resolutely turned to the door. There wasn't enough money in the world to make her stay. With the baby's wails ringing in her ears and a look of abject horror on her playboy boss's face firmly embedded in her mind, she went outside.

Faye hadn't realized she was shaking until the door closed at her back. The baby's cries even made it through the heavy wood. Faye blinked away her own tears. She. Would. Not. Cry. Ignoring her need to provide comfort might rank up there with the hardest things she'd ever done, but at least this way no one would get hurt—especially not her. Piers had resources at his disposal; there were people constantly ready to jump at his beck and call. And if all else failed, there was always Google.

Stiffening her spine, she headed to the garage, got into her SUV and started down the drive. It might only be four in the afternoon, but with the storm it was already gloomy out. Despite the snow tires and the chains, nothing could get her used to the sensation of driving on a snow-and-ice-covered road. Nothing quite overcame that sickening, all-encompassing sense of dread that struck her every time the tires began to lose purchase—nothing quite managed to hold off the memories that came flooding back in that moment. Nothing, except perhaps the overpowering sense of reprieve when the all-wheel-drive kicked in and she knew she wasn't going to suffer a repeat of that night.

And then, as always, came the guilt. Survivor's guilt they called it. Thirteen years later and it still felt a lot more like punishment. It was part of why she'd chosen to live in Southern California rather than her hometown in Michigan or anyplace that got snow and ice in winter. It didn't make the memories go away, but sunshine had a way of blurring them over time.

The sturdy SUV rocked under the onslaught of the wind and Faye's fingers wrapped tight around the steering wheel. She should have left ages ago. Waiting a couple extra hours at the airport would have been infinitely preferable to this.

"Relax," she told herself. "You've got this."

Another gust rocked the vehicle and it slid a little in the icy conditions. Faye's heart rate picked up a few notches and beneath her coat she felt perspiration begin to form in her armpits and under her breasts. Damn snow. Damn Piers. Damn Christmas.

And then it happened. A pine tree on the side of the road just ahead toppled across the road in front of her. Faye jammed on the brakes and tried to steer to the side, but it was too late—there was no way she could avoid the impact. The airbag deployed in her face with a shotgun-like boom, shoving her back into her seat. The air around her filled with fine dust that almost looked like smoke, making her cough, and an acrid scent like gunpowder filled her nostrils.

Memories flooded into her mind. Of screams, of the scent of blood and gasoline, of the heat and flare of flames and then of pain and loss and the end of everything she'd ever known. Faye shook uncontrollably and struggled to get out of the SUV. It took her a while to realize she still had her seat belt on.

"I'm okay," she said shakily, willing it to be true. "I'm okay."

She took a swift inventory of her limbs, her face. A quick glance in the rearview mirror confirmed she had what looked like gravel rash on her face from the airbag. It was minor in the grand scheme of things, she told herself. It could have been so much worse. At least this time she was alone.

Faye searched the foot well for her handbag and pulled out her cell phone. She needed to call for help, but the lack of bars on her screen made it clear there was no reception—not even enough for an emergency call.

With a groan of frustration, she hitched her bag crosswise over her body and pushed the door open. It took some effort as one of the front panels had jammed up against the door frame, but eventually she got it open wide enough to squeeze through.

She surveyed the damage. There was no way this vehicle was going anywhere anytime soon, and unless she could climb over the fallen tree and make it down the rest of the driveway and somehow hail a cab at the bottom of the mountain, she was very definitely going to miss her flight.

She weighed her options and looked toward the house, not so terribly far away, where light blazed from the downstairs' windows and the trees outside twinkled with Christmas lights. Then she looked back down—over the tree with its massive girth, the snowdrifts on one side of the driveway and the sheer drop on the other.

She had only one choice.

Piers stared incredulously at the closed front door. She'd actually done it. She'd left him with a screaming baby and no idea of what to do. He'd fire her on the spot, if he didn't need her so damn much. Faye basically ran his life with Swiss precision. On the rare occasions something went off the rails, she was always there to right things. Except for now.

Piers looked at the squalling baby in the car seat and set it on the floor. Darn kid was loud.

He figured out how to extricate the little human from his bindings and picked him up, instinctively resting the baby against his chest and patting him on the bottom. To his amazement, the little tyke began to settle. And nuzzle, as if he was seeking something Piers was pretty sure he was incapable of providing.

Before the little guy could work himself up to more tears, Piers bent, lifted the tote his traitorous PA had dropped on the floor and carried it and the baby through to the kitchen.

Sure enough, when he managed to one-handedly wrangle the thing open, he found a premixed baby bottle in a cooler sleeve.

"Right, now what?" he asked the infant in his arms. "You guys like this stuff warm, don't you?"

He vaguely remembered hearing somewhere that heating formula in a microwave was a no-no and right now he knew that standing the bottle in a pot of warm water and waiting for it to heat wouldn't be quick enough for him or for the baby. On cue, the baby began to fret. His little hands curled into tight fists that clutched at Piers's sweater impatiently and he banged his little face against Piers' neck.

"Okay, okay. I'm new at this. You're just going to have to be patient a while longer."

With an air of desperation, Piers continued to check the voluminous tote—taking everything out and laying it on the broad slab of granite that was his kitchen counter.

The tote reminded him of Mary Poppins's magical bag with the amount of stuff it held—a tin of formula along with a massive stash of disposable diapers and a couple of sets of clothing. In the bottom of the bag he found a contraption that looked like it would hold a baby bottle. He checked the side and huffed a massive sigh of relief on discovering it was a bottle warmer. Four to six minutes, according to the directions, and the demanding tyrant in his arms could be fed.

"Okay, buddy, here we go. Let's get this warmed up for you," Piers muttered to his ungrateful audience, who'd had enough of waiting and screwed up his face again before letting out a massive wail.

Piers frantically jiggled the baby while following the directions to warm the bottle. It was undoubtedly the longest four minutes of his life. The baby banged his forehead against Piers's neck again. Oh, hell, he was hot. Did he have a fever? Piers felt the child's forehead with one of his big hands. A bit too warm, yes, but not feverish. He hoped. Maybe he just needed to get out of that jacket. But how on earth was Piers going to manage that? Feeling about as clumsy as if attempting to disrobe the baby while wearing oven gloves, Piers carefully wrestled the baby out of the jacket.

"There we go, buddy. Mission accomplished."

The baby rewarded him with a demanding bellow of frustration, reminding Piers that the time had to be up for warming the bottle. He lifted the bottle, gave it a good shake, tested it on his wrist and then offered it to the baby. Poor mite must have been starving; he took to the bottle as if his life depended on it. And it did, Piers realized. And right now this little life depended on him, too.

So where on earth had he come from?

Remembering the note Faye had left with him, Piers walked to the entrance of the house and shifted the blanket until he found the crumpled piece of paper. Carefully balancing the baby and bottle with one hand, he went to sit in the main room and read the note.

Dear Mr. Luckman,
It's time you took responsibility for your actions. You've ignored all my attempts to contact you so far. Maybe this will make you sit up and take notice. His name is Casey, he was born on September 10 and he's your son. I relinquish all rights to him. I never wanted him in the first place, but he deserves to know his father. Do not try to find me.

There was an indecipherable signature scrawled along the bottom. Piers read the note again and flipped the single sheet over to see if the author had left a name on the other side. There was nothing.

His son? Impossible. Well, perhaps not completely impossible, but about as highly unlikely as growing a market garden on the moon. He was meticulous about protection in all his relationships. Accidents like this did not happen to him. Or at least they hadn't, until now.

Piers did the mental math and figured, if he was the child's father, he had to have met the baby's mother around the New Year. He was always in Jackson Hole from before Christmas until early January and hosted his usual festivities around the twenty-fourth and on the thirty-first. But he'd been between girlfriends at the time and he certainly didn't remember sleeping with anyone.

The baby had slowed down on the bottle and he stared up at Piers with very solemn brown eyes. Eyes that were very much like Piers's own. His son? Could it somehow be true? Even as he mentally rejected the idea, he began to feel a connection to the infant in his arms. A connection that was surely as unfeasible as the idea that he was responsible for this tiny life.

The bottle was empty and Piers removed it from the baby's mouth. So now what?

Casey looked blissed out on the formula, the expression on his face making Piers smile as the baby blew a milky bubble. In seconds the infant was asleep. Piers laid the kid down on the couch and packed some pillows around him like a soft fortress. Then he got to his feet and reached for his phone. Someone in town had to know where the baby belonged. Because as cute as Casey was, he surely didn't belong to him.

He dialed the number for one of the café and bar joints in town, a place where the locals gathered to gossip by day and party and occasionally fight by night. If anyone knew anything about a new baby in town, it would be these guys. Except the call didn't go through. He checked the screen—no reception. He reached for the landline only to discover it was out of action, too.

"Damn," Piers cursed on a heavy sigh.

The storm had clearly grown a lot worse while he was occupied with his unexpected guest. Maybe he should go and check on the backup generator. He was just about to do so when he heard a knocking at the front door. Puzzled, as he wasn't expecting any of his guests for a few more days yet, he went across to open it.

"Faye? What happened to you?"

His eyes roamed her face as he took her arm and led her inside toward the warmth of the fireplace. She was pale and she had a large red mark on her face, like a mild gravel rash or something, and she shivered uncontrollably. Her jacket, which was fine for show but obviously useless in actual snowy conditions, was sodden, as were the jeans she wore, and her sneakers made a squelching sound on the floor tiles.

"A t-t-tree came d-d-down on the driveway," she managed through chattering teeth.

"You're going to have to get out of these wet clothes before you get hypothermic," he said.

"T-too late," she said with a wry grin. "I think I'm already th-there."

"Come on," he said leading the way to a downstairs bathroom. "Get in a hot shower and I'll get you something dry to put on. Where's your suitcase?"

"St-still in the b-b-back of the SUV," she said through lips tinged with blue.

"And the SUV?"

"It's stuck against the tree that came down across the drive about halfway down."

"Are you hurt anywhere other than your face?"

"A f-few bruises, maybe, b-but mostly just c-cold."

No wonder she looked so shocky. A crash and then walking back up the drive in this weather? It was a miracle she'd made it.

"Let's get you out of these wet things."

He reached for her jacket and tugged the zipper down. Chilled fingers closed around his hands.

"I-I can m-manage," she said weakly.

"You can barely speak," he answered firmly, brushing her hands away and tugging the jacket off her. "I'll help you get out of your clothes, that's all. Okay?"

Faye nodded, her hair dripping. Beneath her jacket, Faye's fine wool sweater was also soaked through and her nipples peaked against the fabric through her bra. He bent to undo the laces on her sneakers and yanked them off, then peeled away her wet socks. She had pretty feet, even though they were currently blue with cold and, to his surprise, she had tiny daisies painted on each of her big toes. Cute and whimsical, he thought, and nothing like the automaton he was used to in the office. Near her ankle he caught sight of some scar tissue that appeared to be snaking out from beneath her sodden jeans.

"We've got two options," Piers said as he reached for the button fly of her jeans. "The best way to warm you up is skin-to-skin contact, or a nice hot shower."

"S-shower," Faye said emphatically.

Piers smiled a little. So, she wasn't so far gone she couldn't make a decision. For that he could be thankful, even if the prospect of skin-to-skin contact with her held greater appeal than it ought to. At least the under-floor heating would help to restore some warmth to her frigid feet. He peeled the wet denim down her legs. He always knew she was slightly built but there was lean muscle there, too. As if she did distance running or something like that.

He'd always been a leg man and a twitch in his groin inconveniently reminded him of that fact. Now wasn't the time for those kinds of thoughts, he reminded himself firmly. But then he noticed her lower legs and the ropey scar tissue. Faye's hands had been on his shoulder, to help her keep her balance as he removed her jeans. Her fingers tightened against his muscles when he exposed her damaged skin.

"I can take it from h-here," she said, her voice still shaking with the effect of the cold.

"No, don't worry, I've got it," he insisted and finished pulling her jeans off for her.

No wonder she always wore trousers in the office. Those were some serious scars and she was obviously self-conscious about them. Still, they were the least of their worries right now. First priority was getting her warm again.

"Okay." He stepped away. "Can you manage the sweater and your underwear on your own? I'll get the shower running."

Faye nodded and began to pull her sweater up and over her head. For all that she lived in Los Angeles, she had the fairest skin of anyone he'd ever seen. And were those freckles scattering down her chest and over the swell of her perfect breasts? Suddenly disgusted with himself for sneaking a peek, Piers snapped his attention back to his task before she caught him staring, but he knew he'd never be able to see her in her usual buttoned-up office wear without seeing those freckles in the back of his mind.

The bathroom soon began to fill with steam and he turned to see Faye had wrapped a towel around herself, protecting her modesty. Even so, he couldn't quite rid himself of the vision of her as she'd pulled her sweater off. Of the slenderness of her hips and thighs and how very tiny her waist was. Of the scar across her abdomen that had told of a major surgery at some time. Of that intriguing dusting of freckles that invited closer exploration—

No, stop it! he castigated himself. *She's your PA, not your plaything.*

"Shower's all ready. Stay in there as long as you need. I'll be back with some clothes, then I'll warm up something to eat."

For a second he considered trekking down the drive to retrieve her suitcase, but that wasn't a practical consideration with both her and the baby needing his supervision. Which left him with the task of finding her something out of his wardrobe. An imp of mischief tugged his lips into a grin. Oh, yes, he knew exactly what he'd get her.

"You can't be serious!" Faye exclaimed as she came through the bathroom door. "Surely you could have found me something better than this to wear!"

Now that she was warm again she was well and truly back to her usual self.

Piers fought the urge to laugh out loud. She was swamped in the Christmas sweater he'd chosen for her out of his collection and the track pants ballooned around her slender legs. At least the knitted socks he favored while he stayed here didn't look too ridiculous, even if the heel part was probably up around her ankles. It was a relief to see her with some natural color back in her cheeks, though.

"You needed something warm." He shrugged. "I didn't have time to be picky. Besides, you look adorable."

Faye snorted. "I don't do adorable."

"Not normally, no," he agreed amicably. "But you have to admit you're warmer in those clothes than you would be in your own."

"Speaking of my own... Where are they?"

"In the dryer—except for your coat, which is hanging up in the mudroom."

Faye nodded in approval and looked around. "What have you done with the baby?"

As if on cue, a squawk arose from the sofa. A squawk that soon rose to a high-pitched scream that was enough to raise the hairs on the back of Piers's neck. He groaned inwardly. One problem solved and another just popped right back up. It was like playing Whac-A-Mole except a whole lot less satisfying.

"Well, aren't you going to do something?" Faye asked with a pained expression on her face.

"I was going to get you something to eat. Perhaps you could see to Casey."

"That's his name?"

Piers winced as the baby screamed again and he rushed over to the sofa to pick him up. The little tyke's knees were pulled up against his chest and his fists flailed angrily in the air. For a wee thing, he sure had bushels full of temper.

"According to the note, yes." He held the baby up against him, but Casey wouldn't be consoled. "What do I do now?"

"Why would you expect me to know?" his currently very unhelpful PA responded.

"Because..." His voice trailed off. He'd been about to say "because you're a woman," but saved himself in time. It was an unfair assumption to make. "Because you seem to know everything else," he hastily blurted.

"You deal with him. I'll go find us something to eat."

"Faye, please. What should I do?" he implored, jiggling Casey up and down and swaying on the spot. All things he'd seen other people do with babies with far greater success than he was currently experiencing. If he didn't know better, he'd think the child was in pain, but how could that be so?

Faye gestured to the empty bottle he'd left on the coffee table. "Did you burp him after you fed him?"

"Burp him?"

"You know, keep him upright, rub his back, encourage him to burp."

"No."

"Then he's probably just got gas in his stomach. Put a cloth or a towel on your shoulder and rub his back firmly. He'll come around."

"Like this?" Piers said, rubbing the baby's tiny little back for all he was worth.

"Yes, but you'll need a towel—"

Casey let out an almighty belch and Piers felt something warm and wet congeal on his shoulder and against the side of his neck. He fought a shudder, almost too afraid to look.

"—in case he spits up on you," Faye finished with a smug expression on her face.

If he didn't know better he'd have accused her of enjoying his discomfort, but, never one to let the little things get him down, Piers merely went through to the kitchen and grabbed a handful of paper towels to wipe off his neck and shoulder. His nostrils flared at the scent of slightly soured milk.

"Try not to let it get on his clothes if you can help it. Unless you want to bathe and change him, that is."

Yes, there was no mistaking the humor in her tone. Piers turned on her, the now silent baby cradled in one arm as he continued to dab at the moisture on his shoulder.

"You do know about babies," he accused her.

She shrugged in much the same way he had when she'd protested the clothing he'd given her. "Maybe I just know everything, like you said."

"Can you hold him for me while I go and change?"

"You could just get me something decent to wear and I can give you this abominable snowman back," she answered, tugging at the front of the sweater he'd given her. "Seriously, do you have an entire collection of these things?"

"Actually, I do. So, back to my question, can you hold him for me?"

"No."

She turned and walked away.

"Then what am I supposed to do with him?"

"Put him on a blanket on the floor or lay him on your bed while you get changed. Although, if you've fed him you might want to check his diaper before you put him on the bed. You wouldn't want anything to leak out on that silk comforter of yours."

Piers shuddered in horror. "Check his diaper? How does one do that?"

Faye sighed heavily and turned to face him. "You really don't know?"

"It doesn't fall under the category of running a Fortune 500 company and keeping thousands of staff in employment. Nor does it come under the banner of relaxing and enjoying the spoils of my labors," he answered tightly. "Seriously, Faye. I need your help."

A look of reluctant resignation crossed her dainty features. "Fine," she said with all the enthusiasm of a pirate about to walk the plank into shark-infested waters. "Give him to me, go get changed and come straight back. I'll give you a lesson when you're ready."

Faye reluctantly accepted the infant as Piers handed him over and was instantly forced to quell the instinctive urge to hold him close and to nuzzle the fuzz on the top of his head. Instead she walked swiftly over to the Christmas tree, where there were more than enough ornaments and sparkling lights to hold his attention until Piers returned.

She could do this, she told herself firmly. It was just a baby. And she was just a woman, whose every instinct compelled her to nurture, to protect, to care. Okay, so that might have been the old Faye, she admitted. But the reinvented Faye was self-sufficient and completely independent. She did not need other people to find her joy in life, and she was happier with everyone at a firm distance. She did what she could on a day-to-day basis to ensure Piers's life ran smoothly, both in business and personally, and that was where her human interactions began and ended. She did not need people. Period. Especially little people, who in return needed you so much more.

"You look comfortable with him. Has he been okay?"

Faye hoped Piers hadn't seen her flinch at the unexpected sound of his voice. Give the man an inch and he took a mile. No wonder it had become her personal mission to stay on top of their professional relationship every single day.

"What? Did you expect me to have carved him up and cooked him for dinner?"

Piers cocked his head and looked at her. "Maybe. You don't seem too thrilled to be around him."

Faye pushed the child back into his arms. "I'm not a baby person."

"And yet you seemed to know what was wrong with him before."

Faye ignored his comment.

Of course she knew what was likely wrong with little Casey. Hadn't she helped her mom from the day she'd brought little Henry home from the hospital? Then, after the accident, hadn't she spent three years in foster care, assisting her foster mom as often as humanly possible with the little ones as some way to assuage the guilt she felt over the deaths of her baby brother, her mom and her stepdad? Deaths she'd been responsible for. Hadn't her heart been riven in two as every baby and toddler had been adopted or returned to their families, taking a piece of her with them every time? And still the guilt remained.

"Knowing what to do and actually wanting to do it are two completely different things," she said brusquely. "Now, you need to learn to change his diaper. By the way, did that note explain who he belongs to?" She switched subjects rather than risk revealing a glimmer of her feelings.

"Me, apparently. Although I have my doubts. Quin was here at the time he was likely conceived. Casey could just as easily be his."

More likely be his, Faye thought privately. While Piers was a wealthy man who enjoyed a playboy lifestyle when he wasn't working his butt off, his identical twin brother had made a habit of taking his privileged lifestyle to even greater heights—and greater irresponsibility—always leaving a scattering of broken hearts wherever he went. Faye could easily imagine that he might have been casual enough to have left a piece of himself here and moved on to his next conquest with not even a thought to the chaos he may have left behind. Still, it didn't do to think ill of the dead. She knew Piers missed his brother. With Quin's death, it had been as though he'd lost a piece of himself.

"What do you plan to do?" she asked.

"Keep him if he is my son or Quin's."

"What if he's not?"

"Why would his mother have any reason to bring him here if he wasn't?"

She had to admit he had a good point, but she noticed he'd dodged her question quite neatly. Almost as neatly as she might have done in similar circumstances.

"How long do you think it'll be before the phones are back up and we can get some help to clear the driveway?"

"A day. Maybe more. Depends on how long before the storm blows over, I guess."

"A few days! Don't you have a satellite phone or a backup radio or *something*?"

Faye began to feel a little panicked. Being here alone with her boss wasn't the problem. They had a working relationship only and she would never presume to believe she came even close to his "type" for anything romantic, not that she wanted that, anyway. But alone with him and a baby? A baby that even now was cooing and smiling in her direction while Piers held it? That was akin to sheer torture.

Three

"No, no radio."

"Well, I plan to get right on that as soon as I get home. You can't be stranded here like this. In fact, I'm not sure how an event like this is even covered under your protection insurance for the firm."

"Faye, relax," Piers instructed her with a wry grin. "We're hardly about to die."

"I am relaxed."

"No, you're not. You know, to be honest, I don't think I've ever seen you relaxed."

"Of course you have. I'm always relaxed at work."

His brows lifted in incredulity. "Seriously?"

"Seriously," she affirmed, averting her gaze from his perfectly symmetrical face with its quizzical expression and the similar expression on the infant so comfortable in his arms. For a man who had no experience with babies, he certainly looked very natural with this one.

Fay willed her heart rate back to normal. Right, so they had no external communication. It wasn't her worst nightmare, but with a baby on hand it came pretty darn close. What if something went wrong and they needed medical assistance? What if—

The lights flickered.

"What was that?" she demanded.

"Just a flicker, that's all. It's perfectly normal, considering the weather. How about you show me how to do this diaper thing?"

"Diaper. Yes. Okay. Fine." Faye looked around the room, searching for the tote bag. "Where's the bag with his things?"

"It's in the kitchen," Piers said.

"Great."

Faye marched in the direction of the kitchen and retrieved what she—correction, what Piers—would need, and detoured past the massive linen closet near the housekeeper's quarters for a thick towel to lay the baby on. She wondered what Meredith, Piers's housekeeper, would think of the situation when she arrived. When she actually could arrive, that was. Faye felt a flutter of panic in her chest again. She thought she'd overcome her anxiety issues years ago, but it was a little daunting to realize that all it took was being stranded with her boss and a baby and they all came flooding back.

"Okay," she said on her return to the main room. "Pick a nice, flat spot and lay the towel down, double thickness."

Piers took the towel from her and did as she instructed, spreading it with one hand on the sofa where he'd put Casey to sleep earlier.

"Good," Faye said from her safe distance at the end of the couch. "Open the wipes container and put it next to where you'll be working, then lay him down on the towel and undo the snaps that run along the inside of the legs of his onesie."

"Okay, that's not so bad so far," Piers said.

"Keep one hand on his tummy. It's a good habit to get into so when he starts to wriggle more, or roll over, he's less likely to fall and hurt himself."

"How *do* you know this stuff?" Piers asked, doing what he was told and looking up at her. "Jokes aside, I didn't see anything about baby wrangling in your résumé."

Faye ignored the question. Of course she did. She wasn't about to launch into the bleeding heart story of her tragic past. The last thing she wanted from Piers was pity.

The last thing? What about the first? a tiny voice tickled at the back of her mind.

There was no first, she told herself firmly.

"Now, do you see the tapes on the sides of his diaper? Undo them carefully and pull the front of the diaper down and check for—"

A string of expletives poured from Piers's lips. "What on earth? Is that normal?"

Faye couldn't help it. She laughed out loud. As if he knew exactly what she found so funny—and he probably did—Casey gurgled happily under Piers's hand.

"I'm sorry," she said, getting herself back under control. "I shouldn't laugh. Yes, it's entirely normal when a child is on a liquid-only diet. His gut is still very immature and doesn't process stuff like an older child begins to. Watch out, though, don't let his feet kick into it."

She continued with her instructions, stifling more laughter as Piers gagged when it came to wiping Casey's little bottom clean. But that was nothing compared to his reaction to the water fountain the baby spouted right before he got the clean diaper on.

Faye couldn't quite remember when she had last enjoyed herself so much. Her usually suave and capable boss—the lady slayer, as they called him in the office—was all fingers and thumbs when it came to changing a baby.

Eventually the job was done and Piers sat back on his heels with a look of accomplishment on his face.

"You do realize you're probably going to have to do this about eight to ten times a day, don't you?" Faye said with a wicked sense of glee. "Including at night if he doesn't sleep through yet."

"You're kidding me, aren't you? That took me, how long?"

"Fifteen minutes. But then, you're a newbie at this. You'll get faster as you get used to it."

"No way. There aren't enough hours in a day."

"What else were you planning to do with your time? It's not like you were planning to work this week."

"Entertain my guests, maybe?"

"If we can't get out, they can't get in," Faye reminded him, ignoring the little clench in her gut at the thought.

She hated the idea of being trapped anywhere, even if it was in a luxury ten-bedroom lodge in the mountains.

"True, but I expect once the storm blows through we'll have the phones back, mobiles if not the landline, and we can call someone to come and clear the road and retrieve your car."

"And then I can head back home," she said with a heartfelt sigh.

"And then you can head home," Piers agreed. He balanced Casey standing on his thighs, smiling at him as Casey locked his knees and bore his weight for a few seconds before his legs buckled and he sagged back down again.

"Why do you hate Christmas so much, Faye?"

"I don't hate it," she said defensively.

"Oh, you do."

Piers looked her square in the eye and Faye shifted a little under his penetrating gaze. Against the well-washed wool of the snowman sweater her bare nipples tightened and she felt her breath hitch in her chest.

No, she wasn't attracted to him. He wasn't at all appealing as he sat there wearing a mutant Rudolph sweater and cuddling a tiny baby on his lap as if it was the most natural thing in the world. The lights flickered again.

"I'd better find some flashlights. Where do you keep them?"

"In the kitchen, I suppose. Usually, Meredith takes care of all that," he answered, referring to the housekeeper who'd been due to arrive this evening.

Overhead, the lights dimmed again before going right out. Faye shot to her feet.

"It's dark!" she blurted unnecessarily.

"Let your eyes adjust. With the fire going we'll be able to see okay in a minute," Piers soothed her.

Faye felt inexplicably helpless and that was something she generally avoided at all cost. Not being in control or being able to direct the outcome of what was going on around her was the tenth circle of hell as far as she was concerned. Where was her mobile? She had a flashlight app she could use. Better yet, she could use Piers's. His was undoubtedly closer.

"Give me your phone," she demanded.

"No reception, remember?" he drawled.

She could just make out that he was still playing with the baby, who remained completely unfazed by this new development. Mind you, after being abandoned by your mother, facing a power outage was nothing by comparison in his little world.

"It has a flashlight function, remember?" she sniped in return.

Piers stood, reached into his pocket and handed her the phone.

It held the warmth of his body and she felt that warmth seep into the palm of her hand, almost as intensely as if he'd touched her. She swapped the phone into her other hand and rubbed her palm over the soft cotton of the track pants, but it did little to alleviate the little tingle that warmth had left behind. The realization made her exhale impatiently.

"Faye, they'll get the power back on soon, don't worry. Besides, I have a backup generator. I'll get that going in a moment or two. In the meantime, relax—enjoy the ambience."

Ambience? On the bright side, at least the Christmas lights were also out and the carols were no longer playing. Okay, she could do ambience if she had to.

"I'm not worrying, I'm making contingency plans. It's what I do," she replied.

After selecting the right app on his phone, she made her way into the kitchen and searched the drawers for flashlights. Uttering a small prayer of thanks that Meredith was such an organized soul that she not only had several bright flashlights but spare bulbs and batteries, as well, Faye returned to the main room. Piers was right, with the firelight it didn't take long for her eyes to adjust to the cozy glow that limned the furnishings. But the flickering light reminded her all too quickly of another time, another night, another fire—and the screams that had come with it.

Forcing down the quiver juddering through her, Faye methodically lined up the flashlights on the coffee table, then sat.

"I guess you're not a fan of the dark, either, then?" Piers commented casually, as if they'd been discussing her likes and dislikes already.

"I never said that. I just like to be prepared for all eventualities."

In the gloom she saw Piers shrug a little. "Sometimes it pays to live dangerously. To roll with the unexpected."

"Not on my watch," she said firmly.

The unexpected had always delivered the worst stages of her life, and she'd made it her goal to never be that vulnerable to circumstances again. So far, she'd aced it.

Across from her, Piers chuckled and the baby made a similar sound in response.

"He seems happy enough," Faye observed. What would it be to have a life so simple? A full tummy, a nap and clean diaper, and all was well with the world. But the helplessness? Faye cringed internally. No, she was better off the way she was. An island. "What are you going to do with him?" she asked.

"Aside from keep him?" Piers asked with a laconic grin. "Raise him to be a Luckman, I guess. According to the note, he's mine."

Faye shot to her feet again. "We both know that's impossible. You weren't even going out with anyone around the time he was conceived. You'd broken up with Adele and hadn't met Lydia yet. Unless you had a casual hookup over the Christmas break?"

Piers snorted. "I can't believe you know exactly who and when I was going out with someone."

"Of course I keep track of those details. For the most

part I've had a closer relationship with any of those women than you have, remember?"

"I do remember, and you're right. I wasn't with anyone, in any sense, that holiday."

"Then why would his mother say he's yours? Surely she knew who she slept with that holiday?"

Or had she known?

Piers's twin had been at the lodge since before that New Year's Eve when Piers had flown to LA for two days to countersign a new deal he'd been waiting on. While Quin had always been charming enough, he'd very clearly lacked the moral fiber and work ethic of his slightly older twin. Faye privately thought part of Quin's problem was that everything in his life had come too easily to him—especially women—and that had left him jaded and often cynical. Not for the first time she wondered if he'd masqueraded as his brother sometimes, purely for the nuisance factor. And this baby development was nothing if not a nuisance.

"If we ever track her down, I'll make sure to ask her," Piers said with a wry twist to his mouth. "We don't have much to go on, do we?"

No, they didn't. Faye made a mental note to add speaking to their private investigators to her to-do list the moment she returned to civilization.

Piers shifted Casey into the crook of his arm and the baby snuggled against him, his little eyes drifting closed again. The picture of the two of them was so poignantly sweet it made Faye want to head straight out into the nearest snowdrift and freeze away any sense of longing that dared spark deep inside her.

She moved toward the fireplace and put her hands out to the flames.

"Still cold?" Piers asked.

"Not really."

"I should get that food I promised you."

"No, it's okay. I'll get it. You hold the baby," she said firmly and grabbed a flashlight from the table. "I'll be back in a few minutes."

Piers watched her scurry away as if the hounds of hell were after her. Why was his super-efficient PA so afraid of babies? It was more than fear, though, he mused. On the surface, it appeared as if she couldn't bear to be around the child, but Piers wasn't fooled by that. He hadn't doubled the family's billion-dollar empire by being deceived by what lay on the surface. His ability to delve into the heart of matters was one of his greatest strengths, and the idea of delving into Faye's closely held secrets definitely held a great deal of appeal.

Casey was now fast asleep in his arms. He settled the baby down inside the cushion fort he'd created earlier and covered him with his blanket. As Piers fingered the covering—hand-knitted in the softest of yarns—he wondered if the baby had other family who cared about him. Family who might be wondering where he was and who was caring for him.

While Piers projected the image of a lazy playboy, beneath the surface he had a quick mind that never stopped working. It frustrated him that there was nothing further he could do to solve the question of how Casey had come to be delivered to his door.

But he could certainly delve a little deeper into Faye's apparent phobia when it came to infants. She intrigued him on many levels. Always had. He'd always sensed she bore scars, emotional if not physical, because she was so locked down. But now he knew she had scars on her body, too, and suddenly he wanted to know why. Were the two linked? And how did she know her way around a diaper bag so well?

Satisfied the baby was safe where he was placed, Piers rose and made his way through to the kitchen, where he could hear Faye clattering around. From the scent that tweaked his nostrils, she'd found one of Meredith's signature rich tomato soups in the freezer and was reheating it on the stove top, tiny blue flames dancing merrily beneath the pot. Ever resourceful, she'd lit some candles and placed them in mason jars to give more light.

Faye was in the middle of slicing a loaf of ciabatta and sprinkling grated cheese onto the slices when she became aware of his presence.

"Bored with the baby already?"

"He's asleep, so I thought I'd come and annoy you instead."

"It takes a lot to annoy me."

"Casey seemed to manage it," Piers said succinctly, determined to get to the root of her aversion to the infant.

"He doesn't annoy me. I'm just not a baby person," she said lightly, turning her attention back to putting the tray of sliced bread and cheese under the broiler. "Not every woman is, you know."

"Most have a reason," he pressed. "What's yours?"

Sometimes it was best to go directly to the issue, he'd found. With Faye, it was fifty-fifty that he'd get a response. Tonight, it seemed, he was out of luck.

"Did you want a glass of wine with the meal?" she asked, moving to the tall wine fridge against the wall.

"No, thanks, but go ahead if you want one."

She shook her head. Piers watched her move around the kitchen, finding everything she needed to set up trays for them to eat from. He'd always appreciated her competence and reliability, but right now he wished there was a little less polished professionalism and little more about her that was forthcoming. Like, who was she really? How did she get to be so competent around babies and yet seem to detest them at the same time? No, *detest* was too strong a word. It had been fear in her eyes, together with a genuine need to create distance between her and little Casey.

"Are you scared of him?" Piers asked conversationally. "I can understand if you are. I was always terrified that I'd drop a baby if I ever had to hold one."

"You? Terrified?" she asked, raising a skeptical brow at him as she turned from checking the bread under the broiler.

Under the candle glow, he could see the hot air had flushed her cheeks and was reminded again that Faye was a very attractive woman. Not that he was into her or anything. *Liar*, said the small voice at the back of his head. Half of her appeal had always been her looks, the other half had been her apparent immunity to his charms. It didn't matter what he said, did or wore—or didn't wear—she remained impervious to him. She also wasn't in the least sycophantic—and not at all hesitant to bluntly tell him when his ideas or demands were outrageous or unreasonable.

He realized she'd managed to deflect the question away from herself again.

"You're very good at that, you know," he commented with a wry grin.

"What, cheese on toast?" she answered flippantly, presenting her back to him as she bent to lift the tray of toasted golden goodness from the oven. Faye began piling the cheese toast slices onto a plate on his tray, taking only two small bits for herself.

No wonder she was so slender. She barely ate enough to keep a bird alive.

"I meant your ability to avoid answering my questions."

"Did you want cream in your soup?"

And there she went again. She was so much better at this than him, but he was nothing if not tenacious.

"Faye, tell me. Are you scared of babies?"

She sighed heavily and looked up from ladling out the steaming, hot soup into bowls.

"No. Did you want cream or not?"

He acceded. "Fine, whatever."

As with everything Faye did, she paid meticulous attention to presentation, and he watched with amusement as she swirled cream into his bowl and then, using a skewer like some kind of soup barista, created a snowflake pattern in the cream before sprinkling a little chopped parsley on top and setting the bowl on his tray.

"That's cute. Where did you learn to do that?"

"Nowhere special," she said softly. But then a stricken expression crossed her face and she seemed to draw herself together even tighter. Her voice, when she spoke, held a slight tremor. "Actually, that's not true. I learned it as a kid."

She bit her lower lip, as if she'd realized she'd suddenly said too much.

Piers pressed home with another more pointed question. "From your mom?"

She gave a brief, jerky nod of her head.

Piers sensed the memory had pained her and regretted having pushed her for a response. But he knew, better than most people realized, that sometimes you had to endure the pain before you could reap the rewards. Oh, sure, he'd been born into a life of entitlement and with more money at his disposal while he was growing up than any child should ever have. Most people thought he had no idea as to the meaning of suffering or being without—and maybe, on their scale, he didn't. Yet, despite all of the advantages his life had afforded him, he knew what emptiness felt like, and right now he could see a yawning emptiness in his PA's eyes that urged him to do something to fill it.

But how could a man who had everything, and yet nothing at the same time, offer help to someone who kept everyone beyond arms' length?

Something hanging from the light fitting above Faye's head caught his eye. Mistletoe. Before he knew it, Piers was rising and taking her in his arms. Then he did the one thing he knew he did better than any man on earth. He kissed her.

Four

Shock rippled through her mind, followed very closely by something else. Something that offered a thrill of enticement, a promise of pleasure. Piers's lips were warm and firm, and the pressure of them against hers was gentle, coaxing.

Even though her mind argued that this was wrong on so many levels, a piece of her—deep down inside—unfurled in the unexpected warmth and comfort his kiss offered. Comfort, yes, and another promise layered beneath it. One that told her that *she* decided what happened next. That she could take this wherever she wanted to.

In her bid to protect herself from further emotional pain, she'd always kept her distance from people. She knew how much it hurt to lose the ones you loved—how it had torn her apart and left her a devastated shell. How her attempts to fill that emptiness had only left her hurting all over again. How she'd shored up her personal walls until nothing and no one could get back inside into the deepest recesses of her heart ever again. And yet, here she was, being kissed by the man she worked for and *feeling* emotions she'd been hiding from for years. Wanting more. It was exhilarating and terrifying in equal proportions.

Even as Faye's mind protested, her body reacted. Her heart rate kicked up a beat. An ember of desire flickered to molten life at her core. Oh, sure, she'd been kissed before, but nothing in her limited experience had prepared her for this onslaught of need and heat and confusion.

Finally her mind overruled her body, reminding her that this was not just any man in any situation. This was her boss. In his house. With a baby in the next room.

Faye put a hand against Piers's chest, her palm tingling at the heat that radiated from behind his shirt—at the firmly muscled contours that lay beneath the finely woven linen. Her fingers curled into the fabric, ever so briefly, before she flattened her palm and pushed against him.

To his credit, he reacted immediately—stepping back with a slightly stunned expression in his eyes for a moment before it was masked. If she hadn't seen that brief glimpse in his eyes, seen the shock that had briefly mirrored her own reflected there, she would have believed the good-guy smile that now curved those wicked lips and seemed to say that the kiss had been no big deal.

Faye fought to calm her rapidly beating heart—to not betray even an inkling of the chaos that rattled through her mind over what had just happened. She bent her head to avoid looking at him, to avoid betraying just how much she'd enjoyed that kiss. She took in a deep breath and chose her words very deliberately.

"If you want me to continue to work for you, that had better be the last time you ever do something like that to me," she said in a voice that was surprisingly even. "Here, your tray is ready."

She picked up the tray with his supper and handed it to him, then turned away to finish preparing her own.

"Faye, I—"

"Really, there's no need to rehash it. Or apologize, if that's what you were thinking. Let's just drop it, hmm?"

"For the record, I do want you to keep working for me."

"Good, then there won't be a repeat of that, then."

"Was it so awful?" he asked, a glimmer of uncertainty flickering briefly in his dark brown eyes.

"I thought we agreed not to rehash it."

"Actually *we* didn't agree on anything. But, fine, if you don't want to talk about it, we won't talk about it."

Had she offended him? That hadn't been her intention...but if it meant he wouldn't do something as insane as try to kiss her again, that was a very good thing. Wasn't it? Of course it was. And he wasn't the kind of guy to carry a grudge. It was one of things she'd always admired about him.

Faye finished fussing over her tray and checked that the stove was turned off.

"Let me take that for you," Piers said, easily balancing his tray on one hand while sliding hers off the countertop with his other. "You can lead the way with the flashlight."

He was laughing at her. Oh, not in any obvious way, but she sensed the humor that hovered beneath the surface of his smooth demeanor. What she'd said had actually amused him rather than offended him, she was certain.

Determined to avoid too much further interaction, she decided the best course of action was to do as he'd suggested rather than fight over her tray. It wasn't as if they had far to walk, and if she chose one of the deep armchairs to sit in by the fire she wouldn't have to sit next to him.

By the time she was settled in the chair, with her tray on her lap, she was back to thinking about that kiss and the man who'd chosen the seat opposite her.

The glow of the fireplace cast golden flickers of light and contrasting shadows across his face, highlighting the hollows beneath his cheekbones and the set of his firm jaw. He'd lost some weight this past year, since the death of his twin. She was shocked to realize she hadn't noticed until now. She'd been too busy avoiding letting her eyes linger on any part of him. In simply taking instructions, preempting others and basically just doing her job to the best of her ability. For a personal assistant, though, she'd hadn't paid much attention to the actual personal side of Piers Luckman.

Oh, sure, she'd organized his social calendar, ensured none of his engagements clashed, seen off unwelcome interest from women who saw him as a short road to a comfortable future and, more recently, forwarded his farewell gift to the girlfriend who'd stuck longer than so many others.

But even though she'd done most of the coordination for Quin Luckman's funeral, she hadn't offered more than the usual cursory expression of sympathy to his twin. How had it felt for him, losing that half of himself that had been there from conception? She'd been so locked under her own carapace of protection that she'd rendered herself immune to his grief once the initial shock of Quin's death had blunted.

And why on earth was she even worrying about it? It wasn't as if he was about to lay his sorrow at her feet now that he'd kissed her. Without thinking, she pressed her lips together, catching her lower lip between her teeth in an unconscious effort to relive the pressure of his lips on hers. The clatter of a spoon on an empty bowl dragged her attention back to the man sitting opposite and a flush of embarrassment swept across her cheeks.

"That was good. Remind me to thank Meredith for having the foresight to lay in such tasty supplies."

"I'll do that," Faye said, reaching automatically for the small tablet that she kept in her bag to note his command immediately.

"Faye, I'm kidding. You're off the clock, remember?"

His voice held that note of humor again and it made the back of her neck prickle. She looked him squarely in the eye.

"You don't pay me to be off the clock. Besides, I'll just call this overtime."

Piers sighed, a thread of frustration clear in the huff of air he expelled. "You can relax, Faye. On or off the clock, I'm glad you're here."

He cast a glance at the sleeping baby and even with the shadows she could see the concern that played across his features. She felt compelled to reassure him.

"He'll be fine, you know. You're doing a good job with him so far."

"I can't help feeling sorry for him. His mother abandoning him. His father gone." Piers's voice broke on the last word. "I miss Quin so much, you know? I kind of feel that having Casey here is giving me another chance."

"Another chance?" Faye asked gently when he lapsed into silence.

"At a real family."

"You have your parents," she pointed out pragmatically, "and I know you have extended family, as well. They're all quite real."

"And yet, for as long as I can remember, I always felt like Quin and I only had each other."

Faye shifted uncomfortably on her chair. This was getting altogether too personal for comfort. Piers had never really talked about his family at great length. She'd always privately envied him that they, until Quin's sudden death, were all still there for him. But were they really?

When she thought back, her dealings with his parents and other relatives had hinged around what Piers could do for them, never the other way around. Even thinking about his annual house party here, Piers had always instructed her on what gifts to ensure were under the tree for whom. But, aside from his great-aunt Florence's questionable Christmas sweaters, had Faye ever heard of anyone bringing him a gift in return?

"I'm sorry," she said for lack of anything else to say to fill the sudden silence that fell between them.

"This little one isn't going to grow up alone. I will always be there for him."

"You don't even know for sure he's your brother's child," Faye protested.

"It fits. You know what Quin was like. I'm only sorry I didn't know about Casey sooner—then I could have helped his mom more."

Faye saw his shoulders rise and fall on a deep sigh. There was a resoluteness to his voice when he spoke again.

"She needed help and Quin couldn't be there for her. I'll find her, Faye. I'll make sure she's okay before going any further with Casey but I want to offer him the kind of life he deserves."

Piers's words made something twist deep in Faye's chest. Made her see another side of him that was all too appealing. It was the baby, it had to be. After her infant brother's death thirteen years ago she'd spent some time subconsciously trying to fill that gaping hole in her life. Tried and failed and learned the hard way to inure herself to getting involved, to forming an emotional bond. And here she was, stranded with a man who appealed to her on so many levels—despite her best efforts to keep her reactions under control—and a helpless infant who called on those old instincts she thought she'd suppressed.

Faye rose to take their trays back to the kitchen.

"Here, let me do that. You cooked."

She swiftly maneuvered out of reach. "I hardly would call reheating soup and making grilled cheese on toast cooking. Besides, he's waking up. You'll need to check his diaper."

"Again?"

"Yup," she said and, with her flashlight balanced on a tray to light her way forward, she made her way to the kitchen.

Piers watched her go before turning his attention to his charge. He was determined to get to the root of why she was so unwavering about having nothing to do with the baby.

"I can't see the problem, can you?" he said softly to the little boy who was now looking up at him and kicking his legs under the blanket.

But maybe it wasn't the baby she was avoiding now. Maybe it was just him. At first, he could have sworn she was reacting favorably to that kiss he'd given her under the mistletoe. Hell, favorably? She'd been melting under his touch, but that had been nothing compared to how their brief embrace had made him feel. Even now, thinking about it, it still had the power to leave him feeling a little stunned.

He'd kissed a fair few women in his time but, so far, none had moved him the way that simple touch had. The sensations that had struck him from the minute his lips touched hers were electric—curious and demanding at the same time. He'd had to hold back, had to force himself not to pull her hard against the length of his body. Had to fight every instinct inside him to keep the kiss simple, light, when what she'd awakened in him demanded so much more.

"Who would have known?" he said under his breath and lifting Casey in his arms. "Just one kiss, eh? What do we do now?"

What had he unleashed in himself with that embrace? He'd been trying to distract her. Her face, always composed and serene even in the most trying circumstances in the office, had looked stricken. His instinct had been to divert her thoughts, perhaps even to provide comfort. Instead he'd ticked her off—probably just as effective at distracting her, even if it didn't quite lend itself to them repeating the exercise, as much as he wanted to.

Did he pursue it further when she'd made it categorically clear that she wanted no further intimacy between them? He wasn't the kind of man who gave up when he reached the first obstacle, but there was a lot riding on this. Faye was the best assistant he'd ever had. Her very aloofness had been instrumental in keeping his mind focused on the job and his busy workdays on an even keel. Her ability to anticipate his needs was second to none. In fact, sometimes he felt like she knew him better than he knew himself.

He'd found her attractive from the get-go. From the interview selection process right through to the day she'd started she'd intrigued him, but he'd respected the boundaries they'd had between them as boss and employee.

Boundaries he himself had insisted on after his last two assistants—one male and one female—had complicated things by declaring their love for him. He'd worked with Faye for three years now. He respected her, relied on her and trusted her. But now that he'd kissed her… Well, it had opened the door on something else entirely.

For all her cool and inscrutable manner at work, she'd been different here from the moment he'd arrived. Maybe it was because it was the first time he'd seen her in anything other than her usual neatly practical and understated office attire. He had to admit, despite the horrible sweater he'd forced on her, the sight of her in his clothing appealed to him on an instinctive level, as if by her being dressed in something of his she'd become more accessible to him. As if, somehow, she belonged to him.

And she had, for that brief moment. They'd connected both physically and, he liked to think, on some emotional plane, as well. He'd felt the curiosity in her response, the interest. Right up until that moment she'd pushed him away, she'd been as invested in their kiss as he had been.

"I'm not dreaming, am I?" he said to the baby in his arms.

Casey looked at him with solemn dark eyes and then his little mouth curled into a gummy grin.

"Maybe, just maybe, it's time to see if dreams really can come true," Piers said with an answering smile of his own.

He'd have to approach this carefully. The last thing he wanted was for Faye to actually turn around and quit. But surely he could push things forward without pushing her to that extreme. He was a resourceful kind of guy. He'd think of something. He wasn't afraid of hard work. Not when something was important, and he had the strongest feeling that Faye had the potential to be far more important to him than she already was. And, he realized with a sense of recognition that felt as if it came from deep at his center, he wanted to be equally as important to her, too. If only she'd let him.

When Faye returned to the main room he stood with Casey and held him out to her. She looked as if she was going to instinctively put her hands out to take him, but then she took a step back.

"What are you doing?" she asked warily.

"Handing him to you. He doesn't bite. He hasn't even got teeth. It's not like he'll gum you to death."

Faye rolled her eyes in obvious exasperation. "I know he doesn't bite, but why would I hold him?"

"I need to check on the generator, see if we can get some power running."

"Perhaps I can do that for you," she said, still avoiding taking the baby.

"It's easier if I do it. I know exactly where it is and how to operate it. I'll be quick, I promise."

"Fine," she said, her irritation clear in her tone. "Be quick."

Piers watched as she nestled the baby against her, her movements sure and hinting of a physical memory that intrigued him. He liked seeing this side of her, even though she was so reluctant to display it.

It didn't take long to check the generator, which was housed in a small shed at the back of the house. Getting it going, however, took a little longer. In the end he'd had to pull his gloves off to get the job done. His fingers were turning white in reaction to the cold by the time he wrestled the shed door closed and reentered the house.

He'd expected the house to be blazing with light and sound when he got back in but instead all he could hear was a gentle humming coming from the kitchen. He followed the sound and discovered Faye in the kitchen with the baby, one-handedly making up a bottle of formula for Casey while humming a little tune that seemed to hold the baby transfixed. The humming stopped the instant she saw him.

"I thought you were going to be quick. Problems?"

"Nothing I couldn't handle." He glanced out into the main room. "No tree lights?"

"I thought it best not to draw too much on the generator if we could avoid it," Faye replied, ducking her head.

He suspected her decision may have more to do with her unexplained and very obvious disdain of the festive season than with any need to conserve power. His backup generator could keep a small factory running, but he wasn't about to argue.

"Where were you planning to have Casey sleep tonight?" she asked, her back turned to him.

"I hadn't actually thought that far. I guess in the bed with me. He'll be warmer that way, won't he?"

"There's a lot of data against co-sleeping with a baby. To be honest, I think you'd do better to make him up a type of crib out of one of your dresser drawers or even a large cardboard box. You'll need to fold up a blanket or several towels to make a firm mattress base and he'll probably be okay with his knitted baby blanket over him. Your room should be warm enough with the central heat."

Piers couldn't help it, his eyebrows shot up in surprise. She could have been quoting a baby care manual. How did she know this stuff?

"Okay, I'll get on it right away, but before I go I have to ask. How do you know these things?"

She shrugged her slender shoulders beneath the overlarge sweater he'd given her. "It's just common sense, really. By the way, I'll make up an extra bottle for Casey in case he needs a night feeding. It'll be in the fridge here."

"A night feeding?"

She sighed and shook her head. "You really know absolutely nothing about babies, do you?"

"Guilty as charged. They haven't really been on my radar until now. Do you think it's safe for me to look after him on my own tonight? Don't you think it would be better if you—"

"Oh, no, don't involve me. I'm already doing more than I wanted to. Here." She passed him the baby. "You feed him. I'll go make up a bed for him in your room."

And before he could stop her, she did just that. Piers looked down at the solemn little boy in his arms.

"We're going to get to the bottom of it eventually, Casey, my boy. One way or another, I'm going to get through those layers she's got built up around her."

Five

The sun was barely up when Faye gave up all pretense of trying to sleep. All night her mind had raced over ways she could get out of this situation. By 3:00 a.m. she'd decided that, no matter the dent in her savings, she'd call a helicopter to come rescue her if necessary. Anything to get out of there. In the literally cold light of day that didn't appear to be such a rational solution to her dilemma. After all, it wasn't as if she was in an emergency situation.

At least the storm had passed, she noted as she shoved her heavy drapes aside to expose a clear sky and a landscape blanketed in white. There was a tranquil stillness about it that had a calming effect on her weary nerves, right up until she heard the excited squawk of an infant followed by the low rumble that was Piers's response.

She had to admit that he'd stepped up to the plate pretty well last night. By the time she'd made up the makeshift crib in Piers's room and returned downstairs, he'd competently fed and changed the baby. And later, when she'd instructed him on how to bathe Casey, he'd handled the slippery wee man with confidence and ease and no small amount of laughter. For the briefest moment she'd forgotten why she was even at the lodge and had caught herself on the verge of laughing with them. But she didn't deserve that kind of happiness. Not after what she'd done to her own family.

It was true, people said the crash hadn't been her fault. But she had to live every day with her choices, which included pestering her beloved stepdad to let her drive home that Christmas Eve. Her mom had expressed her concern but Ellis had agreed with Faye, telling her mother the girl needed the experience on the icy roads. And now they were all gone. Her mom. Ellis. And her adorable baby brother.

Tears burned at the backs of Faye's eyes and she looked up at the ceiling, refusing to allow them to fall. She'd grieved. Oh, how she'd grieved. And she'd borne her punishment stoically these past years. Rising with each new dawn, putting one foot in front of the other. Doing what had to be done. And never letting anyone close.

She turned from the window and her memories and went to the bathroom to get ready for the day. Thankfully, she'd be able to wear her own clothing today, but as she passed Piers's neatly folded sweater on top of her dresser she couldn't help but wistfully stroke the outline of the crooked snowman on its front.

"What's the matter with you, woman?" she said out loud. "You hate Christmas and you're not in the least bit interested in Piers that way."

Liar.

Her fingertips automatically rose to her lips as she remembered that kiss, but then she rubbed her fingers hard across them, as if by doing so she could somehow wipe away the physical recall her body seemed determined to hold on to. She turned on the shower and stripped off the T-shirt Piers had given her to sleep in. Hoping against hope that the symbolic action of peeling the last thing of his off her body would also remove any lingering ideas said body had about her boss at the same time.

Now that the storm was gone, with any luck she'd be able to get away from there, and Piers and Casey, before she fell any deeper under their spell. But even the best laid plans seemed fated to go awry.

As she crunched down the snow-covered private road to her car she was forced to accept that even in broad daylight the road remained impassable. In fact, she was darn lucky she'd escaped without serious injury, or worse.

The tree could have struck her vehicle. She could have swerved off the driveway and down into the steep gully on the other side. The realization was sobering and left her shivering with more than just the cold as she opened the trunk of the SUV and pulled out her suitcase before trekking back up to the house.

"I was beginning to think you'd decided to hike cross-country to get away from us," Piers remarked laconically when she returned.

"I thought about it," she admitted. "I see we have cell phone reception now."

"Yes, I've called the authorities and requested assistance in removing the tree and getting your car towed. There are a few others in more extreme circumstances needing attention before us."

"And the police? Did you call them about Casey?"

"I did. Again, not much anyone can do until they can

get up to the house. I also called my lawyer to see where I stand legally with custody of Casey. Under the circumstances of his abandonment, they're drawing up temporary guardianship papers."

"You're not wasting any time," Faye commented, not entirely sure how she felt about this version of her boss. "What if his mom changes her mind? It's only been a day."

"I'll cross that bridge if that happens."

Over the next couple of days, if she wanted to get away from Piers's interminable holiday spirit, she had to tuck herself away in her room to read or watch movies. Otherwise she'd find herself sticking around downstairs and watching Piers interact with the baby. It was enough to soften the hardest shell and, shred by shred, her carefully wrapped emotions were beginning to be exposed and she could feel herself actually wanting to spend time with the two males.

Watching Piers fall in love with the baby was a wonder in itself. Sometimes she found it hard to believe that this was the same man who usually wore bespoke suits and steered a multibillion-dollar corporation to new successes and achievements each and every year. It was as if the world had shrunk and closed in around them—putting them in a cocoon where nothing and no one could interrupt.

Piers's comment a few days ago about heading away cross-country should be beginning to hold appeal. She'd kept her feelings wrapped up so tight for so long that the thought of being vulnerable to anyone was enough to make her hunt out a pair of snowshoes and find her way down the mountain. Except as each day passed, she found her desperation to get away growing less and less.

One night, three days after the storm, Faye was preparing dinner when Piers joined her in the kitchen.

"A glass of wine while you work?" he asked.

"Sure, that would be nice," she admitted.

She'd avoided having anything to drink these past few days because she didn't trust herself not to lower her barriers, or her inhibitions, should Piers try to kiss her again, but since that first night he hadn't so much as laid a hand on her shoulder again.

Piers poured them each a glass of red wine in tall, stemmed glasses and put hers next to her on the countertop.

"Thank you," she acknowledged and reached for the glass to take a sip.

"What can I do to help you?"

Piers leaned one hip against the counter and raised his glass to his lips. Faye found herself mesmerized by the action, his nearness making her feel as though she ought to back away. And yet she didn't. Instead her eyes fixed on his mouth, on the faint glisten of moisture on his lips. That darn mistletoe was just to the right of him. All she had to do was to rise up on her toes and kiss him and that would be—

Absolutely insanely stupid, she silently growled at herself as she reached for a knife to chop the vegetables she'd taken from the refrigerator earlier.

"Nothing," she snapped. "I've got this."

Piers's eyebrows rose slightly. "You okay?"

"Just cabin fever, I guess. Looking forward to getting out of here."

Even as she said the words she knew she was lying. Truth was, she had begun to enjoy this enforced idyll just a little too much. She had to get away before she lost all reason.

"Look, why don't you sit down? Let me finish making dinner. You sound a bit stressed."

"Stressed? You think I'm stressed? It's all this doing nothing that's driving me crazy," Faye said on a strangled laugh. "Seriously, I don't need you to pander to me."

"Everyone needs someone to pander to them from time to time."

"Not me," she said resolutely and started to chop a carrot with more vigor than finesse.

She stiffened as gentle hands closed over hers, as the warmth of Piers's body surrounded her from behind.

"Everyone," he said firmly. "Now, go. Sit. Tell me what needs to be done and just watch me to make sure I don't mess anything up, okay?"

He picked up her wine, pushed the glass into her hand and steered her to a stool on the other side of the kitchen island.

"So I'm guessing these need to be diced?" he asked, gesturing with the knife to the irregularly sized chunks of carrot.

She nodded in surrender and took another sip of her wine.

He followed her instructions to the letter and soon their meal was simmering on the stove top. Piers topped up their glasses, took a seat beside her and swiveled to face her.

"Now, tell me what's really bothering you. Why do you hate it here so much? Most people would give their right arm to be stranded with two gorgeous males for a few days."

"I'm not most people," she said bluntly.

"I noticed. Is there someone waiting for you at home? Is that what it is?"

"No, there's no one waiting for me at home."

No one. Not a pet. Not even a plant since she'd managed to kill off the maidenhair fern and the ficus she'd been given by one of her colleagues who'd jokingly said she needed something less inanimate than four walls to come home to each day.

"Then what is it?"

"This." She gestured widely with one hand. "It just isn't me, okay? I like California. I like sunshine. The beach. Dry roads."

"It's always good to have some contrast in your life," he commented, his face suddenly serious. "But it's more than that, isn't it? It's Casey."

Faye let her shoulders slump. "I don't hate him," she said defensively.

"But you don't want anything to do with him."

"Look, even you, if you had the chance, would have run a mile from a baby a few days ago."

"True." Piers nodded. "But I'm enjoying this time with him and with you more than I ever would have expected. C'mon, you have to admit it. Even you've enjoyed some of our time together."

She felt as if he'd backed her up against a corner and she had nowhere to go. "Look, this is an unusual situation for us both. Once you're back in Santa Monica you'll be back to your usual whirl of work, travel and women— no doubt in that order—and Casey will be tucked away to be someone else's problem."

"Wow, why don't you tell me how you really feel?" Piers said, feeling a wave of defensiveness swell through his whole body.

Her blunt assessment of his priorities angered him, he admitted, but he couldn't deny she'd hit the nail very squarely on the head.

"So you don't think I'll be a suitable parent to Casey?" he pressed, fighting to hold on to his temper.

"To be honest, I think it would be a huge leap for you to learn to balance your existing lifestyle with caring for a child. Of course, it all seems so easy when you're here. There's nothing else for you to do all day other than look after him. But what about when you're in negotiations in your next takeover and you're working eighteen-hour days and he's had his immunizations and he's running a low fever and he wants you? What about when you're attending a theater premiere in New York and he wakes with colic or he's teething and grumpy and inconsolable? What about—"

"Okay, okay, you've made your point. I'm going to need help."

"You really haven't thought this through, Piers. It's going to take more than help," Faye argued, putting air quotes around the last word. "There's more to raising a child than feeding it and changing a diaper, and you can't just expect to be there when it suits you and leave him to others when it doesn't. It's just not right or fair."

Piers wanted to argue with her, to shout her accusations down. But there was a ring of truth in her words that pricked his conscience and reminded him that the very upbringing he'd endured was likely the kind of upbringing he'd end up giving to Casey.

For all that he wanted to raise Quin's son as his own, and give him all the love that he and his brother had missed out on growing up, how could he continue to do what he did—live the life he led—and still give Casey the nurturing he would need? The little boy was only three and a half months old. There was a lifetime of commitment ahead. Could he really do that? Be the person Casey needed? Be everything his own parents had never been?

His mom and dad had loved the attention that being parents of twins had brought them, but they'd left the basics of child rearing to a team of nannies and staff, and as soon as he and his brother were old enough they'd been shipped to boarding school. At least they'd always had each other. Who would Casey have?

Piers felt a massive leaden weight of responsibility settle heavily on his shoulders. "You're right."

"I beg your pardon?"

"I said, you're right." He turned the stem of his wineglass between his fingers and watched the ruby liquid inside the bowl spin around the sides of the glass. "I haven't thought this through."

"What will you do then? Surrender Casey to child services?"

"Absolutely not. He's my responsibility. I will make sure he doesn't want for anything and if I make a few mistakes along the way then I'm sure you'll be there to remind me how things should be done."

"Me?" she squeaked.

"Yes, you. You're not planning to leave my employ anytime soon are you?"

The question hung on the air between them.

"Leave? No, why should I? But I'm not a nanny. I'm your assistant."

"And as such you can guide me in making sure I don't work longer than I ought to and you can help me ensure that I employ the right people to help me care for Casey."

He looked into Faye's blue-gray eyes, noticing for the first time the tiny silver striations that marked her irises. Realizing, too, that the thick black fringe of her eyelashes were her own and not the product of artifice created by some cosmetic manufacturer.

Tension built in his gut. He needed her and it was daunting to admit it. She'd become such an integral part of his working life that he now found it difficult to imagine his days without her keeping his course running smooth. She did such an incredible job in the office, the idea of having her extend her reach even deeper into his personal sphere, as well, was enticing. But could he convince her to do it? Could he show her that he was serious about being a suitable parent for Casey and that he was equally serious about her, too?

She got up from her chair, walked over to where she'd left her trusty tablet on the countertop and made a notation.

"I'll get on it when I get back. If I ever get out of here, that is."

Piers surprised himself by laughing at her hangdog expression and bleak tone.

"It's no laughing matter," she stressed.

"Hey, we're hardly suffering, are we? We're warm and dry. We have food and my wine cellar at our disposal—"

"And we're running out of diapers, or hadn't you noticed? I took the liberty of checking Meredith's linen supply. If we can't get out of here by late tomorrow, we're going to have to start using cloth napkins. It's going to create a lot of laundry."

"We'll manage," he said grimly, irked by her not so subtle reminder that he really didn't have the first idea of what was needed to care for Casey.

But he had her and she very obviously did.

Again he wondered where she'd gotten her knowledge from. Her CV had said she was from Michigan but she'd attended college in California and had worked in and around Santa Monica since graduation. She had no family that he knew of, and had never worked in child care. All the dots had connected. There were no significant gaps in between her education and work histories. So where had she learned so much about babies?

Six

The following evening, Piers was playing with the baby on a blanket on the floor when he took a call on his cell phone. It was a contractor with very good news. The road up the mountain would be cleared in the morning and a crew would remove the fallen tree. Piers had taken a walk to look at it a couple of days ago, while Casey had slept back at the house under Faye's supervision. Seeing her SUV crunched up against the solid tree trunk had made him sick to his stomach. The outcome could have been so very different for her and the thought of losing her sent a spear of dread right through him.

"Good news," he said as Faye came through to the main room with a basket of laundry tucked under one arm.

The sheer domesticity of the picture she made brought a smile to his face.

"Oh? What is it? By the way, here's your laundry,"

she said, dumping the contents of the basket on the sofa. "You do know how to fold it, don't you?"

The domestic picture blurred a little.

"How hard can it be, right?" Piers said, reaching for one of his Christmas sweaters and holding it up.

Was it his imagination or had the thing shrunk? Santa looked a lot shorter than he'd been before. He wouldn't put it past Faye to have shrunk it deliberately, but then he'd been the one to put the load into the dryer.

"What news?" Faye prompted, tapping her foot impatiently.

"The road will be cleared tomorrow morning."

"Oh, thank goodness."

The relief in her voice was palpable. Piers fought back the pang of disappointment. He'd known all along she couldn't wait to leave and realistically he knew they couldn't stay snowbound together forever, even if the idea was tempting. Baby logistics alone meant they had to venture out into the real world.

He dropped the sweater back onto the pile of clothing. "We should celebrate tonight."

"Celebrate?" She frowned slightly then nodded. "I could celebrate but I'll be more inclined to do so when my plane takes off and heads toward the West Coast."

"Skeptic."

"Realist."

He smiled at her and felt a surge of elation when she reluctantly smiled in return.

"Well, I plan to celebrate," he said firmly. "Champagne, I think, after Casey is down, and dancing."

"I hope you have fun. I'm going to pack," Faye said, turning and heading for the stairs.

"Oh, come on," Piers coaxed. "Let yourself relax for once, Faye. It won't hurt. I promise."

"I know how to relax," she answered with a scowl.

Casey squealed from his position on the blanket.

"Even Casey thinks you need to lighten up."

"Casey is focused on the stockings you've got hanging over the fireplace," she pointed out drily.

"Yeah, about those. I know it's only a day's notice but I think we should cancel the Christmas Eve party—in fact, cancel the whole house party. I don't think a lodge full of guests will be a good environment for the little guy here and, to be honest, I think I'd rather just keep things low-key this year."

Faye looked at him in surprise. He'd been adamant that, despite the fact that the last time he'd been here with his friends it had been the last time Quin had partied with them all, he wanted to keep with his usual tradition.

"Are you certain?" she asked.

"Yeah. Somehow it doesn't feel right. I know it's short notice and people will be annoyed but, to be honest, if they can't understand that my change in circumstances makes me want to change my routine then I don't really want to be around them."

"Okay, I'll get right on it."

"Thank you, Faye. I know I don't say it often enough, but I couldn't function properly without you."

"Oh, I'm sure you'd do just fine."

"No," he answered seriously. "I don't think I would. You're important to me, Faye. More than you realize."

The flip response she'd been about to deliver froze on the tip of her tongue. The expression in Piers's eyes was serious, his brows drawn lightly together. Her heart gave a little flip. Important to him. What did he mean by that? She'd sensed a shift in their relationship in the time they'd been stranded but she'd put it down to the bizarreness of their situation. That pesky flicker of desire shimmered low in her body and she felt her skin tighten, her breathing become a little short, her mouth dry. She swallowed and forced her gaze away from his face.

What could she say? The atmosphere between them stretched out like a fog rich with innuendo. If he took a step toward her now, what would she do? Would she take a step back or would she hold her ground and let him come to her? And kiss her again, perhaps?

The flicker burned a little brighter and her nipples grew taut and achy. This was crazy, she thought with an edge of panic. He'd just been thanking her for her dedication to her job. That was all she had to offer him. And yet there was heat in his dark brown gaze. This wasn't just a boss expressing his gratitude to his employee; there was so much more subtext to what he'd uttered with such feeling.

Faye fought to find some words that would bring things back to her kind of normal. One where you didn't suddenly feel an overwhelming desire to run your fingers along the waistband of your boss's sweater and lift it up to see if the skin of his ridged abdomen was like heated silk. Her fingers curled into tight fists at her sides.

As if he could sense the strain in the air, Casey had fallen silent. Faye forced herself to look away from Piers and her gaze fell on the baby.

"Oh, look," she cried. "He's found his thumb."

It took Piers a moment or two to move but when he did a smile spread across his face.

"Hey, clever guy. I guess that means no more pacifier?"

"I guess. It may help him to self-settle better at night."

"I'm all for that."

"But it can lead to other issues. You can always throw

a pacifier away but it's not so easy when a kid gets attached to sucking their thumb."

"Hey, I'm prepared not to overthink it at this stage."

She watched as Piers settled back down on the floor beside the baby and started talking to him as if he was the cleverest kid in the world. This time when her heart strings pulled, it was a different kind of feeling. One that made her realize all that she'd forsaken in her life with her choice not to have a family. Faye made herself turn away and take the basket back to the laundry room. She couldn't stay here another second and allow herself to—

She cut off that train of thought but a persistent voice at the back of her mind asked, *Allow yourself to what? To fall in love with them?* That would be stupid. Stupid and self-destructive.

Faye made herself scarce during Casey's bath time and final feeding, leaving Piers to settle him for the night. Now that she knew she'd be leaving at some stage tomorrow, she didn't trust herself not to indulge in little Casey's nearness just that bit too much. It would be all too easy to nuzzle that dark fuzz of hair on his head, to pepper his chubby little cheeks with kisses, to coax just one more smile from him before bedtime, to feel the weight of his solid little body lying so trustingly in her arms. Just thinking about it made her ache to hold him, but she held firm on her decision to keep a safe distance between them. Piers was perfectly capable of seeing to Casey's immediate needs right now. The baby didn't need her any more than she wanted to be needed.

But you do *want to be needed*, came that insidious inner voice again. The voice that, no matter how resolute she determined to be, continued to wear at her psyche. It had been easy enough for her to keep away from situations where interaction with babies was inevitable, but in this enforced, close atmosphere here at the lodge, all her hard-fought-for internal barricades had begun to crumble.

She needed some distance. Right now.

Faye turned on her heel and left the room, checking the laundry to ensure she hadn't left anything behind before taking the back stairs up to the next floor. She closed the door behind her when she reached her bedroom, leaned against it and let out the pent-up sigh she'd been holding.

Tomorrow, she told herself. She'd have her life back tomorrow. Just a few more hours. She could do this. How hard could it be to continue to resist one exceptionally adorable baby and a man who made her breath hitch and her heart hammer a rapid beat in her chest? For now, though, she had work to do and she had a whole lot of people to contact on Piers's behalf to cancel the house party.

When that task was done, she decided to get the ball rolling with the private investigation firm Piers used on occasion to collate data on a prospective property development. They were discreet and detailed. Everything you needed an investigator to be.

She explained the situation with Casey and what little information they had about his mother, and asked if they could look into things. After hitting Send on the email, she lay back on her bed and wondered if she could simply hide out there for the rest of the night. But a knock at her bedroom door drew her up on her feet again.

Piers leaned against the doorjamb with a sardonic smile on his face.

"It's safe to come out now," he said. "Casey's down for the night."

"I wasn't hiding from Casey."

"Oh, you were hiding from me, then?"

"No, of course not. I was working," she protested, earning another devastating smile from her boss.

She detailed what she'd done and he nodded with approval.

"Thanks for taking care of all that. I'd have gotten onto the investigators myself, but I got busy with Casey."

"That's why you have me, remember."

The words tripped glibly off her tongue but her job truly meant the world to her. She actively enjoyed the sense of order she could restore when things went awry and, for her, the skill she'd developed for anticipating Piers's needs—whether professionally or personally— was something to take pride in. Doing her job well was important to her. Basically, when it came down to it, it was all she had.

Sure, she had a handful of friends, but they were more acquaintances really. She tended to keep people at arm's length because it was so much easier that way. She'd even lost touch with Brenda, her best friend from high school. Brenda had tried so hard to be there for Faye after the crash, but no one could truly understand what she'd been through, or how she'd felt, and eventually Brenda, too, had drifted out of her sphere. Now they occasionally exchanged birthday cards, but it was the sum total of their contact with one another.

"Yes, that's why I have you," he answered with a note of solemnity in his voice she couldn't quite understand. He held out a hand. "Come on downstairs. The fire's going, the music's playing and I have a very special bottle of champagne on ice."

"Champagne?" she asked, reluctantly giving him her hand and allowing him to tug her along the hallway.

"Yeah, we're celebrating, remember?"

"Ah, yes. Freedom."

"Is that all it is to you? A chance to run away?"

Was it?

"I had other plans, too, you know," she said defensively.

So what if those plans included allowing herself to go into deep mourning for her family the way she did every year. It was how she coped—how she kept herself together for the balance of the year. It was the only time of year she ever allowed herself to look through the old family albums that ended abruptly thirteen years ago. It hurt—oh, how it hurt—but they were snapshots of happier times and that one night was all she'd allow herself— it was all she deserved.

They reached the bottom of the stairs and Faye noticed he'd put lighted candles around the main room and turned the Christmas tree lights off. Piers spun her to face him, his expression serious.

"I'm really sorry you ended up stuck here. I mean it. I should have realized you'd have plans of your own. It's just that you're always there at the end of the phone or in the office working right next to me. I guess I'm guilty of taking you for granted."

"It's okay. I love my work, Piers. I wouldn't change it for the world."

"But there's more to life than work, right?"

She smiled in response and watched as he reached down and pulled a bottle of French champagne from the ice bucket that stood sweating on a place mat on the coffee table.

"The good stuff tonight, hmm?" she commented as he deftly popped the cork.

"Only the best. We've earned it, don't you think? Besides, we're celebrating the road being cleared."

Faye accepted a crystal flute filled with the golden, bubbling liquid. "It's not clear yet," she reminded him.

"Always so pedantic," he teased. "Then let's just say we're celebrating the *prospect* of the road being cleared, and of Casey not needing to use my good linen as diapers."

"To both of those things." Faye smiled and clinked her glass to his.

She cocked her head and listened to the music playing softly in the background.

"What? No Christmas carols?" she said over the rim of her glass.

"I know you don't like them. I thought tonight I'd cut you some slack," he said with a wink.

"Thank you, I appreciate it."

She sipped her champagne, enjoying the sensation of the bubbles dancing on her tongue before she swallowed. The sparkling wine was so much better than anything she allowed herself to indulge in at home. Piers turned to put another log on the fire and she found herself swaying gently to the music as she watched him. When he straightened from the fireplace, she realized she'd already drunk half her glass and it was already beginning to mess with her head. She was such a lightweight when it came to drinking, which was part of the reason she so rarely indulged.

"Enjoying that?" he asked. Without waiting for her answer, he reached for the bottle and topped off her glass.

"I am," she answered simply.

"Good, you deserve nothing but the best. Take a seat, I'll be right back."

He was as good as his word, returning from the kitchen a moment later with plate laden with cheese and crackers.

"Sorry there's not much of a selection," he said with a wink. "I haven't had a chance to get out to the grocery store."

Faye laughed out loud. "As if you ever go to the grocery store yourself."

"True." He nodded. "I've led an exceptionally privileged life, haven't I?"

But he'd known loneliness and loss, too, despite all that privilege. And, while he hid it well, she knew that he missed his brother more than words could ever say.

"On the other hand, you also provide employment to hundreds of people, with benefits, so I guess you can be forgiven for not ever doing your own shopping."

Faye put her glass down and helped herself to some cheese and crackers. It was probably better to put some food in her stomach before she had any more champagne. She had a fast metabolism and the light lunch she'd prepared hours ago had most certainly been burned up by now. A delicious aroma slowly began to filter through from the kitchen.

"Have you been cooking?" she asked.

"Just a little thing Casey and I threw together." He chuckled at her surprised expression. "No, to be honest, it's one of Meredith's stews that I found in the freezer. I thought we could eat here, in front of the fire. It's kind of nice to just chill out for a bit, don't you think?"

Faye nodded. It wasn't often that she chilled out completely. Maybe it was the champagne, or maybe the knowledge that she'd be leaving soon, but she felt deeply relaxed this evening. The plate with cheese and crackers seemed to empty itself rather quickly, she thought as she reached for her glass again. Or maybe she'd just been hungrier than she'd realized. When she apologized

to Piers for having more than her share, he was mag-
nanimous.

"Don't worry. You have no idea how many of them I
had to sample before I got the combination of relish and
cheese right on the crackers," he assured her.

He poured her another glass of champagne and she
looked at the flute in her hand in surprise. Had the thing
sprung a leak? Surely she hadn't drunk all that herself?

As if he could read her mind, Piers hastened to reassure her. "I won't let you drink too much. Responsible
host and all that. Besides, I know how much you like to
remain in control."

"I'm not worried," she protested.

In fact, she'd rarely felt less worried than she did right
now. A delicious lassitude had spread through her limbs
and there was a glowing warmth radiating from the pit
of her belly. She curled her legs up beside her on the sofa
and watched the flames dance and lick along the logs in
the fireplace. She'd hated fire since the accident—hated
how consuming it could be, how uncontrolled. But being
here at the lodge these past few days had desensitized
her from those fears somewhat. The curtain grille that
Piers always pulled across the grate created both a physical and mental barrier to the potential harm that could be
wrought. Of course, he'd have to put stronger barriers in
place once Casey became mobile, she thought. If he stuck
with his plans to keep the baby, she reminded herself.

But that was a problem for another time. And not hers
to worry about, either, she told herself firmly. Tonight's
goal was to chill out, so that's what she most definitely
was going to do.

The latter part of Piers's remark, about her liking to
remain in control, echoed in her mind. Was that how she
portrayed herself to him? In control at all times? It was

certainly the demeanor she strived to create. It was her protection. If she had everything under control, nothing could surprise her. Nothing could hurt her.

Being totally helpless in the face of the gas tanker skidding toward their car on the icy road that night had left scars that went far deeper than purely physical. Her whole life had imploded. By the time she'd recovered from the worst of her physical injuries, the emotional injuries had taken over her every waking thought.

Faye's transition into foster care had been a blur and, as a salve to her wounded, broken heart, she'd poured herself into the care of the younger children in the home. The babies had caught at her the most, each one feeling like a substitute for the baby brother she'd lost. The baby brother who may have still been alive today if she hadn't begged her stepdad to let her drive that night. For the longest time she'd wished she'd died along with her family. That the tanker driver hadn't been able to pull her free from the burning wreckage of their family sedan.

Subconsciously she rubbed her legs. The scar tissue wasn't as tight as it used to be, but it remained a constant reminder that she'd survived when her family hadn't.

"You okay? Your legs sore?" Piers asked.

It was the first time he'd said anything about her injuries since he'd seen her undress the night he'd arrived.

"They're fine. It's just a habit, I guess."

She waited for him to ask the inevitable questions, like how she'd gotten the scars, had it hurt and all the other things people asked.

"Would you like me to rub them for you? I guess massage helps, right?"

She looked at him, completely startled. "Well, yes, it has helped when I've tried it before—but I'm okay, truly."

A flutter of fear, intermingled with something else—

desire, maybe—flickered on the edges of her mind. What would it be like to feel his hands on her legs, to feel those long, supple fingers stroking her damaged skin? She slammed the door on that thought before it could gain purchase and swung her legs down to the floor again.

"Shall I go and check on dinner?" she asked, rising to her feet.

"Not at all, sit down. Tonight, let me wait on you, okay?"

Reluctantly, Faye sat again. "I'm not used to being waited upon."

"Then this will be an experience for you, won't it?" Piers said with a quick grin. "Now, relax. Boss's orders."

He went to the kitchen and she caught herself watching his every step. She couldn't help herself. From the broad sweep of his shoulders to the way his jeans cupped his backside, he appealed to her on so many forbidden levels it wasn't even funny. It was easy in the office to ignore his physical appeal. After all, at work she was too busy ensuring everything ran smoothly and that potential disasters were averted at all times to notice just how good Piers looked. So exactly when had her perception of him changed? When had he stopped simply being her boss and become a man she now desired?

Seven

As Piers sliced a loaf of bread he'd defrosted earlier, he wondered if Faye had any idea of how much she revealed in her expression. These past few days it was as if the careful mask she wore in her professional life had been destroyed and he was finally getting to see the woman who lived behind the facade. He put the slices in the basket he'd put on a large tray earlier and turned to lift the lid from the pot simmering on the stove.

The scent of the gently bubbling beef-and-red-wine stew made his mouth water. It was funny how living in isolation like this made you appreciate things so much more. He'd never take any of his staff for granted again. Not that he'd made a habit of it up to now, but it was time to show additional gratitude for the foresight the people around him displayed. Of course, that's why he employed those very people in the first place—without them he could hardly do his job properly, either.

Which brought him very firmly back to the woman

waiting for him in the main room. Tonight he'd seen a window into her vulnerability that he hadn't noticed before. It kind of made him feel as though it left a gap for him to fill. Some way to be of use to her, for a change, instead of being the one being shepherded and looked after all the time. It made him feel a little on edge. As if this was his one shot to make things change between them. If he screwed it up, that would be it. He'd not only lose any chance they had of genuinely forming a relationship together, but she'd no doubt hightail it out of the workplace, as well. Nothing had ever felt quite so vital to him before.

He couldn't understand why things had changed between them, but he wasn't about to question it. He already knew he trusted Faye with everything that was important to him. She'd been his absolute rock when his brother had died, ensuring everything continued to run while he was away dealing with tying up Quin's estate. Over the three years they'd worked together they'd formed a synchronicity he'd never experienced with anyone else. Did he dare hope that same synchronicity could spread into the personal side of their lives, too? And this snowstorm, their being stranded together—albeit with a miniature chaperone—it all conspired to open his eyes to what they really could be.

Realizing he was allowing himself to get thoroughly lost in his thoughts, he quickly ladled two large servings of the stew into bowls. After a final check of the tray to ensure he had sufficient cutlery and napkins, et cetera, he took the tray through to the main room.

Faye was staring vacantly into the flames. What was she thinking? She didn't hear him until he put the tray down on the coffee table and sat beside her on the sofa.

She straightened and moved a fraction away from him,

which only made him spread himself out a little more, closing the distance between them. He leaned forward, picked up one of the bowls and passed it to her with a fork.

"Dinner is served," he said.

"Thank you."

"Bread?"

He offered the bread basket and was relieved when she took a slice. She hardly ate a thing that he could tell, certainly far less than he did. Clearly she needed better looking after. It was a good thing he was just the man to do it. The thought made him feel a rising sense of anticipation build inside.

Some things were best savored slowly, he reminded himself, and together they ate their meal in companionable silence. It was later, when he'd cleared their plates away and tidied the kitchen, that he made his suggestion.

"Come on, let's dance some of that dinner off," he coaxed as he rose and held out one hand.

Faye eyed him dubiously. "Dance?"

"Oh, come on, Faye. Relax. I won't bite."

Even as he said the words he felt an almost overwhelming urge to lower his mouth to the curve of her neck and do just that, gently bite her fair skin, then pepper it with kisses to soothe away any hurt. The very idea sent a surge of something else coursing through his veins. Desire. Slick and hot and demanding. He clenched his jaw tight on the wave of need that overtook him. And waited.

It felt like forever but, eventually, she placed one small, pale hand in his and allowed him to tug her to her feet. Piers led her to an open area of the main room and pulled her into his arms. It came as no surprise to him that she fit as though she belonged there. He caught a faint whiff of her fragrance as he held her close. Her choice held a subtle suggestion as to the potential sensuality that lay beneath her carefully neutral surface. The sandalwood base note was warm and heady, and totally at odds with the woman he thought he knew. He'd have thought she'd wear something more astringent, sharper. Something more in keeping with her persona in the office—not that he'd ever had that many opportunities to get close enough to her to smell her perfume, he noted silently.

But right now, right here, on what he fervently hoped would not be their last evening together, they were *very* close. Piers began to move to the music, enjoying the way she moved with him and relishing the brush of their hips, the sensation of her hand in his and the feel of the subtle movement of her back muscles beneath his other hand. And all the while, those delicate hints of her scent teased and tantalized his senses.

The initial resistance he'd felt in her body began to soften. Her steps became more instinctive, losing the stiffness that showed she was overthinking every move. It was hardly as if they were in a dance competition, but to him it felt as though there was a unity to their movements that led his mind to temptingly explore how well they could move together under other circumstances.

He bent his head and kissed the top of hers. Faye pulled back and looked up at him with wide eyes. Did he dare follow through on what he truly wanted—what he suspected that deep down she wanted, too? Of course he did.

When he took Faye's lips with his, he felt the shock of recognition pulse through his body. As if this woman in his arms was the one he'd been looking for all his adult life. The need that had been simmering under his carefully controlled behavior ever since their first kiss flamed to demanding life as her lips parted beneath his and she began to return his kiss with equal fervor.

This was more than that incident under the mistletoe the night he'd arrived at the lodge. This was incendiary. Consuming. He wanted her so much he had begun to tremble. He raised his hands to her hair and tugged at the pins that confined it into a knot at the back of her head. The pins dropped unheeded to the floor and her hair fell in thick, wavy tresses past her shoulders. He pushed his fingers through the silken length until he cupped the back of her head and angled her ever so slightly so he could deepen their embrace.

That she let him was more speaking than any words they'd ever shared. That her hands had knotted in his sweater at his waist, as if she had to somehow anchor herself to something solid, told him she was as invested in what was happening as he was.

Relief coursed through his veins. He didn't know how he'd have coped if she'd pulled away from him completely or if she had asked him to stop. Of course he'd stop, but it would probably strip years off his life to have to do so.

She felt so dainty in his arms, so fragile, and yet he knew she had a core of steel that many people never developed. She was tough and strong, yet vulnerable and incredibly precious at the same time.

Her hands released their grip on his sweater and he felt her tug at the garment before sliding her hands underneath it. Then he felt the incredible sensation of her warm palms against his skin. He groaned ever so slightly and lifted his mouth from hers so he could look again in her eyes—to receive confirmation once again that he wasn't demanding anything from her that she wasn't willing to give.

The sheen of desire that reflected back in her blue-gray

gaze was almost his undoing. The semi-arousal he'd been hoping wouldn't terrify her into running away stepped up a notch. He couldn't help it. He flexed his hips against her. Her cheeks flushed in response and her eyelids fluttered as if she were riding her own wave of sensation.

Piers lowered his mouth and kissed her again, this time sweeping her lips with his tongue and teasing past the soft inner flesh to titillate. She was making soft sounds of pleasure and when he pressed his hips against her again, he immediately felt the hitch in her breath. Her fingers tightened on the muscles of his back, her short, practical nails digging into him ever so lightly. His skin, already sensitive to her touch, became even more so, and a thrill tingled through him.

He gently pulled one hand free of her hair and stroked it down her back to the taut globes of her butt. She was so perfect and she felt so right against him. His hand drifted over her hip and up under her sweater. He felt tiny goose bumps rise on the smooth skin of her belly. Felt each indentation between her ribs, then felt the slippery-smooth satin of her bra. His hand slid around to her back and he deftly unfastened the hooks that bound her.

"I want to see you," he groaned against the side of her throat. "I want to touch you. All of you."

"Yes," she whispered shakily.

It was all the encouragement he needed. He moved away from her only enough to tug her sweater up over her head and to slide the straps of her unfastened bra down her arms, freeing her breasts to his hungry gaze. And there they were—those freckles that had so inappropriately tantalized him only a few nights ago.

Piers reached out with the tip of his forefinger to trace a line from her collarbone, connecting the dots until they disappeared and her flesh turned creamy white. Creamy white tipped with deliciously tantalizing pink nipples that were currently tight buds begging for his touch, his mouth. Action immediately followed thought. One hand went to her tiny waist, the other supported her back, as he lowered his mouth to her and teased one nipple and then the other with the tip of his tongue. He felt her shudder from head to foot and saw the blush of desire that bloomed across her skin.

Knowing he did this to her gave him a sense of joy he'd never experienced before with another woman. She was so responsive, so honest in her reactions. It was as refreshing as it was enticing and it made him want to make this evening even more special for her, more memorable.

Maybe there was a stroke of selfishness in his purpose. If he got this right, then maybe she wouldn't hightail it out of there when the road was open. Maybe she'd want to linger, to explore just how great they could be together in every way possible.

She deserved the best of everything and he would see to it that she got it. It was as simple as that.

It was one thing to touch her, but he wanted to *feel* her, as well. He moved away slightly so he could tug his sweater off. The instant he was free of it he pulled her to him, skin to skin. The delicious shock of it made him feel giddy in a way he hadn't experienced since he was a crazy teenager with too many advantages and a whole lot of testosterone. He savored the sensation and stroked the top of Faye's slender shoulders.

Her arms closed around him and she pressed her breasts against his diaphragm.

"Your skin, it's so hot. It's like you're on fire," she said so softly he had to bend his head to hear her.

"I'm on fire, all right. For you."

* * *

Faye ran her fingers up the bumps in Piers's spine then let her nails trace down his arms. She'd seen him topless before. When she'd worked with him while he'd been closing a business deal in France, on the Côte d'Azur, it wasn't unusual for him to declare his poolside patio his office for the day. She'd marveled at the chiseled lines of his body but she'd never imagined they would feel like this to the touch. That beneath the golden tan of his heated skin his muscles would feel both hard and supple at the same time.

It was thrilling to caress him. Forbidden and yet not at the same time. Faye pushed away the confusion that clouded the back of her mind. The voice of reason that told her this was a very stupid idea. That she was merely a temporary amusement for him. But there was something about the way he looked at her, and the way his hands touched her with such reverence, that made her feel as though even if she only got to have him this one time, this interlude could still be an experience that would chase away the darkness and the loneliness that dwelled inside her.

Was it wrong to want, to need, this physical contact with another person? To want to feel cherished? Under normal circumstances the logical side of her brain—the one that had endured years of guilt, grief and recovery—would say that, of course, it was wrong. She didn't deserve that kind of happiness.

But these were not normal circumstances and tonight that inner voice had been silenced. Wooed by champagne, dinner by firelight and dancing in the arms of a man whose breathtaking physical beauty was only transcended by the care he'd showed her tonight. Tonight? No, at all times. He might tease her and try to wheedle her secrets out of her, but he'd never been unkind or un-reasonable. In the office, while he was very firmly the boss, he'd always treated her as a valued equal. Considering her ideas and suggestions and giving credit where credit was due when he followed through on something that had been her brainchild.

Maybe she hadn't simply been wooed by tonight. Maybe she'd been wooed by Piers for the whole three years she'd known him and been working by his side, becoming more a part of his life than his parents and extended family. Certainly more a part of his life than the women he'd paraded in and out of his bed. For a brief moment she wondered, *If this went any further, would I be categorized as one of those women?* Okay, so maybe the inner voice wasn't completely silenced—she smiled gently to herself—but it was about to be.

Faye traced her fingertips up to the broad sweep of Piers's shoulders and back down over his biceps and forearms before shifting to his ridged abdomen. She heard his sharp intake of breath as she let her fingers slide lower, to the waistband of his trousers. One of his hands closed over hers as she started to tug at his belt.

"Let's take this slow." He practically ground out the words.

"Okay," she said in a small voice.

But she wanted him so much. She was almost afraid to acknowledge to herself just how deeply she was affected by him. How the heat of his body penetrated through her to warm her where she'd believed she'd never feel warm again. How that heat infiltrated to the depths of her very soul. How the strength of his arms made her feel protected and how his very presence made her feel so much less alone in the world.

His hips began to sway and she followed his lead as

they started again to dance. It felt so incredibly wicked to be dancing topless like this, but as his chest brushed against her breasts, as their bellies touched, as she felt his arousal press against her, it became less wicked and more and more right by the second.

When Piers tilted her face up to his and kissed her again, she felt as if she was melting from the inside out. His touch was magical, sending feathers of promise and delight singing along her veins. When he slowed their steps and reached for the fastener on her jeans to slowly slide her zipper down, she felt as though her entire body was humming like a tuning fork. She helped him push the denim to the floor and stepped out of the pool of fabric.

For a second she felt self-conscious about the burn scars that snaked over her lower legs, but then he kissed her and all thoughts of scars and the past fled.

His touch was so gentle, so reverent, she wanted to beg him to go further, harder, faster. But she was new at this. While she'd certainly been out with other men, even kissed a few, she'd never gone this far before. And what Piers was doing to her was making her insides quiver with a building tension that ached and demanded release.

Piers's fingers skimmed her mound through her panties and she pressed against him.

"Eager, hmm?"

"You make me feel so much," she acknowledged shyly. "But I… I want to feel more."

"I promise I will make you feel everything you can imagine and that you will enjoy every moment of it."

She chuckled softly, feeling a little self-conscious again. "Every moment?" she asked.

He pressed against her, his fingers cupping firmly between her thighs, leaving her quivering as an intense spear of longing pierced her.

"Every. Moment." He kissed the side of her neck to punctuate each word.

The sensation of his lips on her skin sent a sizzling tingle through her body. Who knew you could feel this much from something as simple as a caress?

"I will hold you to that, then," she said with all the solemnity she could muster.

"You know me. I love a challenge."

She shivered a little as she felt his lips pull into a smile against her sensitive skin. And, yes, she did know him. So why was she letting him touch her like this? His relationships in the past three years had been many—more than enough for her to recognize the similarities. The women all beautiful. Statuesque. Worldly. Experienced. Nothing like her. Her mind started ticking overtime. Was he simply amusing himself with her? Looking for someone to scratch an itch with and she was "it" purely by proximity and lack of other options?

And then his hands skimmed her rib cage and cupped her breasts, his fingers gently kneading the softness while his lips and tongue traced a line from the curve of her neck down to the tips of her tightly budded nipples. His teeth grazed one nipple as he drew it into the heated cavern of his mouth and all thought fled her mind as his tongue rasped her flesh. A moan escaped her and she clung to his broad shoulders as if her very ability to stand depended on him. And maybe it did. Maybe he was all that anchored her to this reality, these feelings, the need that pulsed an insistent demand through her body.

When Piers lifted her and laid her on the large sofa, she felt a ripple of anticipation undulate through her. She watched as he undid his trousers and pushed them down with his underwear, kicking off his shoes and socks with the grace that was inherent in everything he did. When he straightened, she found her gaze riveted to his arousal, the hard length of him jutting proudly from a nest of curls. A primal tug pulled through her body. An ancient answer to an equally ancient unspoken question. Piers bent and slid her panties down her legs, tossing them to the floor before lowering himself over her.

She reached for him, her fingers closing around the length of him, sliding gently up and down. His skin was so very hot and silky smooth. He groaned as she reached the tip and her fingertip met the drop of moisture that had gathered there.

"Damn it," he muttered. "Protection. I'll be right back."

He pulled away swiftly and she heard him leave the main room and head to one of the guest rooms. He was back in a moment, the rustle of foil barely audible over the crackle of the fire behind them. She watched, intrigued, as he rolled the sheath over his penis—her eyes flickering to the concentrated expression on his handsome face. His cheeks were flushed, his eyes shining with a fervor she'd never seen before. It took a moment to realize it was his desire for her that put that expression there.

The knowledge gave her strength. She knew that what came next could be uncomfortable, but she also knew that beyond the discomfort would come delight and gratification such as she'd never known. Her body already told her so. She knew she was ready.

When Piers settled over her, he looked her straight in the eye.

"Tell me if I'm taking this too fast," he urged as he nestled his hips between her open thighs.

Faye was aware of the blunt tip of his shaft nudging the soft folds of her skin, aware of his hand as he expertly guided himself to her entrance. A tiny sliver of apprehension pierced the veil of desire that gripped her, but it was soothed in the moment his fingers touched her just above that point where their bodies met.

He circled her clitoris, pressing gently against the nub and making her squirm against him. She moaned again as a fresh spiral of bliss began to radiate from her core. A spiral that grew in force commensurate with the pressure he applied until she felt her entire body become consumed with the strength of it. She surged against him and beneath the pleasure that racked her she was aware of a searing sensation as he entered her and filled her completely.

The pain was instantly forgotten as aftershocks of satisfaction rippled through her, making her inner muscles clench against him and, in turn, sending continued jolts of delight that spread from her core.

Piers didn't move and Faye slowly became aware of the strain that scored his face.

"What is it?" she said softly, her hands reaching up to cup his face. "Did I do something wrong?"

To her shock and surprise Piers withdrew from her body. He shook his head. "No, you did nothing wrong. Nothing except neglect to tell me you were still a virgin."

Eight

A virgin!

Piers's mind was in turmoil even as his body screamed at him to seek the release he'd been so close to attaining.

"Does it make a difference?" Faye asked beneath him in a small voice.

Her skin was still flushed with the aftermath of her orgasm, her eyes still glowed with the confirmation of the satisfaction he'd made it his mission to give her. But it wasn't enough. It had been her first time and if he'd known... Well, suffice it to say he wouldn't have taken her on a sofa the way he had.

"Piers?"

"Yes, it makes a difference."

He was disgusted with himself.

She was his employee. She should have been completely out of bounds. But these past few days he'd allowed himself to push all of his scruples out the door and to focus only on what he'd wanted. And he'd decided he'd wanted her. He still did. His blood still beat hot and fast through his veins with ferocious desire for her, every throb a painful reminder that he hadn't reached completion. But this wasn't about him anymore. It should never have been about him. The only person who mattered right here and now was the precious woman who'd trusted him with her virginity. Now it was up to him to make it right.

Without saying anything he rose, scooped her into his arms and began to head up the stairs.

"What are you doing?" she asked as she automatically hooked her arms around his neck.

Her room was just off the gallery. He toed the door open and walked through the darkened room toward the bed. Piers set her on her feet and swept the covers down.

"What am I doing? Well, I'm going to make love to you the way you deserve."

"But…but…" She sounded confused. "I know you didn't finish downstairs but you made me—"

Her voice broke as if she couldn't quite find the words to describe what she'd felt.

He'd have smiled at this—the first time he'd ever seen her at a complete loss for words—if he hadn't felt so damned serious.

"Lie down on the bed," he instructed her and reached over to switch on a bedside lamp. "That was nothing."

"Well, it felt like a whole lot more than nothing to me."

This time he couldn't help it. A twinge of male pride tugged his lips into a smile.

"Then you're really going to enjoy what I have planned for you this time."

"Oh?" she said with an arch to her brow that made her look a great deal more coquettish and experienced than he'd ever seen from her. "Well, it'll have to be something else to beat the last time."

He couldn't help it. He laughed and then realized this was first time he'd ever actually laughed in a situation like this.

"You know what I said about a challenge," he murmured as he settled on the mattress and began to stroke her body. "Nothing gives me more satisfaction than beating it—nothing except maybe this."

He moved to the base of the bed and began to run his fingertips from her feet up her legs. He felt her stiffen as he skimmed over the ropey scars on her feet and lower legs. Understanding her reluctance for him to focus too much attention on them, he moved upward, to her thighs, taking his time as he touched her. He chased each caress with a brush of his lips, a lick of his tongue or a nip of his teeth. Beneath his touch Faye began to quiver again, her thighs becoming rigid beneath his touch.

Yes, she thought he'd showed her pleasure, but that would pale in significance now.

His fingertips brushed the neatly trimmed patch of curls on her mound. He liked that she kept herself natural when so many went hairless these days. He tugged gently before letting his touch soothe again.

Faye squirmed against the sheets. He was drawing closer to the object of his goal and let his fingers drift across her clit.

She went still beneath him, as if trying to anticipate where he'd touch and what he'd do next. Piers smiled to himself as he bent his head lower. He could smell her scent, that wonderful musk of woman—a scent rich with promise that made his erection ache with a pleasure-pain that demanded he hurry this up. But he wouldn't be hurried. He was a man on a mission.

He touched her again with a fingertip, then let his hand trail to the top of her thighs. Her skin shivered with goose bumps and she clenched her hands in the sheets beside her. It was time. Piers lowered his mouth to her bud, flicking it with his tongue and relishing the taste of her. Faye uttered a startled gasp as he flicked his tongue across her again before blowing a cool stream of air on her heated flesh.

Again she gasped, her hands letting go of the sheets and tangling in his hair instead. He nuzzled her and traced his fingers higher, to the moist folds of skin that hid her entrance and beyond until he gently penetrated her. He felt her muscles tighten around his fingers, felt the shudder that racked her body. Yes, it was definitely time. He closed his mouth around her bud, swirling his tongue around the tiny nub and sucking gently until she was pressing against his mouth with abandon. He withdrew his fingers and then entered them into her body again, mimicking the action his arousal craved.

He tracked every indication of the escalating sensations that grew within her. Knew the exact moment she broke apart into a million pieces of pleasure. She looked so beautiful in her utter abandon that he had to fight to stay under control. He gentled the movement of his tongue, his fingers, until he felt her body begin to relax.

Faye's legs eased farther apart as she sank deeper into the mattress, and Piers moved between them, positioned himself and slowly slid into her molten heat. There was no resistance this time. No reminder that she had chosen to give herself to him and only him. Even so, he would eternally treasure that gift, treasure her, and make sure she realized just how incredibly special she was to him.

This time he coaxed her slowly to her peak, holding on to his control with every last thread of concentration and only letting himself go as he felt the deep, slow ripple of her climax undulate through her body. And then he let go, allowing his own pleasure to roll like thunder through him.

Spent, he finally collapsed on top of her, his heart pounding in his chest. He wrapped his arms around her slender form and rolled onto his side so that she was nestled up against him.

He pressed his lips to her forehead, feeling closer to her than he'd ever felt to anyone in his life. And he knew he wanted this new closeness between them to continue. He couldn't imagine his life without her in every aspect of it now.

"Are you okay?" he asked gently, nuzzling her hair and relishing the scent of it.

"Okay? I don't think I've ever felt more okay in my entire life." Faye's voice sounded thick and heavy, as though she was drugged with a combination of satisfaction and exhaustion. A soft chuckle escaped her. "I always knew you were a man of your word, but I didn't expect you to take things quite so literally. I think you can safely say your challenge has been met."

He smiled in response. "Well, you know what that means, don't you?"

She stiffened slightly in his arms, and though he wasn't sure what had triggered that response, Piers stroked the skin of her back to soothe her again.

"What does it mean?" she asked, fighting back a yawn.

"It means I have to do better next time."

"If there is a next time," she answered.

"Oh, there'll be a next time. And a time after that. But for now I think we should rest."

"Yeah, rest. That's a good idea. I don't think my body could handle all of that again too soon."

"Did I hurt you?" Piers asked, suddenly concerned.

He'd done his best to be gentle. To ensure her body was completely ready for him before he'd entered her.

"No, not at all. You were…you were amazing. Thank you."

He reached for the bedcovers and drew them over her, leaving the bed only long enough to dispense with the protection he'd worn before diving back under the covers and pulling her to him again. He felt that if he let her go she'd simply slip away like an ephemeral creature— there one minute, gone the next.

"Are you comfortable?" he asked.

"Very. I didn't know it could be like this, sharing a bed with someone else. It's cozy, isn't it?"

He laughed softly. "Very cozy." He fell silent a minute before asking the question that kept echoing in the back of his mind. "Why me, Faye? Why did you let me be your first?"

The minute he allowed the words to fall on the air he knew he'd made a mistake. He could feel her retreat, mentally if not physically.

"Why not?" she answered. "You did seem to be very good at it."

Now she was using humor to shield herself from revealing the truth. He'd have to tread carefully if he was to work his way past her protective shields without damaging the fragile link they now shared.

"For what it's worth, I'm honored I was your first. I—" He took a deep breath. Was it too soon? "I care about you, Faye."

She remained silent for what felt like forever but then he heard her indrawn breath and her voice softly filtered through the darkness around them.

"I care about you, too."

As admissions went, it was hard-won, and he allowed

a swell of relief dosed with a liberal coating of satisfaction to ride through him. It was a good start.

She snuggled right into his chest and he could feel the puffs of her breath against his skin.

"I haven't had many boyfriends," she admitted. "After my family died in a car wreck, I just wasn't interested in much of anything anymore. I was fostered in the same district where I'd grown up, so there was as little disruption to my routine as possible once I was released from hospital. Some of my friends at school…they tried to include me, but as we all got older we drifted apart."

"I'm sorry about your family, Faye. That must have been tough."

The words sounded so inane. Not nearly enough to describe his sorrow at the thought of what she must have been through. What would it have been like to suddenly be alone at fifteen? To be without the anchors that kept you feeling safe and loved. Growing up, his parents had been uninvolved, but he'd always had Quin by his side. The grief he'd felt at the loss of his brother had sent him to a dark, lonely place in his mind and it had forced him to reevaluate a lot of things in his life. But at least he'd been an adult while learning to cope with his loss. For Faye, just a teenager, how could she make decisions about her future when everything she'd ever known, every parameter she'd lived her life by, had been gone in a flash?

"Tough, yeah. That's one word for it. I had lovely foster parents, though. And my mom and stepdad had established a college fund for me so when I aged out of foster care I could choose where I went from there. I didn't want for anything."

Anything except for a family. Piers thought about the little boy sleeping down the hall in his bedroom, considered the ready-made family that he and Casey could offer

Faye. But he weighed that up with her obvious reluctance to have anything to do with the baby. Did that stem from the losses she'd suffered when she was still a teenager? How on earth did a man wade past that?

Encircled in Piers's arms, Faye didn't feel the usual searing pain that scored her when she thought about her family. Instead it was kind of a dull ache. Still there, still hurting, but muted, as if the edges had softened somehow. The realization made her feel disloyal to their memory. She didn't deserve this. Didn't deserve to let any aspect of the memory of their loss slide away. Guilt hammered at her with all the subtlety of a sledgehammer.

This was why she hadn't encouraged any relationships beyond friendship in the past. And it was why she should never have allowed things between her and Piers to go as far as they'd gone—no matter how fantastic it had been.

She'd made a mistake tonight—several mistakes. From the minute she'd accepted the glass of champagne from Piers to the second she'd allowed him to touch her. What had she been thinking?

Maybe that, for once in her life, she should reach out and sample what others took for granted?

No. She mentally shook her head. She had no right to do that. It was best that she get back on her path alone and leave in the morning as she'd planned. Leave before her heart became too heavily engaged with the man who had drifted to sleep beside her, not to mention the child he was determined to claim for his own.

Decision made, she closed her eyes, willing herself to drift to sleep. Goodness knew her body felt so sated and weary that sleep should have come easily. But for some reason her mind wouldn't let go, wouldn't allow her to find peace.

Instead she found herself concentrating on the smallest of things, like the way Piers's fingers continued to stroke her bare back every now and then, even though he was asleep. Like the deep, regular sound of his breathing and the scent of his skin. She would store these memories and lock them away, and maybe one day she'd be strong enough to think about them, about this magical night, again.

Faye woke to an empty bed and felt a rush of relief. At least the whole morning-after thing could be delayed until she was showered, dressed, packed and ready to leave. She shifted in the bedsheets, catching a drift of Piers's cologne. Just that tiny thing made her body tighten on a wave of longing so piercing that it almost brought tears to her eyes.

Instead of giving in to her emotions, Faye did what she'd always done. She focused on what needed to be accomplished first. That, at least, was something she could control.

Once dressed and packed, she double-checked the bathroom and bedroom to ensure she was leaving nothing behind and headed down the stairs to put her suitcase by the front door. She could hear Piers and Casey in the kitchen. With her stomach in knots, she walked toward the sound. Piers had his back to her and was talking a bunch of nonsense to the baby, who was staring up at him in rapt attention.

Faye would never have thought her heart could break any further than it already had, but the sight of those two was just about her undoing. Once again, tears sprang to her eyes. She blinked them back fiercely and turned to a cupboard to drag a mug out for her morning coffee.

"Good morning," Piers said. "Did you sleep well?"

"Better than I expected," she answered shortly.

"Me, too," he answered with a smile that sent a curl of lust winding through her.

This is impossible, she thought as she grabbed the carafe from the coffee machine and poured the steaming liquid into her mug. Just a look from him, a smile, and she was as pathetically eager for his attention as all his other women. Did that mean she was one of them now? She straightened her shoulders. No, it most certainly did not. One night did not change anything as far as she was concerned. If she could just get back to her apartment and back to a routine, everything would be okay.

She watched as Piers took the baby bottle from the warmer and gave it a little shake before testing a few drops on his wrist.

"Sir, your breakfast is served!" he said to the infant with a delightfully dramatically flourish.

Casey gave him a massive gummy grin in return. His little legs kicked wildly as Piers offered him the bottle.

"You're good with him," Faye observed. "Are you still going to keep him?"

"Yes."

The answer was simple and emphatic. No fluffing about responsibilities or honoring his brother's memory or anything like that. Just a simple yes.

She envied him his conviction.

Piers looked up at her and she saw something new in his gaze.

"Is it ridiculous to say that I love him already?" he asked.

She'd never known him to sound insecure about anything. Ever. That he should feel that way about Casey just made him even more human, more attractive. She shook her head.

"No, it's not."

Piers nodded in acceptance and turned his attention back to the little boy.

Faye took advantage of the shift in focus to start making breakfast. "Have you eaten?" she asked.

"Yeah, I ate when I got up. It was early, though. I could go a second round."

She busied herself making omelets with the last of the ingredients she could find in the refrigerator. It was a good thing the road would be cleared today and that Meredith, who'd been waiting at a motel in town, would be able to come through with supplies.

Faye was just plating up the food when the phone rang with the news that a crew had cleared the road up to the fallen tree and was now working to clear the log. The news made Faye feel as if every nerve in her body had coiled tight, ready to spring free the moment she could leave the building.

The next two hours were an exercise in torment as she tried to catch up on emails while Piers lay on the floor and played with the baby before putting him to bed for another nap. The moment she heard a sound near the front door she was up and all but running to let the newcomer inside.

"Ms. Darby! Are you all right? I saw your car. It's a miracle you're still alive!"

Piers's housekeeper bustled inside and grasped Faye by her upper arms, giving her a once-over as if checking for injuries. "Oh, Ms. Darby—your face!"

"It's okay, Meredith. It's what happened when the airbag went off. I wasn't hurt aside from that, and I'm almost all healed," Faye said as brightly as she could.

Satisfied Faye hadn't been seriously injured, Meredith gave her a nod and then drew her in for a quick hug, which Faye endured good-naturedly. She wasn't a hugger but she was used to Meredith's overwhelming need to mother everyone in her sphere.

"I'm fine, Meredith. I take it the road is clear now?"

"Yes, they've moved your wreck to the side and taken away most of the tree. Some of it will have to wait until they can get some heavier equipment up, but there's room to squeeze by."

Faye had expected to feel relieved at the news. Actually, she'd expected to feel jubilant. Instead there was a hollow sense of loss looming inside her. She shoved the thought away before it could take hold.

"Well, that's a relief!" she said with all the brightness she could muster. "I think I'm suffering a bit of cabin fever. I can't wait to get home."

"Mr. Luckman! I'm so glad to see you!" Meredith gushed effusively over Faye's shoulder.

Faye turned and saw the swiftly masked look of disappointment in Piers's eyes. Had he really thought that a spectacular night of sex would change her mind about leaving? She already knew there was a flight out early this afternoon. She had to be on it. She couldn't stay another minute or maybe she would change her mind and stay—and what then? More risk? More chance of loss? More joy and pleasure that she didn't deserve and couldn't allow herself to enjoy? No, it was far better that she left now.

"Meredith, good to see you, too."

"How have you been managing?" Meredith said, fussing over him.

"Just fine, thanks, Meredith. You left us so well stocked we could have stayed here a month on our own."

Faye suppressed a shudder. A month? She could never have lasted that long and still left with her sanity intact.

In a month Casey would have grown and changed and wound her completely around his pudgy little fingers. And a whole month confined here with Piers? She tried to think of the reasons why that was a bad idea but her newly awakened libido kept shouting them down. Every last one. Which in itself was exactly why she needed to put distance between her and Piers.

"We have run out of diapers, however," Piers continued. "I hope you got my text to add them and baby food to the groceries."

"I did. But why on earth…?" Meredith looked from Piers to Faye for an explanation.

Faye shrugged and looked at Piers. "You can explain it. I really need to get going. Meredith, after we've unloaded your car, can I borrow it to get to the airport? I'll organize for someone to return it for you."

Over Meredith's iron-gray curls, Faye saw Piers looking at her again. His expression appeared relaxed but she could see tiny lines of strain around his eyes.

"Do you really need to run away right now?" he asked.

"I can't stay. You know that. I have things to do. Places to go. People to see."

He knew she was lying, she could see it in the bleak expression that reflected back at her. Faye turned away. She couldn't bear to see his disappointment and it irritated her that it mattered to her so much.

She grabbed her coat, scurried down the front steps to where Meredith had left her station wagon and started to take bags of groceries from the rear. Piers was at her side before she could make her way back to the house.

"You know you're running away."

"I'm doing nothing of the kind. I wasn't supposed to be here in the first place, remember?"

"You're running away," he repeated emphatically. "But are you running away from me or from yourself?"

"Don't be ridiculous. I'm not running anywhere," she snapped and pushed past him to take the groceries to the house.

He was too astute. She'd always admired his perceptiveness in the workplace but she hated it when he applied it to her. Behind her she heard him grab the remaining sacks of supplies and follow her up the stairs.

She made her way swiftly to the kitchen, where Meredith was already taking inventory of what needed to be done.

He was close behind her, and as he brushed past he whispered in her ear, "Liar. I'd hoped you might change your plans and spend Christmas here with Casey and me. We don't have to worry about anyone else."

Words hovered on the edge of her lips—acceptance and denial warring with one another.

"Thanks, but no thanks," she eventually said, hoping she'd injected just the right amount of lightness into her tone.

"Faye, we need to talk. C'mon, stay. It's Christmas Eve."

The last three words were the reminder she needed. Christmas Eve. The anniversary of the death of her family. Shame filled her that she'd lost track of the days.

"I really need to go," she said, her voice hollow.

Meredith handed her the set of keys to the station wagon. "There you go, Ms. Darby. There's plenty of gas in the tank."

"Thanks, Meredith. I'll take good care of it, I promise. I'll leave Mr. Luckman to explain why he needs all these diapers," Faye answered, patting the bumper pack she'd carried in with the bags from the car.

Before Piers could stop her, she slipped out of the kitchen, through the main room and out the front door. The finality of pulling the heavy door closed behind her sent a shaft of anguish stinging through her, but she ignored it and kept going. It was the only way she could cope. She was used to loss. Used to pain. She'd honed her ability to survive, to get through every single day, on both those things. And, somehow, she'd get through this day exactly the same way.

Nine

Blue skies, sand and sunshine had never looked better, Faye decided as she opened the drapes of her sitting room on Christmas morning and stared out at the vista below. She'd paid a fine premium for this apartment with its tiny balcony overlooking the beach, but even though she'd chosen it because it was nothing like what she remembered of home, she never could quite shake off the memories.

Take last night. She'd started her movie marathon; the way she'd done every year since she'd lived alone. But for some reason the gory plotlines and the gripping action couldn't hold her attention and in the end she'd turned off the player. At a loss, she'd sought out the box of precious possessions among her parents' things. The entire household had been packed up and stored in a large locker after the accident and held for her until she turned eighteen—fees had been paid out of her parents' estate.

This particular box she saved for Christmas Eve alone.

Filled with photo albums of her throughout her childhood, starting as a baby, with her mom, then with her stepdad and finally the unfinished album with the precious few photos she had of her baby brother. He'd have been just over thirteen years old by now. Maybe he'd have been an irritating teenager, pushing his boundaries—or a sports star in his favorite game. Or maybe he'd have been more bookish and quiet like she'd been as a child. She'd never know. The empty pages at the back of the album were an all-too-somber reminder of the lack of future for baby Henry.

Last night's visit to her past had reduced her to a shaking, sobbing mess, but when she'd woken this morning, instead of the yawning abyss of loss that had consumed her heart for so many years, she felt different. Yes, there was grief, and that would never completely go away. But overlaying that grief was a sense of closure, as if she'd finally been able to completely say goodbye.

She knew she'd never be able to stop thinking about her family, never stop loving them, but she felt less of a hostage to her grief than she'd been before. It was part of her. It had made her grow into the adult she was now and it had driven so many of her decisions, leading her to this point in her life. But maybe it was time for her to stop letting it direct her life. Maybe it was even time to let go of her grip on the guilt she felt for not having been able to avoid the crash that night. Perhaps she didn't deserve to be unhappy, after all. Maybe it was even time to take a risk on loving someone else again. Someone like Piers, perhaps, who now came with a ready-made family?

The thought struck terror into her heart, but before long she managed to push past it to examine the thought carefully.

The analytical side of her brain asked her if she thought she might genuinely be falling in love with Piers.

If she entered into a relationship with him, she'd be doing it with her eyes open. After all, she probably knew the man better than his own mother did. She'd been an integral part of his life for the past three years, managing both his work world and his private life in as much as he needed her to. And she admired him. He could so easily have been more like Quin. So easily have lived off the obscenely large trust fund that previous generations of Luckmans had provided for him, but he'd chosen to work and he worked hard. The business and residential property developments he'd undertaken since she'd worked with him had become among the most sought after anywhere in the world.

Yes, he had a playboy background and, yes, she'd seen how easily he discarded a lover when he'd felt a relationship had run its course. But he'd definitely been different since Quin had died. Quieter. More thoughtful. And, slowly, she'd begun to see yet another facet to him. One that had undoubtedly begun to unravel the bindings around her heart.

But was she actually falling in love with *him* or was she instead falling in love with the idea of being part of something bigger than just herself? A family? A new start? A chance to make amends for what she'd done?

Faye squeezed her eyes closed and growled out loud in frustration. So many questions. So few answers.

Piers returned from Wyoming in the second week of the new year. She heard his voice as he came down the corridor from the elevators and every nerve in her body stood to attention. She'd avoided all his calls since she'd left Jackson Hole, keeping their communications strictly to text messages and email. She'd sensed his frustration with her immediately but she hadn't been ready talk to him. To hear the timbre of his voice. To relive the intimacy they'd shared—the memory of which still took her by surprise every now and then and stole her breath away.

But there was no hiding now. Any second he'd round the corner and walk straight into the open-plan area they shared.

And then there he was.

The impact of seeing him was just as shocking as she'd anticipated. A flush of heat spread through her body as her eyes flew up to meet his. She swallowed hard against the sudden lump that formed in her throat when she realized he bore a baby car seat in one hand, with Casey sound asleep inside it, and his briefcase in the other.

"Good morning," she finally managed to squeeze the greeting past the constriction and stepped out from behind her desk. "Coffee?"

"Why wouldn't you answer my calls?"

"Coffee it is, then," she answered smoothly and turned her back on him.

"Faye, you can't keep avoiding me."

"I wasn't avoiding you. We spoke."

"Through the written word only. And, yes, before you remind me *again*, I have been in touch with Lydia and, not so surprisingly, she canceled dinner. It seems she wasn't quite ready for instant motherhood.

"But, back to you—after you left I was worried about you and until I was certain I could take Casey out of state with me, I couldn't exactly drop everything and come running to check on you, either."

She'd been aware of all that. She automatically went through the motions of making his coffee from the espresso machine in the corner. Once it was made to his preferred specifications, black and sweet, she carried his mug across to his desk.

"As you can see, you had nothing to worry about. I'm fine."

Piers put the carrier with the sleeping baby on his desk and turned to face her. His hand shot up and his fingers captured her chin lightly, tilting her face toward his. A shiver of anticipation ran through her. Was he planning to kiss her? Here, in the office?

"Still too many shadows, Faye. Too many secrets. I don't want there to be any secrets between us," he said gently. "Not anymore."

"Secrets? I'm sure I don't know what you're talking about. I'm an open book."

He laughed, a short, sharp sound that expressed his disbelief far more eloquently than any words could have done.

"Okay, so you want to play it that way for now. Fine. We'll get back to business, but you won't be able to hide from me forever."

Casey chose that moment to wake and squawk his disapproval with his new surroundings. Faye was riveted by the sight of Piers, in full corporate splendor, lifting the child from the car seat and holding him to him as if he'd been doing it from the day Casey had been born. The little guy settled immediately.

"You're spoiling him," Faye noted, settling behind her desk.

"According to Meredith, you can't spoil a baby. You can only love them. I'm inclined to agree."

Faye felt that all too familiar clench in her chest. She knew very well how it felt to love babies. And to lose them.

"Have you had any more news from your lawyers?"

"They tell me they're going to attempt a case based on abandonment. As Quin's next of kin, they believe I stand a strong chance of being able to adopt Casey outright. At the very least the emergency guardianship application has been approved."

"Are you sure that's what you want to do? Adoption? It's a big commitment. What if his mom changes her mind? What if even now she's looking for him?"

"She knew where to find me the first time, she can find me again. If she does reach out, then maybe we can get to the bottom of why she didn't see fit to contact us earlier about Casey."

Faye thought back to the note. "Do you think she knew that Quin had…?" Her voice trailed away.

"To be honest, no. I think she heard I was coming back to the house for Christmas and acted impulsively. Maybe she thought I was Quin. Who knows? From what we've been able to glean, she worked on a temporary basis for the company that catered for me. She's very young, only nineteen. She's from Australia and had been backpacking her way across the country and picking up casual work where she could. I don't even know if Casey was born in Wyoming. Whatever the case, his place is with me."

Piers's voice was emphatic on that last statement.

"Well, as long as you realize he's not like a toy you can pick up and put down at whim. He's a lifetime commitment. When you start a new relationship, I hope, whoever she is, she's on board with having a baby in her life."

Piers shot her a searing glance. She could see the banked irritation in his eyes.

"What are you implying, Faye? That I'll just ignore Casey when it suits me?"

"I'm not implying anything. But, let's face it, you've only had a few weeks with a baby, part of which you had with me and the rest with Meredith who probably hardly let you hold him once she got there. You didn't have any work or other priorities to deal with, so you could focus completely on him. It's not the real world. The reality involves dealing with fevers and colds, teething, colic, potty training, tantrums, sleepless nights on top of the busy schedule you usually keep. You seem to think it's going to be a walk in the park, but it's not like that. Raising a child is damn hard work."

"And you'd know because?" He pinned her under a hard stare, silently demanding she answer him.

"I know because I'm not some Pollyanna who thinks everything is always going to be all right. Bad things happen. Life doesn't always go the way you expect to."

As soon as she said the words she wished them back. It was almost the anniversary of Quin's death. Piers knew as well as anyone else who'd suffered great loss that life could deliver unexpected blows along with the highs.

She hastened to make amends. "Look, I'm sorry. I'm out of line. I'll get out of your way. I have a meeting with the new brand manager at ten so I'd better get down to marketing."

"Yeah, you do that," he said, his voice carrying a note of determination that made Faye's stomach lurch a little. "And while you're at it, ask yourself why you keep such strong emotional barriers up between you and everyone else. It's not just me, is it? It's everyone. Because while you're questioning my ability to commit to Casey, I think perhaps you ought to be asking yourself why you're not capable of committing to anything but your work."

She looked at him in shock. His acuity cut straight through everything and got immediately to the point. She took in a deep, steadying breath and met his gaze, but even as she did so she could feel the sting of tears burning at the backs of her eyes.

Piers saw the moisture begin to collect and his expression turned stricken. "Faye, I'm sorry, this time *I* overstepped."

"No, it's okay," she said, blinking fiercely and waving a hand between them. "I'd better go."

Piers watched her leave, feeling as if he was little more than a slug that had crawled out of a vegetable patch. What on earth had spurred him to be so cruel to Faye like that? Was it because she'd hit a nerve when questioning his commitment to Casey? Or had it been her comment about bad things happening to people? *Which she apologized for*, the voice at the back of his mind sternly reminded him. Either way, he knew he'd done wrong. He couldn't afford to lose her and it wasn't just because she knew his company almost as well as he knew it himself.

The last two weeks without her had been oddly empty. Sure, he'd been busy with the baby, who'd already grown and changed in that short time. Yes, Meredith had helped him, but he'd made sure he'd been Casey's primary caregiver. But Faye's absence had made him all the more aware of what she'd come to mean to him on a personal level. If only he could get past that barrier she kept so firmly between them. He sensed the only way that would happen would be if he learned what had occurred in her past to make her so closed off and wary.

Obviously his people had done a background check before she'd been offered the job here, but it had focused on her credentials and experience, and had been peripheral to what he needed to know about her now. Maybe he needed to delve a little deeper. A part of him cautioned him about digging into her past without her knowledge—warned him that if she wanted him to know that much about her, she'd tell him herself. But Piers didn't get things done by waiting for other people. Sometimes you just had to take control and steer the course yourself. This was one of those times.

By the time Faye returned from her meeting, Piers was satisfied that before long he'd get to the root of why she held herself so aloof. Of course, it didn't mean that he wouldn't keep trying to glean what he could from her in the meantime. As soon as she was back in the office, he rose from his desk and walked over to her.

"Everything go okay with the brand manager?"

"Yes, perfect in fact. You made an excellent choice there."

"I know people," he said without any smugness.

It was one of his greatest strengths and he wasn't afraid to admit it. It was also the reason why he knew Faye had unplumbed depths he needed to explore. She deserved more in her life than the shell of existence he knew she lived. She deserved to feel, to laugh—to love.

"You do seem to have a knack there," she admitted wryly.

"I'm glad you think so, but I'd like your help with the meetings I've scheduled for the afternoon. An agency is sending over some nannies for interviews. I want to establish a nursery for Casey on this floor. I was thinking of repurposing the archive room a couple of doors down, actually. Archives can be moved to another floor. I'll need someone who can be here with Casey during the day and at home when I have to make an overnight trip anywhere—although I plan to minimize travel where possible from now on."

Faye looked at him in surprise. "You want me to help you with interviews?"

"Of course, you're my right hand here."

She looked uncomfortable. "But choosing a nanny… Surely that's something you should do on your own."

"Why?"

She was running again, moving into classic avoidance mode, although perhaps not quite as literally as she had back at the lodge.

"Well… I…"

"I trust your judgment, Faye. Will you help me?"

He'd chosen his words carefully, knowing her pride in her work wouldn't allow her to say a flat-out no if he phrased it like that.

"Why me? Maybe you should ask someone else on staff who already has children and has hired nannies before."

"But you know what I need. You always do. First appointment is after lunch."

He saw her visibly sag. "Fine, I'll be ready. Is there anything in particular you want me to look out for?"

"No, just use your judgment like you always do. I know you won't be shy in telling me what you think. And, Faye," he continued just as she started to turn and walk away, "I want to apologize for my comment earlier about commitment. It was unkind of me to say that especially when you've always been there for me when I needed you."

"It's fine. Consider it forgotten."

"No, I can't forget it because I know I hurt you and it hurts me to know I did that. That said, things have changed between us and I'd like to see where we go from here."

"Changed?"

"You've forgotten our lovemaking already?" he teased. Even though he kept his tone light, deep down he felt a slight sting at the idea she'd put that incredible night to the back of her memory.

"Oh, that," she said, coloring again. "No. I haven't forgotten. Any of it."

"And it doesn't make you curious about maybe exploring that side of our relationship further?"

She shook her head firmly. "No. To be honest, I've thought about little else since I came home and, frankly, I think we should forget it."

"I can't forget it. I can't forget *you*." He stepped closer to her and took her hands in his. "I want to know you better, Faye. Sure, I know how great you are here at work. I also know how you sound when we make love. I know how to bring you pleasure, but…" He let go of one hand to tap gently at her forehead. "In here, I don't think I know you at all—and I really, really want to. Will you let me in, Faye? Will you let me know you?"

She looked shaken, uncertain…but he believed he was having an impact, that she was at least considering the idea.

A phone on her desk began to ring and Piers bit back a curse. Faye pulled loose from his hold.

"I'd better get that," she said, her voice sounding choked.

"Sure, but we will finish this discussion, Faye. I promise you. I won't give up. You mean too much to me."

And leaving that statement ringing in her ears, he left the room.

Ten

The nanny interviews went extremely well. So well, in fact, that Faye couldn't fault any of the women or the highly qualified male pediatric nurse who'd applied. When Piers suggested they discuss the applicants over dinner at his house, Faye sensed a rat, but she knew he wouldn't back down and decided the easiest thing would be to face him and get it over with.

She went home after work, showered and changed into a loose pair of pants and a long-sleeved silk blouse that drifted over her skin like a lover's touch. Huh? Where had that thought come from?

She frowned as she checked her reflection in the mirror. The cornflower blue of the silk with its darker navy print in a tribal pattern here and there made her eyes look more blue than gray. Was this too dressy? she wondered. Maybe she should just put on something she'd wear at work.

A glance at the time scotched that idea. Piers was expecting her in twenty minutes and it would take her all of that to get to his place in the Palisades. She slid her feet into low-heeled sandals, grabbed her bag and headed out the door. She took the Pacific Coast Highway to the turnoff, letting the view of the sea calm her—a comfort she badly needed when the prospect of spending the evening with Piers, and likely Casey, was the least relaxing thing she could think of.

Piers answered the door himself when she arrived, his cell phone stuck to his ear. He gestured for her to come in and take a seat in the living room off the main entrance. Rather than sit, Faye strolled over to the large French doors that opened to the gardens and looked out toward the pool. Despite the elegance and expense he'd put into furnishing the house, it looked and felt very much like a home. Although she'd been there many times for work, somehow this visit felt different. A tiny shiver ran down her back and she rubbed her arms before wrapping them around herself.

"Cold?" Piers asked from behind her, making her jump a little.

"No, it's nothing."

"You're nervous then."

"I am not," she protested. "I have nothing to be nervous about."

He studied her for a few seconds before quirking his mouth a little, as if he'd accepted what she said on face value and nothing more. It made her instinctively bristle, but she was prepared to let it drop if he was.

"Sorry I was on the phone when you arrived. It was my lawyer's office. They've tracked down Casey's mom. Turns out she's back in Australia."

"And? Is she okay?"

"That was the first thing I asked them. Apparently she's doing fine and she remains adamant that she wants nothing to do with Casey."

Faye felt a strong tug of sympathy for the little guy. "Why did she have him then, if she didn't want him? What was she thinking?"

"I get the impression she wasn't thinking much at all. She came to the US after ditching her boyfriend in Australia. She fell into a relationship with a new guy here, but he left her when they found out she was expecting. He said it couldn't be his baby because he was infertile, which, according to her, left Quin as the only other possible father.

"She says she tried to get ahold of Quin but never got an answer when she called his phone, which would make sense, of course." Piers's eyes grew bleak and he drew in another breath before continuing. "According to what she told the lawyer, she stayed in Wyoming, drifting from casual job to casual job until she had the baby. By then she'd saved enough to go home again. She'd originally believed Casey to be her boyfriend's child but when he told her he was infertile and their relationship broke down *and* she couldn't get ahold of Quin, she honestly didn't know where to turn. She hadn't wanted to call on her family back in Australia and, living a transient lifestyle here, had no idea of how to seek help. Now, she only sees Casey as a hindrance and, also according to my lawyer, is willing to sign off all her rights to access."

"She is getting legal counsel about her decision, isn't she?"

"I've insisted on it and agreed to pay all her expenses. I've also requested she have a psychological assessment. I would hate for her decision to be based on any possible psychosis as a result of having Casey."

Faye nodded in agreement. "That's a good idea. I'm glad you've done that."

"She insisted it wasn't necessary and that she simply wants to close the door on this episode of her life, but when we said we'd cover all costs, she reluctantly agreed."

"Did she know Quin had passed away?"

"Apparently not. She heard that I was coming up to the house and assumed I was the guy she'd had a relationship with. Although 'relationship' is a bit of a misnomer. It seems they were nothing more than a few brief liaisons during and after New Year's Eve.

"Anyway," Piers continued, "I'm leaving everything I can in the hands of my lawyers and my most pressing concern right now is choosing who I trust the most to be able to help me provide the best care for Casey."

He poured them both a drink. A Scotch on the rocks for him and a mineral water for her. They sat side by side on the sofa and pored over the folders he'd brought home.

"I think you should go with these two," Faye said, putting her finger on the guy's CV and one of the slightly older women.

"Tell me why."

"Well, I think they both have some very strong experience. Jeremy's worked in pediatrics and needs more regular hours to support his wife while she completes her degree, and Laurie has excellent references from all of her past positions. In fact, she's only leaving her current role because the family is moving to the UK and Laurie doesn't want to go. They could rotate from week to week between the office and the house. One week, day shifts. The next, nights."

"Do I really need two nannies? I plan to be on hand in the evenings and if Casey needs me during the night."

"I know you plan to minimize travel, but what about when you do site visits and you're away for several days, or if you're called to troubleshoot a problem at short notice and can't get home at night? Not to mention business dinners and other events that you can't skip that could take you away for hours at a time. Getting a sitter for him every time would be a hassle, and it would be rough for Casey, too. He needs continuity—to feel familiar with the person caring for him. Babies respond better to routine."

Piers fell silent and angled his body to face her, one arm resting along the back of the sofa.

"I asked you this before but this time I want an answer. How come you know so much about babies? I know you act like you want nothing to do with them but your advice is always spot-on. You talk about child care like you really understand it."

Faye felt the all too familiar lump solidify in her throat. She swallowed to try to clear it but it barely made any difference.

"I've seen kids in the care system. Some of them abandoned, some of them taken from their families through hardship or abuse. It gave me an insight, that's all."

The half lie made her heart begin to race in her chest. An insight? That was far too mild a description for what it had been like in her foster home when a baby was brought to the house for care—and in her years there, there had been several. She vividly remembered the first one who'd come into the home after her placement. Remembered hurrying home from high school each day so she could help her foster mom with the little boy's care. She didn't understand then, but now she knew that she'd poured all of her love for her dead baby brother into that child. When he was eventually returned to his parents, she'd felt the aching loss of his departure as if it was a physical pain.

She'd promised herself she wouldn't get so involved the next time, but she'd been unable to help herself. Each child had called to her on one level or another—each one a substitute; a vessel open to receive all the love she had inside her. Her foster mom had seen it all, had talked with Faye's caseworker about it, but the woman had told her it was a good thing. That it was allowing Faye to work through her grief for her family. But it hadn't. In the end, when she'd aged out of the system at eighteen and gone to college, she was just as broken as she'd been when she'd arrived.

A touch on her cheek made her realize she'd fallen deep into her reveries—forgotten where she was, and why. To her horror she realized she was crying. She bolted up from the sofa and dashed her hands across her face, wiping all trace of tears from her cheeks.

"Faye? It's more than that, isn't it?" Piers probed gently. "How did you see those kids in the system? Was it when you were placed in foster care yourself?"

She stopped at the French doors. Maybe this would be easier if she couldn't see him. Couldn't feel his strong reassuring presence so close beside her.

"Yes."

A shudder shook her. Warm hands settled on her shoulders but he made no move to turn her around.

"It must have been hell for you."

She didn't want to go into details, so she did the only thing she knew would distract him. She spun and slipped her hands around the back of his neck and gently coaxed his face to hers.

He didn't pull away; he didn't protest. He simply closed

his arms around her waist, let her take his mouth and coax his lips open.

The second she did, she felt a jolt of need course through her. A need that demanded he fill all the dark, empty spaces inside. The spaces she barely even wanted to acknowledge existed. She wanted him so badly her entire body shook with it, and when his hands began to move, one cupping her buttocks and pulling her more firmly into the cradle of his hips, she let herself give over to sensation.

She couldn't get enough of him. His taste, his scent, the strong, hard feeling of his body against hers. Her mind blazed with heat and longing, remembering the intense gratification he'd wrung from her. The feeling of him reaching his own peak and knowing he'd found that delight in her.

"Dinner is served in the conservatory, Mr. Luckman. Oh!"

Faye ripped her lips from his and tried to pull away, but Piers wouldn't let her go. Instead he firmly rubbed her back, as one would when trying to settle a skittish animal.

"Thank you, Meredith. We'll be along in a moment."

Faye ducked her head, unable to meet the housekeeper's eyes. Ashamed of what she'd done.

Piers tipped her chin so she'd looked up at him again.

"As a distraction tactic, I have to say, I admire your strategy. Shall we go through to dinner?"

Faye pulled away again and Piers let her go this time.

"No. Look, I'd better go. Meredith—"

"No more running away. Meredith won't say a word. You should know as well as anyone that she's the soul of discretion. Besides, she likes you."

Like her or not, Faye felt horribly uncomfortable as she let Piers tug her down the hall to the family room and through to an informal dining area in the conservatory, where Meredith had arranged their meal. A succulent-looking tri-tip roast nestled in its juices on a carving plate and a roasted vegetable salad was piled in a serving dish beside it. The scents of balsamic and garlic made Faye's mouth water hungrily.

Meredith looked up from tweaking a napkin at one of the place settings. "I've left the roast for you to carve, Mr. Luckman. The baby is down for the night, so I'll be off now. The monitor is on the sideboard over there. *Bon appétit!*" And, with a warm and knowing smile in Faye's direction, she bustled her way back to the kitchen.

Faye felt herself begin to relax. Okay, so Meredith didn't judge her for what she'd seen back there in the living room. *And why should she?* a little voice asked. *She's probably seen Piers kissing women every day.*

Across the table, Piers picked up the carving knife and fork. "What's your pleasure?" he asked with a hooded look.

Her insides clenched on a wave of heat at his simple question. "I… I beg your pardon?"

"Do you prefer the crispy end or something from the middle?"

"Oh, the end bit, please."

"Your wish is my command."

Faye watched, mesmerized, as Piers deftly carved the tri-tip into slices and then served her. The evening sun caught the hairs on his arm and instantly she was thrown back to Wyoming. Remembering how his body hair had felt under her fingertips. More, how the silky heat of his skin had felt against hers. She pressed her thighs together as another surge of need billowed through her.

What on earth had she been thinking, kissing him before? It had awakened a monster within her. A demanding monster that plucked at her psyche, drawing on select memories that would eventually drive her mad.

Mad with lust, perhaps, that thoroughly inconvenient droll little voice said at the back of her mind.

In an effort to distract herself, Faye served a large helping of balsamic-roasted vegetables onto Piers's plate and a smaller helping for herself. She tried to direct the conversation toward a project nearing completion in San Francisco but Piers wasn't having any of it.

"Let's leave work at the office for today, hmm?" he said, spearing some food on his fork and lifting it to his mouth. "What do you think of the vegetables? Meredith uses a secret ingredient that she refuses to disclose to me. Maybe you can help me figure out what it is?"

Was he serious? Apparently so, judging by the expression on his face. She'd never really stopped to watch him eat before, but now, with a faint glisten on his lips and a rapt expression on his face, she was reminded all too much of how seriously he took other pleasures. Biting back a moan, Faye sampled some of the vegetables herself.

"Tell me," Piers insisted. "What do you taste?"

"Well, balsamic vinegar, of course. And garlic. And…" She let the flavors roll over her tongue. "Rosemary. Definitely rosemary."

"Yes, but there's something else in there. It's subtle but sweet. Meredith obviously uses it sparingly."

Faye concentrated a little longer, closing her eyes this time as she sampled another mouthful.

"Honey!" she exclaimed. "It's barely there, like you said, but I just get a hint of it before I swallow."

Across the table Piers beamed at her. "You know, I've been trying to figure that out for the better part of two years. It's been driving me crazy."

"Really? That's been the driving question behind everything you do?" Faye teased, laughing softly.

"You're beautiful when you laugh like that. Actually, you're beautiful all the time, but when you let go and laugh—" He paused, his face growing serious and his eyes deepening into dark pools.

"Stop it," Faye insisted. "You're making me uncomfortable."

"I can't help it, Faye. I have feelings for you. I want to talk about them. About you. About us."

"The only *us* is the *us* that works together," she said adamantly and carved a piece of meat to put in her mouth.

"I'd like there to be more than that. Wouldn't you? Don't you think we owe it to ourselves to explore what we shared back at the lodge?"

She chewed, swallowed and set her knife and fork down before looking at him. It took all her control to keep her response short and to the point.

"No."

"Don't you ever get tired of hiding from your feelings, Faye?"

"I'm just being pragmatic. Look, your track record with women speaks volumes to your inability to commit long-term, even if I was interested in anything long-term. Which I'm not. Ever."

Faye looked at the skillfully prepared food on her plate and felt all appetite flee. She hated having to talk like this to Piers and fervently wished they'd never gone and complicated everything by having sex.

"That's a shame. As to my track record, perhaps I've been searching for the one who has been under my nose all the time?"

"You're being ridiculous," she scoffed.

But deep inside a little piece of her began to wish she

could reach out and accept what he was offering. She wondered what it would be like to belong to someone. To be a part of more than just one.

The monitor on the sideboard near the entrance to the conservatory crackled into life and Casey's cry broke into the air.

"You'd better go and see to him," Faye said.

Piers looked as if he wanted to say more to her but he couldn't ignore the growing demands of the baby upstairs.

"Don't you dare leave," he said. "I'll be right back."

"I—"

"Don't. Leave."

And with that demand he rose and walked quickly to the doorway.

A few minutes later, through the monitor, Faye heard Piers enter the baby's room. He made soothing sounds as he obviously picked the little boy up and tried to settle him. She felt as though she was eavesdropping on something precious and wished like crazy she could get up and walk away. That she could forget the man upstairs and the child he cared for. But she knew that both of them had somehow inveigled their way into her heart. She shook her head at her own stupidity. How had she let that happen? Why?

Casey had obviously soiled his diaper, and she could hear Piers gagging in the background as he cleaned the little boy up. Obviously he was going to be a while. Faye gathered their plates and took them through to the kitchen where she put them in the oven, which she set on warm. No need for cold dinner, she thought.

She went back to the table and played with her water glass, trying not to listen as Piers struggled through the diaper change. There was something about hearing her handsome, capable boss being so completely out of his element that really appealed to her. Her hand to her mouth, she tried to hold back the chuckle that rose from deep inside.

Eventually, Piers resettled the child and returned to the conservatory.

"I hope you washed your hands," she teased.

"As if my life depended on it." Piers shook his head. "I still can't believe a baby can do that."

Faye felt a smile pull at her lips but fought to hide it. "Just wait till he projectile v—"

"Don't!" Piers barked, holding up a hand in protest. "Just don't."

Faye shrugged. "It's not all roses, is all I'm saying."

"I've discovered that," Piers replied ruefully.

"I'll get our plates," she said, rising. "That's if you're still hungry?"

Piers pulled a face. "I guess I could still eat. Especially after Meredith went to all that effort."

"Good choice." Faye tossed the words over her shoulder as she went through to the kitchen to retrieve their meals.

"Thanks for keeping it warm for me," Piers said as he picked up his knife and fork.

"It's nothing."

"You do that all the time. Did you know that?"

"Do what?"

"Diminish what you do."

"Do I?"

Faye stopped and thought for a bit. She had to concede he was probably right.

"Why is that? Don't you think that what you do is good enough? That *you're* good enough?"

Faye just looked at him in surprise. She'd never really stopped to consider it before.

Piers continued, "Because you are. You're better than good enough. You're the best assistant I've ever had and I know you apply yourself one hundred percent to everything you do."

She looked away, uncomfortable with the praise. Wasn't it enough that she just did her job? Did he have to talk about it?

"But what about your personal life, Faye?" He pressed on. "You have friends, don't you?"

"Of course I do," she answered automatically.

"You never talk about them."

"I thought I'd made it clear. My private life is private."

"Faye, I want to be a part of your private life. I want to be a part of your life altogether."

"I can't do that," she answered, shaking her head.

"So far you haven't given me a decent reason as to why not. And I won't back down without one. You know I don't give up when I want something."

She pushed her chair back from the table and stood. "I'm not just something to be wanted, Piers. And I don't have to give you a reason for anything. You're my boss. So far, you've been a good one, but I'm beginning to revise my opinion on that."

"Is that why you won't let anything develop between us?" he said, swiftly coming around the table to stand between her and the exit. "Because I'm your boss? Because if it is, then I'll fire you here and now so we can be together."

There was another sound from the monitor and Faye went rigid.

Piers looked at her with questions in his eyes. "Is it Casey? Or is it me?"

"No, it's neither of you," she lied, her voice a little more than a whisper. "I just don't want to get involved. With anyone. Look, thanks for dinner. I have to go."

She pushed past him and all but ran to the living room, where she grabbed her bag and headed for the front door. Piers was a second behind her. She spun around to face him.

"Yes, before you say it, I am running away. It's how I deal with stuff, okay? If I don't like a situation I'm in, I remove myself from it."

"But you do like me, don't you, Faye?" He stepped a little closer, his strong, warm hands clasping her upper arms and pulling her gently to him. "In fact, you more than like me. You're just fighting it. If it makes it any easier, I more than like you, too. In fact, I—"

"Don't!" Faye pressed her fingers to his mouth before he could say another word. "Don't say anything, please. I don't deserve it."

And with that she tugged loose from his grasp, pulled open the front door and hightailed it to her car.

Eleven

Piers watched her leave in a state of shock. He'd been on the verge of declaring he loved her. In fact, right now he was probably more stunned by that almost-admission than she was.

He closed the door and slowly walked back to the conservatory, automatically clearing the table and putting away the leftovers. Meredith had her own suite downstairs in the house, with its own entrance, but she was away at a community college course tonight. Something he'd offered to fund for her when he'd heard of her long-held dream to study English literature. It certainly didn't hurt him to look after himself for one night a week, especially if that only meant cleaning up his dinner dishes.

Helping people achieve their dreams made him feel good. Whether it was at work and assisting them to develop further in their role or whether it was through the generous donations he made to various charities in the area. But never had he wanted to help someone as badly as he wanted to help Faye. What would it take to make her feel good? Something held her back. He could sense she wanted more—just as he did—but every time she started to reach for it, she yanked herself away. Almost as if she felt she had to punish herself for wanting it in the first place. The why of it might elude him forever if she didn't open up, unless the private investigator he'd contacted came up with what he needed to know.

Thinking about what he'd done, requesting the investigation, made him question his morals. Faye had a right to privacy and if she didn't want him to know about her past then he ought to respect that. In any other instance he would. But this was Faye. This was the woman who'd let him be her first lover. This was the woman he'd fallen in love with. Not a sudden headlong lunge into love, but a long and growing respect that had evolved into so much more while they'd been snowbound at the lodge.

He couldn't just ignore what they could potentially have together. They both deserved to know exactly where they could go with the feelings she so determinedly kept shoving away.

Piers went up to his master suite and stood at the window, looking out at the night sky. Ethics could take a hike. He had to know what he was dealing with here. How could he fight it, overcome it, if he didn't know what *it* was? Knowing would at least allow him to metaphorically arm himself for what would be the most important battle of his life. The battle to win Faye's heart.

The next few days passed in a blur of activity. The archive room next to the office Piers and Faye shared had been emptied and converted into a nursery for Casey. Thankfully the two nannies that had been both his and

Faye's top picks had been free to start working immediately and the roster system seemed to be working well.

As to Faye, she appeared determined to spend as little time with him in the office as possible. She was constantly in another part of the building or out at meetings
on his behalf for one thing and another. Normally he
wouldn't have questioned it, but in light of how she'd
left his house earlier in the week he saw this as exactly
what it was. Avoidance. Well, it didn't matter. She had
to come back to the office eventually and, when she did,
he'd be waiting.

There was still no news from the investigator regard-
ing Faye's past. Piers had begun to question whether he'd
done the right thing—whether he shouldn't just cancel
the whole inquiry—but a niggling need to know now
wouldn't leave him.

Another question had also taken up residence in his
thoughts. Something his lawyer had discussed with him
when he'd relayed the information from Casey's mom.
Greg, his lawyer, had asked what it could mean if the in-
fertility angle from the woman's other lover had just been
something he had said to avoid responsibility. Or what if
she'd made the whole thing up? She'd worked at the lodge
that night and no doubt had some idea of the wealth behind the Luckman family. Maybe claiming Quin was the
father was just an attempt to get a share of that wealth in
exchange for the child?

Piers rejected one of the questions immediately. If
money had been Casey's mom's goal, she would have
asked for it outright. She would hardly have left the baby
with him the way she had. And while the fact that she'd
had sex with Quin while apparently involved with someone else didn't exactly speak volumes as to her reliability

or her integrity, he didn't believe her actions in abandoning Casey had been for her own financial gain.

While Piers was convinced that Casey was his brother's son, Greg had thrown another scenario at him. What if the boyfriend was the real father and decided to demand access to Casey? Greg had strongly recommended Piers have DNA testing done to ensure that there would be no future threats to Casey's stability and his position in Piers's life. If Piers could prove his biological link to the baby, there could be no questions asked, ever. Hell, with the fact that as identical twins he and Quin shared identical DNA, even Piers couldn't be ruled out as Casey's biological father.

When Greg had first thrown that into the conversation Piers hadn't been in a hurry to follow his recommendation for the DNA test. But his lawyer had sown a seed. Piers wanted to be certain that Casey's stability would never be threatened. That he'd never become involved in a tug-of-war between parents the way Piers and Quin so often had with their own parents. Even though they'd never separated, they'd spent most of their marriage living very separate lives and constantly battling over their assets. Their children, though uninteresting to them personally, were often pawns used in their bickering.

No, Casey would have the stability he deserved. There would be no question about who was responsible for him or who would raise him. Piers would get the testing done and settle any doubt once and for all.

"Faye, I need you to do something for me," he said the moment she returned to the office from a meeting.

She raised one brow in question.

He explained what he needed and, true to form, within fifteen minutes she'd gathered the information he'd requested and ordered the test kit to be couriered directly to their office.

"Are you sure you want to do this?" she asked after she hung up the phone.

"I don't want any nasty surprises in the future," he answered firmly.

"But what if Casey's not Quin's, after all? Isn't that why you're keeping him rather than relinquishing him to state care?"

"It won't make any difference."

"Won't it?"

"Of course not. He's mine now. Forever."

"If he's not Quin's child, you can change your mind."

Piers felt the weight of her statement as if it was placed directly over his heart. "What are you suggesting?" he demanded, his voice hard.

"It wouldn't be the first time someone decided parenthood wasn't for them. I saw it at least twice when adoptions failed while I was being fostered. It's heartbreaking for everyone concerned."

He looked at her in shock. Was that a measure of how she saw him? Was that why she showed no inclination to take a risk on him? Did she truly think he was incapable of commitment to anyone—a woman or a child?

"Wow. Why don't you just tell me what you really think of me, Faye?"

He couldn't hide the hurt in his voice. Her words had scored deep cuts, whether she'd intended them to or not.

"I'm sorry, but it happens. This is all very new for you now and you're deeply invested in the whole idea of raising Casey. I can see that."

"But?" he prompted when she fell silent.

"There is no but. Before you complete the adoption

process you need to be certain, for all your sakes, that you're in this for the right reasons."

"And they would be?"

"That Casey gets the best and most loving home and upbringing he possibly can."

There was a note in her voice that surprised him. A passion that spoke volumes as to why she was playing devil's advocate so persistently. Was it possible that she'd allowed herself to develop feelings for Casey, too? That it would distress her if the adoption didn't work out?

The very idea that it mightn't made Piers feel sick to his stomach, but he forced that feeling aside, focusing instead on Faye.

"Those are my very reasons for adopting him," he said finally. "It heartens me that you care so much for his welfare."

He watched as myriad expressions raced over her fine features and as those features finally settled into a frown. She was just about to speak when Piers's cell phone chimed in his pocket.

"You'd better get that," she said before turning back to her computer.

Whatever the call was, it must have been important because with just a short "I'll be back by lunch," Piers headed out of the office.

She sagged in her office chair, the tension she hadn't even realized she'd been carrying in her shoulders finally letting go.

Faye closed her eyes for a moment and bowed her head, then took in a deep breath before letting it go slowly. She'd overstepped when she'd talked to him like that but someone had to advocate for Casey. From where she sat, Piers had lived a golden life. Born into money, given the best education that money could buy, raised in luxurious indulgence—even his position here at work had fallen into his lap after his father had declared his retirement.

While he was more than capable of hard work, he'd always started each battle with every advantage on his side. He didn't know true hardship. Sure, yes, he knew grief. He knew that life could change in an instant, but she'd seen very little about his world that showed he truly understood personal commitment. Casey deserved that.

"Ms. Darby?"

Faye's eyes flew open and she looked up to see Casey's male nanny, Jeremy, standing in front of her.

"Hi, Jeremy. Sorry, I was away with the fairies," she said with a smile of welcome. "What can I help you with?"

"I'm really sorry, but I've just received a call to say my wife has been in a car accident and she's being taken to the hospital. I've called Laurie and she's coming in to cover for me, but she won't be here for another half hour, at least. I wouldn't ask normally, but my wife is in a lot of pain and she needs to be seen as soon as possible.

"Could you listen for Casey? He's sleeping and I don't expect he'll wake until after Laurie gets here but—"

"Leave me the monitor and go. Your wife needs you. There are plenty of us who can listen out for when Casey wakes. Don't worry, okay? And let me know how your wife is doing after you've seen a doctor."

"Thanks, Ms. Darby. I really appreciate it."

"Faye. Please, call me Faye."

Jeremy smiled in response and popped the baby monitor on her desk. "Thanks, Faye. I owe you one."

"No problem, just go and see to your wife."

He was gone almost before the words had left her mouth.

Faye stared at the monitor he'd left on her desk with a wary expression. Even though she'd made sure she had no direct contact with him since returning from the lodge, she knew Casey's schedule by heart. Usually a good little sleeper, he wasn't due to wake for at least another hour, and by then Laurie would definitely be here. She could cope with this, she told herself. All care and yet no responsibility.

She returned her attention to her computer screen and studied the building cost analysis figures for a proposed refit of a collection of old warehouses in North Carolina. Something was off, but she couldn't put her finger on it. She sighed and scrolled back to the beginning. She'd find the discrepancy and deal with it. Details were what she did best.

Faye had been lost in numbers and projections for the better part of fifteen minutes when she heard an enraged howl through the monitor. A chill washed through her and she looked at the time on her computer screen. No way. Casey shouldn't be waking now. Another scream bellowed through the speaker on her desk, forcing her to her feet and out of the office. A few yards down the hall she stopped at the door to the nursery. Her hand trembled as she reached for the doorknob.

This was ridiculous, she told herself. He was just a baby. Just a helpless, sweet thing needing comfort. And yet she could barely bring herself to turn the knob and let herself into the room. Another cry from inside pushed her into action.

She opened the door and stepped into the nursery and was instantly assailed with an array of scents. Soothing lavender in an electric oil burner in one corner was overlaid with the powdery scent of talcum powder. Over that again was something sharper, more sour.

She hurried across the room to discover Casey had been sick in his bed.

"Oh, you poor wee thing," she cooed to him in an attempt to soothe him with her voice.

At the sound of her voice, Casey's cries lessened. She lifted him from the crib and took him across to the change table, swiftly divesting him of his dirty clothing and wiping him clean. She checked his diaper, which was thankfully dry, and then redressed him in a clean onesie.

"There we go," she crooned, lifting him into her arms and resting her cheek on the top of his downy head. "All tidied up. Now we just have your bed to sort out, don't we?"

He didn't feel feverish, she noted with relief. Hopefully his throwing up wasn't a precursor to something serious. With one hand she stripped the dirty linens from the crib, balled them up with his soiled clothing and put them in a hamper in a corner of the room. All the while she kept talking softly to Casey, who'd grown quieter in her arms—just emitting a grumble every now and then. Faye put him in the stroller—in the room for when the nanny took him out for fresh air a couple of times a day—so she could remake the bed, but he wasn't having any of it.

"Silly boy," she chided gently, picking him up again. "I can't make your bed if you don't let me put you down for a couple of minutes."

Casey settled against her, his little body curling up against her chest and his head resting on her shoulder. A fierce wave of emotion swept over her. So much trust from one so small. For as long as she held him, his world was just as it ought to be. Secure. Safe. Loved.

Loved? Tears sprang to her eyes and she blinked them away fiercely. No, she didn't deserve to love or be loved.

Her baby brother had loved her, as had her mom and her stepdad. And she'd let them down. Living without love was her punishment for destroying their future together. And Casey's trust in her was obviously misplaced.

She rubbed his tiny back with one hand and closed her eyes—allowing herself to pretend for just a minute that it was her brother, Henry, she held. That it was his little snuffles she heard. His sweet baby scent that filled her nostrils. The weight of his chubby little body that felt so right in her arms.

"Oh, Henry," she whispered brokenly. "I'm so sorry. I'm so very sorry."

Tears began in earnest now, rolling down her cheeks as though the floodgates had truly been opened. Faye reached for a box of tissues and wiped at the moisture, but it was no good. The tears kept on coming.

She had no idea how long she stood there, rocking gently with the infant in her arms and tears streaming down her face. He'd fallen asleep again, she realized, but she couldn't put him in the bassinette because it wasn't ready. At least, that's what she told herself. It was the only reason why, now that she held him, she couldn't let him go.

A movement at the door caught her gaze and then Piers's strong, male presence was in the room with them.

"Faye?" he asked gently, reaching a hand to touch the tear tracks on her cheek. "I heard you on the monitor. Are you okay?"

His touch, his words, they were the reality check she needed. She shouldn't be there. Shouldn't be holding this child like this.

"He was upset. He'd been sick," she choked out even though her throat felt as though it was clogged with cotton wool. "Here, take him. He doesn't need me."

She deftly transferred the sleeping child to Piers's

arms and tried to ignore the aching sense of emptiness that overcame her the second she let him go. Faye turned to make up the crib, keeping her back firmly to Piers. The moment she was done she left the room, not even trusting herself to speak another word.

Instead of returning to her office she took refuge in the ladies' restroom on their floor. She turned on the faucet and dashed cold water over her wrists and then her face before straightening and looking at her reflection in the mirror. Her face was pale—her eyes shadowed, haunted. Somehow she had to pull herself together, go back to her desk and get on with her day, but she knew something had irrevocably changed for her back there in the nursery.

She couldn't stay at this job. She couldn't face every day watching Piers bond with Casey, watching Casey grow and develop from baby to toddler. It hurt too much. It was a constant, aching reminder of all she'd lost. Of the pain she'd endured for so long now. She'd thought she had it under control. She lived her life the way she wanted it, by creating distance between herself and others. There was no risk that way. No chance she'd lose her heart and face the hazards that loving someone else brought.

But now she was lost on a sea of change and swirling emotion that threatened to drown her. She had to go. Had to leave this place—leave Piers, the job she looked forward to every day. Leave the baby who'd stolen her heart despite her best efforts to remain aloof. She reached for a paper towel and wiped her face one last time before straightening her shoulders and setting her mouth into a grim line of determination.

She'd hand in her notice today. And she'd survive this. Somehow.

Twelve

"You're resigning?" Piers couldn't keep the shock from his voice. "But why? Are you unhappy here? I thought you loved your job."

"I'm sorry, Piers. I'm giving you the required four weeks' notice, effective from today, and I'll contact HR straight away to begin recruitment."

She was still pale and he could see she was holding on to her composure by the merest thread. Everything about her urged him to take her into his arms and to say that whatever it was that worried or frightened her so very much back there in the nursery, he would make it okay—if only she'd let him. And there was the rub. She wouldn't let him, would she? She'd made being an island an art form. Though she was cordial and worked well with everyone, she had no true friends among the staff and, to the best of his knowledge, few, if any, close friends outside of work, either. Certainly, she was respected here in the office, but she was always strictly business and didn't allow herself to be included in any-thing personal.

He'd returned to the office today much sooner than he'd expected. Halfway to meet his mother for an unex-pected and apparently urgent meeting during a layover at LAX, she'd called and said she'd changed her mind and could they make it dinner on her way home from Tahiti in ten days' time instead. He'd rolled his eyes and told himself he wasn't disappointed. That he hadn't dropped everything to spend some time with the woman who'd borne him. But he'd suggested that on her return she come to the house to meet Casey at the same time. It was rare that she was on the West Coast and he hoped to encourage some form of relationship between her and her grandson.

Upon his return, he'd been surprised to hear Faye through the monitor—to hear the raw emotion in her voice as she'd made an apology to someone. What was that name again? Henry. That was it. Was he the rea-son why she held herself so separate from everyone? He tucked the name away, determined to pass it on to his investigator the moment he'd dealt with the situa-tion right now.

"I don't want to lose you, Faye. You're the best PA I've ever had, but you're so much more to me than that. I'd hoped we could be—"

"I never asked for anything more than to be your assis-tant," she interrupted. "I never made you any promises."

"No, you didn't. Why is that, Faye? What has you so scared that you'll distance yourself from me like this? Seriously, resigning from your position here is ludicrous. You don't have another job to go to, do you?"

She shook her head. "I can't stay, Piers. I can't do this anymore."

"Why not? Why won't you open up to me and tell me what is holding you back? Until I know what I'm dealing with, I'm in the dark. I don't know how to fix things between us."

"That's half the issue. There can't be any *us*. I've told you over and over again. Why won't you listen to me?"

The note of sheer desperation in her voice made him take a step back and give her space. But hadn't he done enough of that since she'd left him in Wyoming? They'd made love, damn it. Love. It was so much more than just sex. They'd shared something special, something that should have drawn them closer than ever, not driven an insurmountable wedge between them.

He knew she was hurting. He could see it in every line of her beautiful features, in the shadows that lingered in her expressive eyes, not to mention in the rigid lines in which she held her body. Somehow he needed to take action, to help her face the fear that was holding her in its claws, so she could face up to the feelings he knew she had for him.

A woman like Faye didn't just give herself to a man on a whim. The fact that she'd been a virgin the night they'd made love had been irrefutable proof of that. Right now, he was terrified he was on the verge of losing the only woman he'd ever truly loved, but what could he do? He was working in the dark, grasping at straws. He hated that he couldn't just bark a command and have everything fall into place, but he was prepared to keep working at this. If Faye still wanted to leave Luckman Developments after this, that was fine, but he couldn't let her leave him.

He had four weeks to somehow change her mind and Piers knew without a single doubt that it would be the toughest negotiation of his entire life.

* * *

Six days later he had his answers. The wait had almost driven him crazy, especially loaded on top of the growing pile of recommended applicants for Faye's position. But now he knew and he hoped like hell that somewhere in this information delivered privately to his home tonight, he'd have the answer to why Faye was so determined to keep her distance from him.

The reading was sobering. Her background began like so many other people's. Solo, hardworking mom—no father on the scene. A lifestyle he would have considered underprivileged when he was a kid, but now realized was likely rich in nonmaterial things like love and consistency. Faye's mom married when Faye was about thirteen and, from all accounts, the little family was very happy together. A happiness that, according to the report, grew when Faye's baby brother was born. Piers flipped through the notes, looking for the baby's name. Ah, there it was. Henry. The name he'd heard her whisper through the baby monitor last week. Things were starting to fall into place now.

It appeared the family had been involved in a tragic wreck on Christmas Eve. Faye had been the only survivor. Details about the wreck were scarce and Piers had an instinct that there was a great deal more to the event than the brief description on the file. He could understand why losing her entire family in one night would make a person put up walls. But surely those walls couldn't hold forever.

Piers skimmed the rest of the report, reading the summary of her time in foster care and her subsequent acceptance into college. At least she hadn't suffered financial hardship. Her stepdad had been very astute with his finances and her mom had been putting savings aside in a college fund from the day Faye had been born. Following the crash, all the assets had been consolidated. By the time the family home had been sold and life insurances paid out, and after three years of sound management by the executor of her family's estate, Faye had had quite a healthy little nest egg to set her up for her adult life.

He closed the file with a snap. Words. That's all it was. Nothing in there gave him a true insight into why Faye was so hell-bent on leaving him. Yes, yes, he could see the similarities between Casey and her brother Henry. He understood Casey was the same age as her brother had been when he'd died. He could, partially at least, understand why she'd steered clear of involvement with his soon-to-be adopted son. But to keep herself aloof from love and from children for the rest of her life? It was living half a life. No, it was even less than that.

Piers locked the file in a drawer in his home office. Somehow he had to find a way to peel away the protective layers Faye had gathered around her to get her to show him what truly lay in her heart. His future happiness, and hers, depended on it.

It was the kind of day where logic went to hell in a handbasket. Pretty much everything that could go wrong, did. Two new projects being quoted by contractors had come in way over the estimated budgets and asbestos had been found on another site, which had shut the operation down until the material could be safely removed.

Faye and Piers had been juggling balls and spinning plates all day, and it was nearly 8:00 p.m. when their phones stopped ringing.

Faye leaned back in her office chair and sighed heavily. "Do you think that's it? Have we put out enough fires for one day?"

"Enough for a year, I'd say. I want an inquiry into how those estimates were so far off track—"

"Already started," she said succinctly.

It was one of the first things she'd requested when the issue had arisen at the start of the day.

"I love that about you," Piers said suddenly.

Faye looked at him in shock. "I beg your pardon?"

"Your ability to anticipate my needs."

"Hmm," she responded noncommittally.

She looked away and refreshed the email on her screen, hoping something new had arisen that might distract her from what she suspected would be another less than subtle attempt to get her to change her mind about leaving.

"Faye, what would it take to make you stay?"

And there it is. She closed her eyes and silently prayed for strength.

"Nothing."

"Would love make you stay?"

"Love? No, why?"

"I love you."

"You love what I can do for you. Don't confuse that with love," she said as witheringly as she could manage.

Inside, though, she was a mess. He loved her? No. He couldn't. He only thought he loved her because she was probably the first person ever to say a flat-out no to him, and he loved a challenge. Of course he wanted her. And once he had her he'd lose interest because that's the way things went. Either that or he'd realize he never loved her, anyway.

Would that be so bad? her inner voice asked.

Of course not, she scoffed. She wasn't interested in love. Ever.

Liar.

"You think I don't know what love is? That's interesting," Piers continued undeterred. "You know what I think, Faye?"

She sighed theatrically but continued staring at her computer screen. "Whether I want to know or not, I'm sure you're going to tell me, aren't you?"

She heard him get up from his chair and move across the office to stand right beside her. Strong, warm hands descended on her shoulders and turned her chair so she faced him.

"I think you're too scared to love again."

"Again?"

"Yes, *again*. I'm pretty certain you have loved, and loved deeply. I'm also pretty certain you've been incredibly hurt. Faye, not wanting to take a risk on love is a genuine shame. I never really knew what love felt like, aside from the brotherly bond Quin and I shared. But now I think I've finally learned what love is."

"You seem to think you know a lot about me," she said. Her words were stilted and a knot tightened deep in her chest. She had a feeling she really wasn't going to like what he was about to say next so she decided to go on the attack instead. "Piers, please don't kid yourself that you love me. You're just attempting to manipulate me into staying because that's what would make your life easier."

He genuinely looked shocked at her words. "That's the second time recently you've made your perception of me clear—and I haven't been happy with the picture you've painted either time. Tell me, Faye. Is that why you slept with me back at the lodge? Because it meant nothing to you and because you thought it would mean nothing to me?"

His words robbed all the breath from her lungs. Wow, when he wanted to strike a low blow he really knew how and where to strike, didn't he? That night had meant everything to her, but she wasn't about to tell him that. It would only give him more ammunition in this crazy war of his against her defenses.

Faye pushed against the floor and skidded her chair back a little. She stood. "I don't need to take this from you. I'm leaving, remember?"

"And you're still running."

"Oh, for goodness' sake! Will you stop it with the running comments? So I choose to remove myself from situations I'm uncomfortable with. That's not a crime."

"No, it's not a crime." He closed the distance between them. "Unless by doing so you continue to hurt yourself and anyone who cares about you every time you do it. Faye, you can't keep living half a life. Your family would never have wanted that for you."

An arctic chill ran through her veins, freezing her in place and stealing away every thought.

"M-my family? What do you know of my family?"

The sense of anxiety she'd felt before had nothing on the dark hole slowly consuming her from the inside right now. Aside from the police, she'd never spoken to anyone about exactly what had happened on the night of the wreck. How could he know? Why would he?

Piers's next words were everything she'd dreaded and more. "I know everything. I'm so sorry for your loss."

His beautiful dark eyes reflected his deep compassion but she didn't want to see it. Even so, she remained trapped in the moment. Ensnared by his words, by his caring.

"Everything, huh?" she asked bitterly. "Did you know I killed them? That I was the one behind the wheel that night? I killed them all." She threw the words at him harshly, the constriction of her throat leaving her voice raw.

Shock splintered across his handsome features.

"I thought as much," she continued bitterly. "That information wasn't in any report you could commission because it was sealed. So, how much do you love me now that you know I'm a murderer?"

Piers shoved a hand through his hair. His brows drew into a straight line, twin creases forming between them. "How can you say you're a murderer? You know you didn't deliberately kill anyone. It was an accident."

"Was it? I'm the one who pestered my stepdad to let me drive that night. Mom didn't want me to. She said it was too icy on the road, that I didn't have the experience. But my stepdad said experience was the only way I'd learn."

"Even so, from what I read, the gas tanker skidded on the road, not you. You didn't stand a chance."

Her mouth twisted as she remembered seeing the tanker coming toward them, relived the moment it jack-knifed and began its uncontrollable slide toward their car. She'd been petrified. She'd had no idea what to do, how to avoid the inevitable.

"You're right, I didn't. But when it happened, I froze— I didn't know what to do. If my stepdad had driven instead… If I'd listened to my mom…" Faye's voice broke and she dragged in a ragged breath before continuing. "If I'd listened to my mom, we might all have been alive today."

"You don't know that."

"No, I'll never know that. The one thing I do know is

that my decisions that night killed my family. And that's something I can never forget or forgive myself for. My stepdad and my brother died instantly. Henry was only three and a half months old. Don't you think he deserved to grow up, to have a life? And my mom—I can still hear her screams when I try to sleep at night. The only reason I didn't burn to death right along with her was because people pulled me from the wreck before the flames took complete hold of the car."

"Your scars," Piers said softly. "They're from the fire?"

Faye nodded. "So you see, I'm not worth loving."

"Everyone deserves to be loved, Faye. You more than anyone, if only for what you've been through. Don't you think you've paid enough? You need to learn to forgive yourself and rid yourself of the guilt that is keeping you from living."

"I live. That's my punishment."

He shook his head emphatically. "You exist. That's not living. The night we shared at the lodge—*that* was living. That was reveling in life, not this empty shell of subsistence you endure every day. Take a risk, Faye. Accept my love for you. Learn to love me."

She'd begun to tremble under the force of emotion in his words.

"I can't. I can't care. I won't."

"Why?" He pressed her.

"If I love someone again, I'll lose them. Can't you see? I did try to love after the crash. I cared for every baby that came into the foster home as if every single one of them was my chance to redeem myself for what I did to Henry. I poured my love and care into each one and you know what happened? Each and every one of them was taken from me again. Either they were re-homed or they were returned to their parents. Every.

Single. Time—I lost my baby brother all over again."
Faye hesitated and drew on every last ounce of strength
she possessed. "So you'll forgive me if I don't *ever* want
to love again."

Thirteen

Piers watched as she retrieved her bag from her bottom drawer and slung the strap over her shoulder. She still shook and her face was so very pale that her freckles stood out in harsh relief against her skin.

"Now, if you don't need me for anything else tonight, I'd like to go home."

He looked at her, desperate to haul her into his arms, to hold her and to reassure her that she didn't need to be alone anymore. That if she could only let go of that cloak of protection she'd pulled around her emotions and let him inside, everything would be all right. But even he couldn't guarantee that, could he? Accepting that fact was a painful realization. But even so, he was willing to take that chance because surely the reward far outweighed the possibility it would all go wrong?

"Faye, please, hear me out."

"Again?"

"For the last time. Please. After this, I'll let you go, if that's what you truly want me to do."

He saw the muscles working in the slender column of her throat, saw the tension that gripped her body in the set of her shoulders and her rigid stance.

"Fine. Say your piece."

"Look, I know I've had a charmed life compared to yours. I never wanted for anything. But in all my years growing up, those people who professed to love me— my own mom and dad—never showed any hint that their emotions went below the surface. Quin and I had each other, but we were just trophies to our parents. Either something to show off or something for our parents to fight about.

"I thought I was okay with that. That I could live my life like that. But it wasn't until Quin died that I began to take a good, long, hard look at myself and I didn't like what I saw anymore. In fact, I think Quin's thrill-seeking lifestyle was a direct result of how he coped with our parents' inability to express or feel genuine love for us, as well.

"His whole life he pushed the envelope. He took extreme risks in everything he did. Someone would climb a tree—he'd climb a taller one. Someone would ski a black-diamond trail—he'd go off piste. Right up until he died, he was searching for something. Whether it was praise or acceptance or even, just simply, love or a sense that he was deserving of love—I'll never know. But I do know that his dying taught me a valuable lesson about life. It's worth living, Faye, and in living it you have to make room for love because, if you don't, what are we doing on this earth?"

Was he getting through to her? She made no move to leave. In fact, was that a shimmer of tears in those blue-gray eyes of hers? Sensing he might have created a crack in her armor, he decided to continue to drive whatever kind of wedge in that chink that he possibly could.

"Do you know why I'm so crazy about Christmas?" When she rolled her eyes and shook her head, he continued. "I've spent my whole adult life trying to create a sense of family and to experience what Christmas can be all about. My family may have been wealthy, but we were so fractured. Dad living most of his retirement playing golf around the gators in Florida, Mom in New York. While they remain married, they've lived separate lives ever since Quin and I were carted off to boarding school. For the longest time I thought that was normal! Can you imagine it? Six years old and thinking that was how everyone did it?"

"I'm sorry, Piers. So sorry you didn't know a parents' love." Faye spoke softly, and he could see her understanding, feel her sympathy as if it was a physical thing reaching out to fill the empty spaces inside him.

"Then you'll understand when I say this. I want more than what I had growing up. I want Casey to have that, too. Quin's son will never know another minute where he isn't loved. And that's what I want, too, and I want to have it with you, Faye. I love you. I want you in my life, my arms, my bed."

He drew in a breath and let it out in a shudder. "But it has to be all or nothing. I don't want you to come to me with any part of you locked away. I'm prepared to lay everything on the line for you because I want you to be a part of the family I'm trying to create, the future I want to have. I will help you and support you and love you every day for the rest of my life—if you'll let me.

"So, what's it to be? Are you going to take what's

freely and openly offered to you? Will you take a chance on me and on yourself, and let yourself be happy?"

Faye just stood there, staring at him. Piers willed her to respond, willed her to say something. Anything. Hope leaped like a bright flame in his chest when she took a step toward him. This was it. This was when she would accept the offer of his heart and hopes and his promises for their future. Then she hesitated. Her head dropped.

"I can't."

She walked away and, despite every instinct in his body screaming at him to stop her, he let her go. He had to. He'd understood what she was doing when she took that single step toward him. She'd wanted him to meet her halfway. But in this, he had to know she was totally committed. It wasn't just his happiness that was at stake here, nor just hers. It was Casey's, too, and if she couldn't commit wholeheartedly, then they were destined to fail.

He hadn't realized letting her go could hurt so much.

After a night fraught with lack of sleep and an irritable teething baby to boot, Piers wasn't surprised to arrive in the office to discover a message for him from HR saying that Faye had requested urgent personal leave in lieu of working out the rest of her notice. He hated to admit it, but her decision was probably for the best. It would be absolute torture to be around her every day knowing that she'd closed the door on any chance of them having a future together.

He set to dealing with the fallout from the problems that had arisen the day before and, with every call, every email, every decision, he missed her more and more. It wasn't just her ability to do her job as well as he did his, nor her intuition when it came to what he needed. It was, quite simply, her. All through the day he found himself staring at her empty desk, or starting to say something to her only to realize she wasn't there. Nor would she be, ever again.

Had he been wrong to push her? A part of him agreed that he most definitely was every kind of fool. Surely half having her was better than not having her at all? But the other part of him, the part that still remained after the poor little rich boy had grown up, knew that he deserved more than that. And so did she. By her own admission, she didn't want what he could offer her. She didn't want his love or his soon-to-be adopted son. She didn't want the security he could offer her. The prospect of more children. She didn't want him, period.

He was at the end of his tether by day's end and decided it was time to head home. There was no need to work late tonight. He'd dismiss Laurie, who was caring for Casey at the office this week, and take the baby home.

Piers was at the door of his office when his cell phone vibrated in his pocket. He slid it out and, not recognizing the number, debated diverting the call to voice mail. But something prompted him to accept it.

"Mr. Luckman? This is Bruce Duncan from the lab. We have the results of the DNA testing you requested."

"That was quick. I wasn't expecting them for another week at least."

"Your assistant requested we handle the testing as promptly as possible. I understand there is an adoption in process?"

"Yes, that's right. My brother's son."

"Ah," Bruce Duncan said on a long sigh. "The results are quite clear on that. I'm sorry to inform you that the infant being tested is not your brother's son."

Piers staggered under the shock of the man's words. Not Quin's son? At the back of his mind he'd known it was a possibility, but he'd convinced himself that Casey was Quin's flesh and blood.

"Mr. Luckman? Are you still there?"

"Yes, yes. I'm here. And you're absolutely certain about that?" His voice was raw but not as raw as his bleeding heart.

Duncan began to rattle on about markers and strands and all manner of technical data to support the bombshell he'd just dropped, but it all just washed over Piers until Duncan made one last statement.

"The results are conclusive. The infant has no biological link to your family."

"Thank you," Piers managed to say through a jaw clenched against the pain that washed over him. "Please send the final report to my office addressed to my attention."

After receiving an assurance that a copy was already on its way, Piers severed the call. He put one hand against the door frame and leaned heavily against it. He'd said it didn't matter, that he'd go ahead with the adoption anyway—and he would—but the knowledge that he now had nothing left of Quin scored across his heart like a tiger's claw.

Losing his brother had come as such a shock, and the hope that Quin had left something of himself behind had buoyed Piers along these past several weeks. He hadn't realized how much it had lifted the pall of grief he'd carried with him since Quin's death. Or how much it had eased the shock of realization that his carefree brother was not as bulletproof as they both had always thought. That Piers now was, for all intents and purposes, alone.

He would have to let his lawyer know, although it would not change his wishes about the adoption process. But Casey's real father, if he could be found, would need to be notified. The whole process could open up a whole new can of worms. The thought of making that call right now was a mountain too far for him. Piers pushed off from the frame, straightened his shoulders and headed down the hall toward Casey's nursery.

Laurie looked up from where she was playing with the baby on the floor.

"Look, here's your daddy!" she cooed to the squirming infant on the play mat on the floor. "Just in time to see what a clever boy you are."

Laurie looked up from the baby and smiled at Piers. "He's coming along so well, Mr. Luckman. You must be so proud. His hand/eye coordination is improving every day. He can strike the hanging toys and even grip them at will from time to time."

"That's wonderful, Laurie."

"Mr. Luckman, is everything okay? You sound different."

Piers forced a smile to his face. "Just a little tired, is all. This little tyke had me up a few times last night."

"Oh, was Jeremy not on duty?"

"His wife had an early appointment to follow up on her injury from last week. I gave him the night off."

"Well, you know if you need me, I'm more than happy to take an extra duty. I just adore this little man. He's such a joy to care for."

"Thank you, Laurie, but we'll be okay. Jeremy is back on duty tonight. I'm finishing early for the day. You can head on home now."

Laurie quickly finished straightening the nursery while Piers settled on the floor with Casey. The moment he sat beside the little boy, the baby turned his head toward him and began to babble and pump his legs in excitement.

"He knows you," Laurie said with an indulgent smile. "He's always so happy to see you."

Some of the pain that had cut him so viciously at the news from the lab, eased a little. He scooped his wee charge up into his arms and held him close. As if sensing Piers's need for comfort, Casey settled immediately, his little thumb finding its way into his mouth and his head nestling under Piers's chin.

Child of his blood or not, he loved this little boy so very much. No matter what, he would fight to keep him.

Faye sat in the rental car opposite the house that had been her home for most of her childhood. With the engine still running and the heater blasting hot air into the car's cabin, she should have been warm. Instead she felt as though a solid lump of ice had solidified deep inside her. Coming here had been a mistake. She wouldn't find any answers here. There was no resolution to be found. Her family was gone.

She let her eyes drift over the house that was obviously still very much a home. It was still well-kept. The walk had been shoveled clear of snow and the driveway looked as though a car had been on it recently. Lights burned at the downstairs windows, glowing welcomingly from inside. She looked up to the window that had once been hers and wondered who slept in that room now. Did they stare out that window at night and gaze at the stars, wondering where life would lead them?

Did they ever imagine that everything could be torn away from them in an instant? That they could lose everything they held dear?

A movement at the window caught her eye. A woman, with a small child on her hip, moved from room to room downstairs and tugged the drapes closed. Cutting the coziness of their world off from the harsh winter night outside.

Faye swallowed against the lump in her throat. There was nothing to see here. Nothing to gain.

Life moved on.

But you haven't.

That pesky small voice was back. She put the car in gear and eased away from the curb, not really knowing what she'd been looking for. The only thing she was sure of right now was that whatever it was, it wasn't here anymore.

She'd thought coming back to Michigan, to her hometown, would give her a sense of closure. She'd visited with her foster parents, who'd now retired, and they'd been glad to see her—proud of her achievements in the years since she'd left their care. She'd even caught up on the phone with her old friend, Brenda, from high school. The only one who hadn't awkwardly withdrawn from her and her grief when she'd finally returned to class.

At the time, Faye had felt as though she was being justifiably punished by the other children. No wonder they'd shunned her. After all, they hadn't killed their parents and siblings, had they? They still lived their lives. Went to sport or band practice. Went to one another's houses to do homework and eat junk food and watch movies together. But looking back now, she realized she'd been to blame for most of the distance that had widened between her and her friends. They'd had little to no experience with death and loss, especially on the scale Faye had endured. And, subsequently, they'd had no idea of what to say, or how to cope with her withdrawal from them. Only Brenda had tried to maintain their friendship up until they'd gone their separate ways to college.

She was due at Brenda's for dinner soon, Faye realized

as she got to the end of the street and came to a halt at a stop sign. She started to roll forward, only to slam on her brakes as a large tanker bore down the cross street toward her. Her tires slipped on the icy road. Her heart began to race in her chest. She slid to a halt, the tanker continuing past her completely oblivious to the turmoil that rolled and pitched inside her.

An impatient honk of a horn behind her made Faye force herself to concentrate, to continue through the intersection and to keep on driving. To overcome her fright and to keep on going. And wasn't that what she'd done every day since that night?

Be honest with yourself. You haven't kept going. You've been hiding. Running. Just like Piers said.

"Damn it!" she muttered out loud. "Stop that."

Refusing to listen anymore to her inner voice, Faye focused on the drive to Brenda's house. It wasn't far from where Brenda had grown up, the house where her parents still lived—a blessing since Brenda's mom and dad cared for her little ones while she worked in her role as a busy family medicine doctor at a local practice. Faye had been surprised to hear that her career-focused friend now had two small children and a husband who adored her. By the sounds of things, her life was chaotic and full, and everything she'd never known she always wanted. And most of all, from talking with Brenda on the phone yesterday, it had been obvious that despite the chaos, her life was filled with love.

Faye drew to a halt outside Brenda's house and got out of the car. The front door flung open, sending warmth and light flooding onto the front porch.

"Come on in!" Brenda urged. "It's freezing out there."

The moment Faye was on the porch she was enveloped in a huge hug.

"Oh, I've missed you! I'm so glad you called," her old friend sighed happily in her ear.

She led Faye inside and introduced her to her husband and eighteen-month-old identical twin boys.

Faye felt tears prick at her eyes as she looked at the dark-haired miniatures of their father. Was this what Piers and Quin had been like as kids? she wondered. She shoved the thought aside. Piers had been on her mind constantly since she'd walked away from him that night, even though she'd tried her hardest not to think about him.

Despite her attempts to remain aloof, Faye was quickly drawn into the chaos of the young family, and when Brenda's husband went to put the boys to bed after dinner, Brenda led her into the sitting room where they perched on the sofa together.

"So, tell me. What have you been doing with yourself? And this isn't a general inquiry. This is me with my doctor's hat on. Something's not right, is it?"

"I'm fine. I've been working hard lately. You know how it is."

Brenda reached out and squeezed Faye's hand. "It's more than just work, isn't it? How did you cope this last Christmas? Was it as awful for you as it used to be?"

Faye started to brush off Brenda's concern but then somewhere along the line the words began to fall from her mouth. She told her old friend all about the lodge and having to decorate it. Brenda had laughed, but in a sympathetic way and urged her to keep talking. When she got to the part where she'd found Casey, Brenda was incredulous.

"How could anyone do something like that? The risks were terrible. He could have died!"

"In her defense, she waited until I was there before she left. To be honest, I don't think she was in a rational state of mind."

Brenda shook her head. "I've seen a lot of sad cases but this really makes me wonder about people's choices. There are so many avenues for help available if people would only ask."

"But sometimes it's too hard to ask. Sometimes it's easier just to keep it all in and deal with it however you can."

Brenda looked at her carefully. "We're not talking about the abandoned baby anymore, are we?"

Faye tried to steer Brenda's interest in another direction but her friend wasn't having any of it.

"Did you ever have any counseling after the accident, Faye?"

"I didn't need counseling. I knew what I'd done. I learned to deal with it."

"Deal with it, yes. But accept it? Move on from it?"

"Of course," Faye insisted, but even as she spoke she knew the words were a lie.

"I'm worried about you," Brenda said softly. She moved closer and took both of Faye's hands in hers. "You can talk to me, Faye. I know we haven't been close in years but I know what you went through. I watched you withdraw from everyone more and more until no one could reach you. I should have said something then, but we were still so young and clueless. So busy with what we were doing."

"There's no shame in that. Everyone had their life to live," Faye said in defense.

"As did you." Brenda gently squeezed Faye's fingers. "Think about it. If you want to see someone while you're here, I know several really good grief counselors. It's time you took your life back, Faye. You can't remain a victim of that dreadful accident forever."

Faye wanted to protest. Wanted to insist that this was her cross to bear. But then she thought about the new family living in the house where she'd grown up. Thought about Brenda and her busy life and her growing family. Thought about Piers's comment about what her family would have wanted for her.

Suddenly it was too hard to hold on to the guilt and the responsibility she'd borne on her shoulders for all this time. She felt a tremor rack her body, then another, and then the tears began to fall.

Brenda gathered her into her arms and held her as she wept. At some stage Brenda's husband entered the room but a fierce look from his wife sent him straight back out again. Eventually, Faye regained some semblance of control of her wayward emotions.

"I'm sorry," she said, blowing her nose on a wad of tissues Brenda had thrust into her hand. "I didn't come here to cry on your shoulder."

"I'm glad you did. You've needed it for far too long."

Her friend looked at her with concern in her eyes and a small frown creasing her forehead. "So, about that counselor?"

Faye found herself nodding. "Okay, yes. I think it's time."

"You won't regret it," Brenda said firmly, giving her hand another squeeze. "Now, let's go have a coffee and rescue Adam from the kitchen."

"Thank you, Bren. I mean that. I've missed you."

Her friend smiled back. "I've missed you, too. I'm glad you're back."

And she was. For the first time in forever, Faye felt as though she really was fighting her way back.

Fourteen

Piers hung up the phone and felt his body sag in relief. The adoption petition had been reviewed by the judge and his lawyer had assured him that despite the DNA findings two months ago, the adoption should still proceed unhindered.

Casey's mom had signed the papers and there'd been no protest from her family. Her ex had been tracked down in prison in Montana and had given his written and notarized statement that he wanted nothing to do with the baby. In fact, he had gone to great lengths to insist Casey wasn't his child and had refused to allow his DNA to be compared. Everything remained on the fast track his lawyer had promised.

Except he didn't feel as though he was on track at all. He felt as though he'd been derailed completely and he didn't quite know how to fill the chasm of Faye's absence. He'd tried to call her, if only to check on her to ensure she was okay, but there'd been no answer at her apartment and his calls to her cell had gone straight to voice mail. If he didn't think she was simply avoiding him, he would have asked his people to track her down. But surely he'd have heard by now if something had happened to her.

He tried to tell himself it wasn't his problem, but he couldn't let go of the concern. You didn't just turn love off like a faucet.

A sound at the door to his office made him turn around. Relief flooded through him as Faye stepped through the doorway. He didn't know what to say or to do. All he could do was stare at her as if he was afraid to look away in case she disappeared again.

"Hello, Piers," she said, looking straight at him.

"Long time no see," he said stiffly.

His eyes raked over her. Something was different about her, but he couldn't put his finger on it. Sure, her hair was slightly longer than it had been two months ago, but that wasn't it. There was something about her face, her expression, that had changed. She looked less severe somehow and it wasn't just because she wore her hair in long, loose waves that cascaded over her shoulders.

The last time he'd seen her hair unbound like that had been when they'd been in bed together back in December last year. She'd still been asleep and he'd had to force himself from the bed to attend to Casey. The memory sent a shaft of longing through him. They'd been so good together. But she'd chosen to leave him. Which made him want to know—what was she doing here now?

"Have you got a minute?" she asked shyly.

There was a hitch to her voice, betraying her nervousness. He was unused to seeing her like this. Soft. Unsure. Unguarded even. It made every one of his protective urges rise to the fore, compelling him to close that distance between them and to hold her in his arms and kiss her until every uncertainty was soothed and they were both senseless with need. Instead he stood his ground. He'd meant what he said two months ago. Every last word. If she couldn't commit to him fully and freely, they had no future.

Was the fact that she was here an indication that she was ready? That she'd found a way to pull down the walls she'd kept around herself for almost half her life? Was she ready to give her all? He wanted to believe it but, despite the open expression on her face, he couldn't read her.

"I can make time," he answered. "For you."

"Thank you. Do you, um, want to talk here?"

He looked around his office. "It's as good a place as any, isn't it?"

She firmed her lips and nodded.

"Would you rather go somewhere else? A restaurant, maybe?"

"No, this is fine. Can we...can we sit down?"

He'd never seen her this unsure of herself before. Her calm confidence had been such a strong part of who she was that he found himself worrying for what had caused this change in her.

"Sure," he said, gesturing to the twin sofas set adjacent to the window that looked out over the city.

He waited for her to sit, then took the other end of the sofa. "Can I get you anything?"

She shook her head. "I'm fine, but grab something if you want it."

"No, I'm good."

He stretched one arm across the back of the sofa and angled his body to face hers while he waited for her to speak. Silence thickened in the air between them, coercing him into saying something, anything, to fill it. But this was her time to speak, not his. He'd said all he could say the last time he'd seen her. Now it was her turn.

Faye cleared her throat and her fingers tangled with the strap of her purse. "How's Casey doing?"

"He's home today. He has a cold and I didn't think he should come into the office."

A glow of concern filled her eyes. "Poor wee guy. His first cold?"

"As far as I'm aware," Piers conceded. "He's pretty miserable."

Miserable had been an understatement. All blocked up, Casey had woken, crying, four times last night, which in turn had only made things worse. Jeremy had been on duty and between him and Piers they'd taken turns to soothe Casey back to sleep. Even so, it had been a tough night for all of them.

Faye twisted the purse strap into a tight coil, then let it go again before threading her fingers through the leather to start all over again.

Frustration bubbled to the surface for Piers. She'd come here of her own volition. There must be a reason for that. So why the hell didn't she just come out with what she wanted to say?

"I guess you're wondering why I'm here," Faye said in a rush.

Piers simply nodded.

Faye scooted to the edge of the sofa and put her bag on the floor, then she stood and stepped over to the window. With the afternoon light streaming around her, he could see she'd lost weight. Another point of concern but not his problem, he reminded himself firmly. Not unless she was willing to allow it to be.

"I'm sorry for leaving the way I did. I see my old desk is unused. Don't you have a new assistant yet?"

"Faye, you didn't come here to talk about whether or not I have a new assistant, did you? Because if so, I have somewhere I need to be."

She spun around to face him, worry streaking her pale face. "I'm holding you up? You should have said."

"I told you I could make time for you and I can—but please, get to the point of why you're here."

It pained him to be so blunt but he couldn't bear to have her beat around the bush any longer. He'd left message after message for her. Worried about her welfare, where she was, what she was doing. And she hadn't responded to him. Not even so much as an email or a text. It had alternately concerned and then angered him before rolling back to concern all over again. He hoped that whatever she was here to say, it would let him off this crazy roller coaster of emotion.

She drew in another breath. "Like I said, I'm sorry for how I left you. You deserved better than that, but I didn't know how to give it to you. I just knew I needed to get away, so I did. Just like you always said, I ran. Except this time, instead of running away from my problems, I decided to run right to the root of them. To face them."

"You went back to Michigan?"

Faye nodded and clasped her fingers tightly together. "It wasn't easy but I knew I had to face everything I'd left behind. One of my old high school friends—she's a doctor now—put me in touch with a grief counselor who has helped me put a lot of things into perspective."

"I see. And now?" he prompted when she fell silent again.

"Now I think I'm ready. Ready to be honest with myself and with you about everything. You see, I've been carrying so much guilt since the night of the crash. What I'd never told anyone before was that I'd been an absolute bitch to my stepdad in the weeks leading up to Christmas. He'd always done his best by me and always allowed me to take the lead in how our father-daughter relationship developed. To be honest, he was too good, too kind, too patient. For some stupid reason that made me lash out. Teenagers, huh?" She gave Piers a wry smile. "Anyway, when I started pestering him about allowing me to drive home from the carol singing I could see he was torn. I almost wanted him to say no, just so I'd have something to complain about."

"But he said yes," Piers said heavily.

Faye nodded again, her eyes washing with sudden tears. She wiped at them and accepted a handkerchief from Piers when he dragged it from his pocket.

"Thanks. I'm sorry. It seems in the past two months I've cried a lifetime of tears and I don't seem to be able to stop."

"It's okay, Faye. Sometimes we just need to let go."

"Do we? Do you?"

He thought of the days and nights he'd endured since she'd walked out on him, of the pain of losing her and not knowing where she was. It had been a different kind of grief to that of losing his brother, but it had been grief nonetheless.

"Yes, it's only natural. We might not like it, we might not be able to always control it, but sometimes we have to give in to it."

"That's another thing I've had to learn. And here I thought I was all grown up." Faye gave a self-deprecating laugh. "Anyway, I was doing okay on the road that night. Maybe going a little too fast for the conditions, but Ellis, my stepdad, just cautioned me gently to be aware of where I was and what I was doing. Henry was fussing in his car seat and Mom said he needed to be fed.

Ellis had just turned around to say something to Mom when I saw the tanker take a curve in the road in front of our car. He lost traction and jackknifed—then he slid straight into us.

"If I had been going slower, we'd have been farther back, I'd have had a longer time to react... Or, if I'd only let Ellis drive, we'd probably have been past that spot already, instead of wasting time bickering in the parking lot about who'd drive, and the truck would have missed us altogether."

"Faye, you can't torture yourself with the what-ifs and maybes. You don't know that it would have made any difference at all."

She wiped her eyes with his handkerchief again and nodded. "I understand that now, but fifteen-year-old me certainly didn't and, unfortunately, it has been fifteen-year-old me—still fighting to make sense of what I did—that's been driving my life for most of the past thirteen years."

Faye came back to the sofa and sat again. "I was told later that Ellis and Henry died on impact, but Mom and I were both trapped. The car caught fire almost immediately." She shuddered. "I still see the flames licking up over the hood and coming from under the dash. I can still smell my legs starting to burn. Mom was screaming in the back, telling the people who arrived on the scene to save her babies. Someone managed to drag Henry out in his car seat, but by that point, there was nothing they could do. Another man wrenched my door open and pulled me free. The last thing I remember is begging him to save my mom and dad—then I passed out. When I woke up, they told me I was the only survivor."

"It sounds like a nightmare. I'm so sorry you had to go through that, Faye."

She stared unseeingly out the window, her mind obviously lost back in that awful, tragic night. "It's taken me a long time to realize that so much of what happened was out of my control. It seemed like I should be able to blame someone for me losing my family—even if the only target I found was myself.

"When I helped with the babies at my foster home, they were my substitutes for the brother I lost. In them I saw that chance again to love him, to make up for what I'd done—until they left, anyway."

"It's why you were so reluctant to let yourself near Casey, isn't it? Because you were afraid of loving him and possibly losing him all over again," Piers said with sudden insight.

Faye inclined her head and clenched the sodden handkerchief in her hand. "My counselor has helped me understand why I behaved the way I did. Helped me realize that I was still trying to protect my teenage heart—the one that had lost everything and everyone. But she also helped me understand that it's okay to try again—to trust in my feelings and give them a chance to blossom. To open my heart to others. To accept that while things won't always work out, not everyone will be taken from me. It…it hasn't been easy and I'm not all the way there yet, but I'm determined to win this time. Because, if I don't, I will lose the most important thing in my life for good, if I haven't already."

Piers felt a spark of hope flicker to life in his chest. "And that is?"

"You," she answered simply. "You offered me your love—heck, you offered me everything that's always been missing since that night—and I was too afraid to take it. Too afraid to trust you. It was easier to walk—" Faye made a choked sound in her throat that almost sounded like a laugh "—okay, *run* away, than it was to accept what you promised me."

"And now?" he prompted.

"Now I want to be selfish. I want you. I want Casey. I want it all." She hesitated, uncertainty pulling her brows together and clouding her blue-gray eyes to the color of the sky on a stormy day. "If you'll still have me, that is. I know I've had my walls up and I know you've done your level best to scale them or break them down. I just hope you're still prepared to help me—to continue to fill the missing pieces in my life like you've been trying to do all along. Will you, Piers? Will you have me back?"

Piers reached out his hand and traced the line of her cheek, staring deeply into her eyes. He'd waited for these words, hoped against hope that one day she'd be ready to say them. But there was one thing still missing.

"Like I told you before, Faye, I want it all, not just pieces of you. Like you, I want everything, too. Maybe it's selfish of me, but I need to know you're in this all the way. It's been hell with you gone. Not just in the office, but here, too." He pounded a fist on his chest. "Some nights I couldn't sleep for wondering where you were or what you were doing. And every time Casey passed another milestone, I wanted to share it with you, and you weren't there."

Faye swallowed, the muscles in her slender throat working hard as she accepted what he had to say.

"I can only say I'm so sorry I've hurt you, Piers. I love you and I never want to hurt you in any way ever again."

All the tension he'd been holding in his body released on those oh-so-important three little words. She loved him. It was enough. He knew Faye wasn't the kind of person to toss that simple phrase around lightly. If she said it, she meant it.

"I know you never will. As long as you love me, I will have everything I ever need," he murmured.

Piers pulled her into his arms, every nerve in his body leaping from the sheer joy of having her back where she belonged.

"You know I'm going to want to formalize this. You're going to have to marry me," he pressed. "And you're going to have to adopt Casey, too. We come as a package deal, you know."

"Marry you? Are you sure?"

She sounded hesitant but it only took a second for Piers to realize she wasn't stalling because of her own feelings, more that she was seeking confirmation of his.

"Completely and utterly certain," he said firmly. "It might surprise you to know, I've never told anyone that I loved them. Ever. Except for you. It was a leap of faith when I admitted to you how I felt. You'd become such an integral part of so many aspects of my life that I didn't blame you for accusing me of using the L-word to manipulate you into staying with me. But admitting I loved you came as a bolt out of the blue for me and, once I understood it, I knew that would never change. You're it, for me. The first, the last, the only."

"Oh, Piers!" Faye lifted a hand to cup his cheek and a sweet smile tugged at her lips. "You've given me so much already and now this? I'm so very lucky to have you in my life. I never want to spend a day without you by my side. So, I guess that means you forgive me for running out on you?"

"I will forgive you anything provided you never leave me again."

"I never will," she promised and pulled his face to hers.

* * * * *

"Something happened in the water today. Something changed between us."

No, Delia wanted to protest. Yet Jager was right and they both knew it.

"We can't let that happen." She needed to maintain the balance of power. Rebuild some guise of professionalism before it was too late. "This job is too important to me."

"And your professional skills are valuable to me, as well. But we can work around that. Besides, do you really believe ignoring it will make it go away, Delia?"

"If we both make an effort, yes. Of course. We're both adults with professional agendas. We can keep those work goals front and center when we're together."

"Like we did today."

"Today was an aberration." It had to be. "Emotions ran high. We were both scared for Emily." She wanted it to be as simple as that. "Just an adrenaline moment."

"So what about this moment, right now?" he asked. "Adrenaline?"

She willed a logical answer to explain the way the air simmered all around them.

Any answer she might have given was a moot point, however, since Jager chose that moment to lower his lips to hers.

* * *

Little Secrets: His Pregnant Secretary
is part of the Little Secrets series:
Untamed passion, unexpected pregnancy…

LITTLE SECRETS: HIS PREGNANT SECRETARY

BY
JOANNE ROCK

First Published in Great Britain 2017
By Mills & Boon, an imprint of HarperCollins*Publishers*
1 London Bridge Street, London, SE1 9GF

© 2017 Joanne Rock

ISBN: 978-0-263-92846-4

51-1217

For my sister-in-law, Kate,
thank you for joining our family!
My brother is lucky to have you, and so are we.
Wishing you much love and happiness.

One

Sun glinted off the brilliant blue Atlantic, full of sailboats bobbing on the calm water. For Delia Rickard, the picturesque island scene meant only one thing. It was the perfect day to ask for a raise.

Delia mentally gave herself a pep talk as she rushed around the marina in Le François, Martinique. She anticipated meeting her boss at any moment. Her father desperately needed her help and that meant forcing herself to push for that raise. Her quiet nature and organizational skills made her great at her job but sometimes posed a challenge when it came time to stand up for herself.

She hadn't seen Jager McNeill in the last six months. Would he be impressed with the changes she'd made both at his family's marina and the nearby McNeill mansion where she'd taken over as on-site property manager a year ago, on top of her responsibilities assisting Jager?

She'd worked tirelessly for months just to be worthy of Jager McNeill's trust in her. He'd given her the job as a favor since she didn't have a four-year degree—showing more faith in her than anyone else in her life. At first, it had been enough to work hard to repay Jager for giving her a chance. But now, considering the hours she put in to manage both properties and the effort she made to execute every facet to the best of her ability, she knew it was time to approach her employer about a bump up in her paycheck. Her father couldn't afford his portion of the taxes on the Rickard family lands this year and Delia needed to help to keep the small plot in the family. Her former fiancé had tried to trick her out of her share of the land once and she wouldn't give his greedy corporate backers any chance to swoop in now and take it from her or her dad. But unless she made more money, the Rickard home would be up for auction by springtime.

Delia sidestepped a family loading their cooler onto a skippered sailboat as she hurried toward the dockmaster's office for an update. Just as she got there, guests on one of the new superyachts dialed up its sound system far more than the noise regulations allowed, alerting Delia to a sunset party just getting underway.

"Cyril?" she called into the small office, raising her voice to be heard. "Any word on Mr. McNeill's arrival?"

The sun-weathered dockmaster turned to her. "His seaplane just landed. The skiff picked him up a moment ago."

"Thank you." She smiled quickly before turning to glare out toward the party boat, wishing the group would take their ten-decibel fun out to sea for a few hours. She wanted Jager's arrival to be perfect. "I'll go speak to our guest about the noise."

Cyril shouldered his way out of his office. He shaded his eyes to peer down the dock past the multimillion-dollar boat blasting house music, toward the open water. "Do you know why Jager wants to meet here?"

Delia had been puzzled about that too. Why would their boss want to step off a plane and go straight to work after being away from home for over six months?

The McNeill family had been through a harrowing year. The three brothers, Jager, Damon and Gabriel, had all relocated to Los Altos Hills, California, a year ago to establish their tech company in the heart of Silicon Valley. The software start-up had been Damon's brainchild, but both Jager and Gabriel played roles in managing the business as it grew. Shortly afterward, Damon had married. He planned to stay out West once the company took root, and Gabe and Jager would return to Martinique, where the family had a small hotel resort and the marina, in addition to the main house they sometimes rented out for upscale corporate retreats.

But then their lives had been turned upside down when Damon's new bride was kidnapped and held for ransom. All of Damon's focus had turned to getting his wife back, leaving Jager and Gabe to run the fledgling business. Eight months after the kidnapping—even after ransom had been paid—Caroline McNeill had not been returned. Damon's father-in-law insisted the ransom note had been a hoax and that Caroline had left of her own volition. Damon refused to accept that story even though police refused to investigate. Damon had left the country and hadn't been heard from since. To save his brother's company before the value dropped with rumors of instability in the leadership, Jager had quietly shopped the software start-up to potential buyers. He hoped to sell the business as soon as possible.

"I'm not sure why he wants to visit the marina first," Delia answered Cyril, her gaze trained on the water for signs of Jager's arrival. "Maybe after the year his family has had, work is the only thing getting them through the days."

Someone had threatened her family once and Delia had never forgotten the bite of betrayal. She couldn't imagine the pain the McNeills had been through.

"I just hope he doesn't decide to sell the marina too," Cyril admitted before he retreated into the dockside office, leaving Delia with a new worry to add to her list.

It was bad enough she needed to ask for a raise. What would she do if Jager unloaded his Martinique assets?

Delia felt the thrum of bass in the repetitive technocrap blaring from the deck speakers as she rushed up the long wooden dock as fast as her wedge-heeled sandals would allow. The superyacht had only been docked at Le François for three days and Cyril had already talked to them once about the noise and the parties.

"Excuse me!" Delia called up to the bow, which was at least ten feet above her head. She waved her arms to try to catch someone's attention. A handful of swimsuit-clad couples lounged on big built-in sofas or milled around the bar. A few kids ran around the deck, squealing and chasing each other. "Hello!"

Delia backed up a step to make herself visible to the group. She could hardly hear herself shout; they were completely oblivious. She glanced behind her to make sure she had more clearance, well aware that the docks were narrow at the far end where the larger watercraft tied off.

She peered back up at the party boat just in time

to see one of the kids—a girl in a fluttery white bathing suit cover-up—lose her balance near the rail. Her scream pierced the air right before she pitched headlong into the water with a splash.

Terrified and not sure if anyone else even saw the child go in, Delia scrambled to the edge of the dock. She toed off her shoes and tugged her phone out of the pocket of her simple sundress, never taking her eyes off the ring of rippling water where the girl had landed. Jumping in feetfirst to avoid hitting her head on any hidden debris, Delia rotated her arms to pull herself deeper.

Salt water stung her eyes when she tried to open them. Her hair tangled in her face as she whipped her head from side to side. Scanning. Searching.

Fear robbed her of breath too fast. Her lungs burned as she grew light-headed. Had anyone else even seen the girl fall? What if Delia was the only one looking for her, and what would happen now that even she'd lost sight of her?

Breaking the surface, she hauled in a giant gulp of air, then forced herself to dive deeper. Legs kicking fast, she felt something tickle her outstretched hand. Forcing her body deeper, she couldn't quite catch the blur of white she spotted in the water through burning eyes.

And then another swimmer streaked past her as if powered by scuba fins. There was a rush of water as strong limbs sluiced by. Though her vision was distorted by the sting of salt, she could tell the new arrival was on target for the flash of white she'd spotted. Even as her chest threatened to explode from lack of air, she remained underwater long enough to be sure the diver retrieved the child.

Thank you, God.

The fear fueling her strokes leaked away. Relief kicked in along with a wave of weariness. By the time she got to the surface, she could barely drag in air, she was so woozy and exhausted, yet she could see through painful eyes as the victim was pulled to safety on the dock.

But now it seemed that Delia was the one in trouble. Gagging, gasping, her arms flailing, she reached blindly for the side of the boat or anything, clawing for support…

"Whoa!" A deep, masculine voice sounded in her ear at the same moment two arms wrapped around her midsection. "I've got you."

Only then did she realize she'd somehow clawed him too. The arm that held her was bleeding from three shallow scratches. Sense slowly returned as oxygen fed her brain again.

The house music had been silenced. The only sound now was the murmur of voices drifting from the marina. She glimpsed the drenched little girl on the dock, already surrounded by family. A woman—a local with a houseboat who happened to be a retired RN—was on her knees at the victim's side, lifting her gently as she coughed up water. The relief in the crowd was palpable. Delia felt the same overwhelming gratitude throughout her body. Her shoulders sagged.

Bringing her breasts into intimate contact with the arm around her. She collapsed like a wet noodle against the slick, hot body of a man built like iron. Her dress floated like seaweed around her thighs, making her suddenly aware of the way her soaked bikini panties were all that separated her from him.

"Are you okay, Delia?" The voice in her ear was familiar; she'd heard it nearly every day for the past year, even if she hadn't seen the man in person for weeks on end.

Her boss. Jager McNeill.

"Fine," she spluttered, the word ending in a cough.

Of course, it was foolish to be embarrassed since she had dived in the water to save a child. And yet, it still felt terribly awkward to be caught with her dress up around her waist today of all days when she'd wanted to make the perfect professional impression.

Also, she'd scratched him.

Coughed all over him.

If she hadn't had a crush on him once upon a time, maybe she wouldn't be tingling from head to toe right now in spite of everything. But she feared if she tried to swim away from him to escape all the feelings, she just might drown. She was surprised to notice how far she'd drifted from the dock in her search. Behind them, she noticed the transport skiff that Cyril had sent out to meet Jager's seaplane. Jager must have been arriving at the same time she'd jumped into the water.

"Hold onto my shoulders," he told her, shifting their positions in the water so he faced her. "I'll tow you to the dock."

Nose to nose with him, Delia stared up into his steel-blue eyes. She thought she'd gotten used to his good looks in the past two years that they'd known each other. His dark hair and sharp, shadowed jaw made for enticing contrasts to those incredibly blue eyes. His hair had grown longer in the past months, as if barber visits were the last thing on his mind. But the way the damp strands curled along the strong column of his neck only added to the appeal.

This close, she had the benefit of sensing the wealth of muscle in his athletic body where he held her. Feeling the flush of heat course through her, she ducked deeper into the cold water to hide her reaction to him.

"I can make it." Shaking her head, she scattered droplets from her wet hair. "I just needed to catch my breath."

She attempted to paddle away, but Jager only gripped her tighter.

Oh. My.

Feeling the warmth of his chest through their clingy clothes roused an ache she should not be feeling for her boss. Adding to the problem, the strapless bra she'd been wearing had shifted lower on her rib cage, where it did absolutely no good.

"Humor me," he ordered her, his voice as controlled as his movements. "You're exhausted and dry land is farther away than it looks." He took one of her hands and placed it on his right shoulder. Then, turning away from her, he very deliberately set her other hand on his left shoulder.

He began to swim toward the dock with measured strokes, towing her along behind him. Water lapped over them in light waves. She felt every ripple of his muscles under her palms as the light waves swished over them. She debated fishing one hand down her dress to haul up her bra before they reached land, but decided the potential scolding from Jager if she let go of him wasn't worth it. So she clung to him and gritted her teeth against the friction of her pebbled breasts rubbing against his back. By now he had to be as keenly aware of her as she was of him.

The only positive of this awkward reunion?

Any anxiety she had about talking business with him was utterly eclipsed by physical awareness. So when they reached land, she clamped onto the dock, evenly met his blue gaze and said, "I definitely deserve a raise."

* * *

Two hours later, when they were safely back at the McNeill family estate in Le François, Jager still couldn't erase Delia Rickard from his mind. After pouring himself an aged whiskey from the cut crystal decanter on his desk and taking a sip, he stared out his office window through the slats of the open plantation shutters. His gaze kept returning to the guest cottage lit by white landscape lights. He was waiting for Delia to emerge. When he'd first asked her to manage the Martinique household for him, he'd offered her the cottage on the British Colonial style property for expediency's sake.

Not only could she keep track of the staff better onsite, but at the time, she had also been trying to put some distance between herself and her past. Her former fiancé, Brandon Nelson, was a particular kind of son of a bitch Jager had run into often in business—always looking for a way to cheat the system. In this case, the guy had attempted to scam Delia out of her rightful inheritance—a plot of land belonging to her father that was in the way of a proposed landing strip for private aircrafts serving a luxury hotel development. The investors had offered Brandon a cash payment if he could convince her to sign over the rights. He'd decided to simply marry her and obtain the rights for himself.

Unethically.

Jager leaned a hip on the dark hardwood desk, remembering how Delia had discovered the truth on the morning of her wedding. She'd fled the seaside venue on a Jet Ski and run it aground on a small island where Jager had been fishing. It had been the start of a friendship that had benefitted them both.

He'd been in a relationship at the time, and Delia

had been running from an awful one, so he'd tamped down the attraction for both of their sakes. Instead, he'd offered her a job. Very quickly, she'd proven an excellent assistant, invaluable in helping him repurpose a portion of the family estate for private parties and occasional corporate retreats as a way to support local businesses—in particular, his marina. After Delia trimmed the household budget the first year and made a local farm-to-table initiative on McNeill lands a success, Jager had asked her to expand her role to review the operations at the marina as well.

Leaving things in her capable hands, he'd moved to California with his brother to take Damon's start-up to the next level. Just thinking about the hell that move had caused for all of them made his shoulders sag with grief for Damon and the loss of his vibrant and beautiful wife.

Now Damon had disappeared too. He'd left to travel two months ago and at the time, Jager had agreed it would be wise for him to get away. But days after his departure, Damon had shut off his phone and hadn't been in contact since.

To make it worse, around that time Jager had been contacted by their father, who'd barely acknowledged him as a child and whom Jager hadn't seen in fifteen years. Now, suddenly, he was offering the help of his wealthy family.

Too little. Too late.

As if Jager had any desire to spend time with the dirtbag who'd walked out on their mom. Apparently Jager's paternal grandfather—whom he'd never met—was determined to reunite all his grandsons. Bastard offspring and otherwise. Jager had told them hell no.

He finished off the whiskey and set aside his glass.

His world was a giant mess. The one moment of clarity in it all?

When Delia had been in his arms in the water just two hours ago. The dark churn of thoughts that had plagued him for nearly a year suddenly quieted, burned away by an attraction grown more intense since that first day when she'd washed up on his island. Nothing prohibited them from being together now. He was so distant from the Martinique-based businesses that he could make a move without worrying about the impact on their working relationship. Or he'd simply transfer her to another part of the company where Gabe could monitor her job performance, eliminating the conflict of interest. Gabe could make the decision about that raise she wanted.

His conscience clear, Jager watched her step from the cottage, her fair hair glowing golden under the porch light as she locked the dead bolt with a key. Now he could allow himself to think about the possibilities of being alone with her. Of forgetting the hell of the past year for a night in her arms.

Backing away from the window, Jager watched as Delia strode toward the main house. She wore a rose-colored tank dress, with a thin white sweater thrown over her shoulders. A simple gold bangle wrapped around one wrist. She worried her lip with her teeth as she stared down at the dusky gold pavers that led to the stone steps up to the house.

If he could have a taste of that soft pink mouth, he would indulge as often as possible. Was she nervous about spending the evening with him? Or was she looking forward to it as much as he? She had to have known she was getting to him today in the water. Soaking wet and hard as hell for her, he'd been unable to hide his fast reaction to feeling her breasts pressed to his chest. He'd felt her reaction too though. The attraction wasn't one-sided.

"Hello, Jager." He couldn't believe how long he'd allowed himself to ruminate over her body. She'd entered the house and his office while he was preoccupied.

Of course, she had domain over the whole place while he was gone. And he'd left the double doors to his office open. He was more than ready to let her in.

"I trust you're feeling better after the impromptu swim?" He turned to greet her but did not approach, hoping to put her at ease. She'd pinned her golden-blond hair up, leaving only a few stray pieces around her face. The rest bounced in a loose knot as she walked.

He gestured toward the seating arrangement near the fireplace. A wrought iron candelabra with fat white pillar candles had been laid in the cold hearth at some point in his absence. A homey touch. Delia perched on the edge of a wide gray twill armchair near the rattan chest that served as a coffee table, her posture stiff even though she gave him a smile.

"I'm almost warm again, thank you." She tugged the shawl sweater more tightly around her while he took a seat on the couch adjacent to her chair. "Tourists may swim in November, but I don't usually go in the water this time of year."

"Yet you didn't even hesitate." He'd been watching her from the deck of the skiff carrying him from the seaplane to the marina. "I saw how fast you jumped in after Emily fell." He'd spoken to the girl's family briefly after reaching the dock, to make sure she was going to be fine and that they would focus more on parenting and less on partying.

"You were in the water almost as quickly as me."

She shook her head and briefly closed her hazel eyes as a delicate shudder passed through her. "I don't even want to think about what might have happened if you hadn't arrived when you did. I was never so panicked as those few seconds when I couldn't find her."

"I only spotted her because you were just above her in the water." He'd swum faster than he'd known he was capable of. "Although I would have searched the whole damn marina for her if I had to. I've had enough sleepless nights thinking about how different our lives might be if someone had been there to haul Caroline out of the water."

He hadn't meant to share that, but the loss of his sister-in-law had overshadowed everything else for their family. Delia's hand on his forearm cut through some of the darkness though, providing an unexpected comfort.

"I'm sorry," she said simply, her eyes filled with genuine empathy.

Empathy that didn't even rightfully belong to him. It was Damon who'd been through hell. Suddenly Jager was reminded that he needed to focus on his family and not whatever he was feeling for his assistant right now. At least until they'd cleared up some business.

"Thank you." He acknowledged her kindness before redirecting the conversation. "Which reminds me that I won't be staying in town long, so I'd like to come up with a plan to review any new business over the next week."

"You're leaving again? Why?" Delia's touch fell away from his arm. Her lips parted in surprise.

"I need to find Damon." He'd never imagined his brother as the kind of man who might do himself harm, but Damon had been through more than any man should have to bear.

"I understand." Delia nodded, but her expression remained troubled. She spun the gold bangle around her wrist.

"I won't leave until we address any concerns you may have about the business." Or Gabe did. But there was enough time to share his plan with her. He still hoped to put her at ease first.

"Of course." She quit spinning the bracelet and glanced up at him. "I know how committed you are to this place. You're always quick to respond to any of my questions about the business."

Leaving him to wonder if she'd ever had questions of a more personal nature that he'd overlooked? He studied her features, trying to read the woman who'd become so adept at managing his affairs. A woman who had become a professional force to be reckoned with despite a lack of formal training.

She deftly changed the subject.

"Have you eaten?" she asked, straightening in her seat. "Dinner is ready. Chef texted me half an hour ago to say he'd prepared something—"

"Will you join me?" he asked, wanting her with him.

"I don't want to monopolize your time on your first day home." She scooted to the edge of her seat as if looking for the closest exit. Cautious. Professional. "I can bring you up to speed on the house and marina in the morning so you can enjoy your meal."

"My brother Gabe is in Los Altos Hills for another week," he reminded her. "There's no one else in Le François waiting to spend time with me, I'm afraid."

Still, she hesitated. No doubt about it, those chilly moments wrapped around one another in the Atlantic today had shifted the dynamic between them. She'd never been uneasy around him before.

"We can make it a working dinner, if you wish." He reached for his phone and began to type out a text. "I'm requesting that the meal be served in here."

"That's not necessary," she protested.

"I insist." He needed them to clear away an important piece of business. To remove any barrier there was to being together. "Besides, I've been meaning to discuss something you brought up in the water today."

"I…" Her eyes went wide. She swallowed visibly. If she were any other woman, he wouldn't hesitate to end the suspense and kiss her.

But he wouldn't rush this.

"You mentioned needing a raise?" he reminded her, clearing a place for their plates on the rattan chest by moving aside a fresh flower arrangement of spiky red blooms he recognized as native to the island.

Already, a uniformed server hesitated at the office door, a tray in hand. He waved the young woman in.

"Sir?" The woman's starched gray uniform was cinched tight by apron strings. She carefully set the tray down where he indicated. "Chef said to tell you there is a visitor at the gate."

"There is?" Delia tugged her phone out of a long brown leather wallet that she'd deposited on the chair beside her. The call button at the gate on the main road was hooked up to an app Delia and Jager could access. "I'm sorry I didn't hear the bell. I turned off notifications for our meeting."

Curious, Jager spun his own phone toward him and clicked on the icon for the security system while the server went to retrieve another tray from a rolling cart in the hallway.

Before Jager pulled up the video feed from the front gate, Delia gasped.

"What is it?" Jager asked.

She lost color in her face, her fingers hovering above her lips as if to hold in the rest of her reaction.

"It's not your ex, is it?" Jager shot to his feet, moving behind her chair to view her screen.

"No." Delia lifted the phone to show him. "It's your brother. Damon."

Two

Steel-blue eyes stared up into the security camera. Mc-Neill eyes. Delia had seen the three brothers together often enough to appreciate the family resemblance. The striking blue eyes and dark hair. The strong jaw and athletic build. Damon was the tallest of the three. He looked a bit thinner than she recalled, which was no surprise given the year he'd had.

"That's not Damon." The cold harshness of Jager's voice stunned her as he tugged her phone from her grip, his strong hands brushing over her fingers. "Let me speak to him."

Confused, she let go of the device while Jager pressed the talk button. Her skin was still humming from his touch as he straightened.

"I've made it clear I don't want to see anyone from your family," he barked into the speaker while he gently closed the office doors to keep their conversation private from the staff. "If you need accommodations in town, I can send someone out to the gate with a list of recommendations."

"Jager!" Appalled, Delia leaped from her seat and reached to take her phone back. "What are you doing?"

The voice of the man at the gate rumbled through the speaker. "You're not getting rid of us, dude. Now that my grandfather knows about you, the old man is insistent that you and your brothers join the fold."

Delia froze as she absorbed the words. After hearing him speak, she questioned her own eyes. The man didn't have Damon's voice. Or his reserved, deliberate manner. The voice was bolder, more casual, even a bit brash.

Her gaze found Jager's, searching for answers. The air sparked between them, making her realize how close she was standing to her boss. She was painfully aware of how handsome he was in a pair of khakis and a long-sleeved dark tee that showed off his toned body. She caught a hint of his aftershave: pine and musk. Her heartbeat quickened before she stepped back fast.

"Not going to happen, Cam." Jager spoke softly, but there was an edge to his voice she couldn't recall hearing before. Clearly, he knew the man. "You can tell your grandfather that your father made the best possible decision when he walked out on my mother. We're better off without him."

Delia backed up another step, processing. The men looked so much alike. The man at the gate wanted Jager and his brothers to *join the fold* and said his grandfather knew about them now.

The man *was* Jager's brother. Just not the brother that Delia had assumed he was. This was a relation she'd never known about—a half brother.

"We have a lead on Damon," the visitor countered in a more guarded tone. "My brother Ian knows an excellent private investigator—"

"Damon is not your concern," Jager told him shortly, still studying Delia with that watchful gaze. "Goodbye."

He lowered the phone and pressed the button to end the connection and shut down the security app. Sudden silence echoed in Jager's office.

"You have more family than just Damon and Gabriel," she observed, feeling shaken from the encounter. From the whole day that had left her exposed in more ways than one.

It seemed as if Jager had whole facets of his life that she knew nothing about. If he didn't trust her with that information, how well did she even know him? Her former fiancé had left her more than a little wary of men who kept secrets.

"My father was a sporadic part of my childhood at best, and I haven't seen him once since my thirteenth birthday." Jager set her phone on the sofa table next to a platter of food covered with a silver dome.

She'd forgotten about the dinner, but the spices of island cooking—French Creole dishes that were Jager's favorite—scented the air.

"He had other children?" She felt she was owed an answer because of their friendship but she also needed to know about this to do her job. "This can have an impact on all your businesses. You'll want to protect yourself from outside legal claims."

"And so we will." His lips twisted in a wry expression. "But the Manhattan branch of the McNeill family is far wealthier than we can imagine thanks to their global resort empire, so they certainly don't need to alienate their own relatives by forcing their way into our businesses." He gestured to the sofa. "Please sit. We should eat before the meal is cold."

"McNeill Resorts? Oh, wow." The name was as familiar as Hilton. Ritz-Carlton. It was too much to process. She sank down onto the soft twill chair cushion.

Jager took the opportunity to lift the domes from the serving platters and pass her a plate and silverware. The scent of *accras*, the delectable fritters the McNeills' chef made so well, tempted her, rousing an appetite after all.

"Yes. Wow." His tone was biting. "I believe my half brothers expected Gabe and me to swoon when they informed us we were now welcome into the family." He dished out a sampling of the gourmet offerings onto her plate—spiced *chatrou*, the small octopus that was a local delicacy, plus some grilled chicken in an aromatic coconut sauce.

His arm brushed hers. The intimacy of this private meal reminded her she needed to be careful around him. She needed this job desperately. Her father relied on her and good opportunities were difficult to come by locally for a woman with no college degree. She couldn't afford to leave the island to find more options. Balancing her plate carefully, she shifted deeper against the seat cushion to try to insert some space between her and her tempting dining companion.

"Damon doesn't know about them?" she asked, trying to focus her scattered thoughts on his last comment.

"Only in a peripheral way. We were aware of their existence for years, but they didn't contact us until recently." Jager filled his plate as well. "Cameron McNeill and his brother Ian flew out to Los Altos Hills last month to introduce themselves and make it clear their grandfather wants to unite the whole family. Including the bastard Martinique branch."

Delia took her time responding, biting into the tender chicken and taking a sip from the water glass Jager passed her. She knew that he had no love for his father after the man disappeared from their lives—refusing to leave his wife for Jager's mother—when Gabe, the youngest son, was just ten years old. Their father had only visited the boys a few times a year before that, making it impossible to build a relationship. They'd lived in California back then. But after the father quit coming to visit, their mother sold the house and used the proceeds to buy an old plantation home in Martinique, purposely making it difficult for the boys' father to find them even if he'd wanted to. As far as Jager was concerned, however, his father had abandoned their family long before that time.

Jager had shared all that with Delia in the past, but the latest developments were news to her.

"It's the right thing for your grandfather to do," she said finally. "You, Damon and Gabe have as much claim to the McNeill empire as your father's legitimate sons."

"Not in the eyes of the law." Jager scowled down at his plate.

"The business belongs to your grandfather." She knew the rudimentary facts about the hotel giant. They owned enough properties throughout the Caribbean to warrant regular coverage in regional news publications. "Malcolm McNeill gets to choose how he wants to divide his legacy." She waited a moment, and when he didn't argue, she continued, "Have you met him?"

"Absolutely not. That's what they want—for me to get on a plane and go to New York to meet the old man." He speared a piece of white fish with his fork. "They claim Malcolm McNeill is in declining health, but if it's true, they're keeping a tight lock on the news since I haven't seen a whisper of it in the business pages."

Her jaw dropped. How could he be so stubborn?

"Jager, what if something happened to him and you never got to meet him?" She only had her father for family, so she couldn't imagine what it might be like to have more siblings and family who wanted to be a part of her life. "They're family."

"By blood, maybe. But not by any definition that matters in my book." Reaching for a bottle of chilled Viognier the server had left for them, Jager poured two glasses, passing her one before taking a sip of his own.

"And does Gabe feel the same way?" She had a hard time imagining the youngest McNeill digging his heels in so completely. Whereas Jager resolutely watched over his siblings like a de facto father, Gabe went his own way more often than not. He'd only invested in Transparent—Damon's tech company—after considerable urging from his siblings. Gabe preferred to stick close to the hotel he owned on Martinique and was renovating the place by hand.

His older brothers had scoffed at the manual labor, but Delia noticed that Gabe was having a hard time finishing the hotel work because his craftsmanship skills had developed a following, making him in demand for other restoration projects around the Caribbean, all the way to Miami.

"Gabe is outvoted by Damon and me." He took two more bites before he noticed she hadn't responded. When he turned toward her, she glared at him.

"Meaning he disagrees?" she asked.

"Meaning Damon would feel the same way I do, so if Gabe chooses to disagree, he's still outnumbered."

Delia set her plate aside on the rattan chest, then put her wineglass beside it.

"Damon might have a very different opinion about family after losing someone," she observed quietly.

Jager went still.

"You have a lot to say about something that doesn't concern you, Delia." He set aside his half-eaten meal as well, and turned to face her.

"Doesn't it?" She shifted toward him, their knees almost brushing. "I could give you an update on my plans for next year's community garden or how to increase profits at the marina, but it's hard to ignore the fact that you just turned your back on a family member who looks eerily like your missing brother."

"It's not eerie." His tone softened. "It's simple genetics. And I find you a whole lot tougher to ignore than my half brother."

She opened her mouth to deliver a retort and found herself speechless. The air in the room changed—as if the molecules had swollen up with heat and weight, pressing down on her. Making her far too aware of scents, sounds and him.

"That's good," she said finally, recovering herself— barely. She needed to tackle his comment head-on, address whatever simmered between them before they both got burned. "Because I don't want to be ignored. I would have hoped you'd listen to my opinion the way I once listened to yours when I was having some rough times."

She hoped that it was safe to remind him of the start to their relationship. She'd felt a flare of attraction for him that day too, but she'd been too shredded by her former fiancé and too mistrusting of her own judgment to act on it. For his part, Jager had seemed oblivious to her eyes wandering over his muscled chest and lean hips covered by a sea-washed pair of swim trunks. He'd quietly assessed the situation despite her tearful outburst about her thwarted marriage, and he'd given her direction, plus a face-saving way out of her dilemma at the time.

She hadn't been able to pay the taxes on the family's land that year either. Her dad had been injured in a fishing accident three years ago and couldn't earn half the living he used to selling fresh catch to local restaurants. But Jager had given her a job and the income had staved off foreclosure. Plus, Jager had given her a place to stay far away from her ex, and time to find herself.

Now, he looked at her with warmth in his blue eyes. A heat that might stem from something more than friendship.

"Maybe I liked to flatter myself that I was the one doling out all the advice in this relationship." His self-deprecating smile slid past her defenses faster than any heated touch.

"I don't think any of us exercise our best judgment when our world is flipped upside down." She'd been a wreck when they'd met. Literally. She'd almost plowed right into him on a Jet Ski she'd taken from the dock near where she'd planned to say her vows.

"Is that what's happening here?" he asked, shifting on the sofa cushions in a way that squared them up somehow. Put him fractionally closer. "The world is off-kilter today?"

The low rasp of his voice, a subtle intimacy of tone that she hadn't heard from him before, brought heat raining down over her skin. Her gaze lowered to his mouth before she thought the better of it.

"That's not what I meant." She felt breathless. Her

words were a light whisper of air, but she couldn't draw a deep breath without inhaling the scent of him.

Without wanting him.

"It's true though." He skimmed a touch just below her chin, drawing her eyes up to his. "Something happened in the water today. Something changed between us."

No, she wanted to protest. To call it out for a lie.

Yet he was right and they both knew it.

His touch lingered, the barest brush of his knuckles beneath her jaw. She wanted to dip her cheek toward his hand to increase the pressure, to really feel him.

Madness. Total madness to think it, let alone act on it.

"We can't let that happen." She needed to maintain the balance of power. Rebuild some guise of professionalism before it was too late. "This job is too important to me."

Shakily, she shot to her feet. She stalked to the window on legs that felt like liquid, forcing herself to focus. To get this conversation back on track. Why hadn't she simply spoken to him about the community garden?

"And your professional skills are valuable to me as well. But we can work around that." Behind her, his voice was controlled. Far more level than she felt. "Besides, do you really believe ignoring it will make it go away, Delia?"

She felt him approach, his step quiet but certain. He stood beside her at the window, giving her personal space, yet not conceding her point. The soft glow of a nearby sconce cast his face in partial shadow.

"If we both make an effort, yes. Of course." She nodded, hoping she sounded more sure of herself than she felt. "We're both adults with professional agendas.

We can keep those work goals front and center when we're together."

"Like we did today." His gaze fixed on some point outside the window, but his eyebrows rose in question.

"Today was an aberration." It had to be. "Emotions ran high. We were both scared for Emily." She wanted it to be as simple as that. "Just an adrenaline moment."

Her heart fluttered oddly as he turned toward her again, taking her measure. Seeing right through her.

"So what about this moment, right now?" he asked. "Adrenaline?"

She licked her suddenly-dry lips. Willed herself to come up with a logical explanation for the way the air simmered all around them. The way her skin sensed his every movement.

Any answer she might have given was a moot point, however, since Jager chose that moment to lower his lips to hers.

Jager couldn't walk away from her tonight. Not after the hellish year he'd had. He needed this. Needed her.

Her lips were softer than any woman's he'd ever tasted. She kissed with a tentative hunger—gentle and curious, questing and cautious at the same time. She swayed near him for a moment, her slender body as pliable as it had been in the water today, moving where he guided her. So he slid his hands around her waist, dipping them beneath the lightweight cotton sweater to rest on the indent just above her hips.

She felt as good as she tasted. Something buzzed loudly in his brain—a warning, maybe, telling him to take it slower. But he couldn't do a damned thing to stop it.

Instead, he gripped the fabric of her dress in his

hands, a tactic to keep from gripping her too hard. He tugged the knit material toward him, drawing her more fully against him.

Yes.

Her breasts were as delectable as he remembered from in the water today. High. Firm. Perfect. And Delia seemed to lose herself in the contact as much as he. She looped her arms around his neck, pressing her whole body to his in a way that made flames leap inside him. Heat licked over his skin, singeing him. Making him realize how cold he'd been inside for months.

Delia's kiss burned all that away. Torched everything else but this incredible connection. The warning buzz in his brain short-circuited and finally shut the hell up.

Letting go of her dress, he splayed his fingers on the curve of her ass, drawing her hips fully to his. The soft moan in her throat sounded like approval, but he was so hungry for her he didn't trust what he heard.

"Delia." He broke the kiss and angled back to see her better, trying to blink through the fog of desire. "I want you. Here. Now."

"Yes. Yes." She said it over and over, a whispered chant as if to hurry him along, her hands restlessly trolling his chest, slipping beneath his shirt. "Definitely now. If you lock the doors," she suggested right before she lowered a kiss to his shoulder, "I can get the blinds."

"I'm not letting you go for even a second." He walked her backward toward the door, kissing her most of the way until he needed to focus on the bolt. Even then, he kept one palm on her lower back, at the base of her dress's zipper.

"And the blinds?" she reminded him, her hair starting to fall from the topknot she was wearing. "The switch on your desk is closest."

"Right. Of course. Lady, you do mess with my brain." His brain—and other parts of him.

Jager moved with her in that direction, but he used his free hand to sift through her silky hair, pulling out pins and one jeweled comb, letting them fall to the dark bamboo floor. He'd been wanting to do this forever, he realized. Ever since he'd held her that first day when she wore that wet wedding gown and cried her eyes out against his bare chest.

She reached to find the switch, lowering the blinds electronically, shutting the room off from the well-lit grounds. Now just a few low lamps illuminated his office, casting appealing shadows on her creamy pale skin. With her tousled hair falling over one eye and the shadows slanting over her, she looked decidedly wanton. Altogether appealing.

He wanted her so much his teeth ached. He tugged the zipper down on her dress, peeling the cotton knit away from her body, sliding it right off her shoulders to pool at narrow hips. One quick shimmy and she kicked free of the dress; now she was clad only in ice-blue satin panties and a matching strapless bra. She was even more beautiful than he'd imagined, and he'd had some dreams where he'd thoroughly fantasized about her over the past two years.

Before he could contemplate how best to savor her, she slid a finger between her breasts and loosened the tiny clasp of her bra, baring herself. He froze for an instant to take in the sight of her—then his body unleashed into motion. His arms were already moving as he hauled off his shirt so he could feel her against him.

Kissing her, he cupped her breasts in his hands, teased one taut peak and then the other. Licking, nipping, drawing her deep into his mouth. He backed her into the desk and then lifted her, settling her there. She wrapped her legs around his waist, hooking her ankles and keeping him close.

"Do you have…protection?" she asked, her breath a warm huff of air against his shoulder.

Hell, yes. He might not have been with anyone in months, but he always kept a supply of condoms here. Pulling away, he opened the middle desk drawer. Thumbed past the last file. Emerged with a packet.

Their eyes met over the condom before she plucked it from his fingers and kissed him. No hesitation. No reservations.

He tunneled his hands through her hair, tilting her head back to taste his way along her jaw and behind one ear. She shivered sweetly against him, deliciously responsive. She smelled sweet there, like vanilla. He lingered, inhaling her, relishing the way her breath caught.

Too soon, her touch along his belt, the backs of her knuckles grazing his erection through his fly, called his attention from her delicate neck. Later, he would return to her neck, he promised himself. He wanted to linger over every part of her, but right now, the need was too fierce to ignore. While he unfastened the belt and carefully freed himself from the zipper, Delia was already tearing open the condom packet, her fingers unsteady as she rolled it into place. Her palm stroking over him there sent a fire roaring inside. He touched her through the blue satin panties she still wore, and he found the hidden dampness just inside and teased a throaty moan from her, stilling her questing hands long enough to let him catch his breath.

He wanted her ready for him. Really ready. Sinking a finger inside her, he felt the deep shudders of her release and kissed her moans quiet as she rode out the storm of sensation.

Damn, but she was beautiful. Her cheeks were flushed and eyes dazed, her hair a golden banner in the low lamplight.

When she was still again, he eased inside her slowly, gripping her thighs with his hands to guide himself home. She wound her arms around him again, nipping his lower lip before drawing it between hers. She arched against him, her breasts flattening to his chest. He knew he wouldn't last long this time. The day had stolen his restraint long before he started peeling her clothes off.

So he let himself just feel the slick heat of her body around his, her warm vanilla scent making his mouth water for a fuller taste. He cupped one breast and feasted on the taut nipple, finding a rhythm that pleased them both and riding it to…

Heaven.

His release crashed through him, trampling his body like a rogue wave until he could only hold on to Delia. He buried his face in her hair, the shudders moving up his back again and again. Her nails bit pleasantly into his shoulders and he welcomed the sweet hurt to bring him back to earth. Back to reality.

A reality that felt…off, somehow.

Straightening with Delia still in his arms, his body tensed.

"What is it?" The sultry note in her voice told him she hadn't realized what happened yet.

His satiated body was only beginning to get the message too, but his brain had already figured out what was wrong.

"It broke."

Three

Delia's brain didn't compute.

Her limbs still tingled pleasantly from the first orgasm a man had ever given her. Her whole body hummed with sensual fulfillment. And yet…panic was just starting to flood through her nervous system, rattling her from the inside out.

"What do you mean, *it broke*?" She knew what he meant, of course. But she didn't understand how it had happened. How she could have let herself be so carried away by the man and the moment. Even if the man in question was Jager McNeill.

"I don't suppose you're on the pill?" he asked, instead of answering her question, as he gently extricated himself from her arms and legs.

"No." She shook her head while reality slowly chilled the residual heat right out of her veins.

"You should stand up," he urged her, lifting her off

the desk and settling her on her feet. "Do you mind if I carry you into the shower?"

His matter-of-fact response to a potential grenade in both their lives only rattled her further, making the possible consequences feel all the more real. And frightening.

"I'll walk there," she assured him, wondering what the rest of his staff—her coworkers, for crying out loud—were going to think of her walk of shame through his house into the nearest bathroom.

She would headline local gossip for weeks. Or, quite possibly, nine months.

Oh, God. What had she done?

"We could try emergency contraception," Jager suggested carefully. "If you're amenable to taking the medication."

Would that work? She'd never had a need to investigate the option. "I can call my doctor."

Jager was putting a blanket around her. The throw from the back of the couch, she realized. Gratefully, she sank into the gray cashmere, veiling her tender body from the cool calculation she now saw in her lover's eyes. He'd pulled on his pants and shrugged into his long-sleeved black shirt. Only his dark hair, disheveled from her fingers, gave away the less guarded man who'd made passionate love to her just moments ago.

Not that it was love, she reminded herself sharply.

"I'm sure I can find a pharmacy with the over-the-counter variety." Jager was all efficiency. "I'll get you settled and make a trip to the store."

"Thank you." She would still want to talk to her doctor. Double-check the side effects given her medical history. But she wasn't sure how much to disclose about that right now with her thoughts churning.

"The guest room is closest," he told her, tucking her under one strong arm as he opened the double doors of his office and steered her into the hallway.

Of course she knew the guest room was closest. She'd been in this house every day for two years. Would she lose her job now if she was carrying his child? Or even if she wasn't? Only pride kept her from blurting out how much she needed this job.

When they arrived in the downstairs guest suite, Jager locked the door behind him and she scurried toward the bathroom.

"Delia." His voice halted her just before she shut the door behind her.

Peeking out through a crack—not that it mattered since he'd already seen her very naked—she waited to see what he wanted. And wished she saw some hint of warmth in his eyes to reassure her.

"I believe emergency contraception has a high rate of effectiveness. But based on where you are in your cycle, how strong of a chance would there be that this would have—" He hesitated, and she wondered if this was rattling him more than he let on. But he blinked, and any hint of uncertainty vanished. "Resulted in pregnancy?"

"Based solely on my cycle?" She had no idea if she was a fertile woman. But if so? "We would want to come up with a contingency plan when I get out of the shower."

Delia felt marginally calmer when she emerged from the bathroom in a pair of navy cotton shorts and a tee with McNeill Meadows printed on one pocket—promotional items given away to school groups who visited the community garden. She'd found a stack of clean items still in the packaging in the back of the guest bathroom's linen closet. Indulging herself, she'd helped herself to two tees to make up for the fact that her bra still lay on the floor of Jager's office.

She used a hand towel to dry her hair a bit more as she padded across the thick Persian carpet toward the king-size bed with its pristine white duvet. This bedroom overlooked the gardens, its deep balcony almost as large as the room itself. The sliding glass pocket doors were open now, and she followed the floral-scented breeze to where Jager sat on a padded chaise longue, looking out at the lit paths of the rock garden. The table nearby was set for two, a hurricane lamp glowing between the place settings of all white dishes. New serving platters undoubtedly held an entirely new meal. Sandwiches, maybe. Or fruit and cheese. Not even the McNeills' talented chef could turn out five-star cuisine on an hourly basis.

The travertine tiles were cold on her bare feet as she padded outside to join Jager. He turned when she'd almost reached him, then stood.

"Would you be more comfortable in your own clothes?" he asked. "I brought them from the office and put your things in the closet."

She winced to think of her wrinkled dress neatly hung in one of the gargantuan closets. "No, thank you. I've always liked these McNeill Meadows tees. I chose them last year for when school groups visit. At long last, I'll have my own."

"You wear it well." His blue gaze slid over her and she felt it as keenly as any touch. "I had some food brought up in case you're hungry. I wasn't much of a host the first time around."

Her stomach rumbled an answer at the same time she nodded. Needing to stay cool and levelheaded, she focused on slow, calming breaths. She draped the damp hand towel over one of the stone railings surrounding the balcony, then let him lead her to the table. The outdoor carpet was warm against her bare toes. He held out a chair for her and she sank into the wide seat. Once he tucked her chair in, he opened the platters, offering her each so she could help herself to a selection of fruits, cheeses and warm baguettes. Jager poured them both glasses of sparkling water over ice and lemons, then sat in the seat beside her. The hurricane lamp sent gold light flickering over the table while night birds called in the trees just off the balcony.

To a bystander, it would look like the perfect romantic setting. She guessed romance couldn't be further from either of their minds.

"Based on your comment going into the shower earlier, I thought it would be wise to discuss a plan for the future. Just in case." He slid a paper bag across the table. "Although I was able to obtain the contraception option we discussed."

She eyed the bag dubiously, but took it after a moment. "I'd like to check with my own doctor in the morning, but if he gives me the okay, I'll take it then."

"That sounds fair." He nodded.

"Thank you." She congratulated herself on her calm tone that belied the wild knot of fears in her belly. She focused on her wedge of brie, spreading the cheese on a thin slice of baguette.

Jager laid a hand on her knee, an intimacy she hadn't expected after how quickly he'd pulled away following the encounter in his office. It felt good. Too good. She couldn't allow herself to fall for him. One moment of passionate madness was one too many when she needed this job and the good will of the McNeills to help keep the Rickard home and land.

"Let me begin by assuring you that I would never abandon my child." Jager spoke with a fierceness that gave her pause. "My father taught me well the damage a parent inflicts with his absence."

The candle flame leaped and the glow was reflected in his eyes. She wasn't sure how to interpret his words, however.

"Neither would I," she told him evenly. Family loyalty meant everything to her. Her father had raised her by himself, on the most meager means, after losing his wife in childbirth.

Some of the intensity faded from Jager's expression. He lifted his hand from her knee and sipped his water before replacing the glass on the white linen tablecloth.

"Then we'll have to stick together if tonight has consequences," Jager observed. "In the meantime, I think I should fly out as soon as possible to begin the search for my brother. I want to find Damon so I can return here next month or in six weeks, whenever you think we might learn one way or another about a possible pregnancy."

Her knife clattered to her plate as she lost her grip. She fumbled to retrieve it, but couldn't hide her dismay at his quick abandonment. "I have set a new record for chasing a man out of my bed." Resentment stirred. "I can email you the test results, if it comes down to that."

"Delia." He set down his own cutlery to reach across the table, his hand circling one of her wrists. "It never occurred to me you might want to travel with me, but I can arrange for that. Our chemistry is undeniable."

Defensiveness prickled. She wasn't planning to be his mistress.

"What about my job? I need the work, Jager. My father relies on my income. That's why I asked about the raise before things got…complicated."

"I had already planned to ask Gabe to supervise your work from now on. To eliminate any conflict of interest for me. But in light of what's happened—"

"You already had a plan in place to have an *affair* and didn't tell me?" She wondered when he'd decided that. Or when he would have clued her in to the fact. It might have put her more at ease about being with him.

Then again, what did it say about the beginnings of a relationship between them when he made all the decisions?

"I wanted to be with you, Delia." His jaw flexed as he spoke and she had a memory of kissing him there. "I knew it in the water today that we weren't going to be able to continue a productive working relationship with so much tension between us."

She worried her lip, unsure how she felt about that. What if she didn't like working with Gabe? More to the point, what if Gabe didn't need her? If she was pregnant as a result of this night, how could she possibly maintain any independence when she worked for the family of her child's father?

Most important of all? She wasn't sure how she felt about an affair with Jager. Of course she was tempted. She couldn't deny their time together had been incredible. One touch from him and she'd been lost, swamped by a desire so heated she'd forgotten her common sense. But she had a few obvious reservations straight out of the gate.

"I'm not sure we can have a productive personal relationship either if we're not equal partners. I'd like to be a part of the decision-making." She nibbled a straw-berry, hungry despite the anxiety.

"I agree," he surprised her by saying. But then, was he just trying to pacify her? "If there's any chance we need to parent together, we'll have to figure out how to share that responsibility in a healthy way."

Determined to at least appear calm and in control, Delia lifted her glass in a silent toast. "We're making progress then. I appreciate you hearing my opinions."

"I value your input. Would you really want to travel with me for the next few weeks? The last I knew, Damon was in Marrakesh."

She took a deep breath, steeling herself for a conver-sation he wouldn't want to have. But he said he'd share the decision-making power. She didn't plan on accept-ing his offer to extend this affair if he didn't mean it.

"Your half brother said he knows where Damon is," she reminded him. "On the off chance that it's true, shouldn't you find him as quickly as possible in case he needs you?"

Jager's shoulders tensed. "You're going to make this about my family?"

"Isn't this whole conversation about the possibility of more family? A McNeill child?" Straightening in her seat, she tried to maintain some composure, but she could see him pulling away fast. It was in his shut-tered expression.

"I know Damon. That means I can locate him faster than anyone else." He'd sidestepped her question, she noticed. "The only thing left to decide now is if you want to join me in my search, or if you prefer to wait in Le François until we find out for certain if there will be another McNeill in our future?"

Four

Pacing the floor of the cottage bedroom, Delia paused to check her desk calendar for the third time, making sure her dates were right while she waited for the results of the at-home pregnancy test.

The calendar told her the same thing it had before. It was now two weeks until Christmas, and almost six weeks after that fateful night when she'd let her attraction to Jager run wild.

Nearly six weeks since she'd had unprotected sex with her boss, and no sign of her period. She'd ended up taking the morning-after contraception Jager had purchased for her after speaking to her physician, so she'd honestly thought they'd be in the clear, even though she hadn't been able to take the pill within the first twenty-four hours as would have been ideal. But it was still supposed to be highly effective within the first seventy-two hours, so she hadn't panicked when her doctor hadn't gotten back to her personally until the next day.

Still, she'd delayed this test, fearing a false negative result. Better to wait longer and be certain, even if Jager had been texting her daily from Morocco, asking her for updates, tactfully suggesting a blood test at an appointment he'd helpfully arranged. She'd been ducking his calls, which was totally unprofessional given that he still had some sway over her job, despite Gabriel McNeill now technically being the one signing her paycheck. But the longer she went missing her expected period, the more her anxiety spiked.

Because honestly, she was scared to know the truth.

In Jager's last text, he'd informed her he would fly home tonight, insisting they find out for certain one way or another. Knowing she couldn't handle discovering the result in front of him, she'd surrendered and pulled out one of the pregnancy tests she'd purchased two weeks before.

Now she just had to wait three minutes.

Thirty more seconds, she corrected herself after checking her watch. Skin still damp from her bath, Delia tightened the bathrobe tie around her waist and returned to the steamy bathroom where the garden tub was draining. The clove-and-cinnamon-scented bubble bath, which she made from her own recipe during the holidays, was a small decadence she allowed herself at times like this.

The pregnancy test lay facedown on the white tile countertop beside the sink. She'd left it there while she reread the instructions to be sure she understood. One line meant not pregnant. Two lines—however faint— meant she was going to have a child with Jager McNeill.

She'd read online that high tension and stress could

delay a period. That *had* to be why she was late. So, holding her breath, she closed her eyes. Flipped over the stick on the cool tile.

Two. Lines.

One bright pink. One paler pink.

There was no denying it. And according to the package, this was the most reliable at-home pregnancy detection kit.

"Oh, no. No." Her legs turned to jelly beneath her. She felt so dizzy she clutched the narrow countertop with both hands to steady herself. The stack of rolled yellow hand towels swayed against the wall as she stared at it.

No, wait. That was her swaying.

She stumbled back to sit on the edge of the garden tub, the last of her bubble bath gurgling down the drain with a sucking swish. Kind of like all the plans she'd had for independence once she had her father more securely settled. Plans to get a college degree one day. To travel somewhere beyond this tiny island where she'd been born.

Plans for a future where she called the shots and dictated her own life. She must not have taken the morning-after medicine soon enough, but at the time, she'd really wanted her doctor's advice about the pill considering her health history.

Wasn't it enough that she'd screwed up by nearly marrying a guy who didn't care about her? Nope. She had to compound her foolishness by succumbing to a moment of passion with a man who would never see her as more than…what? A company employee? A former friend turned sometime lover?

Her child deserved better than that.

That simple truth helped her emotions to level out.

Made the dizzy feeling subside a bit. She couldn't afford to wallow in a pity party for what she'd wanted in life. She was going to be a mother, and that was something tremendously significant.

She might have messed up plenty of times on her own behalf, but Delia Rickard was not going to be the kind of woman who made mistakes where her baby was concerned. That didn't mean she had a clue what to do next, but she sure planned to take her time and figure it out.

Deep breath in.

Deep breath out.

Before she even finished the exhale, however, a swift, hard knock sounded on the front door of the cottage.

"Delia?" The deep rumble of the familiar voice caused panic to stab through her.

Jager McNeill had come home.

Jager stood under the cottage porch light, waiting. He knew Delia was here. His housekeeper had seen her enter the carriage house an hour ago and Delia's lights were all on. Soft holiday music played inside.

She'd been avoiding any real conversations with him for weeks. He'd tried to give her some space, knowing she was even more rattled about the possibility of being pregnant than he was. Besides, the search for his brother had been intense, leading him on a circuitous path around the globe. Now he was certain, at least, that Damon was alive. But he'd seen signs that his brother was hell-bent on revenge and that scared him.

Still, Jager should have made Delia his first priority before now. Either she was delaying taking the pregnancy test for reasons he didn't understand or—worse—she'd been hiding the news from him. Whatever the truth, he needed to earn her trust. He couldn't afford to alienate her when their futures might be irrevocably bound.

He lifted his hand to knock again, only to hear the deadbolt slide free on the other side. The doorknob turned and there she was.

Delia.

Wearing a white terry-cloth robe and a pair of red-and-green-striped knee socks, she was scrubbed clean, her wet hair falling in dark gold waves onto her shoulders. Worry filled her hazel eyes. The rosy color he'd grown used to seeing was missing in her cheeks.

Hell.

He hadn't seen her look so upset since that first day they'd met. And that comparison put his own behavior into perspective. He wasn't a loser like her former fiancé. He should have come home before now. Been there for her.

"May I come in?" He hadn't even changed his clothes when he stepped off the plane. He'd flown eight hours to be here today, the six-week anniversary of the passionate encounter in his office.

Six weeks hadn't dimmed how much he wanted her. Not even when they were both stressed and worried about the future. If he had his way, she'd be in his arms already, but he didn't want to pressure her.

"That would be wise." Nodding, Delia retreated while he stepped over the threshold, closing the door behind him.

He hadn't been inside the cottage for over a year. He'd overseen the delivery of a few basic pieces of furniture when she'd first taken up residence in the renovated carriage house. But it bore no resemblance to what he remembered.

To say she painted flowers on the walls didn't come close to describing the way she'd made the interior look like an enchanted garden. Yes, there were flowers of all colors and varieties—some not found in nature—growing from a painted grass border along the floor. On one wall, a full moon glowed in white phosphorescent paint, shining down on a garden path full of rabbits and hedgehogs, all following a girl in a dark blue dress. On another wall, there was a painted mouse hole on the baseboard, with a mouse with a broom and apron beside it, as if the tiny creature had just swept her front mat. Above the couch, framing a window overlooking the garden, someone had painted an elaborate stained-glass frame, as if the window view itself was a painting. The white curtains were drawn and a holiday wreath hung from the curtain rod on a bright red ribbon. He could only imagine the effect in the daytime.

From the living room, Jager spied her small bedroom; a white queen-size bed dominated the space. A canopy made of willow branches around the headboard was covered in white fairy lights that made the whole room glow. The unexpected glimpse into Delia's private space was so distracting that for a moment he'd forgotten his purpose.

"I took the test," Delia announced, passing him a white plastic stick. "Two pink lines. I'm pregnant."

She collapsed down onto the narrow white love seat, her robe billowing out at her sides. Her head dropped into her hands, and she planted her elbows on the bare knees visible just above her knee socks.

For his part, Jager felt like he'd just taken a roundhouse kick to the solar plexus. He'd tried to mentally prepare himself for this outcome for the past six weeks, but he hadn't come close to doing an adequate job.

"You're pregnant." He stared blindly at the two pink lines for a moment before setting the test aside on a glass-topped wrought iron coffee table. He needed to focus on Delia.

Lowering himself to the love seat beside her, he placed a hand on the center of her back, hoping to reassure her. Or maybe himself. He wasn't feeling too steady either.

"I only just found out." She lifted her head from her hands. Her eyes were rimmed with red but there were no tears. "I should have taken the test weeks ago, but I was scared of a false reading. I knew I just wasn't ready for the relief of getting a negative result, only to find out three days later that it hadn't been accurate."

"It's okay." He rubbed circles on her back, trying to remember the to-do list he'd typed into his phone for just this scenario. "I was worried you've known all week and couldn't figure out how to tell me."

"No." She shook her head, damp gold strands of hair clinging to one cheek. "When you texted that you were coming home tonight, I knew I couldn't wait any longer. Bottom line, I've probably been delaying just because I was worried."

"That's why I wanted to be here for you when you found out," he reminded her, wondering how they were going to come to any agreement about the future of their child when they couldn't coordinate something so simple. "I wish you would have responded to my messages."

A determined expression appeared in her eyes. "I hope you can appreciate that we're going to have a new dynamic between us now and I can't be expected to have a sixty-minute window to respond to your texts. You ensured we wouldn't be working together when you handed over my performance reviews to your brother."

Surprised at her response, Jager realized there were many facets to this woman that he knew nothing about. Her whimsical love of gardens for one. And this steely, willful side that he'd never suspected lurked beneath her cooperative professional demeanor.

"I never said you needed to reply to my texts within the hour," he answered, his hand going still on her shoulders where he'd been touching her.

"Perhaps not, but it's a level of responsiveness I prided myself on when I was your assistant." She suddenly shot up off the cushions to pace about the small living area, her stocking feet silent on the moss-colored area rug. "Maybe you never noticed, Jager, but not once in two years was I delinquent with a reply."

He supposed that could be accurate. In truth, he'd never taken that much note. He tucked aside the information to consider later, once they'd gotten through the emotionally charged moment. For now, he focused on remembering the items on the checklist from his phone.

"Fair enough. I realize our relationship has changed radically in a short amount of time. We'll find our way forward together." He kept his tone gentle, unwilling to upset her any more than she already seemed. "I hope you'll agree our next step is a doctor's appointment to confirm the result of your test and ensure you're off to a healthy start."

She stopped her agitated pacing and stared at him blankly for a moment before she resumed.

"Of course." She nodded, but she appeared distracted. She paused beside her wireless speaker and flicked it off, quieting the classical Christmas music. "I'll call my doctor first thing in the morning."

"I'd like to go with you."

She stopped again, her gaze wary. "Why?"

Frustration ground through him at the realization that she could shut him out at any time. Sure, once the child was born he had a way to exercise legal rights. But until then, she could cut him out of a large part of the baby's life—ultrasounds, heartbeats—things he wanted to be a part of. The lack of control in this situation was alien to him.

"To be a part of the process, Delia. I've tried to give you the space you craved these last six weeks." It was tough even now staying in his seat while she paced the floor. He wanted to pull her against him, hold her and remind her how good they could be together in the most fundamental way, but he knew it wasn't the time. "This child is every bit as much my responsibility as yours. I tried to explain to you on the night we made this baby that I will take this duty very seriously." Jager would not be the kind of father Liam McNeill had been.

"Okay." Delia nodded, then bit her lip. "I should warn you though, there's a bit of medical history I'll be sharing at that time. I'm not necessarily worried, but in the interest of taking every precaution—" she hesitated, her fingers massaging her temple gently before she continued "—my own mother died in childbirth."

The revelation speared through him hard. "I should have remembered." She'd shared that with him once, long ago. He tried to recall what little he knew about her past and her family. "You said she went into labor early, while she was out sailing with your father."

He'd met Pascal Rickard once, a stern-faced fisherman who'd stared down Jager when he'd visited Delia's home village to collect some of her things. Jager hadn't wanted her to return home alone after the incident with her ex. Pascal had been in his seventies then, but even with his weathered face, gray hair and half an arm amputated, he'd been an imposing figure. His broad shoulders and burly muscles attested to the hard work he'd done all his life. The man had little to say to his only child when Delia had packed up her small room for good.

"They were having me late in life. My father was fifty at the time, and my mom was forty-two." Delia hugged her arms around her waist; there was a new level of anguish in the story now that she was going to be a mother too. "Her uterus ruptured. The doctors told my dad afterward there was nothing he could have done to save her. She would have been in critical danger even if she'd been close to a hospital at the time."

The thought of something like that happening to Delia floored Jager. No matter what happened between them romantically, she had been more than just an assistant to him these last two years. Even though they'd seen little of each other these last several months, he considered her a friend.

"Did her doctors know she was at risk?" He would spare no expense to keep Delia safe. He would call specialists. Hire extra help if she needed rest. His mental to-do list grew exponentially.

"She would have been considered high-risk anyway because of her age, but I'm not sure what caused the rupture." Delia swiped a hand through her damp hair, pulling it away from her neck. "Talking about my mother—and particularly my birth—always left my father sad, so I avoided the topic in the past. But now that the events are extremely relevant to me, I will visit him as soon as possible and find out everything I can about what happened."

"I'll drive you there." Jager would clear his schedule and look into hiring someone to follow up on the lead he had to find Damon. Until he knew more about Delia's condition, he wasn't leaving her side.

"I'll be fine." She shook her head, waving away the offer.

"I insist." He rose to his feet, needing to make it clear that he was involved with this pregnancy and staying that way. He closed the distance between them. He didn't reach for her the way he wanted to, but he stood close enough to catch a hint of cinnamon and cloves.

She smelled good enough to eat, reminding him of how long it had been since he'd tasted her. Touched her. He planned to pursue her again as soon as she had the all clear from her doctor.

"Jager, I understand you want to be a part of this, but I won't compromise my independence." Frowning, she huffed out an impatient sigh.

"Giving you a ride is hardly taking away your independence. You can drive us in the Hummer if it makes you feel more in control." He didn't use the huge SUV often, but the vehicle had just the right amount of metal to keep her safe. Delia had driven it before.

"This isn't about who's in the driver's seat." Her chin tilted up. She was stubborn. Fierce. "It's about sharing decision-making. Remember we discussed that? If we're going to be effective co-parents, we need to find a way to share responsibility."

"I remember very well." He couldn't help but feel stubborn on this subject as well, damn it. Raising a child together was too important.

Which brought him to the second item on his list, every bit as important as the doctor visit.

And even more likely to put that wary look in her eyes.

"Since we want to share responsibility, I suggest we

approach co-parenting through the time-honored legal channel that gives us equal rights in the eyes of the law."

He lifted her left hand in his and held it tight. Her gaze followed the movement, brows knitting together in confusion. As he bent over her left hand, he kissed the back of her knuckles. When he straightened, her lips had formed a silent O of surprise. But he didn't even hesitate.

"Delia Rickard, will you marry me?"

Five

Was he serious?

Delia studied Jager's handsome face, trying to understand his motive. He had to know how fiercely she would resist that kind of bloodless arrangement, especially now that she'd had a glimpse of what real passion felt like. She wasn't going to accept anything less than true love if she ever returned to the altar again.

"How can you ask me that after what I went through with my engagement?" Delia slid her fingers free of Jager's hand. Though her skin tingled pleasantly from the contact, her brain rejected his matter-of-fact proposal. She needed time to process all of this. Rushing headlong to make another mistake was not the answer, and she felt like she was hanging on by an emotional thread right now. "I already had one man try to marry me for purely business reasons."

"Our child is hardly a business reason," Jager reminded her. She noticed how he was still wearing his travel clothes: dark jeans, white tee and simply cut black jacket.

She would bet he'd driven here directly from the airport. His face was rough with a few days' whiskers too, making her wonder what his trip chasing Damon around the globe had been like.

"A legal reason then," she told him flatly. "I believe that's the very language you used when you tendered the offer. Marriage as a *legal channel* to raise our child jointly."

He drew a breath, no doubt to launch a counteroffensive, but she was simply not ready for this conversation tonight. His presence already loomed too big in her small living room, and with his child literally growing inside her, it was simply too much.

"Jager, I'm sorry." She stepped closer, hoping to appeal to him as a friend. "I'm still reeling from all of this. Since we'll be spending time together tomorrow to speak to my father and visit the doctor, maybe we could table this discussion for tonight to give us both a chance to get a handle on it?"

"I understand." He nodded but made no move to leave. His blue gaze skimmed over her. "Will you join me for dinner? We can unwind and relax. No need to talk about anything you don't wish to discuss."

She hesitated. And in the small span of silence, he picked up her hand and slid his thumb across the center of her palm in a touch that was deliberately provocative. Or maybe she was just especially sensitive to his caress.

Either way, it gave her shivers.

"Delia, we were together the last time I was here for a reason." His voice wound around her senses, drawing her in. "There is no need to deny ourselves a connection we couldn't resist then either."

She swayed in limbo, hovering between wanting to lose herself in his touch, and wanting to set new parameters for a relationship grown way too complicated. In the end, she wasn't ready to do either. Taking a deep breath, she extricated her fingers from his.

"That connection caused me to make a reckless decision that I'm unwilling to repeat."

Yet.

She knew resisting the pull of Jager McNeill was going to be a Herculean task, but for the sake of their child, she needed to sort out her feelings and make a plan before she ran headlong into another unwise decision.

"Very well." He tipped his head in the barest concession of her point. "I'll wait to hear from you in the morning. Let me know what time to pick you up."

"Thank you. I'll text you." She knew tomorrow she'd face the same temptations all over again—to simply fall back into a heated relationship with Jager and indulge herself. But maybe after a good night's sleep, she'd feel stronger. More ready to think about what kind of preparations she needed to make for her child's future.

"Until then, I hope you bear in mind that I'm sleeping close by and I'm here for you, Delia." He reached out and ran his finger along a damp strand of hair, tucking it behind her ear. Then, lowering his voice, he brushed the back of his knuckles along her cheek. "Day or night."

She felt the sexy promise low in her belly, where desire pooled, thick and hot. All at once, she was reminded of how very naked she was beneath her robe. Of how easy it would be to shrug her way out of it and take the pleasure Jager's touch offered.

For a moment, she didn't dare to breathe, her whole body weak with longing. She guessed that he knew. His blue eyes turned a molten shade for a moment, before he allowed his touch to fall away.

When he departed, bidding her good-night before he closed her door behind him, Delia slumped onto the sofa, her heart beating wildly. Resisting her former boss wasn't going to be easy. How long would he hold back because she asked him to? Another day? A week?

Because she knew with certainty that she would have lost herself in him all over again tonight if he'd pressed his advantage and used all that chemistry to woo her. That meant she needed to be smart. Strong. Resolute.

She couldn't possibly invite Jager back into her bed unless she meant more to him than a passing pleasure. With a child on the way, the stakes were too high to give him that kind of power over her since she wasn't the kind of woman who could simply indulge herself for the sake of…indulging.

Starting tomorrow, there wouldn't be any more impromptu meetings in private spaces where they could be totally alone. She needed allies. Distractions.

She needed family.

With that kind of buffer to romance, Delia would carefully insulate herself from temptation until Jager saw reason. Until he understood how much it hurt her to think about marrying for purely legal reasons. She'd already been a means to an end for one man. Now? She would never marry for anything less than love.

Jager stared at his cell phone as his call went through to the Manhattan number.

He didn't want to speak to any of his half brothers and hated relying on anyone else to find Damon.

But tonight's discovery that Delia was pregnant left him with limited options. He needed to be with her to press his suit for marriage and, even more important, to make sure she remained in good health throughout her pregnancy. The realization that her mother had died in childbirth had left him reeling far more than the news that he was going to be a father.

He wouldn't let anything happen to Delia, or to their child. And if that meant making a deal with his father's other sons in New York, Jager would do it. He couldn't search for his missing brother and win over Delia too.

"Cameron McNeill," his half brother answered. It was a name Jager might never get used to hearing.

Until two months ago, Damon, Gabe and he were the only ones in his life who shared the same last name and the same useless father.

"It's Jager," he announced, pacing around his upstairs bedroom balcony. He could see a corner of the carriage house below. Delia's lights were all out now.

"Hello, brother." The greeting wasn't exactly sarcastic. But not entirely friendly either.

Hell. Maybe it was simply awkward. Jager could totally empathize with that, at least.

"I've decided to call in the favor you offered last time you were here." He lowered himself to sit on the giant chaise longue—another new addition to the house's furnishings under Delia's supervision. Everything about the historic Martinique property was warmer and more comfortable since she'd taken over.

"The favor I offered the time you locked me out and refused to see me?"

"Correct."

While he waited for Cam to respond, Jager could hear the familiar music from a popular video game.

He'd read—during a brief, unwelcome need to acquaint himself with the other branch of the family—that Cameron had founded a video game development company.

"I'm glad you're willing to have this conversation," Cameron finally said as the triumphant music that signaled he'd completed another game level played in the background. "Gramps is going to be psyched."

Jager stared out over the cottage and the gardens beyond just as some of the landscape lights shut off for the night.

"I'm not going to New York anytime soon," he warned his half brother. His grandfather had been pushing for a visit, but he had too many things to focus on at home. "I want to see if your investigator has any more luck than I've had finding Damon."

"Fine." A series of electronic chimes sounded on the other end of the call. "But when Bentley finds your brother, you're getting on a plane and meeting Malcolm."

He'd been expecting this, of course, but didn't appreciate being dictated to.

"Or Malcolm can get on a plane and meet all of us at once." Jager made the counteroffer mostly because he didn't like caving on this point. But he knew Delia wanted him to make peace with his family.

"Not happening," Cam said flatly. "It's not his fault Liam is a tool."

That shocked a laugh out of Jager. Not enough to concede the point, however.

"We can revisit the subject after your investigator finds my brother. There's no use planning for an event that could be totally hypothetical anyhow. And I'm not going to see any of you unless I've got Damon back." It would take something major to get him to change his mind. He fisted his hand against the lounger cushion, then pounded it twice.

"Very well. I'm texting you Bentley's contact information. He has reason to believe Damon's in Baja." Even as Cameron said the words, Jager heard the message notification chime in his ear.

The words confirmed what Jager had already feared. Damon had circled back to North America without telling anyone.

"He's trying to find the men he believes kidnapped his wife." A cold pit widened in his stomach.

Though he and Damon hadn't always seen eye to eye, Damon remained his younger brother. And, to an extent, his responsibility. He'd understood that even before their mother died of breast cancer when Jager was a senior in high school. With no father in the picture, it had always been Jager's job to make sure his siblings were safe.

"Or else he believes Caroline is still alive," Cameron offered, "and he wants to find her."

The words chilled him. Mostly because he feared that wasn't possible. He'd seen for himself how in love Caroline had been with his brother. He couldn't imagine her leaving of her own free will.

"For Damon's sake, I hope the latter is true." He needed some shred of positive news. "I'm going to phone Bentley now."

"Jager?" Cam said in a rush. "One more thing?"

He waited.

"You remember the terms of Malcolm's will? That we can only claim a share of his legacy if we've been married for twelve months?"

Jager's gaze shifted back to the cottage where Delia must be sleeping by now. He felt a pang of guilt that she'd taken the pregnancy test alone, that he hadn't been with her. What would she think about his wedding proposal if she discovered that marriage fulfilled one of the stipulations Malcolm McNeill had outlined for his heirs? Would she be so enthusiastic about a McNeill family union then, if she discovered another "business reason" for marriage?

"We don't want your company." He was more interested in profiting from his own projects—work he'd invested in personally.

"Right." Cameron huffed out a long sigh. "Between me and you, I'm grateful about that, so thanks. But our grandfather is a stubborn individual and he is determined to make us all fall in line."

"You're welcome to be his puppet. But not me." He was already grappling with feeling a lack of control where Delia was concerned. He wasn't about to relinquish more power over his own life to Malcolm McNeill.

"So consider a cash settlement," Cam suggested. "Meet Malcolm, shake his hand, let him feel like you're going to be a part of the family. But if you don't want the company, let my brothers and me buy you out."

"You can't be serious." The net worth of McNeill Resorts was staggering to contemplate. Far more than they'd make on the sale of Transparent, Damon's software company.

"Dead serious. Don't rob us of the business that has his name on it. The business we've all worked our asses off to further because it means something to him."

That Cameron would even suggest such an offer brought home how much he wanted to keep his grandfather's company intact. Interesting, because all three of the New York McNeill brothers were wealthy in their own right, with diverse business interests. Quinn, the oldest, was a hedge fund manager. He was *made* of money. So good with it, he earned millions showing other people what to invest in.

"I'll talk to my brothers," Jager finally conceded, levering himself off the chaise, needing to make his next call. "No promises though."

"That's all I'm asking."

Disconnecting the call, Jager checked his texts and found the contact information for the investigator Cameron had mentioned. As much as he hated asking for help to find Damon, Jager couldn't deny that he'd benefit from assistance after spending six weeks to find out something that this investigator had apparently known about for over a month. If he'd just given in and taken Cam up on the offer for help back when he showed up at the gate that night, maybe Jager would already have Damon back home.

It seemed stubbornness ran in the family, if what Cameron said about their grandfather was true.

For the first time since learning about his half-siblings, Jager thought maybe it wouldn't be so bad to at least meet them. Especially now that he was having a child of his own. Jager's father might be a two-timing failure as a role model, but that didn't necessarily mean Malcolm would be a negative influence on his heirs.

In less than nine months, Jager would need to make the decision. But first, his main concern was protecting Delia.

A job which would be easier as soon as she was his wife.

Six

With the top down on Jager's sporty convertible roadster, the warm December sun shining on them as they headed south the next day, Delia could almost forget they were driving toward her hometown.

She slicked on lip balm from her purse to keep from fidgeting as she was hit with a small attack of nerves. She'd avoided her father's fishing village for almost two years, preferring to coax him into Le François to visit her so she didn't need to run into people from her hometown. So many of her former neighbors had been at her failed wedding, witnessing the most humiliating day of her life. Understandably, going back home made her nervous. But she took comfort from the scent of the rich leather bucket seats and the smooth purr of the new Mercedes's engine. A local dealer had been all too glad to deliver a vehicle to Jager this morning, encouraging him to take the polar-white luxury car for a "test spin" for a week or two.

The privileged life her former boss led was going to be the kind of life that belonged to her child as well. But not to her. Delia had been lured in by the comforts of excess once. She wouldn't be wooed with superficial things again.

She chucked the lip balm back into her handbag as the vehicle slowed.

"That smells amazing," Jager observed as they stopped at a four-way intersection. "What is it?"

He peered over at her from the driver's seat, his blue gaze moving to her newly-shiny lips. It took all her willpower not to lick them. She felt incredibly aware of him today and she wasn't sure if it had to do with pregnancy hormones or the fact that she hadn't spent much time with him since their single combustible encounter in his office. She knew him differently now, and she wasn't sure she'd ever be able to look at him again without heat creeping all over her skin.

She straightened in her seat, hoping none of what she was thinking showed on her face.

"It's a new addition to the McNeill Meadows gift shop." She hadn't mentioned the product line to him, hoping to see the homemade beauty and bath items start turning a solid profit first. "I've been using the flower petals from the gardens, and beeswax from our beekeeper to make locally sourced lip balms and sugar scrubs. This one is called Coming Up Roses."

His gaze lingered on her mouth. Her heart skipped a beat or twelve.

"May I see?" he asked. With no one else at the intersection, he didn't seem in any hurry to put the car back in gear.

She did lick her lips then. "Um. There's no color or anything. It's just a balm." Still, she tilted toward him slightly so he could have a better look. The consistency of the product was really nice and she was proud of it.

"I meant the packaging." A grin twitched behind those words. "Although it looks very appealing on you."

"Oh." She leaned down to dig through her purse, wishing he didn't make her feel so fluttery inside. How was she going to forge a balanced, even relationship with him when she felt like a swooning teen around this man? "Here you go."

Passing him the tin, she tried to focus, bracing herself for the questions he might ask. But he seemed distracted today. Worried, perhaps. She wasn't sure if it was about the baby news or about his brother, but she understood he was coping with a lot right now. Businesswise, he was brokering a deal for the sale of Transparent, and that alone had to be stressful when it involved so much money.

"This was a great idea," he said finally, handing her back the tin before another car arrived across from them at the intersection. Jager took his foot off the brake and they continued their trip. "I like the way you kept the farm-to-table sensibility with local ingredients."

"And," she couldn't resist adding, "I'm creating a mini exhibit in the gift area about the plantation history of the McNeill home. I think visitors will be interested that we're using our own sugarcane in the lip and body scrubs."

"We are?"

"I sent you some paperwork on it last spring," she reminded him, beginning to see familiar sights out the window as her village neared. "We made an arrangement with a small refinery in Florida, but the end product is very much locally sourced."

The private marina where her wedding would have

been held was ahead on the right. She hadn't seen it since that day she'd stolen a Jet Ski that—thankfully—Jager had returned to the owner on her behalf. It had taken her a full year to repay him for the damages to the watercraft. Her nerves knotted tighter.

"Delia?" Jager said a moment later, making her wonder if she'd missed something he'd said.

"Hmm?" She pulled her gaze off the rocky coastline and back to the too-appealing father of her child.

She had to keep reminding herself of the fact since it still didn't feel real that she was carrying a McNeill heir.

"Are you nervous about seeing your father? Returning home?"

"Is it that obvious?" Her voice was a fraction of its usual volume. She cleared her throat. "I suppose it must be. And I'm not sure what has me more keyed up—telling my father I'm expecting, or seeing that marina where I stole a Jet Ski to escape from my ex."

"Would you like me to take a detour?" Jager flicked on the directional. "We can head inland for the last mile or two."

"No." She reached for him, laying a hand on his arm to stop him. "That's definitely not necessary. It's bad enough I was too insecure to handle things differently two years ago. I won't resort to running away anymore."

Resolutely, she looked out the driver's-side window, where the first boats of the marina were coming into view, bobbing in the crystalline blue water. The scent of the sea drifted through the convertible. Her hand fell away from his strong forearm.

If she touched him too long, she might not be able to stop.

"You didn't run away," he replied, his jaw flexing as he flicked his gaze out the side window for a moment before returning his attention to the road. "You escaped a bad situation. Big difference."

"There's no good excuse for larceny." The guilt over doing something so foolish still gnawed at her on occasion, but her actions that day hadn't just been in response to her fiancé's deception. "Although I might have been able to face my wedding guests that day if I hadn't also learned that my father knew about Brandon's involvement with the investment company."

They cruised past the permanent archway installed on the pier where people traveled from all over the world to say their vows. Today, in fact, a Christmas bride carrying a bouquet of red roses stood beside her tuxedoed groom, a blanket of poinsettias draping the arch. A small crowd filled the pier to watch, just the way Delia's guests had gathered two years ago.

"Your father knew?" Jager asked, his tone incredulous. He didn't even seem to notice the wedding in progress. "Didn't he care that jackass fiancé of yours was going to try to steal away your inheritance?"

That's exactly how she'd felt at the time, but her father had been unperturbed when she approached him in tears.

"Dad said the land was always meant for me, so if I wanted to sell it to developers, that was my business." It had been the way he'd said it that had hurt the most, with a shrug as if it didn't matter to him either way.

It had confirmed for Delia what she'd feared since childhood—that her father watched over her out of a sense of duty, never a sense of love. Pascal Rickard was a hard man, and she'd told herself for years he was simply too stoic to show his softer emotions. On her disastrous wedding day, she'd been confronted with evidence that he really didn't care all that much, and it had been a hurt deeper than anything Brandon Nelson could have ever doled out.

"You never told me." Jager gripped the stick shift tightly as he slowed down the vehicle. "All this time I thought it was a broken heart that brought you to my island that day."

He'd been like a mirage in the desert that day, a too-good-to-be-true vision of masculinity and caring as he helped her out from under the broken Jet Ski. She'd thrown herself into his open arms like he was an old friend and not a total stranger. Funny how she'd worked for two years to erase the horrible first impression she'd made, only to fall right back into those strong arms at his slightest invitation.

"It was a broken heart." She breathed in the scent of spices and fish as they neared the village market near the water. "But Brandon only accounted for part of it."

When Jager didn't respond, she tried to gauge his expression. He turned down the side road that led to her father's property, a tiny white-and-blue fish shack on the corner open for business. A few tourists lined up for whatever they were frying up today, the picnic tables out front already filled.

Tourist season started in December, and even the small fishing villages like this one benefited from the extra traffic.

"No wonder you haven't wanted to return here," Jager muttered darkly. "He would have let you walk right into marriage with a guy who wanted to steal your birthright."

True. But over time, Delia had come to see her father's point of view. He'd assumed that Delia was forsaking the land for the comforts of marriage to a local businessman with more financial means than she'd had growing up. And, sometimes, she feared that he'd understood her more than she understood herself, since walking away from Brandon hadn't been nearly as difficult as it should have been. How much had she loved her former fiancé in the first place?

Clearly, her judgment in men could not be trusted.

"Do you remember which one it is?" She pointed to the bright red house on stilts. "It's over there."

Nodding, Jager pulled off the main street onto the pitted driveway that led to her father's cabin, the simple home where she'd been raised. All around them, she knew, were other families who'd wanted desperately to sell their properties to the development group that had planned to put in an airstrip for a luxury resort. Her father had been the lone holdout.

For as long as he could pay the taxes. Because even though that old deal was no longer on the table, the plans were a matter of public record. Any other developer could swoop in and re-create the plan if they were able to obtain the necessary parcels of land to make it happen.

Tension seized up her shoulders as Jager stopped the car and came around to open her door. It was easier to simply send checks home than to face her father again after all this time. But today, for her child's sake, she needed answers that only Pascal Rickard could provide.

So for just a moment, she took comfort from Jager's hand around hers as he helped her from the Mercedes. She lingered for a moment as they stood close together, her sundress blowing lightly against his legs and winding around him the way the rest of her wanted to. She breathed in the scent of his aftershave—woodsy and familiar—before forcing herself to step away.

She'd allowed too many men access to her heart, and the price for her lack of judgment had been high— broken relationships and too much hurt. She wouldn't make the same mistake with Jager. As the father of her child, he was someone she needed to remain friends with. Only friends.

Forever.

Jager could practically see the mental suit of armor Delia put on as they entered her father's house. Hell, he'd done the same thing long ago himself, back when his family had still been living in the United States and he'd been young enough to care what his father thought of him.

Delia's careful mask of indifference reminded him of things from his own past he didn't want to recall.

So while she made awkward small talk with the serious, graying fisherman, Jager focused on his own agenda for the day. He needed to find out as many details as possible about the cause of her mother's death. Once he had ferreted out all the information, he would consult physicians independently.

Because while Delia had made a doctor's appointment for that afternoon, he didn't trust the local obstetrician to be on the forefront of prenatal and preventative healthcare. The one benefit he could see of a trip to New York—and to the home of the McNeill patriarch— was to ensure Delia had the best possible doctors for this baby.

Their baby.

The idea still threatened to level him every time he thought about it.

Now he followed Delia and her father outside to the deck overlooking the water. The red cabin on stilts was one of many brightly painted houses the village website touted as "charming," but Jager knew Delia's upbringing had been rough. She'd worked hard to help her father make a living, checking nets and making repairs almost daily, manning the fish market when he needed to go back out to sea and cleaning fish for demanding customers.

Still, there was beauty here in the simplicity of a lifestyle rooted in a sense of community. Jager envied that, especially after the McNeill wealth had attracted the kidnappers who'd taken Damon's wife.

Jager would never forget the naked pain in his brother's eyes the day she'd gone missing. The day she'd been presumed dead by the police.

Taking a seat beside Delia, Jager ached to touch her. Hold her hand and tell her father in no uncertain terms that he would be taking take care of Delia from now on. But until she agreed to marriage, what right did he have to stake that claim?

Clamping his jaw shut tight, he studied the older man. Even in his seventies, Pascal Rickard possessed a much younger man's vitality. His half arm didn't seem to hinder him much, and he used the partial limb efficiently enough, easily swinging an extra chair into place at the rickety patio table so that they could all have a seat. When her father didn't offer them anything, Delia returned inside, emerging a minute later with a pitcher of ice water and clear blue glasses. Jager stood to help her pour, passing around the drinks, and then they both sat again.

Had she always taken care of her father that way? Jager wondered. The older man sipped his water without comment while Delia spoke.

"Daddy, I'm here today because I need to ask you a

few questions about my mother. About how she died." Leaning forward in her rusted metal seat, Delia clutched her water glass in both hands, the tension in her arms belying the calm tone of her voice. "I know you don't like to talk about her. But it's important to me now because I'm pregnant."

Jager hadn't expected her to launch right into the heart of the matter. He guessed it must have been nerves that propelled the words from her, because she wasn't the kind of woman to shock an old man on purpose.

Pascal's face paled for a moment while he sipped his drink. Then he lowered the glass to the lopsided wooden tabletop.

"That's why you're here?" Pascal asked Jager, his hazel eyes the same shade as his daughter's but without any of the tenderness.

"I have asked Delia to marry me," Jager pointed out, reaching for her hand on instinct. "I hope that I will convince her to accept before our child is born."

Long before then, actually. Tomorrow wasn't soon enough as far as he was concerned.

Pascal grunted. Some of the color returned to his face, but his expression remained stony. Delia, at least, allowed Jager to hold her hand.

"I'm seeing an obstetrician later today," Delia continued as if Jager hadn't spoken. "And I need more details about mom's medical history in case there could be genetic factors at work we should know about."

The idea punched through Jager again as he turned to watch her. He'd lost his own mother too early, and Delia had never known hers. He guessed the vision of a child growing up without a mother was equally real for both of them. The thought had him twining his fingers through Delia's slender ones, gripping her tighter.

Pascal thrust his lower lip forward in an expression of disapproval before he turned to address Jager again. "Delia doesn't want to get married. Didn't she tell you? She could have been settled by now, but she didn't want to share her inheritance with developers."

Defensiveness rose in him, all the more when he heard Delia's soft gasp of surprise.

"Her fiancé had no plans of 'sharing' it," Jager reminded him. "Something he failed to mention to your daughter. She had to discover on her own." He pressed on, remembering how hurt Delia had been the day she'd wrecked that Jet Ski on the beach. "Didn't it occur to you she'd want to know Brandon's reason for marrying her?"

The old man shrugged, settling his empty water glass on the peeling, planked floor. "She seemed happy enough to put this life behind her when she was dating her big spender."

"That's not fair." Delia shot out of her chair, stalking to the half wall surrounding the deck. "I thought Brandon cared about me."

"And I thought you cared about making a better life for yourself," her father retorted, tipping back in the wooden dining chair he'd dragged outside from the kitchen. "Brandon offered you more than a life as his mistress."

Anger flared hot. Jager deliberately remained seated, facing her father head-on before he replied, "I am prepared to give Delia my home, my name and my life. I thought I made that clear. Right now, I would appreciate your help in protecting her health, so I'd like to know if this pregnancy poses a serious risk for her."

"And if it does?" Pascal set the feet of his chair back on the floor with a thud. "What then? Are you still prepared to give my daughter your life and your name if she can't carry your child to term? Or are you only willing to marry her for a McNeill heir?"

"Daddy, please." Delia stepped closer, not quite between them, but definitely in an effort to placate her father. She touched his knee and dropped down to sit on an overturned milk crate beside him. "I will decide my future, but I need to know what I'm facing. If you don't know about my mother's medical history, maybe you could tell me the name of her doctor—"

Pascal cut her off with a quick shake of his head. "Celine didn't have anything genetic." The words sounded raw in his throat, far different from the taunting tone he'd taken with Jager a minute ago. "She never even told me until that night on the boat when you were born, but Celine had a cesarean as a young woman when she gave birth to a stillborn child. She'd been frightened of something going wrong again. Worried she'd disappoint me." He swallowed hard and looked out to sea, unable to continue for a moment. "By the time I knew about it, it was too late. We'd only been married for two years."

The anger Jager had been feeling toward him seeped away then, his own fears for Delia making it too easy to identify with him.

"Afterward," her father continued, "when I got back to shore with you, the doctors said a cesarean can cause a uterine rupture later in life. It's rare, but it happens. Your mother had no idea of the risk, I'm certain of that, because she wanted you. Desperately."

Jager waited for Delia to ask him more, but she'd gone quiet. She studied her father, who remained silent.

Leaving Jager no choice but to step in again.

"Why was Celine's first child stillborn?" he asked,

wanting to give Delia's doctor a complete picture of any relevant medical history.

Delia spun away from them on the milk crate, grabbing her bag and riffling through the purse before coming up with a tissue.

Had he said something wrong?

Pascal shook his head. "I couldn't tell you. Celine never told me anything about that time in her life until the night she died."

Damn it. Jager kept digging. "Was she from this village? Maybe we can speak to her doctor."

Pascal folded his good arm over the injured limb, his mouth set in a thin line. Delia seemed to read this as a rejection of the question or refusal to reply, because she stepped closer again, slipping her hand around Jager's elbow.

"I can find out about those things," she assured him quietly. Her eyes were bright but there were no tears. "We should go."

Jager wanted to argue, to find out what else they could glean from her father. But seeing the hurt in Delia's eyes—a hurt he didn't fully understand—he followed her outside after a terse goodbye to Pascal. He didn't want to gainsay her in front of her father, a stunt that definitely wouldn't help his efforts to win her hand. He would simply call in every resource to learn more about Celine's medical condition. For now, they had enough information for Delia's obstetrician appointment.

It was good news that the uterine condition wasn't genetic. Yet there was still the worry of why her mother had a stillborn child when she'd been a younger woman. Jager's gut knotted as he opened the passenger door of the convertible for Delia.

No doubt she was upset about that news too, because she retreated to her side of the vehicle and didn't have a single word to say on the ride to her doctor's appointment.

Seven

Stepping out of the exam room an hour later, Delia smoothed a hand through her hair, still windswept from the car ride with the top down. While she was in the cold, antiseptic-scented room with the nurse and her new doctor, Delia had been very aware of Jager's presence in the waiting area outside. The nurse had said she would bring him back to the doctor's private office so they could both speak with the obstetrician at the same time.

After their meeting with her father, Delia had had a fair idea of how that encounter would go. Jager would ask the questions and push for answers.

With the doctor, she wouldn't mind so much. But with her father...

She paused a few steps from the doctor's office, closed her eyes and pulled in a deep breath. Remembering how close she'd been to hearing her father confess something—love for her? That she'd been loved by her mother?—pinched her emotions hard. Today had been the closest her father had ever come to showing some paternal warmth for her when he'd said that her mother had wanted her *desperately*.

How long had she yearned for scraps of his affection, even if that fondness was only a pale reflection of the love her mother might have given her? But the moment when he might have said more had evaporated forever when Jager interrupted, pushing the conversation in a more pragmatic direction.

He didn't know, of course, how much those few words from her father had meant. How much she craved even a few. So she couldn't blame him for stamping out any possibility that the stoic Pascal would share some tender memory from his past.

And yet, she did.

She'd wanted to see her father alone, but Jager had insisted on being a part of her pregnancy. She needed to start building boundaries with him fast before she lost her sense of self to the strong will of this McNeill male. The past two years had been full of hard work to prove to herself she was smart, independent and capable. Being pregnant couldn't take that away from her.

"Ms. Rickard?" The voice of the doctor, a young woman fresh from her residency in Miami, startled Delia.

She opened her eyes and faced Dr. Ruiz. Tall and willowy, the physician wore a light-up reindeer pin on the lapel of her white lab coat over a red tartan dress.

"Yes." Straightening, Delia told herself to get it together. "Sorry. I'm just…excited. About the baby news." She babbled awkwardly, embarrassed to be caught doing relaxation breathing in the middle of the hallway. "It's a lot to process."

"Come on in the office," the doctor urged, opening the door to the consultation room. "I'll do what I can to help you both."

Dr. Ruiz introduced herself to Jager and they settled into chairs around the obstetrician's desk as she talked through the preliminaries. Yes, they'd confirmed her pregnancy. Delia was given a piece of paper with her summer due date written on it in black marker.

Her hand crept to her flat belly while she tried to take it all in. Once more, Jager took the lead with questions, sharing his concerns about her mother's health history and the stillbirth. But when he launched into more questions about the uterine rupture too, Delia interrupted.

"My father made it clear that wasn't a genetic condition," she reminded him before turning to Dr. Ruiz. A filing cabinet behind the obstetrician had a magnet that said Keep Calm and Get Your Pap On caught Delia's eye.

Jager reached over and rested a hand on the back of her chair, so that he was barely touching her. "But your father's not a physician. Perhaps Dr. Ruiz will view the information differently."

Delia felt the sting of defensiveness despite the inevitable rush of heat from Jager's touch. Did he think she was incapable of relating her own medical history? "My mother had a cesarean. I've never had one. I've never even been pregnant."

Dr. Ruiz gave a brisk nod and glanced down at her notes. "I think we'd all rest easier with some more information about your mother's medical history." Her red-polished fingernail trailed down over the chart. "She's from Martinique?"

"Yes. She moved to Le Vauclin after she married my father, but she was raised in Sainte-Anne." Delia knew so little about her mother or her mother's family. According to Pascal, Celine's parents had died in a car crash when she was in high school.

The doctor scribbled a note on a Post-it while her reindeer pin blinked on and off. "I may be able to requisition some more information."

Jager squeezed Delia's hand. "Thank you."

She should be relieved. They did need more information about her mother's health history. Perhaps fear for her baby was making Delia unreasonably prickly when it came to Jager taking command of the conversation with both the physician and her father. He had every bit as much reason to be concerned about this baby's health as she did. Still, something about the way the events had unfolded today made her feel like an afterthought.

He would never cherish her the way he cherished his child, of course. It rattled her to think that; in some small corner of her heart, she nursed a hope that she could be more than just a surrogate for a McNeill baby in Jager's eyes.

He took her hand in his. A show of tenderness for the doctor's sake? Or did the paternal feeling he fostered for his child come through in the way he touched her?

His blue gaze found hers for a moment before flicking back to the physician. "We will be looking for the most advanced care for a possible high-risk pregnancy. Can you recommend the best doctors or hospitals for this?"

Frowning, Delia slid her hand out from under his. "High risk?" Her heart rate sped up. Since when did she need the most advanced care? "We don't have any reason to believe I'm high risk."

"Not yet," Jager conceded with a nod. "But until we

know the rest of your mother's history, it would be wise to have a plan in place."

The doctor paused in her note taking. "We've handled many high-risk pregnancies here. However, the most respected maternal fetal medicine facilities will be in the States. If you'd like a list—"

"We don't need a list," Delia informed Jager.

At the same moment, he nodded. "Thank you."

After a few more tense minutes in the consultation room, they departed. Delia stalked out ahead of him, clutching her file of papers about pregnancy with the due date and a prescription for prenatal vitamins.

She'd left Jager to take the paper containing names of maternal fetal specialists he'd requested.

"Delia." His voice was close behind her as she hurried through the parking lot with its lampposts connected by green garland swags dotted with red berries. "Please wait."

Her toes pinched in her high-heeled sandals. She wanted to be home with her feet up, surrounded by the fairy-tale paintings on her living room walls, a cup of tea in her hand. How had her life spun so far out of control so fast? She slowed her pace.

When he reached her side, he turned her to face him, his gaze sweeping over her in a way that shouldn't have incited a physical reaction and damned well did anyhow. It was like that one fateful encounter with him had stripped away all her defenses where he was concerned. Now she felt naked every time they were together.

"You're angry with me," he observed while a French Christmas carol hummed through a speaker system connected to the lampposts.

The chorus of "Un Flambeau, Jeannette, Isabelle" celebrated the beauty of a newborn child while he lay sleeping in a cradle. Something about the image resonated deeply. The lyrics were so familiar Delia could visualize the villagers admiring the new baby. Soon she would have a child of her own. More than anything she wanted to be a good mother. To stand beside the cradle of her newborn and protect that fragile life with a fierceness no one had ever showed to defend her.

"I'm frustrated that you commandeered our important conversation today." She wondered what Christmas would be like this year.

"Commandeered?" His brows swooped down. "I participated. The same way you did."

"I realize you are used to taking the lead," she continued, feeling more sure of herself as she spoke. If she was going to be an equal partner in parenting, she needed to lay the groundwork for it now. "But we'll need to find a way to rework our relationship so that you're not still trying to be my boss."

"I'm trying to protect you," he clarified. "And our child. That's different."

"And you were so focused on your own agenda that mine fell by the wayside." She straightened the strap on her sundress and felt his gaze track the movement.

She didn't like this confusing intersection point between attraction and frustration.

"I thought we shared the same agenda." Jager covered her bare shoulder with one hand, his fingers stroking a gentle touch along the back of her arm. "To find out answers that could help us protect your health, and the health of our child."

Unwelcome heat stirred from just that simple touch. The classic Christmas carol gave way to a holiday love song.

"I've waited my whole life to have a meaningful con-

versation with my father about the night I was born."
In the past, she'd always backed away from the talk
that he didn't want to have. "There were more answers
I wanted from him."

He'd been close to saying more about that night. She
was sure of it.

"I'm sorry." Jager's simple reply stole away her
anger. She might not be able to read him all the time,
but she recognized the remorse in his voice now, the
obvious sincerity in his eyes. "I didn't know."

Behind them, a young family emerged from the doctor's office. The husband held the door for his wife as
she pushed a toddler in a stroller. The woman's pregnant belly filled the front of a floral maternity dress.

Delia touched her own stomach, still flat. But she
could see that ultrasound image so strongly in her mind.
Would her child ever have a sibling? If she didn't accept Jager's offer of marriage—and she would not accept a business proposal—how soon would he move on
with someone else?

"Come on." Jager wrapped an arm around her waist
and guided her toward the convertible. "Let me apologize by taking you out for dinner."

"That's not necessary," she assured him, ready to
retreat from the world. And the temptation he posed.
"Thank you. But I'm tired."

Discouraged.

She strode ahead toward his car, hearing his steady
steps behind her even as he seemed to take the hint and
respect her need for silence. She needed to be stronger
and smarter tomorrow. To be a worthy advocate for her
unborn baby and weigh her options moving forward.
If she was indeed a high-risk pregnancy, what did that
mean for her? For her father? Would she have to quit

working? Would she and her father lose the family lands after all she'd done to try to protect it?

The plot of Rickard acreage felt like one small offering she had to bring to her baby that was all hers, separate from the McNeill wealth. Perhaps because she had nothing of her mother's, Delia felt the need to be able to give her child something tangible. Something beyond the love she would bear this baby.

Opening the passenger-side door of the bright white vehicle, Jager helped her inside, passing her the seat belt buckle while she tucked her dress around her legs for the breezy ride with the top down. After he closed her door and came around and settled into the driver's seat beside her, he paused before switching on the ignition.

"Can I ask you something, or are we still not talking?" Jager rattled the car key lightly against the gearshift.

"Not funny. But say what you need to." Delia pressed deeper into the leather seat, tipping her neck back into the molded headrest.

"What else were you hoping to learn from Pascal?" He lowered his voice even though there was no one else parked nearby. The family they'd seen earlier was packing into a minivan on the other side of the lot.

She figured she might as well tell Jager the truth since they would be sharing parenting one day and this was very relevant. "It might sound juvenile, but my father has never once said he loved me." She forced a shrug so the words didn't come across as pathetic as they sounded. "I thought today might be the day."

In the moment of silence that followed, she appreciated Jager's restraint. If his response had hinted at any form of pity, she wasn't sure how she could have handled it on such an emotional afternoon.

"Our fathers are very different from one another," he observed finally. "Yours is stoic and undemonstrative even though he was with you throughout your childhood. Mine was fun and fully engaged when he was around, but for the vast majority of time, he was absent." His hand slid over her forearm where it rested on the leather console between them. "I guarantee you I'm not going to be like that with our child. I will be a presence. And I'll do whatever it takes to be a welcome one."

For a moment, she allowed herself to be comforted by the words. This man had been a good friend, after all, before she'd given in to her attraction to him. She could still admire his desire to be a better person.

"We have nine months to figure out a way to be good parents." She had no role model for motherhood, but if she could figure out how to manage and grow McNeill Meadows, which included the historic McNeill mansion and a successful farm-to-table community garden, she would learn about parenting too.

"Less than eight, according to your due date." Jager's hand slid away from her forearm as he moved to start the car. "Since we have a limited amount of time and a lot to accomplish, I'm going to suggest we schedule a trip to New York as soon as possible."

"New York?" The warmth she'd been feeling for him chilled. "Didn't we go over this in the doctor's office? I'm not going to see a specialist or be stressed about a possible high-risk pregnancy until we have some concrete reason to be concerned."

"I completely understand." He backed the car out of the spot. "But you've been adamant that I meet the rest of the McNeills and establish ties with my half brothers." He shot her a sideways glance as he shifted into first, his hand grazing her knee through the thin cotton of her dress. "My relations are going to be our child's relatives too. It makes sense that you visit New York with me and get acquainted with the extended McNeill family."

His words stunned her silent.

Six weeks ago, she had lobbied hard for him to meet his grandfather, Malcolm McNeill. That didn't mean she wanted to be introduced to one of the wealthiest men in the world as Jager's baby mama.

Holding up a trembling hand, she searched for an excuse, any excuse. "I have a lot of arrangements to make here. Things to do to get ready for the baby. And I can't afford to quit my job—"

"Delia." He shook his head. "As the mother of a McNeill, you can afford to do as you please. We'll close up the house in Martinique and spend some time in Manhattan getting to know the rest of the McNeills. If you thought it was a good idea for me to foster those relationships, you must think it's a good idea for our child."

How neatly he'd turned that argument around to maneuver her now. She couldn't think of an appropriate retort as Jager turned the vehicle back onto the westbound road toward Le François. As much as she wanted to retreat into her fairy-tale-painted cottage with her books and dreams, she knew her life would never be the same again. She needed to think like a mother.

Jager slipped his hand over hers, threading their fingers together now that he'd reached a cruising speed and didn't need to shift for a while.

He continued to speak, undeterred by her surprised silence. "If it turns out you need the added care of a specialized facility, we'll already be in New York. If not, you can dictate where you want to be when it comes time to give birth." He gave her hand a gentle squeeze.

"You don't want to be traveling anywhere near the due date."

His words sent a chill through her. Her mother had been out on a boat the night she'd delivered prematurely and had paid the ultimate price. Delia felt sure that she wasn't going to be a high-risk pregnancy. But if she was thinking like a mother—putting her child first— she conceded that Jager had a point.

Accepting his help was in the best interest of their child.

She took a deep breath and let the wind whip through her hair as she tipped her head up to the blue sky. "When do we leave?"

Eight

Stepping off his grandfather's private jet onto the snowy tarmac of Teterboro Airport outside New York City eight days later, Jager wondered if he'd made a deal with the devil to coax Delia out of Martinique.

Jager hadn't wanted any of the McNeill red carpet treatment, and would have damned well preferred making his own travel arrangements, but wily old Malcolm had pulled strings to ensure the trip was exceptionally easy. With his connections, Malcolm had found a way to fast-track Delia as a trusted traveler, a designation Jager already had for himself. That streamlined their arrival process so efficiently that they didn't even need to clear customs in the airport. The minute they got off the plane and went into the terminal, the limo driver was already visible with his white sign bearing the family name.

Jager hadn't been able to refuse his grandfather's

help when it made things easier for Delia. No matter what her doctor said about her pregnancy being normal, he would continue to worry about her health and the health of their baby until they found out more about her mother's medical history. So far, Dr. Ruiz hadn't had any more luck unearthing facts about Celine's first pregnancy than Jager had, but the Martinique physician anticipated speaking to one of Celine's former doctors this week.

"What about our luggage?" Delia asked, shivering slightly as she peered back over her shoulder to stare up at the sleek Cessna, where the two crew members lingered.

Jager tugged her red plaid scarf up higher. He'd bought her warm clothes for the trip, including the long blue wool coat she wore belted tight. At seven weeks pregnant, she looked thinner to him, even in the coat. She insisted she hadn't experienced any morning sickness, but he'd checked it out online to make sure that was normal.

"The driver will make sure they're loaded in the car," Jager assured her, grateful for the cold so he had an excuse to wrap an arm around her and pull her to his side.

The past few days had been busy with preparations to spend Christmas in New York, and he'd tried to give her room to breathe. But he missed her now even more than he had after they'd spent those six weeks apart when he'd been searching Europe for Damon. Seeing her every day, knowing she was carrying his child, only made him want her more. He hoped spending the holidays together would bring them closer.

"Do you always travel like this?" She ducked her head toward his chest, her silky blond hair brushing the lapel of his gray overcoat that hadn't been out of his closet in two years.

"Definitely not." He'd traveled around the world on his own dime—an experience he'd been fortunate to afford—but never with an army of personal staff members. "The added luxury is courtesy of my grandfather."

Did Malcolm think he could bribe him to come into the family fold? Pay him off to accept his father back into his life?

Not happening.

"I know you're only having this meeting with him for our child's sake." She matched her pace to his while the driver hurried over to greet them and send two skycaps out to take their bags.

"And for yours." Jager couldn't help but point that out since he was doing everything in his power to convince Delia he would make a good partner. A good husband. "I wouldn't be in New York right now if it wasn't for you." It was something Delia had really encouraged since she wanted their child to have a bigger family than she'd known growing up.

They walked quickly through the terminal. Christmas trees decorated the crowded lobby, filling the soaring space with the scent of pine. With just a few days left until Christmas, Jager needed to move up his timetable to convince Delia to marry him. Ideally, he'd have a Christmas Eve proposal—one that she'd accept—and a New Year's wedding. Once that was settled, he'd be able to turn his attention back to the sale of Transparent and finding Damon, both of which needed to happen before he could have any kind of meaningful conversation with Malcolm McNeill about their position within the family. Jager couldn't make those decisions without Damon's input. But for now, he could at least meet his grandfather.

"I hope one day you'll be glad you made this concession to come here." Her cheeks were flushed from the cold as they stepped back outside again toward the waiting Mercedes sedan.

The driver, Paolo, directed the loading of their bags while Jager helped Delia into the passenger area in back. Her high-heeled black boots were visible beneath the hem of her coat, the soft suede molded to slim calves. For nearly two weeks, he'd been attuned to small details like that, from the way she tipped her head back when she laughed, to the delicate habit she had of brushing her fingers over her flat belly when she thought no one noticed. As if reassuring herself there was life inside her.

He looked forward to the day she was cleared for intimacy by her doctor, and to the day she trusted him enough to welcome him back into her bed, so he too could lay his palm on the soft expanse of skin between her hips.

Once she was safely inside the vehicle, Jager took Paolo aside.

"We're staying at The Plaza," he informed him. "That's our first stop."

The tall, athletically built driver looked like he could serve double duty as private security on the side with his dark coat and sunglasses. "But Mr. McNeill said to bring you directly to the house."

"Miss Rickard has had a long journey." Jager moved closer to the vehicle. "I'll call my grandfather to explain personally."

The driver's bronzed forehead furrowed, but he nodded. "As you wish."

They had been invited to stay at the McNeill home, a private fourteen-thousand-square-foot townhouse on the Upper East Side. It was a historic piece of local architecture that Jager would normally look forward to seeing, but he had no intention of taking up residence under the family roof. He had tried explaining that to Cameron without much luck. Jager had yet to converse with Malcolm directly.

Inside the limousine, he realized Delia was listening intently to her cell phone.

"Dr. Ruiz?" she said into the mouthpiece as her eyes lifted to meet Jager's gaze. "I'm going to put you on speakerphone. Could you repeat that last part for Jager's sake?"

The obstetrician must have news. About Delia's health? Or about the mystery of Celine's medical history?

"Yes. Hello." The lightly accented voice of the doctor came through the phone. The sound quality was tinny and diminished, but Jager was so glad to hear from her. "Mr. McNeill, I was just explaining to Delia that her mother suffered from lupus. She didn't see a doctor regularly for the condition, and was unaware of the disease with her first pregnancy."

Jager sat knee to knee with Delia in the wide leather seat. At some point, he'd taken her hand, and he squeezed it now. A smile kicked up one side of her mouth, reminding him that it had been too long since he'd seen her happy. They'd both been so worried about this.

"What about Delia? Could she have the condition and be unaware?" His heart lodged in his throat.

"No." Dr. Ruiz sounded certain. "We did a complete blood workup when she was here and I had enough to run additional tests once we received the news about her mother. The test for lupus is one of the most sensitive diagnostic indicators for the disease, clearing Delia with 98% certainty. And since she has virtually no other symptoms—"

Relief coursed through him with a *whoosh* in his ears that drowned out whatever else the obstetrician had to say. He'd been concerned for Delia's health, and for their child's, but he hadn't fully understood how truly scared he was until that moment. His chest constricted. He wrapped his arms around Delia and held her tight. To hell with giving her space.

Inhaling the warm vanilla fragrance of her hair, he smoothed his cheek along the silky strands. Even through the layers of their coats, he could feel the gentle swell of her curves. He traced circles on her back with one hand, soothing himself even as he offered her comfort. Connection.

"Mr. McNeill?" Dr. Ruiz's tinny voice echoed in the limo. "If you have any other questions for me—"

"Just one," he answered, turning his head to be better heard since he wasn't ready to release Delia yet. "I want to be sure I understand. You're saying that Delia is healthy enough for all normal activity?"

Delia turned her face up and peered into his eyes. Her gaze was quizzical for only a moment. And then she must have read his mind, because her cheeks colored with a heat he remembered well. It occurred to him how much he enjoyed her pale complexion that betrayed her so easily.

"Absolutely." Dr. Ruiz's smile was evident in the tone of her voice. "Congratulations to you both. You have all the signs of a healthy pregnancy."

Delia's forehead tipped onto his shoulder, but she

didn't move away from him as Jager thanked the doctor for the good news and disconnected the call.

As the Mercedes sped south on I-95, Jager stroked Delia's hair, the strands clinging from static. When she lifted her face to look at him, her hazel eyes were greener than usual—bright with a mix of emotions he couldn't read.

"Looks like Manhattan is good luck for us." He couldn't help the heated edge in his voice as he unfastened the belt on her bright blue coat and slid a hand over her waist.

Her long gray sweater dress skimmed her subtle curves. If they weren't riding in a car, he would have slid a hand under her knees and tugged her onto his lap.

"Because I'm healthy enough to carry a baby to term, or because I just had the green light for intimacy?" She arched an eyebrow at him, but the rapid tattoo of her pulse at her neck gave away how much the idea intrigued her too.

"My concern is for you and our baby. You know that." He had battled bad dreams for the last week and a half. Every time Delia was in a boat out to sea where he couldn't reach her. Each time, he'd awoken sweating and tangled in his sheets. "But I won't deny that I've thought about being with you again."

She tensed beneath his touch as the limo jockeyed for position on the way into the Lincoln Tunnel. The last rays of afternoon sun disappeared when they descended. Shadows played over her face between flashes of the tunnel's fluorescent lighting.

"I've thought about being with you too." She didn't sound happy about it, and he noticed how she was nervously twisting a button on his coat cuff with her fingers. "But I can't afford to lose perspective where you're

concerned. Not when our relationship is already so con-
voluted and I can't trust my judgment with men."

He hated that her ex had made her doubt herself so
much. Jager willed himself to find the right words that
would make her see his point of view.

"Delia." He took both of her hands in both of his.
"You've known me for two years. I gave you a job because I admired the way you didn't let the pressure of
society sway you into marrying Brandon. I thought es-
caping your wedding on a Jet Ski was kick-ass."

She shook her head. "I was scared."

"But you didn't let fear stop you. You set a course
and got the hell out of Dodge."

A tiny ghost of a smile appeared on her face. "You're
being generous."

"I'm being honest. I liked you right away, and I believe that feeling was mutual from the very first day."
He tipped her chin up when she looked away, needing
to see her eyes to track her reaction to his words. "You
know my brothers. You know my business dealings.
Have I ever given you reason to think I've tried to hide
something from you the way Brandon did?"

"Never." She said the word softly but with a fierceness that made his heart turn over.

"Then trust me when I say that you are the most important part of my life right now." He brought one of
her hands to his lips and kissed it, then the other. "The
last thing I want to do is hurt you, and I can promise if
anything makes you unhappy, I'm going to do everything in my power to fix it."

His heart beat harder, as if he could somehow hammer home the words with the force of his will. He could
see the struggle in her eyes. The worry that another man

had put there. Hell, even her father had made her doubt herself, so he couldn't blame Brandon for that.

Slowly, however, her smile reappeared as the limo hit Midtown. A sexy glimmer lit her hazel eyes as if she'd just started thinking something…naughty.

"I'm going to hold you to that promise, Jager Mc-Neill."

"I hope you do." Desire for her thrummed in his veins, a slow, simmering heat that had him hauling open the door of the vehicle as soon as it pulled up to the curb in front of The Plaza Hotel.

Helping her from the car onto the red carpet underneath the flags that waved over the iconic entrance to the hotel across from Central Park, he was more than ready to bring her to their room. To kiss every inch of her.

And remind her how good they could be together.

But he'd forgotten she'd never been to New York. Let alone Central Park. Or The Plaza Hotel.

At Christmastime.

Her eyes glowed as she stepped out of the limo, and the pleasure he saw there didn't have anything to do with him.

"It's so beautiful!" she exclaimed, doing a slow twirl to take it all in, just like every starry-eyed tourist to ever clog up a city street at rush hour.

Despite his thwarted libido, he couldn't resist the chance to make Delia Rickard happy.

"Would you like a tour?" he asked her, waving off Paolo and the hotel doormen, who were ready to assist with their every need.

"Yes!" She was already gazing at a horse-drawn carriage across the street, her body swaying slightly to the strains of a Christmas tune emanating from a trio of musicians near the park entrance.

Jager forced his gaze away from her and told himself to get a grip. This was the chance he'd been waiting for, and he wasn't about to waste it.

"Don't let go." Delia wrapped a hand around Jager's waist and her other around his neck. "Please. Whatever you do? Don't let go."

Teetering on thin blades, she let Jager tug her around the slippery ice skating rink while other holiday revelers whizzed past them. Even knee-high children skated quickly past, their blades making a *skritch*, *skritch* sound in the cold ice, cutting tiny swaths and sometimes lifting a fine, snow-like spray in their wake.

Her first time on ice skates was a little scarier than she'd anticipated. After a tour of the Christmas lights around Central Park and down Fifth Avenue, she and Jager had stopped at a food cart for gyros. She'd been entranced by the sight of the huge Christmas tree in Rockefeller Plaza. Even better? The ice-skaters skimming the expanse of bright white below the noble fir. She hadn't hesitated when Jager asked if she wanted to test her skills on skates.

Clearly, she'd been too caught up in the holiday spirit to think about what she was getting into. Now Dean Martin crooned about letting it snow on the speaker system, but even with all the laughter, happy shouts and twinkling lights around her, Delia couldn't recapture that lighthearted joy. She was too terrified she'd fall.

"I'm not letting go." Jager whispered the soft assurance in her ear, nuzzling the black cashmere stocking cap he'd bought her in one of the glittering department stores lining Fifth Avenue. "I've been looking for an excuse to touch you for weeks."

Her attention darted from her wobbling skates to his handsome face. He'd been so good to her, helping her to tie up her work responsibilities at the McNeill estate in Martinique by hiring a temporary replacement. His younger brother Gabe—now technically her boss—had given her a surprise holiday bonus that was based on revenue growth for the property. It had given her enough of a financial cushion that she could send the money home to her father to pay the taxes on their small piece of land and keep it safe for another year.

Which was a huge worry off her mind.

Each day for almost two weeks, Jager had asked how she felt, asked what he could do to help make her life easier so she could focus on her health. She'd been touched, especially in light of the pregnancy worries she'd had—at least up until today's call from Dr. Ruiz. And more than anything, she appreciated that he'd given her time to come to terms with being pregnant, without pressuring her about marriage.

That window of time had ended, however. He'd made that clear in the car ride from the airport when he said he wanted to be with her again. That exchange was never far from her mind even as they were sightseeing and enjoying all the Christmas hubbub of New York City just days before the big holiday.

"Are you trying to distract me so I don't fall?" she asked, her heartbeat skipping to its own crazy rhythm.

The scent of roasted chestnuts spiced the air. As the music shifted to an orchestra arrangement of Handel's *Messiah*, Jager swayed on his skates, effortlessly gliding backward so she could remain facing forward.

"I'm one-hundred-percent sincere about wanting to

touch you." The look in his blue eyes sent a wave of heat through her, warming her from the inside out. "But if it helps to keep you distracted, I can share some more explicit thoughts I've been having about you."

She swallowed around a suddenly-dry throat. The sounds, the scents, the night fell away until her world narrowed to only him. Her heart thumped harder.

"I don't want to get so distracted I fall on my face." She was only half kidding. Too much flirting with Jager could be dangerous. "But maybe if you told me just one thing."

Because she had a major weakness where he was concerned.

"Wait until we turn this corner," he cautioned, slowly drawing her body against his while he guided them around the end of the rink in a wide curve.

Pressed against Jager's formidable body, Delia didn't move. She didn't even dare to breathe since breathing would mold her breasts even tighter to his chest. Their wool coats and winter clothes didn't come close to hiding the feel of the bodies beneath. His thigh grazed hers as he skated backward, hard muscle flexing.

She felt a little swoony and knew it wasn't just the skates keeping her off balance.

"There." He checked the skating lane as he moved onto the straightaway for another slow circle around the rink. "You're doing well."

He loosened his hold without letting go and her skates seemed to follow him without any help from her.

"I'm not sure that not falling is synonymous with doing well." Her voice was breathless, a barely there scrape of sound after the close encounter with the sexy father of her future child.

"So we'll get right back to distraction tactics." He

slowed his pace again, letting her close the small gap between them before he lowered his voice. "Do you want me to tell you how sexy you are in the dreams where you pull a pin out of your hair and it all comes spilling down while you straddle me—"

"No." She shook her head, unprepared for the details he seemed only too happy to share. "That is, not here."

He lifted a hand to her cheek and rubbed a thumb along her jaw. "Seeing you blush might be the sexiest thing ever."

"I'm just not used to hearing things like that from the same man who used to demand the Monday morning business briefs by five o'clock the Friday before."

He threw his head back and laughed. "I knew you were secretly opposed to those."

She liked making him smile, something that happened more rarely this year after tragedy had struck his family. Out of the corner of her eye, she saw Santa and a pretty elf walking through the brightly lit café that flanked one end of the skating rink. A family with small children posed for a photo with them.

"Employees want to be out the door at five o'clock on Fridays, not planning for Mondays." She'd been committed to the job though, and to improving herself. She'd never complained.

"I didn't keep you late *every* week." Jager loosened his hold a bit more, but it was okay since she felt steadier on her feet now.

"Only most Fridays," she teased. Despite their light banter, she kept seeing the dream image he'd planted in her mind.

Her. Straddling him.

She might not stop blushing for days at this rate.

"Then I have a lot to make up for." He drew her near

once more so they could navigate another turn. "I hope this trip will be something special that you'll never forget."

"It already is." She lifted her hand from his neck long enough to gesture at the impressive ninety-foot Christmas tree covered in lights above them. "I've always wanted to travel, and New York is…magic."

Certainly, she'd never had a Christmas like this. The holiday had never been easy with her father the fisherman making little effort to spend the day at home most years, let alone play Santa or give special gifts the way other fishing families did.

"I've flown in and out of this city so many times for business, but I will admit I've never had as much fun as seeing it with you."

Her first thought was to argue with him—to call him out on a line meant to romance her. But hadn't he pointed out that he'd never given her a reason to doubt his honesty and sincerity with her?

It was her insecurity that made her not want to believe him. The doubts she felt weren't his fault. If she was going to make this relationship work, with a balanced approach to shared parenting of a child, she needed to start laying the groundwork for trust. More than that, she needed to start trusting herself.

"This has been one of the most fun days of my whole life," she told him honestly.

The fairy-tale images painted on her walls weren't all that different from this—the twinkling lights combined with the myth and magic of New York. In fact, the statue of Prometheus in Rockefeller Center was staring down at her right now, his gilded facade reflecting all the glow.

"Look at you," Jager observed quietly, making her realize she'd been quiet a long time.

"What?" Blinking through the cloudy fog of worries for the future, she peered up into his eyes.

"You're skating."

She glanced down at her feet to confirm the surprising news. Jager still held her, true. But she was gliding forward under her own power, the motion subtle but definite.

Happiness stole through her. She wasn't going to count on Jager being there for her forever. Not yet, anyway. This Christmastime trip would help her decide if he wanted her for herself, not just for the sake of their child.

But no matter what happened for them romantically, she realized that this man had given her a precious gift no one else ever had. He'd believed in her from the moment they met, giving her the courage to have more faith in herself too.

Whatever the future held, she was strong enough to handle it. To move forward. Even if it was on her own.

Nine

Later that night, Delia turned off the gold-plated faucet in the bathroom of their suite at The Plaza.

Gold-plated faucets. Twenty-four-karat gold, in fact, according to the detailed description she'd read in a travel review on her phone while she soaked in the tub.

After toweling off, she shrugged into a white spa robe embroidered with the hotel crest. Everything about the legendary property was beautiful, from the lavish holiday decorations throughout to the tiled mosaic floor in the bathroom. Delia took mental notes, knowing she could upgrade some of their offerings at McNeill Meadows when they hosted private parties and corporate retreats in the public portion of the historic house.

After padding from the bathroom into her bedroom, she scanned the contents of the spacious wood-paneled closet with built-in drawers. The butler service had unpacked for them while they were out sightseeing; her nightgown was neatly folded with the lavender sachet she'd packed on top of it. Even her scarves and mittens were folded.

Dispensing with the spa robe, she dressed in her own nightdress, a wildly romantic gown that had been a rare splurge purchase after her first raise. It was probably the kind of thing a bride wore—diaphanous lemon yellow layers with a satin ribbon through the bodice that tied like a corset. Although it was as romantic as any of her fairy-tale paintings, knowing that she'd acquired it through her own hard work always made her feel like a queen when she wore it. She'd come a long way from the girl who'd nearly bartered her future for a slick businessman who said pretty words but didn't really love her.

Switching off the light, she stepped quietly back out into the living room to admire the view of Central Park. She'd already said good-night to Jager, refusing his offer of room service for a bedtime snack.

She had the distinct impression he was trying to fatten her up, feeding her at every opportunity.

"Did you change your mind about a meal?"

The voice from a dark corner of the room nearly made her jump out of her skin.

"Oh!" Startled, she took a step back, heart racing even though she recognized Jager's voice right away. "You scared me."

"Sorry." He unfolded himself from the chair near the window, a tall shadow that became more visible as he stood in front of the ambient light from the street and the park below. "I thought you saw me."

"No." She became very aware of her nakedness under the nightgown. She hadn't even bothered with underwear, an oversight that made her skin tingle with warmth. "I didn't realize you were still awake."

"I ordered room service while you were in the bath. Just in case." He moved toward the wet bar, where she could see a tray of bread, cheeses and fruits. A champagne bucket held two large bottles of sparkling water chilling on ice.

She was tempted.

Seeing him tempted her even more. She remembered how he'd felt against her in the water that day he'd saved the drowning girl. The way they'd moved together later that same night when desire had spun out of control. She cleared her throat and tried to block out the memories of how his hands felt on her naked skin.

"That was thoughtful of you. Thank you." She reached for a water to quench her sudden thirst; her throat had gone very dry.

"Here, let me." He moved behind the bar, retrieving two crystal glasses. "Do you want me to switch the lights back on?"

"No," she blurted, immediately thinking about the lightweight nature of her nightgown. "We can see the view better this way. That's why I came out here."

While he poured their drinks, Delia walked to the window near the sofa and stared out into the night. The sounds of the city drifted through the closed windows. Horns, brakes, a distant siren provided a kind of nighttime white noise, the unique city sounds all muffled though, since their room was on the eighteenth floor.

Behind her, she heard rustling. Something heavy scraping across the floor. When she turned, she saw Jager had pivoted the couch to face the window, keeping the low coffee table in front of it.

"Come. Have a seat." He was placing the cheese

board on the table, no doubt to tempt her. "We can see for ourselves if this is the city that never sleeps."

The invitation sent pleasurable shivers along her skin as if he'd touched her. The sensation was so vivid she debated scurrying back into her room with her glass of water and half a baguette to prevent a rash decision fueled by this insane chemistry. But running away from him every time this man enticed her was not going to lead to productive parenting for their child.

She bit the inside of her cheek to steel herself, then joined him on the sofa.

He'd never had to work so hard to win a woman's trust before. The way Delia's chin was tilted up and her shoulders were thrown back gave her the look of someone stepping into battle rather than just sharing a couch with him.

As she settled onto the tufted blue cushion, she tucked her bare feet beneath her, her sheer yellow nightgown draping over the edge. His brain still blazed from the way she'd looked while standing in front of the window a moment ago. There'd been just enough light coming through to outline her curves.

Her absolute nakedness underneath.

That vision would be filed away in his memory for a lifetime.

"I love how the lights run in a perfect straight line up either side of the park." Her attention was on the view and not him, her face tipped into the dull golden light spilling through the window. "It's so pretty here."

"You didn't mind the cold today?" He focused on slicing the fresh baguette to keep from thinking about touching her.

"Not one bit. I felt energized. More alive." She

reached for a piece of kiwi and dropped it on a small plate. "I can't believe how much we did today after we landed."

"I think the cold makes you want to move faster to keep warm." She'd looked adorable in that hat he bought her.

She'd told him it was one of the most fun days she could remember, and it had been for him too. He'd never been the kind of guy to cut loose; he was always aware of his responsibility as the oldest brother in a family with no father. And later, no mother.

With Delia, it was different.

"Maybe that's the secret to New York ambition." She added a few more pieces of fruit to the pile, then extended the china toward him for a slice of bread.

"Frigid temperatures?" He layered on multiple pieces of bread and cheese before she pulled the plate back.

"Could be." Her smile faded as she peered out the window into the darkened park. "I never got to ask you much about what it was like to live out on the West Coast. Did you like it there?"

The question chilled him far more than the northeast winds had during their sightseeing. Perhaps some of his reluctance to talk about it showed on his face, because Delia spoke up again.

"We don't have to talk about that time, if you don't want." She chased a slice of cheese around the dish with her bread. "I was just curious how California compared to New York, since it's my first time out of Martinique."

He was never going to put her more at ease if he didn't share some part of himself that wasn't business-related. She knew plenty about his work life. But he'd kept many of the details of what he and his brothers had been through private.

"At first, I was excited to return to California since I'd lived near LA until I was thirteen." He'd been happy enough there, until he understood how unhappy his mother was. Until it occurred to him how his father never visited them anymore, abandoning his illegitimate family for his legal wife and kids.

"That's when your mom decided to ditch Liam and start over somewhere he couldn't find her."

"Right." Jager ground his teeth, the impulse to keep the past on lockdown stronger than he'd realized. He set down his plate and refilled their water glasses to give himself something to occupy his hands. "She'd had enough with his sporadic visits and she knew by then that he'd never leave his wife and other sons."

"Did you know about them back then?" She set aside her plate to lift the heavy crystal goblet. "Your father's other family?"

He studied the way her lips molded around the glass to distract himself from the old anger he always felt thinking about Liam McNeill.

It had been one thing to abandon his kids. Abandoning the mother of his children? Jager found it unforgivable, especially since their mother had fought cancer and died without a partner by her side. Just three devastated sons.

"Not really. As a kid, I had the idea that Liam had another girlfriend and that's why he didn't stay with us more." Remembering the confusion of those years, he had to give his mother a lot of credit for what she'd done when she left the country. "Before she died, Mom told us everything—about Liam's connection to McNeill Resorts, about his other family. But by then, we hated him for not being there when she was battling cancer.

We all agreed after she was gone that we didn't want anything to do with him."

"I can't imagine how hard that must have been for all of you." Delia bit her lip for a moment before continuing, "Liam never knew though, did he? About your mom's illness?"

"No. But keep in mind he lied to two women for over a decade, pretending to his wife that he was faithful and pretending to my mother—at first—that he was a single man, and later that he would leave his marriage for her." Much later, he'd heard that Liam's wife left him shortly after Jager's mother, Audrey, decided to end their affair. So he'd been free. He could have come for his other family, married his mistress if he'd wanted. But he'd never even bothered to search for them.

"After my own experience being deceived, I know that must have hurt both of them deeply." Delia placed the water goblet on the glass coffee table. The soft glow of light from the window played over her delicate features.

"I'll never forgive him," he told her truthfully, unwilling to give her false expectations for their visit. "I'm in New York to meet my grandfather, because I respect that it's important to you that we know my family."

On an intellectual level, he understood that it wasn't Malcolm's fault that Liam had wronged his mother. But Jager couldn't help feeling a sense of disloyalty to his mother for setting foot in Liam's world.

"It is important to me." Her eyes widened as she reached out to lay her hand on his forearm. "But maybe once you reconnect with Liam, you'll feel differently."

"Impossible." Jager knew his own heart, and it was cold where his father was concerned. Still, he regretted his quick response when her hand slid away. Swiftly, he changed the subject before she pursued the topic any further. "But you asked about life in Los Altos Hills. I was looking forward to it when I first got there last year, but after the hell Damon went through soon afterward, I don't think I could ever live on the West Coast again."

His sister-in-law had vanished without a trace after her honeymoon. Damon had punched holes in most of the walls of that big, beautiful home he'd built. Then he'd left town and shut off all means of communication.

Delia smoothed the embroidered satin cuff of her nightgown with one hand, fingering the embellishments stitched in pale blue thread. A placket on the bodice covered her breasts, while two layers of something gauzy and thin created a barely there barrier between his eyes and the rest of her. The urge to touch her had been strong all day, but now—remembering the way Damon's life was falling apart without his wife—the need for Delia was even more fierce.

"I've always wanted to see the Pacific." She had a faraway look for a moment before turning back to him. "Maybe it has to do with being a fisherman's daughter, but I'm more curious about the water than the land."

"I couldn't see the Pacific from the house Damon built in the hills, but the view of San Francisco Bay was impressive."

"There's a lot about the McNeill lifestyle that's impressive," she noted drily, straightening.

It was a welcome change of subject.

"We've been fortunate financially," he admitted, wondering how he could tempt her into eating some more. To keep her strength up. "But I hope you know I'd trade it all to see Damon happy again. Hell. I'd trade it all to *see* him." Jager worried about him. Damon wasn't himself when he'd left.

Jager grabbed the white china plate Delia had set aside and refilled it. It might not be a high-risk pregnancy, but she still needed to take care of herself. He'd read online that exhaustion would kick in over the next few weeks and she could lose her appetite even more.

"I wonder where he went?" She frowned down at the plate as he handed it to her, but she took a raspberry and popped it in her mouth. "Do you think he had a plan?"

"I think he was going to look for Caroline himself. Visit places her credit card was used in the last year. I spoke briefly to the investigator Cameron told us about—the one who said he could find Damon. But ultimately, I know my brother wants to find the men responsible for his wife's disappearance."

"That sounds dangerous. Can you stop him?" Delia set her plate aside again, worry etched in her features. Damn it. He hadn't meant to upset her. "Before he does something rash?"

He hesitated. The truth would only make her more uneasy. But Delia had been lied to before. He had no option besides being completely forthright.

"I'm not sure I'd want to, even if I could." The police had honored a request from Caroline's father that they "respect his daughter's wish for privacy." But Jager didn't believe for a moment that she'd left by her own free will, and neither did Damon.

Unfolding herself from the couch cushion, Delia rose to her feet. Clearly agitated, she paced around the sofa before returning to the window.

"But he could get in serious trouble." She laid a hand on the back of Jager's. "I didn't have time to get to know Damon very well before you all left Martinique, but I spoke with him often enough to realize he's a good person. If you could talk to him, you could convince him to speak to the police again."

Jager came to his feet, wishing he had more comfort to offer her. But his words were unlikely to ease her mind.

"Men came into his house. Took the woman he loved. And, as far as we can tell, those same men let her die alone at sea rather than return her to him after he did everything they asked." Talking about it made him agitated. Putting himself in Damon's shoes lit a fiery rage inside him. "If someone hurt you, I'd turn over heaven and earth to find them too. How can I blame my brother for doing the same?"

His heart slugged hard as he wrapped his arms around her, drawing her close.

"What if he finds the men he's searching for? He could get hurt. Or killed. Or end up in prison for the rest of his life if he—" Delia objected.

He gently quieted the torrent of worries with a finger on her lips.

"He's already suffering more than we can imagine. I'm not sure there's any punishment worse than what he's going through right now."

When she sighed, her shoulders sagging, he shifted his finger away from her soft mouth, feeling his way along her smooth cheek. His hand traveled down her warm neck to the curve of her collarbone, mostly bare above the square neck of her nightgown.

"Damon's in hell." The truth had been apparent to Jager when they parted. "He may never have the chance to touch his wife this way again."

He meant to comfort Delia somehow, but as he glanced up into her hazel eyes, he wondered if he was the one who needed the warmth of this connection. The solace of her touch.

The vanilla scent of her skin beckoned him. Her hair, still damp from a bath, was beginning to dry in soft waves. And damn it all, no matter who needed who, he couldn't deny himself the feel of her any longer.

Gently, he tipped her head back, giving her time to walk away if she chose. But her eyelids slowly lowered, her lashes a dark sweep of fringe fluttering down. He kissed her there. One press of his lips to the right eye. One press of his lips to the left.

Her raspberry-scented breath teased his cheek in a soft puff of air. Her fingers trailed lightly up his arm through the worn cotton of the well-washed Henley shirt that he'd pulled on along with a pair of sweats after his shower. The light, tentative feel of her hands on him seared away the conversation they'd been having. All he cared about was touching her.

Tasting her.

Cradling her face in his hands, he waited for her eyes to open again. He wanted to see acceptance there. When her entranced gaze found his, there was more than just acceptance. He saw hunger. A need as stark as his own.

Ten

Delia's world tilted sideways, her breath catching as she stared up into the laser focus of Jager's blue eyes. She felt herself falling and she was powerless to stop it.

If this night had been just about passion, maybe she could have walked away. But she'd glimpsed Jager's heart tonight, and the stark emotions she'd seen there had ripped her raw too. As the self-appointed head of his family, he took his responsibility to Damon seriously.

How could she argue with him when he would one day give their child that same undivided loyalty that he showed his brother? The power of that devotion was foreign to her, and it took her breath away.

"Kiss me." She whispered the command softly, knowing he awaited her wishes.

The two simple words unleashed a torrent.

He drew her into him, sealing her body to his, chest to thigh. Sensations blazed through her. Her breasts molded to the hard plane of his chest, her heartbeat hammering against him in a rapid, urgent rhythm. He bent to wrap an arm around her thighs, lifting her higher so his sex nudged her hip. Her belly.

She melted inside, the hunger becoming frenzied. Imperative.

When his lips met hers, she speared her fingers into his dark hair, holding him where she wanted him. Every silken stroke of his tongue awakened new fires in her body. A nip to the right made her breasts ache. A kiss to the left caused her thighs to tremble.

The fevered urgency spiked higher. Hotter.

"Delia." He reared away from the kiss abruptly, his eyes blazing. "A kiss won't be enough." His eyelids lowered, shuttering the raw hunger she'd spied. "That is, if you don't want things to proceed—"

"I do want. This. You." Tracing the line of his bristly jaw with her fingers, she inhaled the musky pine scent of his aftershave, then licked a spot in the hollow of his throat to breathe in more. "Very much."

Returning his mouth to hers, he palmed a thigh in each of his hands, wrapping her legs around him. Never breaking the kiss, he charged toward the bedroom. His bedroom. The feel of his muscles shifting against her as he walked provided a sultry prelude to the pleasures she knew came next. Her silk nightgown was a scant barrier to the feel of him, and he felt every bit as amazing as she'd remembered from their first time together.

"I thought I dreamed how good this felt," she murmured, keeping her arms looped around his neck while he toed open the bedroom door and strode into the darkened interior.

His blinds were drawn, the blankets turned down the

same way hers had been. He paused near the dimmer switch on one wall to turn a sconce to the lowest setting.

"It was no dream." Carrying her over to the king-size bed, he lowered her slowly to the center. "Although I've been reliving that night often enough when I close my eyes."

"Me too." The harder she'd tried to forget about it, the more often every touch and kiss replayed in her brain.

He stood up and dragged his shirt up and over his head. Tossing it aside, he untied the drawstring on his sweats, the waistband dropping enough to reveal his lower abs. And…more.

He wasn't wearing boxers.

Lured by the sight of him, she pushed herself up to her knees. Her palms landed on his chest before he could join her on the bed, and she held him there, wanting a chance to explore, needing to imprint the feel of him in her memory.

Hands splayed, she covered as much of him as possible, skimming her palms down his chest, then turning at an angle to line up her fingers with the ridges of his abs. His breath hissed between his teeth, but she couldn't stop until she tested the feel of his erection, trailing her fingers down the rigid length then back up again.

She bent to place a kiss there, her lips following the line of the raised vein.

The harsh sound Jager made was her only warning before he hauled her up by the shoulders. "You play with fire."

"I'm already burning." She reached for the tie on her nightdress, a single yellow ribbon that wound through the satin bodice. "I need to be naked."

His gaze dipped to her body, his hands tunneling under the diaphanous layers of pale yellow to draw the fabric up and over her head, bringing with it the lavender scent of the bath oils she'd used.

Jager set the gown aside and stroked her arms. Shoulders. Breasts. There was a slow reverence in his touch that made her heart turn over, stirring feelings she couldn't afford to have yet. Not with so much uncertainty between them.

So she wrapped her arms around him and dragged him down to the bed with her, losing herself in a mind-drugging kiss. He covered her gently, keeping an elbow on the bed to ensure he didn't put his full weight on her. But she wanted, needed, to feel the full impact of being with him. She kissed him harder and skimmed her leg up one side of his, snaking it around his thigh until she could roll him to the side and lie on top of him.

"You said you had a fantasy about having me here," she reminded him, rubbing her cheek on his chest, soaking up the feel of him. "Straddling you."

"The real thing surpasses it." He captured her hands and held them on either side of his head.

To make sure he remembered it, she rolled her hips against him for emphasis.

He reversed their positions in an instant, flipping her to her back. His move surprised a giggle out of her. When his erection nudged between her thighs, she gripped his shoulders, fire rushing through her veins.

"Please." She needed this. Him. "Come inside me."

"Do you want to use protection? I have it, but—"

"We're both clean." They'd shared medical records for the sake of their child. She shrugged. "And I'm already pregnant. Let's enjoy the benefits."

The last words were muffled by his kiss before he licked his way down to her breast, drawing on the taut crest. She arched against him, wanting more. Everything.

He came inside her then, edging deeper. Deeper.

He lifted his head to watch her, his blue gaze fixed on her eyes. She bit her lip against a rush of pleasure so sweet it threatened to drag her under. She tingled everywhere, her pulse an erratic throb at her throat. Clamping her thighs around his waist, she let the sensations roll through her. Poised on the edge of an orgasm, she simply held on and let herself feel it all.

Jager. Pleasure. Passion.

When he reached between their bodies to tease a finger over the slick center of her, she went completely still. He felt so good. So. Impossibly. Good.

Her release rolled over her like a rogue wave, tossing her helplessly against the bed, having its way with her. She was so lost in her own pleasure that his almost took her by surprise. But his hoarse shout of completion let her know she wasn't alone in the powerful throes of passion.

She clutched him to her hard, her head tipped to his strong chest as she slowly became aware of his heartbeat. It raced faster than if he'd run sprints. She placed a kiss there, smoothing her hand over his skin gone lightly damp.

Closing her eyes, she waited for her breathing to return to normal, her own heart to slow. With the flood of happy endorphins running through her, she couldn't imagine a time when she would regret what they'd just shared. It was nothing short of beautiful. But that didn't mean she could simply allow an affair to continue indefinitely.

She needed to think about her child's future. About maintaining a relationship with Jager that would never put them at odds. Not for all the world would she subject her child to the kind of confusing upbringing Jager had, never seeing his father after his thirteenth birthday.

"Can I get you anything?" His voice broke in on the crowd of worries creeping up on her, his hand tender as he stroked her tousled hair. "Something to eat or drink before bed?"

"I feel like Hansel and Gretel in the witch's cabin," she murmured, exhaustion from their long day starting to take hold.

"Okay. Did I miss something?" He sounded so baffled that she laughed.

"You're trying to fatten me up, Jager McNeill. Don't deny it."

"I've been reading." He tried to fluff the pillow under her head without moving her, then he straightened the blankets as they untangled themselves. "You might experience extreme fatigue in the upcoming weeks. I want you to be ready for it."

Imagining this all-business corporate magnate on his computer doing Google searches of pregnancy symptoms made her smile. He would be a good father. Would she ever measure up as a mother with so little to guide her?

A nervous flutter tripped through her belly at the same time his hand landed there. Right where their baby was growing. Her eyes stung at his tenderness.

"I'll be fine," she reassured him. "And I think the fatigue is starting. I'm so tired all of the sudden."

It was true. Yet she also wasn't ready to think about the implications of what had just happened. About how important it was that she get her relationship with Jager right. Because no matter how tenderly he'd touched her, she had to ask herself if it was really *her* who mattered to him.

Or was he simply honor bound to care for the mother of his child?

Once Delia had fallen asleep, Jager could no longer ignore the notifications on his phone. Or, at least, that was what he told himself; he wanted to let Delia get her rest and he was still reeling from their encounter.

He'd wanted her, that much was damn certain. Still did, even after sex that satisfied him to his toes.

But he hadn't expected being with her to rattle him this way. There had been something deeper at work between them than sex. Knowing the whole time that she carried his child had been powerful.

So maybe he scrambled out of the bed a little too fast once she'd dozed off. But there were a hell of a lot of messages and missed calls on his cell. He'd noticed them earlier, beginning shortly after Paolo dropped them off at The Plaza. Messages from Cameron, Quinn and Ian.

His half brothers were all looking for him. Apparently they'd been summoned to the McNeill mansion to greet him tonight, and he'd never shown. In his defense, he'd tried to warn Cam he needed to have space of his own in New York. And he needed to meet with the family on his own terms. On his timetable. Now, stalking around the dark living room, he debated whom to text first. Before he could decide, the phone vibrated again.

Gabe.

Jager clicked the button to connect them. "I hope you're calling with good news."

"What good news could I possibly have for you?" his brother drawled. Gabe was as unhurried in life as

Jager was Type A. "I know better than to think you'll get excited about the new crown molding I installed in the McNeill Meadows gift shop."

Dropping onto the sofa where he'd sat with Delia earlier, Jager stared out over the lights dotting Central Park and the few low buildings that broke up the dark expanse of trees.

"This is the woodwork you were making?" He'd visited Gabe when he returned from Europe, wanting to update him on the search for Damon.

As usual, Gabe had been in his workshop in the converted boathouse on the small hotel property he ran. The Birdsong had come into his hands as a teen when the older woman Gabe worked for had died. Her family had fought the inheritance for months, but the will had been airtight. Gabe had renovated every square inch, bringing guests from around the world to the Birdsong. He'd either restored or handcrafted all the woodwork himself and quickly got a reputation as a master. Now he had more work than he could handle from businesses that appreciated an artisan's touch.

"That's the stuff." In fact, Gabe had started the project based on a long-ago memo from Delia, when she'd been trying to make over the McNeill Meadows gift shop into a more period-appropriate space. "But I wasn't calling about that. I wanted to see what happened today. Did Cameron have an update on Damon?"

Leaning back into the couch cushions that still held a hint of Delia's scent, Jager ground his teeth at Gabe's impatience. But then, he could hardly blame Gabe for wanting to think about something besides his personal life. Gabe's songstress wife had told him their marriage was over while pregnant with their firstborn. She'd abandoned Gabe—and their son—two weeks after giving birth so that she could pursue her career.

The only thing keeping the guy's bitterness in check was his eight-month-old son.

"I didn't go over there today." He pounded a fist on the arm of the couch. "I'm not going to start reporting to Malcolm McNeill's every summons, and the quicker the old man understands that, the better."

"You went all the way to New York because they said they knew where Damon was, and now you choose to get in a pissing contest to prove some kind of asinine point about how we don't need them?" Gabe's voice lowered, a sure sign he was angry. "We all want the same thing. Bring Damon home."

Frustrated, Jager closed his eyes and counted backward until he could rein himself in.

"They don't want the same thing as us, because they don't even know him. The only reason they're helping us is to flex their muscle and bring us into the fold."

"Dude. This isn't a mob family or something where they're asking us to be part of a gang or start offing their enemies." Gabe's voice broke up on the last few words, probably as a result of poor reception on the island. "They are blood relatives and they'd like to get to know us. It's not their fault Dad is an ass."

Jager had tried telling himself that before, but there was some latent protectiveness of his mom that he couldn't quite shake.

"Still feels disloyal." He didn't have to explain why. Gabe understood him.

"Mom was tough as they come, bro, and she would never hold it against them." Gabe sounded so certain. And he'd had a different relationship with their mother. He hadn't necessarily been the favorite. But the two of them had been alike in a lot of ways. They were more generous and kindhearted than other people.

But you didn't cross them.

"I'll go over there tomorrow." Jager needed to speak to Delia about it, and see what she wanted to do. "I promise."

She'd stressed the importance of meeting his family, and keeping that connection open for their child's sake. But did that mean she wanted to meet all the McNeills too? If so, did he introduce her as his girlfriend? The future mother of his child?

He wished she was already wearing his ring. He had no idea how to tell her that one of the stipulations in Malcolm McNeill's will was that his grandsons had to be wed for at least twelve months to inherit their shares of the family business. Would she view that as him pressuring her? She had to know he didn't want any part of an inheritance from Malcolm, but then again, it seemed too important a detail to omit given that he was going to keep asking her to marry him until she said yes.

"I'll call you tomorrow for an update. If Damon is stirring up trouble somewhere, we either need to talk some sense into him or—"

"Or help him. I know." Jager disconnected the call, and quickly texted with Cameron to make arrangements for visiting the McNeill mansion the next day.

Still, he shut off the phone feeling even more unsettled than when he left Delia's bed.

He had a lot to do to make a more secure world for the child coming in less than eight months' time. Tomorrow, he'd see the McNeills and demand answers about his brother. But first, he needed to have a conversation with Delia about the future. Now that they'd renewed their physical intimacy, she must have recognized how strong their chemistry together could be.

They needed to stay together because he wouldn't be the kind of failure at fatherhood that Liam was. More than that, Jager would never give Delia cause to feel betrayed the way his mother had been. He would be there for her. They could have a Christmas wedding in New York. At The Plaza, if she wanted, surrounded by all the Christmas decorations she loved.

It was a damn good plan. But as he slid quietly into bed beside the beautiful, vibrant woman who'd set him on fire an hour ago, he feared he didn't have enough to offer her.

He had homes. Money. More security than she could ever want.

Yet after hearing about her upbringing with her stoic father, Jager wasn't sure how to convince her he could provide the one thing she wanted most. She longed for love after not receiving it. Jager knew how it felt and understood the way it devastated you when you lost it.

Planting a kiss on Delia's bare shoulder before he covered it with the sheet, he closed his eyes and tipped his head against her back. She sighed sleepily, curling into him. Fitting there perfectly.

Somehow, he would make her see there was more real security in shared goals. In a strong relationship based on trust. And in chemistry that would keep them both satisfied for a lifetime.

Eleven

Sinking deeper in her soaking tub the following afternoon, Delia tipped her head back against the soft bath pillow she'd discovered in a gift package from the hotel spa.

From Jager, of course.

After sleeping soundly for ten hours, she'd awoken to a room service cart near the bed with a veritable breakfast buffet just for her, including two plates of hot food on their own warming stands. She'd also discovered an assortment of gifts lined up on the bedroom's bureau. Jager had gone out to do some Christmas shopping, but left her a note telling her to enjoy herself until he returned. How on earth had she slept through his departure?

She lifted one arm from the water to examine her fingers for their level of pruning and decided she'd probably soaked long enough. She emerged from the bath and stepped into the shower stall to rinse off the spa oils from her skin and deep conditioner from her hair, deciding the only possible explanation for her heavy sleep was the pregnancy. She hadn't experienced any nausea and her breasts seemed to be the same size as normal, so she hadn't felt many effects of carrying a baby. But she wasn't one to sleep so soundly or for so long, and even when she awoke she'd been heavy-limbed and a bit foggy.

The bath and shower were welcome indulgences after the big breakfast. Jager would have been pleased to see how hungry she'd been.

Of course, the voracious appetite might have resulted from the late-night extracurricular activity. She stretched languidly in the shower, remembering the feel of Jager's hands all over her. She was still hypersensitive everywhere, her body pleasantly warm and satiated.

Shutting off the spray, she wrapped herself in fluffy white towels and breathed in the heady fragrances from the bath oils and hair products. The spa package had inspired her to try some new herbal combinations when she got back to work at McNeill Meadows. She would also have to give a lot of thought to how she would balance the responsibilities of her job with the care of her child.

Returning to the spacious closet in her bedroom to choose an outfit, she heard rustling in the living area.

"Jager?" Barefoot, she hurried toward the door adjoining the rooms. Then, recognizing how eager she was to see him, she forced herself to slow down.

"Delia." His voice was teasing. Good-humored. Had he been as stirred by their night together as she?

Cracking open the door, she peered out to see him scoop up a small package gift wrapped in gold foil printed with red holly berries and tied with a red velvet bow.

"I got you a pre-Christmas present," he announced, approaching with the gift held out in front of him.

He wore dark pants and a white dress shirt she happened to know was custom-made for him since she'd been in his office one long-ago day when his tailor had arrived with a garment bag containing that season's wardrobe update. No surprise, it fit him perfectly, molding to his shoulders and tapering to accommodate his athletic frame.

She heated all over remembering how well he'd used that sexy body of his last night.

"That was nice of you," she offered after a pause. "I should dress first."

"Please don't think that's necessary on my account." He stopped just inches from the door but didn't open it the rest of the way.

Letting her set the pace.

"I'm not sure we should make a habit of this." She didn't sound remotely convincing, especially since his nearness made her all hot and breathless.

"Of gift giving?" He arched an eyebrow, a wicked grin curling his lips.

Sweet. Heaven. She wanted his mouth on her.

She released her hold on the door, letting it fall open a bit more.

"Forget what I said." She tipped her head sideways against the door frame. "How about if I thank you for the present first, and then I'll unwrap it?"

His eyes narrowed. His nostrils flared. And he set the package aside on a narrow console table as he understood her meaning.

"That hardly seems fair, but I live to please you."

He reached for her, circling her waist and pulling her close.

His woodsy aftershave acted like an aphrodisiac, calling to mind all the ways she'd kissed him the night before.

Having his hands on her only deepened her hunger.

"I do believe pregnancy is finally increasing my appetite." Delia grazed his mouth with hers once. Twice. Then she tugged his lower lip gently between her teeth. "At least one kind of appetite."

With a growl of approval, he bent to lift her off her feet and cradled her in his arms. He headed for the bed.

"It could be *me* that's driving the new hunger." His fingers flexed lightly against her, squeezing her closer. "Either way, I'm going to be the one to satisfy it."

Her eyes fell shut with the need to concentrate on all her other senses, especially the feel of him. The feel of his powerful body levering over hers when he lay with her on the bed. Of his hips sinking into hers, even through the damp towel around her waist.

He kissed her with a care and attentiveness they'd been too impatient for the previous night. He caressed her face, pressing his lips to her eyelids. Then he slid aside her towel to trail more kisses down her neck. Between her bare breasts.

Lower still.

Pleasure spiraled out from a fixed point inside her, sending ribbons of sensation to every hidden spot on her body. A trembling began in her legs before he laid a kiss on the most sensitive of places, taking his time, clearly in no hurry. Ah, but she was. Eager to ride the tension to completion. She saw stars and never opened her eyes, the pinpricks of light flashing a warning of the pleasure to come. He tasted her and she was lost, her hips arching helplessly against the sensual waves of sweet release.

He didn't let go until the spasms slowed and she sagged into the downy duvet, opening her eyes. Only then did he peel off his clothes and join her on the bed again, seating himself deep inside her. His presence there set off more aftershocks, and she wrapped her arms and legs around him tight.

He held himself still for a long moment, letting her adjust to him. He stroked her hair, kissed her neck. And then he began to move.

She wouldn't have thought it possible to build the hunger again, but when he dropped a kiss on one tender breast, she felt pleasure swell for a second time. Seeing his perpetually shadowed jaw in contrast to the creamy pale skin there made her breath catch. Her nipples tightened more. Had she thought her breasts weren't sensitive from pregnancy? She almost shuddered with release from his tongue's careful attention to each peak.

But then he reversed their positions, letting her sit astride him the way she'd started to do the night before. Now, she didn't take the moment for granted, enjoying the way he let her take control.

She delighted in seeing what pleased him, savored the sensation of his hands on her hips, guiding her when he was ready for more.

And then he stole the rhythm back for them both, taking her where they both wanted to go until her orgasm broke over her. Her thighs hugged his hips, drawing a shout of completion from him. The muscles along his chest contracted against her palms and the knowledge that she pleased him as much as he pleased her sent a fresh ripple of bliss over her tingling nerves until, finally, she slumped against his chest, spent.

Cracking open an eyelid to peer up at him, she was taken aback by a sudden swell of tender emotions. She wanted to wrap her arms around him tight and keep him in her bed for days. She wanted to feed him. Make him smile.

On instinct, she shut her eyes again, knowing she couldn't let herself start caring for him that way. She hoped it was just pregnancy emotions making her so tenderhearted. When she thought she had a handle on her feelings again, she opened her eyes.

Unbelievably, the sun was starting to set again by the time her heart settled into an even pace once more.

"How can it be dark already?" she whispered against his bare shoulder, grateful for a neutral topic to speak about when her heart was beginning to hunger for a different kind of fulfillment. "I only woke up shortly before noon."

"I'm wearing you out." Jager frowned his concern, his blue eyes bright in the slanted rays of the setting sun.

"No. I'm just surprised how much shorter the daylight hours are here versus back home." She hadn't given much thought to it, but it made sense because they were so much farther north. "It's only a little after four o'clock."

He glanced away, and she could see his jaw flex.

"We're invited to the McNeill mansion for dinner tonight, but I will call them and reschedule."

She felt very awake then. A bolt of panic did that to a woman.

"Dinner? As in a meal with your brothers and grandfather?"

"I think they'll all be there, yes. Everyone but my father. They know my feelings where he's concerned." He gripped her shoulder when she would have leapt from the bed. "Delia, we can go another time. You're tired—"

"No. I want to go." She also wanted to look her best. To not embarrass Jager. "I was afraid you wouldn't invite me to go with you when you met them."

He stilled. "You're certainly under no obligation to attend."

Would he have preferred to meet them alone? She was torn between wanting to let him find his own way with his half brothers and wanting to understand the world her son or daughter would one day move in. Maternal concern won out.

"I want to be there. I just need a little time to get ready." She would assess for herself what kind of family her child would have.

She had so little to offer a baby in that regard.

"I'll leave your gift on the bed," he called after her while she hurried to her closet to find something to wear. "You might want to wear it tonight."

She heard the bedroom door open while she took stock of her half-dried hair. She couldn't deny a stab of envy for this baby she carried. A McNeill heir would be surrounded by more than just wealth and luxury, both of which she'd lived happily without.

Her child would have a large, caring family to love him or her, something Delia would never know. Even her father, never a demonstrative parent, seemed to have forsaken her. She'd been hurt by his reaction to her baby news.

She was having a child and, at the same time, her family seemed to be dwindling. Unless, by some chance, Jager McNeill started to feel the same new emotions that she'd experienced.

Christmas was a time of miracles after all, and tomorrow was Christmas Eve. Delia couldn't help a quick, fanciful thought.

What if Jager fell in love with her?

The question halted her, stilling her hand as she reached for a brush. What on earth was she thinking?

She had no business thinking those kinds of thoughts. The fact that the question had floated to the surface of her brain reminded her why it was so dangerous to indulge in a physical relationship. She was already falling in love with him.

Closing her eyes, she acknowledged the simple truth that complicated her life so very much. She'd hoped to use this trip to make a smart, reasonable decision. She was going to be a mother, a duty she took seriously. She couldn't afford to fall victim to foolish, romanticized notions. Again.

She wasn't here because she was Jager's girlfriend, or significant other, so she couldn't allow her new feelings to show. In Jager's eyes, she was simply the mother of his child. She would be wise to remember it.

"The jewelry is stunning, Jager." Delia fingered the diamond drop earrings shaped like snowflakes as she stood beside him in the foyer of Malcolm McNeill's expansive mansion in one of the most jaw-droppingly pricey parts of New York.

The maid who answered the door had taken their coats and then disappeared to announce them. Or so Jager guessed.

He thought he had been prepared for the family's wealth. But he wasn't anywhere near ready for a Cézanne in the foyer or the sheer size of the place in a city where tiny patches of real estate went for millions.

If the house caught him off guard, he could only

imagine what Delia was feeling in her first trip outside Martinique. She was definitely in an unusual mood, something he'd noticed as soon as they'd settled side by side in the back of the chauffeured Range Rover his grandfather sent for them. Jager had watched her open the gift on the ride over, and while he was sure she'd been genuinely pleased, there was something reserved about her this evening. Restrained.

He hoped it was just nerves at meeting the more famous branch of the McNeill family.

"I hope the earrings make you think about how much fun we had watching snowflakes fall on the ice at Rockefeller Center." He kissed her temple just as the maid returned to the foyer, pulling his attention back to the impending encounter with his grandfather and half brothers.

"The family is waiting for you in the library." The older woman gestured to her right as she stepped out of their way. "The elevator is down this hall, and it might be easier than the stairs with your beautiful dress, ma'am."

"The skylight is so lovely over the stairs though, I wouldn't have minded a closer look." Delia peered up the formal staircase to the stained-glass window six stories above. She turned to smile at the woman. "I'll bet you see amazing displays of light depending on the weather."

"Some days are truly breathtaking." The woman nodded before disappearing down a corridor toward the back of the house.

"Speaking of breathtaking." Jager slid an arm around Delia's slender waist, careful not to wrinkle the silk taffeta skirt she wore while he guided her down the hall toward the elevator. "Have I mentioned how incredible you look tonight?"

She was vibrant in the ankle-length crimson skirt, a designer confection he'd bought for her with the help of a shopping service. They'd sent an assortment of outfits particularly fitting for the holidays and the long skirt with beadwork and appliqué was a festive choice. She wore a simple creamy-colored angora sweater with it, letting the skirt shine. The earrings went well with her outfit, dangling against her pale neck since she'd swept her fair hair into a smooth twist.

"You clean up well yourself." Her hazel eyes darted over his crisp white dress shirt and tie, as if scanning for anything amiss. She smoothed her fingers down the lapel of his black jacket and he wondered if she did so to soothe herself or him.

Either way, the caring gesture touched him as they stepped into the elevator cabin and he hit the button for the third floor. When the door closed silently, Jager picked up her hands and kissed the back of one and then the other.

It wasn't until that moment—halfway to the third floor—that he remembered he hadn't informed her about his grandfather's will. Swearing softly, he hit the elevator emergency button, halting their upward progress and making the cabin lurch awkwardly as it stopped.

Delia stumbled a bit, but he caught her against him easily.

"What are you doing?" Frowning, she righted herself by gripping the lapels of his jacket.

An alarm blared inside the car, a red light flashing inside the emergency knob.

"I forgot to tell you something important and I don't want you to be surprised, or think I was trying to hide it." He hated sharing it with her this way. "I meant to

talk to you when I got back from shopping, but then we
got so distracted—"

"Tell me what?" There was a flatness to her voice.
An edge.

He didn't blame her for being upset. The flocked red
paper on the walls around them seemed to close in as
the alarm kept up its insistent wail.

"My grandfather is determined to bring all his grandsons into the business. To carry on his legacy."

She nodded, her hold on his suit jacket loosening. "I
remember your half brother talking about that when he
came to the gate the first time you and I were together."

"Right. What Cam didn't mention was Malcolm's
insistence on his heirs being married for at least a year
to inherit."

"Married." She pursed her lips.

He couldn't read her expression, but it seemed like
the damn elevator alarm was getting louder.

"Yes." He tensed, willing her to understand it meant
nothing to him. "I didn't want you to think that my proposal to you had anything to do with that. I don't care
about the hotel business—"

"Don't you think I know that?" Delia shook her head,
resting her hands on his upper arms as she faced him.
Her words were reassuring but her expression remained
tense. "I know you don't want anything from this family, Jager, but I'm glad you're at least in their home,
hearing what they have to say."

He stared into her hazel eyes, trying to find out if he
was missing something. "You're not upset with me?"

He would swear there was a stiffness about her shoulders. Then again, maybe he was seeing trouble where
there wasn't any. This damn meeting had him uptight.

"I'm a little embarrassed about what your family

might say about our elevator mishap, but other than that, of course I'm not upset with you." She offered a tight smile.

He hurried to explain himself, knowing time was running out and not just because of the elevator. "You know I asked you to marry me because—"

"Because of the baby," she finished for him, straightening as her hands fell away from his arms. "Yes. I'm very clear about that, I assure you."

She pressed the elevator alarm button to set things back into motion again and Jager breathed a mental sigh of relief. She understood him.

And she said she wasn't upset with him.

So he wondered why she seemed to bristle when he touched her as the doors swooshed open on the third floor. He hoped it was simple embarrassment for the awkward situation, as she'd mentioned. He would do whatever it took to ensure this visit went smoothly for her. Because in spite of his grandfather's maneuvering, Jager had his own reasons for wanting to make certain he was married before the New Year.

Twelve

If Delia hadn't been upset about his insistence that he only proposed for the sake of their child, she might have been more appreciative of his anxious attempt to tell her about his grandfather's will. That had been kind and considerate, proving to her that he was a far different man than Brandon and—more important—showing her that he understood how hurt she'd been by her former fiancé's deception.

But instead of putting her more at ease for this first meeting with his grandfather, the conversation only brought home for her that Jager was thinking solely about social convention and his legal claim to their child. That hurt all the more tonight since she'd just come face-to-face with the realization that she loved him. And since she'd made it clear she wouldn't marry for anything less than love, his reminder that they should wed for the baby's sake only deepened the raw ache inside her.

Jager had asked her to marry him because she carried his child. It had nothing to do with any feelings for her.

The blunt truth hurt, but it certainly helped her to be less nervous about meeting the rest of the McNeills. She didn't need to worry about impressing people who would never be *her* family. She could focus on taking their measure because they would be her child's relatives.

"Seriously?" Cameron McNeill, the tall half brother who bore a striking resemblance to Damon, was waiting for them on the third floor when the mansion's elevator doors swished open. "Don't they have home elevators where you come from?"

"Funny." Jager extended his hand and the two men shook. "I figured the old man got wind there was an imposter McNeill in the house and hit the reject button."

"There are no imposters here." Cameron clapped him on the shoulder. "Although I'm more interested in your lovely guest." Expectant and charming, he turned to Delia.

"Delia, this is Cameron. Cam, meet Delia Rickard." Jager wrapped a possessive arm around her waist. "And she is special to me."

She swallowed back the automatic thrill that danced through her at his words, his touch. She tried to focus on his half brother instead. Now that Delia could see Cameron more clearly, she realized she'd never again mistake him for Damon. Though both men were unusually tall, Cameron was probably on the high end of six foot four. And whereas Damon had been a serious man even before his wife's disappearance, Cameron seemed a lighter spirit.

"A pleasure to welcome you, Delia." He grinned as he squeezed her hand briefly. "And no need to worry.

Now that I'm happily wed, I won't be issuing any more impulsive marriage proposals to the beautiful women I meet."

"I'm sure your new wife is glad to know it," Delia replied, remembering well the tabloid frenzy about Cameron's public proposal to the New York City Ballet dancer who later married Quinn—the eldest McNeill. Months afterward, Cameron had wed a concierge who worked for one of the McNeills' Caribbean hotels. The rush to wed made all the more sense in light of what Jager had confided. "And thank you for having me."

"If you're special to Jager, you're special to us. Are you ready to meet the rest of the clan?" Cameron held an arm out, gesturing toward the double doors flanked by carved wood panels at the end of the corridor.

The panels were the kind she'd seen in historic plantation homes, the sort of things that Gabe enjoyed restoring or even reproducing from scratch.

Grateful to have that first encounter behind them—and to have easily brushed aside the matter of the stuck elevator—Delia accompanied the men toward the library. She needed to tamp down the hurt and unease from her conversation with Jager mere seconds earlier.

When Cameron opened the double doors, she only had a moment to take in the richness of the room, with its walls fitted with historic Chinese lacquer panels between the windows overlooking the street. Quickly, she shifted her attention to the six other people she hadn't yet met.

Delia was glad she'd taken time to read up on the family—again—before the trip to New York, since the tidbits she recalled about the various members helped her to keep them straight. Ian was the first to step forward and introduce himself to her. Jager had already met Ian, the brother who was most involved in the hotel business, developing his own specialty properties in addition to his work with McNeill Resorts. Ian's wife, Lydia, a dark-haired beauty with deep furrows in her pale forehead, eyed Delia with an assessing gaze. She was dressed elegantly in a green tartan skirt and black silk blouse, and a velvet choker with an emerald pendant at her throat.

Cameron's wife, Maresa, perched on the arm of a wingback chair, composed and elegant in an ice-blue sweater dress that drew attention to honey-colored eyes, a shade paler than her deeply tanned skin. She was the only one in the group to hug Delia, a gesture that put her a bit more at ease for meeting the rest. Maresa no longer worked as a concierge for one of the McNeill Resorts hotels, but her warm manner made it obvious why she'd been so good at the job in her native Saint Thomas.

The last of the brothers was Quinn, the hedge fund manager who had married the exotic ballerina.

"Good to have you in New York," Quinn greeted them, his navy suit and light blue shirt conservative without being stodgy.

It was interesting to view Jager side by side with this man since each was the oldest of his respective group of McNeill brothers, and she recognized a similar way they had of sizing each other up. While Cam had been open and friendly, Ian was tough to read but warm, and Quinn, the oldest, clearly reserved judgment. That was Jager too. She'd seen it in business meetings.

She saw it in how he related to her.

He held back. He sure didn't rush to embrace people. He'd been as scarred by people in his life—the loss of his mother, especially—as Delia had been. Seeing him that way helped her to understand him better, even if it wouldn't change him.

"Good to be here," Jager replied, offering the barest nod of acknowledgment. "I hope to work more closely with your investigator while I'm here. Bentley."

From the back of the room, the gray-haired gentleman seated in a leather club chair—the patriarch himself, no doubt—finally spoke up. "Bentley will be here before dinner is served."

The crowd of relatives shuffled to give Jager and Delia a better view of Malcolm McNeill. His bearing commanded the room.

With all the attention turned toward Malcolm, the petite blonde beside Delia whispered to her. "I'm Sofia, by the way."

Delia glanced down at the speaker. So this was the ballerina Quinn had married. She was even more beautiful than her photos online, and she didn't even seem to have any makeup on. She certainly had a natural look, and her outfit was a simple black dress, long sleeved with a floor-length skirt that might have been severe on someone else.

Jager strode forward to shake his grandfather's hand, and Sofia continued to speak quietly. "Meeting Quinn's family was more terrifying than any audition I've ever had," she confided, forcing Delia to hide a smile by biting her cheek. "But they're not so bad."

Nearby, Lydia must have overheard because she softly chimed in, "When they're not brawling."

"She's teasing," Sofia rushed to explain, fixing her loose topknot that was slipping from its clasp. "Mostly."

At the other end of the room, Jager conversed quietly with his grandfather. Delia couldn't help but be curious about the exchange; the older man was smiling as Jager held out a hand to help him from his chair. Malcolm shook off the gesture, however, pointing to a silver-topped walking stick nearby.

When he stood, even with his slightly stooped back and bent knees, he was every bit as tall as Cameron. It was clear the brothers had inherited their grandfather's genes. He wore a smoking jacket, of all things, made of dark silk and belted over a pair of black trousers and wing tips. With his thinning hair still damp but combed perfectly into place, he had a debonair quality about him.

"My dear, I'm eager to meet you." His voice boomed the length of the room, and his blue eyes—that matched all the other men's eyes in the room—turned to Delia.

She swallowed hard, grateful for the reassuring pat on the elbow from Sofia.

Stepping forward, she braced herself to meet her child's great-grandfather.

"Hello, sir." Pasting a smile into place, she reminded herself she was good at this. In the same way that Cameron's wife had a warm manner from being a concierge, Delia had honed her skills making people feel comfortable at McNeill Meadows. She could do this. "Thank you so much for inviting me tonight."

Malcom paused a few feet from her, steadying himself on the cane. She wondered if his strength was waning after the heart attack Cameron had mentioned.

Jager might not have believed the story, but Delia did. She guessed the older man's failing health had prompted him to act fast to unify his family.

"I am delighted to know you, Delia." Malcolm McNeill enveloped her hand in his larger one and kept hold of it. "You might have heard that I'm very committed to meeting all my grandsons and ensuring the McNeill legacy lives on through a strong family tree."

Family tree? Delia shifted her gaze to the floor, afraid her face would betray her secret.

"Gramps." Cameron exchanged a look with his wife and then edged forward to stand by Malcolm. "Maybe we should go in for dinner first."

"We haven't even offered our newest members a drink yet, have we?" Malcolm glanced around the room. "Lydia, love, would you bring me mine so we can have a toast?" He let go of Delia's hand to point at the half-empty glass by his abandoned club chair. "And for pity's sake, let's get Jager and Delia something." He nodded toward Ian.

Lydia hurried over to do her part, making no noise in her stilettos. How did some women manage that trick? She had a graceful walk that Delia envied. Delia felt more out of her element with each passing moment, and she most certainly would not have a cocktail to toast anything. Why hadn't she thought of that before she asked to attend this gathering?

"No need to wait on us." Jager beat Ian in his move toward the bar, a freestanding antique that held a few bottles of high-end liquor and three cut crystal decanters. "I'll get it."

Delia touched one of her snowflake earrings to calm herself. She had thought she wasn't nervous when she walked into the room, but Malcolm McNeill's reference to the "strong family tree" stirred anxiety. She felt certain Jager wouldn't have shared their secret with his grandfather.

But was there a chance he'd told one of his brothers? The way Cameron quickly cut off Malcolm's line of conversation made her wonder. Everyone would know soon enough, of course. But she wanted to discuss how to broach the news with Jager before they revealed it to his family.

"What would you like, my dear?" Malcolm asked her suddenly, fixing her with his clear blue gaze. "If Chivas isn't to your taste, there's a bottle of Tattingers we can open."

From the bar, Jager spoke up. "I know her preference. We're all set."

She could see that he'd poured tonic water into a highball glass with an ice cube and a lime wedge. Perfect.

Turning her attention back to Jager's grandfather, she saw the older man's gaze was fixed on Jager's actions as well. And was it her nervous imagination, or had everyone else noticed his discreet pour?

"You're not drinking this evening." Malcolm's observation confirmed her suspicion. He'd seen, all right. "Good for you, my dear." He patted her forearm and then accepted his glass from Lydia as she rejoined the group. "Very good, indeed."

Could he be any more obvious in his implications? Delia felt her cheeks heat and remembered Jager saying how easy it was to read her because of those blushes.

"What did I miss?" Lydia asked, frowning as she peered around at the family.

The men tried to look elsewhere. Sofia gave her sister-in-law a quick headshake as if to discourage a follow-up question.

Jager returned to Delia's side with two drinks, passing her the water before answering Lydia. "Only that Malcolm seemed pleased Delia isn't much of a drinker." He gave Delia's cheek a kiss. "I think we're as ready for that toast as we'll ever be."

Her skin warmed from the brush of his lips. She knew that Jager would have rather skipped the whole formality of a toast that put them at the center of attention. No doubt he'd only redirected the conversation to forestall speculation that she could be pregnant. It was kind of him, and yet the damage had already been done. Malcolm had all but shouted it from the rooftops in his own subtle way.

Unless, of course, Jager really had told his family that she was expecting without letting her know? That was hard to believe given the importance he'd placed on informing her about his grandfather's marriage ultimatum. And yet, she already knew he viewed this baby very differently than he viewed marriage. The former meant the world to him.

The latter? A formality. Different rules might apply in his mind.

She found herself touching the snowflake earring again and forced her hand down to her side. Why should she allow his family to make her feel so uneasy? She might never see them again after tonight. Once the holidays were over, she'd be back on a plane to Martinique.

Around her, the assembled guests retrieved their beverages. Malcolm shuffled backward a step so he could lean against the sofa and set aside his cane. He lifted his tumbler, the crystal glass acting as a prism and reflecting light from the overhead chandelier. Jager's blue gaze landed on her with an unfathomable look. Did he regret bringing her here?

Jager tamped down the urge to tuck Delia under his arm and haul ass out of the mansion and the whole McNeill realm. Although Malcolm McNeill had seemed genuine enough in his words of welcome earlier, Jager didn't appreciate the way the older man put Delia on the spot. What the hell had he been thinking?

Clearly, she was upset. Jager had seen the splotches of color on her cheeks, noticed the way she fidgeted with her earring. He kicked himself for not insisting he meet the family privately first, but she'd surprised him with her emphatic decision to attend the dinner. Besides, his number one goal this week was to make her happy, to change her mind about marriage so they could start building a future together as a family.

Damn. This was not helping.

His grandfather's hand—a surprisingly heavy weight—landed on his shoulder. "I'd like to propose a toast to every person in this room." The older man's voice rumbled with gravelly authority. "My grandsons and the women who stand beside them. I am proud to call you family." His gaze scanned each face around the library. "Tonight, we celebrate a joyous occasion, welcoming even more McNeills into the fold." He nodded at both Delia and Jager. "Cheers to you."

Jager watched Delia, hoping she wouldn't be too upset the toast made it sound like they were already married. Perhaps the family patriarch was referring to Jager's brothers when he mentioned welcoming *more McNeills*. But Jager could see her uneasiness grow even as she raised her glass along with everyone else during shouts of "Cheers!" and "Here, here."

Maybe he was the only one to notice the signs of her agitation. Her time dealing with the public at the McNeill Meadows property had given her easy social skills that hadn't been so apparent when he'd first hired her as an assistant. But he'd known her before she'd developed the ability to put on a public face. He spied the way she waited until she glanced down to bite her lip, hiding the sign of nerves.

The women in the group congregated around Delia; he hoped whatever they had to say distracted her from this debacle in a good way. Quinn moved to speak to Malcolm, shaking his hand and complimenting the toast.

"I should have told you to bring an engagement ring with you to this thing," Cameron muttered in Jager's ear, his tone dry. "We've all been on the marriage fast track here."

"You warned me," Jager admitted, feeling more trapped by the minute. And they hadn't even sat down to dinner yet. "But I underestimated his commitment to his approach."

Cam sipped his drink, his gold wedding band glinting in the light, while he studied his grandfather. "I think when you reach his age, you say what you want and don't give a rip."

"If he sends Delia running, I'm done with him." Jager meant it. Seeing a tentative smile on Delia's face while one of the women spoke to her made him grateful to the females in the group. "I'm only here because of her."

She was all that mattered to him.

And, of course, their child.

It occurred to him that he thought about them—Delia and their baby—in the reverse order of how he'd been used to weighing their importance in his life. Ever since their first impulsive night, when he knew there was a chance she could be pregnant, he'd put all his focus on making plans for an heir.

But there was more to Delia than just her role in this pregnancy, and he wasn't sure how to contend with his growing feelings for her. They were a distraction from the goal. An inconvenience that made him second-guess himself, and he couldn't afford that when he was so ready to close the deal.

Forever.

He had that engagement ring Cam mentioned after all. He'd been working on a Christmas Eve proposal she'd never forget.

Quinn moved away from Malcolm to speak to his wife, and Jager noticed Malcolm retrieve his cane. Jager strode over to intercept him, making sure his grandfather didn't corner Delia to press his family agenda.

"Thank you for the welcome." Jager leaned against the back of the couch beside Malcolm, thinking to keep the two of them separate until the meal. Or to change the subject of conversation.

But Delia was already moving toward them, her diplomatic smile firmly in place.

"It was nice of you to include me," Delia added as she came to face them both. "Even though I'm not family."

There was an edge to her words. No doubt, she'd been pushed to her limit tonight. Jager itched to take her hand. To kiss away her frustrations and make sure no stress touched her. No matter what the doctor said about her pregnancy not being high risk, it couldn't be good for a woman to be upset like this while she was expecting.

It should be a happy time for her.

"Well, I hope my grandson will change that soon." Malcom grinned broadly, unaware of the nervous energy practically thrumming through Delia. "I predict it won't be long until we have another McNeill wedding."

Delia's sharp intake of breath was audible. Jager put a placating hand at the base of her spine and felt for himself how tense she was. The room went silent.

Jager drew a breath, prepared to make their excuses and depart.

Delia beat him in responding.

"We won't be marrying." She smiled sweetly, but her hazel eyes were filled with a steely determination he recognized.

He'd seen it the day she jumped in the sea to save a drowning child.

"My dear." The furrow in Malcolm's brow indicated that—finally—he understood he was out of line. Or that, at the very least, he'd upset his guest. "I only thought, since you are glowing at my grandson's side and you didn't imbibe tonight—"

"You were mistaken," she fired back, standing tall and proud and ready to do battle. "I may be expecting. But we have no plans to wed just for the sake of our child."

If Jager's future didn't hang in the balance of those words, he might have taken some pleasure from seeing this woman, once prone to being insecure, take on the intimidating Malcolm McNeill.

Instead, he felt a kick to the teeth. It reverberated squarely in his chest and every part of him. In spite of his every effort, he'd now be living out his father's legacy of bringing a child into the world without benefit of marrying the mother. That worried him.

But unexpectedly, the pain ran deeper, beyond losing out on a chance at a real family, one with Delia and their child. He was completely leveled by the fact that he'd lost his chance to win over Delia.

The only woman he'd ever loved.

Thirteen

Delia wondered if she would blame this moment on pregnancy hormones later.

It was unlike her to gainsay anyone, especially her host on an important night for Jager. But what made Malcolm McNeill think he could maneuver his family like chess pieces, especially after all these years? Is that what family was about?

In the heavy silence that followed her declaration, she became aware of Jager beside her. His face was a frozen mask she did not recognize. No doubt she had embarrassed him, and she regretted that. Deeply. But he could not have been surprised, as she'd already confided her deep need to marry for love. He, of all people, must understand that. He'd been there for her when she'd been falling apart from Brandon's betrayal. Jager had met her father and seen how that need for authentic emotions went back to her childhood.

Delia became aware of the deep, resonant ticking of the vintage grandfather clock while everyone around her seemed to grapple with what to say next. She understood the feeling, since Malcolm McNeill had put her in that precise awkward position from the moment he'd acknowledged her presence.

"I see that I've upset you, my dear." Malcolm found his cane with one fumbling hand and set down his drink with the other. "And I'm so sorry for that. You should understand I am accustomed to being far too abrupt with my grandsons about my hopes for the future, a flaw they have overlooked because of my age and my health. But that should not excuse poor manners."

When he reached Delia's side, he squeezed her forearm. There was sorrow in his eyes, and she felt contrite. For all she knew, he could still be manipulating her emotions, but she wished she hadn't spoken out.

"Perhaps we should leave," Jager interjected with a terseness that alerted her to how much this had upset him too.

Exhaustion hit her in a wave, making her acutely aware of the stress, the lateness of the hour and a sudden hunger. Her pregnancy hormones may have been late making themselves known, but these last two days had rocked her on a physical level. She felt a bit faint, her vision narrowing to two pinpricks of light.

"I may need to sit," Delia told him, done with caring about how well-liked she was among the McNeills. She'd been foolish to try to be a part of Jager's world. As much as she longed for family, she was not cut out for this.

As one, the McNeills moved to clear a path to the sofa. Jager offered her his arm and steadied her, guiding her toward the couch near the bar.

Ian's wife was suddenly beside her, holding her hand. "Have you eaten? Would that help?"

Delia nodded and someone, Maresa maybe, said, "I'll get it," and left the room. Delia let the soft hubbub of voices wash over her as her vision slowly returned to normal.

"It has to be stressful meeting us all." That voice belonged to Sofia. "Especially everyone at once."

"It's okay, Gramps." That might have been Cameron. "When I'm upset, it always helps me to clear the air. Say what's on my mind and then move past it. She won't hold it against you."

"Delia, would you like me to call for a car?" Jager asked in her ear, his voice kind and yet…distant. "You'd be more comfortable at the hotel."

"I'm fine," she assured him, her vision beginning to clear. "We can't leave now after I put everyone in an uproar."

"Your color is returning." She realized Lydia still held her hand on her other side. Or, rather, Delia was gripping Lydia's hand for dear life.

"Sorry." Delia let go and sat up straighter. "I am feeling better."

"Maresa went to get you something to eat." Lydia lowered her voice for Delia's hearing only. "And we're excited for you, no matter what your plans might be. Babies are the best news."

Sliding a sideways glance to gauge her expression, Delia found a wealth of sincerity in those pretty green eyes. And, maybe, a touch of envy. Did Lydia hope to get pregnant herself? she wondered.

"Thank you. And I am very happy," Delia assured her, realizing how much more attached she grew to this child every single day. What started out as a shock had come to mean more to her than anything else in her life. Although, she had to admit, winning Jager's love would have come very close. Thinking about raising their child separately, losing the close relationship they had, made her heart hurt. But the notion of subjecting herself to a loveless marriage hurt worse. She'd been rejected enough by the people in her life.

Sitting beside him and feeling so apart from him was far worse than any dizziness and exhaustion she may have experienced because of the baby.

Maresa returned with a plate for Delia at the same time two servers entered with hors d'oeuvres for the group at large. The family all seemed as thrilled to see the food as her, probably grateful for a diversion after the tense start to the cocktail hour. Ian asked Jager about McNeill Meadows and the changes he'd made to the property to highlight its plantation history.

She breathed a sigh of relief as Jager allowed himself to be pulled into conversation. Hopefully they could get through the rest of the evening on a more positive note. She crunched into a cracker topped with warm brie and a slice of glazed pear, wondering how many she could devour without raising eyebrows.

As if reading her mind, Lydia winked. "Want me to find a few more of those?"

"Thank you." She nodded. "That would be great."

With Lydia's spot vacated, Delia had a clear view of her host in the club chair, which was situated at an angle to the couch. With both hands folded on top of the cane that rested to one side of his knee, he stared out a window, the lines in his face deeper with his frown.

Unable to leave things festering between them, she set her plate on the coffee table and slid down so that she sat closer to him.

She felt Jager's eyes follow her movement, but she knew what she was doing.

"Mr. McNeill, I began to feel faint while we were speaking and didn't get a chance to say that there is nothing to forgive." She patted his hands awkwardly. "You apologized to me, but I realize that I was unusually prickly, especially at what should be a wonderful reunion for your family. This is about you and your grandsons."

"It's about family. All of us." He shook his head. "I should not have been so forceful."

"But at least I could tell that you were enthused about this baby, and I'm glad for that." She had come here tonight, telling herself the visit was about her child when, really, she had wanted to be a part of Jager's world. To feel the embrace of a long-lost family. Did he know how fortunate he was to have people who wanted to claim him for a brother? For a grandson? "My own father has never expressed much joy in his family, so I may not be adept at navigating the nuances of..." She peered around the room, taking in the faces of so many McNeills, so many people who truly did care about welcoming yet another generation. "All this," she finished lamely.

"And I am so eager for family, I unwittingly push them away. It wouldn't be the first time." When the older man turned his blue eyes toward her, they were bright and shiny. "The mother of any McNeill is family to me," he said quietly.

Malcolm had spoken softly, but Delia could feel Jager's attention focused on them from the other end of the couch. He was listening. She hoped what his grandfather said meant something to him—at least in regard to his own mother, if not to Delia.

"For that, I thank you." The words certainly warmed her heart, even as they underscored all that she would miss by not marrying Jager.

"I had hoped to see all my grandsons married, so I put it in my will." He shook his head, bent in defeat. "Maybe it was not so wise."

She realized it wasn't just Jager who now strained to listen. Conversation around them had stopped once more. This time, Delia didn't feel the need to cross swords with him though, even though she guessed each McNeill in the room wanted to shout that his dictate was horribly unfair.

Yet it seemed to have netted three happy marriages so far.

"You might be better off letting your heirs decide what's best for their future," Delia suggested, reaching for her water glass before remembering she'd left it near her former seat. "Don't forget Damon already lost a wife he loved dearly. A dictate to marry again would only drive him away."

"You make a very good point."

All heads turned toward the open double doors to find the source of the comment.

Damon McNeill had entered the room.

Jager sat with his brother later that night in a second hotel room he'd booked for Damon at The Plaza. Between Delia nearly fainting and Damon showing up unannounced with Bentley, the McNeills' investigator who'd made good on the promise to deliver him, everyone agreed they would share a meal together some other night. Even Malcolm had been too stunned to argue, perhaps feeling abashed between his pushy tactics with Delia and then having Damon, quite possibly a widower at this point, overhear their discussion of the old man's matchmaking tactics.

Jager had had more than enough of the Other Mc-Neills for one night. Cameron had let it slip at some point that that was how they referred to their half brothers. The shoe fit the other damned foot just fine.

Now, as he shared a beer and watched an NBA game with the brother he'd always been closest to, Jager realized his happiness at having Damon back was only dampened by Delia's insistence they wouldn't marry.

And yeah, it dampened his happiness a whole hell of a lot. Still, he was glad to have Damon's big, ugly boots planted in his line of sight on the coffee table while they watched a game being played on the West Coast. He needed this time to decompress after Delia's rejection. Decompress and regroup. He wasn't giving up, but he wasn't sure how to move forward to win her over. She was a confounding, complex and amazing woman.

"If we were still in Los Altos Hills, we'd be at this game right now," Damon observed, looking thinner and scruffier than he had in the fall before he left on his trip. He looked like he hadn't shaved since then; his dark beard hid half his face. "We left behind some good season tickets, didn't we?"

They'd left behind much more than that, but he wasn't sure how to broach the subject with his brother. Jager sucked at expressing himself lately, it seemed. He'd fallen short with Delia when he'd tried his best to be honest and forthright with her—which was exactly what she'd said she'd wanted.

On the TV, a player went for a slam dunk and got rejected at the hoop. It was a perfect freaking metaphor for this day and the ring that burned a hole in his jacket pocket even now. He leaned forward enough to tug his arms from the sleeves and tossed the jacket aside.

When they'd arrived back at The Plaza, he mentioned wanting to spend some time with his brother, and Delia seemed only too glad to find her bed for the night. She was exhausted and happy to have a tray in her room, something he'd ordered for her before he left her two doors down.

"I waited around for you to come home," Jager said now, not sure how much his brother knew about events that had transpired in the past few months. "When I couldn't get in touch with you, I figured I'd better put the business on the market before it lost all value. You know how rumors of the founder's disappearance can make investors nervous."

"I'll take over with the business now. There's no need to sell." Damon clinked his longneck against Jager's bottle. "I just got held up."

Thinking about all the nights he'd been convinced his brother was dead, Jager set the beer down and sat up, barely restraining his anger and—hell, yes—hurt.

"That's all you have to say? After months of not answering your phone and letting us all think the worst?"

Damon traced the outline of the name of the craft beer molded into the glass.

"I needed to find out what happened to my wife." His words were flat. Emotionless. "Unfortunately for me, I've come to agree with the police. She must have wanted out and didn't know how to tell me."

Jager was too stunned to reply for a long moment. Damon had been so certain she'd been kidnapped. "What about the ransom note?"

"Must have been a scheme for cash by someone who

knew she disappeared. I still need to get to the bottom of that."

"You could have called. Or taken me with you. Or—" Jager shook his head. "You shouldn't have left us wondering what happened to you."

"Next time I lose my mind, brother, I'll try to communicate more." Damon tipped back his drink.

Jager stewed for another minute, hoping his brother would offer up the full story. Or at least a few more details. But he didn't want to push him.

Yet.

He'd find out what had happened soon enough. For now, he was so damn glad to have him back and wouldn't risk pushing him away again. There'd been enough screw-ups on that account tonight.

"So what's next for you?" Jager asked, wishing he had a wedding to invite him to. He would have asked him to be his best man.

Then again... No. He couldn't have done that. Not when Damon had been preparing for his own wedding just a year ago.

"I need to launch my software." Damon lifted his bottle to peer through the dark glass. He closed one eye and then the other, watching the TV through the curved surface. "Get Transparent off the ground."

"Sounds good." Jager liked the idea of Damon getting back to work. Before Caroline, he'd been able to lose himself in the business for months at a time.

Jager wished he could be on the West Coast for him. But he had already spent too much time away from McNeill Meadows. Would Delia keep the cottage if she didn't marry him? he wondered. But not marrying was unacceptable. Thinking about her pronouncement during the cocktail hour was driving him out of his mind.

He needed to get back to their room and talk to her if she wasn't asleep.

And if she was, he needed to figure out a way to change her mind about marrying him and convince her first thing when she woke up.

"So." Damon set aside the empty bottle and glanced over at him. "You and Delia Rickard?"

"Yes." Jager ground his teeth. He had been irritated that his brother hadn't said much about where he'd been the last few months, and yet he realized he didn't feel like talking about how he'd spent his time recently either.

They'd never been an overly chatty family. And since their mother had died, they'd been quieter still.

"She's changed since the last time I saw her," his brother observed. "I almost didn't recognize her voice when I heard her from out in the hallway. She's feistier."

Jager had wondered what his brother thought about how she'd confronted Malcolm.

"She contradicted the McNeill patriarch all night long and still won the old man over somehow." Jager had only heard snippets of their conversation as they'd said their goodbyes, but he had overheard his grandfather wresting a promise from her to stay in touch.

The dynamic there was lost on him.

"Did they win you over?" Damon asked, pointing at the television and making the call for a flagrant foul a moment before the game ref did. "Are you going to be joining the petition to merge the families?"

There'd been a time when Jager would have simply barked a *hell no* in his brother's face. But maybe his time with Delia, thinking about a future and family of his own, made him view things differently.

"I think Malcolm is the only one who is psyched

about it. Quinn was polite, but I got the impression he'd rather swallow glass than compromise the empire."

Damon chuckled, a sound rusty from lack of use. "I was there for twenty minutes, and knew in about ten seconds he's a carbon copy of you, dude. That's exactly how you look to the rest of the world."

Jager laughed it off to end the night on an easy note. Finishing his beer, he left Damon to watch the rest of the game on his own. He needed to check on Delia. Make a plan for tomorrow.

But as he strode through The Plaza's empty hallway shortly before midnight, he couldn't help thinking about what Damon had said. Did Delia see him that way? Uncompromising? Unyielding?

If he could figure out how to change her mind, maybe he still had a chance to win her back. Clearly, introducing her to his family had been an epic fail, but he had one last strategy that still might work. A plan he'd put in place before he even left Martinique.

Because to help Jager make his case to Delia, Pascal Rickard was on a flight bound for New York tonight.

Fourteen

Delia slept late on Christmas Eve. She'd been so tired and heartbroken the night before after the failed dinner at the McNeills; she'd forgotten that time was ticking down to the holiday.

And now, it was Christmas Eve and she was alone in her bedroom at The Plaza Hotel.

Through parted curtains, she could see snow falling outside. Fat, fluffy flakes danced down from the sky, taking their time on the way. Her first thought was to share the beautiful view with Jager. Until she remembered their awkward parting the night before.

She'd told his whole family they weren't getting married. She'd hurt him on what had to be one of the toughest days of his life.

He'd been cold and distant, barely speaking to her directly afterward. Of course, he'd had a shock seeing his brother walk into the library. She hadn't blamed Jager for wanting to spend time with Damon when they returned to the hotel. She'd felt deeply tired anyhow. But a part of her had also recognized that Jager was pulling away from her.

From them.

He'd said all along their chemistry was off the charts. He'd made no promises about having feelings for her.

Rolling to her side, she noticed the time—almost 10:00 a.m. *Wow.* She scrubbed her hand across her eyes. She'd slept half the morning away, the pregnancy sleep deep and heavy, as if her body needed plenty of quiet time to nurture the life inside her. Moving a hand to her flat stomach and touching it through the silk nightgown she wore, she marveled to think that her child grew there. One day, she'd be able to share the wonders of snowfalls and Christmases with this baby.

Or Christmases, at least.

Of the many things she would miss when Jager was no longer in her life romantically, snow seemed like a small, frivolous addition to the list. How many times a day would she think about ways she would regret not having him in her life?

As she sat up, her forearm crumpled a piece of paper on the pillow beside her.

Puzzled, she reached for it and discovered Jager's handwriting on hotel stationery.

There is a breakfast tray outside your bedroom. Please take your time getting dressed. I left an outfit for you as I invited a special guest I think you will want to see this afternoon. —Jager

Special guest?

She wondered if he meant Damon. Or someone else in his family. Key word being *his*. Not hers.

Although for a surprisingly touching moment last night, she had wanted to hug Malcolm McNeill tight for his kindness to her. She'd started off the evening so irritated that the older man had put her on the spot, implying she was pregnant when she hadn't been ready to announce anything. Yet by the end of their eventful time together, she'd felt a keen understanding and affection for Jager's grandfather.

Was it the overdose of hormones that made her so emotional? Or was she so hypnotized by the idea of a paternal figure that even Jager's bossy grandparent could win her over that fast?

Planting her feet on the floor, she waited for any sign of morning sickness, but she felt good. Solid. Padding to the door, she opened it and peered out to see if Jager was around, but she spotted only the silver room service tray, as he'd promised.

She also saw a huge, decorated Christmas tree in the living area that hadn't been there the night before. Red ribbons festooned the branches along with multicolored lights and ornaments that looked like…skyscrapers?

Unable to resist, she hurried closer, hugging her arms around herself to ward off the chill from seeing snow outside.

The ornaments were all New York themed. The Empire State Building and the Chrysler Building shone bright in the glow of tree lights. The Statue of Liberty hung from another branch, along with taxicabs, hansom carriages and even The Plaza Hotel with the flags flying on the front. Some of the decorations she'd seen at Rockefeller Center were represented, including the white angels blowing their trumpets and the gilded bronze Prometheus statue that presided over the ice skating rink.

The tree, the scent of pine that filled the room, it all mesmerized her, putting her in the holiday spirit. And outside in Central Park, that dizzying white snowfall coated the trees.

Had Jager done all this? Well, all this except the snowfall? Even a McNeill couldn't make demands of Mother Nature.

Delia wondered if this was his way of... No. She squelched the hopeful thought as she ignored the breakfast tray and jumped in the shower. She was unwilling to build up her expectations all over again. She would speak to Jager. Ask him about realistic goals for co-parenting in the future and plan accordingly. He might break her heart, but she couldn't afford to indulge that hurt. She had to be mature and responsible for her child.

No more running away from her problems on a Jet Ski.

An hour later, she finished drying her hair and dressed in the outfit she'd found on the lower shelf of the room service tray: a simple red velvet dress with a black ribbon sash. As if that wasn't decadent enough, there were red velvet heels with skinny ankle straps. Both boxes were stamped with designer logos from exclusive New York boutiques. And everything fit her perfectly.

She checked her reflection and wondered if it was wrong of her to wear the gifts after what she'd done the night before. Then again, maybe wearing the clothes was a conciliatory gesture. She didn't want to appear ungrateful after all Jager had done for her.

They'd been friends first. She wished there was a way they could maintain that friendship somehow. But there would be no going back now. Not after everything they'd shared.

Blinking fast before her emotions swallowed her whole, she braced herself for whatever awaited her in the next room. She thought she'd heard Jager return when she first emerged from the shower, but she'd done as he asked and taken her time getting ready for whatever special guest he'd brought. Fully expecting to see Damon when she opened the bedroom door, her brain couldn't process what—who—she saw.

Her father?

She blinked, but sure enough the vision stayed the same.

Pascal Rickard sat on the couch in front of the Christmas tree, a glass of eggnog in his hand.

"Dad?" she asked so softly she wasn't sure how he heard.

But he shifted on his cushion, turning toward her before getting to his feet slowly. Behind him, Jager rose as well. It was a sign of how stunned she was that she'd missed him sitting there.

"Hello, Delia." Her father placed his drink on the coffee table to greet her, but didn't move closer.

She looked over at Jager, seeking an explanation, something to account for this visit.

He cleared his throat. "I'm going to leave the two of you to talk." Jager grabbed his long wool coat from a chair by the door. His face was freshly shaven, but there were shadows under his eyes, making her wonder how late he'd stayed up with his brother the night before. "I told Damon I'd meet with him today about the sale of his company. Bring him up to speed."

She nodded, too dazed by her father's presence to think beyond that. When the door closed behind Jager, she moved toward her father, arching up on her toes to kiss his weathered cheek in a rare display of affection.

between them. But if he left his boat to fly halfway around the world to see her, she thought the moment warranted it.

To her surprise, he wrapped her in a hug with his good arm. She laid her head against his chest, noticing his clean new sweater and the heavy sigh he heaved.

She levered away to look up at him. "I can't believe you're here. Is everything all right back home?"

"Things are good. Better than good, actually." He pointed to the couch. "Let's sit."

"I didn't know you were coming." She dropped onto the cushion beside him, facing the Christmas tree that cast a warm golden glow on both of them.

Outside, the snowfall made the day feel cozy, the lack of sunlight making the tree lights more prominent in the room.

"I spoke to Jager last week." He picked up his eggnog and had another sip. Beside his glass there was a plate of sugar cookies shaped like snowmen that must have been delivered by room service. "He came back to town to ask if I would visit you here for Christmas."

"Jager." Of course that accounted for her father being here. He could have never afforded the plane ticket otherwise. "Why? I mean, I'm glad to see you. I'm just surprised he didn't mention it."

"He said he wanted it to be a surprise." Her dad's face had aged in the last few years—more than she'd noticed when they visited to announce her pregnancy. The weathered lines from his years in the sun were deeper, his pallor grayer. "I know I was surprised myself when he showed up. He apologized for being abrupt in the other visit when you both came to see me that day. Asked how he could help out. He said he wanted to provide for you and—for me too."

"That was thoughtful of him," she said carefully, not sure how her proud parent would view that kind of offer.

"It was a damn sight more than thoughtful," he grumbled, swiping a snowman cookie and crunching into it. After a contemplative moment, he said, "He offered to have my boat fixed and my roof patched. And made a deal with me and a few of my friends to provide the seafood for the Birdsong Hotel."

Gabe's resort property.

"He did?" She knew what that meant. Her father could take it easy. There would be no more stress about selling what he caught. Thinking about Jager doing those things for her father—for her—made her eyes sting with sharp gratitude. He'd never even mentioned it to her.

"I told him no—about the boat and roof, not about the seafood deal because I'm still a businessman and I've got bills too, bills I can now afford to pay." He pointed at her with the cookie, the half-eaten snowman taking some of the fire out of his emphatic words.

"But he insisted on the rest too, didn't he?" She already knew the answer. Two years of working for Jager McNeill had shown her that he drove a hard bargain. Weeks of being his lover, even when she'd been ducking his texts and afraid to face him, had shown her he was persistent and caring where she was concerned.

She was so touched. She couldn't stop loving him if she tried.

"Wouldn't take no for an answer. What's more, he gave me this passbook for a bank account with both our names on it—yours and mine." He dug in the pocket of his jacket he'd draped over the couch arm and then slapped a bankbook down on the coffee table. "It's got a balance in it already. Enough to pay the Rickard property taxes for years to come, so we don't have to worry each year about how we'll hang onto the land."

He sounded indignant. But also…amazed.

Her father, the stoic fisherman, had been bowled over by Jager's kindness. She was too. Yet she wasn't at all surprised.

"He's a good man." Her eyes stung more, as she wished there was a way for her to reach Jager's heart.

And wondered now if it was too late.

Had she been foolish to reject him when he had so much to offer beyond the words she longed to hear?

"I wasn't convinced." Her father passed her the tray of cookies. "Have you eaten? These are good."

She took one even though she craved the rest of this story more than the sweet. "What do you mean you weren't convinced?"

"I told him my daughter couldn't be bought." He set the tray down awkwardly, with cookies sliding every which way but somehow managing to stay on the plate. "You know what he said? He said you'd earned far more than what the land was worth doing a CEO's job over at that mansion of his. Any truth to that?"

A flutter of pride swelled her chest to hear Jager's praise. To know that he'd shared it with her father. "I'm not sure, Daddy. But I did run the property for almost a year while he was away."

No doubt about it, she still craved her father's approval.

"Sounds like a CEO to me." There was an assessing light in his eyes. "I told him my daughter and I are cut from the same hardworking cloth. You're like me in that we don't need a lot of recognition or praise. We just quietly get our jobs done."

Is that what he thought? That she didn't need to be told how important she was? Or special? New understanding slid into place.

"I think everyone likes to be recognized sometimes." She set her cookie aside, unable to eat until she told her father how she felt. If she could blurt out her feelings to a total stranger like Malcolm McNeill, surely she could tell her dad. "When I was growing up, I wondered some days if you even noticed what I did to help around the house or prepare the boat for your trips."

"Ah, kiddo," he said brusquely, shaking his head. "I bragged to everyone in town that I had the hardestworking daughter for miles." He stared down for a minute and she didn't say anything.

Waiting.

Needing more from him.

"Delia, I know I wasn't the best father. I was already so damn old when you came along, and I missed your mother so much. Still do. It sounds crazy when I only knew her for a few years before you were born. I've been without her so much longer than I was with her. But I loved her so hard she left a hole."

The anguish in his eyes was the deepest, truest emotion he'd ever let her witness. And while she was grateful for the insight into her father's heart after a lifetime of wishing for his love, a flash of deep self-realization hit her.

She also understood in that moment why she couldn't walk away from Jager.

What if something happened to him and she was the one left with a hole in her heart? How much would she regret the time she wasted that she could have been loving him?

For that matter, maybe instead of worrying about

how her father felt about her, she could simply share how she felt for him. She covered his hand with hers and squeezed.

"Thank you for sharing that. I love you, Daddy," she told him. "I'm going to be so proud to introduce you to your grandchild."

He closed his eyes for a long moment. When he opened them, she saw a new tenderness there. "Love you too, missy. And I never did deserve such a good girl, but I sure am proud of you."

He wrapped his arm around her and kissed the top of her head. Delia let herself rest in the moment, in the gift of finally having a connection to her dad.

"Can I ask you a question?" She angled back to look at him.

"Sure thing." His gaze darted around, as if he was embarrassed by the emotion. When his focus landed on the cookies, he seized another frosted snowman.

"What did Jager say to convince you to come to New York?"

"He said he wanted to give you the best Christmas ever and he thought—for some crazy reason—that meant you might like to see your old man."

"He was right, you know. This is the best Christmas gift he could have given me." Well, one of the best. Having Jager's heart for a lifetime…that was something she couldn't deny she deeply craved and wasn't sure he could give.

But for the first time, she knew she had to risk it.

Her father shook his head. "I know I behaved badly when you told me about the baby, Delia. But you did shock the stuffing out of me when you showed up with that news."

She remembered the way he'd paled at her announcement, no doubt remembering his beloved wife who'd died in childbirth. "I was still reeling myself or I wouldn't have sprung it on you that way. I'm so glad you're here though."

"I got a new sweater out of the deal too." He rubbed a gnarled hand over the cream-colored wool. "It's a fisherman's sweater, you know. And I'll be damned but I never had one before." He flipped his wrist over suddenly to look at his watch. "That reminds me though. I made a deal with Jager to let him know when we finished our talk."

Straightening from the sofa, he reached for his jacket. So soon? She felt off-kilter from this day and it had only just started. But she'd already gotten two wonderful gifts.

An acceptance from her father she'd craved her whole lifetime. And a new determination to share her heart with Jager, no matter the cost.

"I hope we'll have more time to visit than that." She stood too, wondering what kind of arrangement Jager had made with her father. Apparently they'd been conversing often in the last weeks. "You just got here and I've been a neglectful daughter these last two years."

"Nonsense." He brushed aside her worry with a wave. "You had a plantation house to run, for Pete's sake. Besides, I've got some sightseeing to do today while you…do other things." He pointed toward the door. "I've got a room down the hall, you know. And tomorrow is Christmas."

She followed him to the door, the red velvet skirt of her long dress swishing pleasantly around her legs. She'd worn the snowflake earrings too because it was Christmas Eve, after all, and the dress called for festive jewelry even if it was only noontime.

"See you soon then?" she asked, fitting in one more hug before he left.

"For sure. We'll see each other tomorrow. Merry Christmas, Delia."

She smiled, inside and out, to have a holiday to look forward to with her father. How many other Christmases had he spent at sea while she'd been at home by herself?

Peering down the corridor after him, she watched his slightly bent form and his wide-legged seamen's walk as he departed. He barely paused his stride to knock twice on a door down the hall. Damon's room, she guessed, where Jager was visiting with his brother.

Her mind swirling with thoughts, her nerves alight with apprehension, she ducked back into their suite, shutting the door behind her and pressing her spine to it for a moment while she caught her breath. Was Jager on his way back now?

And what should she say about last night and her public refusal to marry him? He'd arranged for her father's trip and the tree before the blow she'd dealt him in front of his family. Had she damaged beyond repair what little chance they may have had together? She wished she could take those words back.

All she could do now was not waste whatever time they had left. To make his Christmas as special as he'd tried to make hers.

Jager knocked before he opened the hotel door with his pass card, wanting to warn Delia he was here. Things had ended so awkwardly between them last night, so he wanted to be as considerate as possible.

Bringing Pascal to New York had been a shot in the

dark, and he had no idea if the surly fisherman had mended his relationship with his daughter. But after hearing her dad's quick knock at Damon's door, Jager knew the time had come for him to face Delia himself. To salvage whatever he could of their relationship.

And while he wanted that to be marriage and forever, he was going to try to be patient. Hear her out. Understand her misgivings before he tackled them, one by one, to show her how good they could be together.

"Delia?" He didn't see her in the living area by the noble fir he'd ordered before dawn. The hotel staff had been excited to help him decorate while Delia slept.

"Coming," she called from her bedroom. "I'm just finishing up something."

"How are you feeling?" He laid his overcoat on a chair, noticing the flurries still swirling outside. It was picture-perfect, snow globe weather.

"Good." Her response was quick, coming a moment before she breezed into the room, looking so beautiful she took his breath away.

"You look...so very lovely." He couldn't imagine not having her in his life—as his wife. Not being there with her to share moments in their child's life.

"It's a gorgeous dress." She swayed slightly, a sweet feminine movement that sent the skirt swirling around her legs. "I love how it feels."

"It's not the dress." He wanted to reach out to her. To hold her. "It's all you."

Her hazel eyes tracked his, as if she was trying to gauge his mood. He remembered what Damon said about how he was hard to read—like his half brother Quinn. So, digging deeper, he stepped closer. Picked up her hand.

She held a paper, still warm from the in-room printer.

he set it hastily aside, making him curious, but mostly grateful that she let him touch her this way. He bent to kiss the back of her fingers.

"I'm so sorry for the fiasco at my grandfather's last night."

"I'm not." She bit her lip. "That is, I'm sorry that I got upset and blurted out words I didn't mean in front of your family. But I'm not at all sorry I moved past that and got to talk with them and get to know them. I actually think Malcolm is kind of great."

Jager hung on to the first part of what she said—about being sorry for blurting words she didn't mean—so he almost missed the rest. Did she regret her announcement that they wouldn't marry? Or something else?

He backed up a step so they could sit near the tree, bringing her with him and drawing her down to the couch.

"You don't mind that Malcolm rudely called out your pregnancy in front of a room full of strangers?" He started there, dealing with the less thorny question first.

The one less inclined to shred him.

"They weren't strangers though. But yes, I did mind. That's why I gave such a knee-jerk response, and I'm sorry for that. Very sorry." She squeezed his hand in both of hers. "Whatever happens with our relationship, I do think it's between us and none of their business, no matter how many wills and contracts he draws up to try to maneuver his grandsons."

"Whatever happens," he repeated carefully, sounding out the words like a kid reading his first book. Damn, but he was far gone for this woman. "Meaning, you haven't closed the door on a marriage down the road."

"No," she said breathlessly, before looking down for

a moment, and when she met his gaze again, her hazel eyes were a brighter green, lit with some new emotion behind them. "All this time, I've been so determined to avoid a loveless marriage. But what I realized today, while I was talking to my father, is that a union between us could never be a loveless marriage. Not even close. Because I love you, Jager."

His chest swelled with love for her, even as he regretted he hadn't been the one to say those words first when he knew how much they meant to her.

Her declaration leveled every plan he'd made to win her back. Detonated the elaborate presents and gestures he'd orchestrated for the best Christmas. Because she'd just given him the most perfect gift of all.

"Delia. My love." He shook his head, scrambling to get this right without all the plans. To go off script for the most important moment of his life. "I have been planning for days to prove my love to you. To *show* you how I feel so that you would believe it, deep in your heart." Damn, but she humbled him. "Yet in a single moment, you showed me how powerful those three simple words are all on their own."

Her smile was happy. Secure. Certain.

"I was almost afraid to hope when I saw the tree. And my father." She bit her lip, but it wasn't nervousness. It was like she was trying to hold back her excitement before it burst right out of her. "Your gift inspired me to take a risk on that hope and to give you something too."

She started to reach for the paper she'd set aside and he stayed her hand.

"Wait. It's my turn to give you something first." He withdrew the ring he'd had made for her. "Delia. Love.

f my life. I would be more honored than I can say if ou would be my wife."

Eyes wide, she gasped when she saw the ring. "It's heart."

"You've had mine in the palm of your hand ever nce the day you nearly mowed me down on a Jet Ski." e held the ring over her left hand, waiting for her per- ission to slide it in place. "It's only fitting you wear here, where you can see it every single day, and re- member how much I love you."

"Yes." She nodded, and then kissed his left cheek nd stroked his right with tender fingers. "Yes, I will arry you, Jager, and be your wife."

As he slid the ring home, he realized he'd been hold- g his breath. She did that to him.

"I'm going to remember, every day, how powerful ose words are," he vowed, so grateful to have her in is life and in his heart.

Forever.

"Do you want to see my present?" she asked, curling ato him, her silken hair clinging to his cheek.

"You've already given me more than any man de- erves. But I'd be glad for any gift from you."

She reached for the paper that she'd been printing hen he walked into their suite. In the warm glow of e Christmas tree lights, he could see that she'd printed e application for a marriage license.

"I wanted to show you that I didn't mean what I said your grandfather's house." She peered up at him.

Jager kissed her nose. "You're going to be the most eautiful Christmas bride."

"Can we invite your family?" She straightened on e couch, so full of hope and happiness that he felt too.

"We'll invite *our* family," he assured her. "Ever
last one of them."

She wrapped her slender arms around him, and h
wondered if she'd ever know how much he loved he
Thankfully, he had a whole lifetime to show her. Star
ing right now.

Epilogue

One week later

"You may now kiss the bride." The young, ruddy-faced justice of the peace closed his officiant's book and grinned broadly at Delia and Jager.

They stood side by side for their New Year's Eve wedding at The Plaza Hotel in the famed Palm Court, which Malcolm McNeill had bought out for a few hours to enjoy a private, late-afternoon ceremony. Delia wore a specially designed gown from an up-and-coming designer friend of Lydia's, who had fully delivered on Delia's request for a fairy-tale dress. Off-the-shoulder chiffon, fitted through the bodice and waist, the dress had a full skirt and short train worthy of any princess. Delia carried red roses and poinsettias, her heart-shaped ring firmly in place on her finger for a lifetime.

"My wife." Jager's quiet words, spoken as his lips

hovered just above hers, gave the happy moment a power and meaning that she understood deeply. "My love."

The kiss that sealed their promise made her lightheaded with joy. Or maybe it was the sentiment he expressed, since it was echoed in her own heart.

"Congratulations, Mr. and Mrs. McNeill." The justice of the peace's words called her back to the reality of the wedding day, and reminded her that they weren't just celebrating their marriage.

Turning toward their small group of assembled guests, Delia knew that promise she'd just made was also a celebration of family. A wonderful new chapter for all of the McNeills, who had taken the first slow steps toward making peace. Toward giving Malcolm McNeill the united kin he dearly craved.

She glanced his way now, and saw the happy tears in his eyes. He didn't even bother to hide them. He was the exact opposite of her father, who of course chose that moment to put his fingers between his teeth and let out a wolf whistle. Cameron McNeill seemed to like this salute to the new couple, and he did the same thing, filling the air with their whistled approval.

"I think that means they want us to kiss again," Jager suggested in her ear. He hadn't let go of her hand since they'd exchanged rings.

Or maybe it was she who couldn't let go of him.

"I think you're right." She kissed her husband again, for longer this time.

She kissed him until the room broke into applause and cheers. But soon decorum prevailed and her cheeks heated just a little.

Jager must have noticed, because he gave one warm cheek a kiss before he drew her over to the dance floor, where they had agreed to share a first dance as man and wife before a meal with the family.

"Shouldn't we thank everyone for coming first? Mingle?" Biting her lip, she peered back at the group seated under an archway of palms outlined with white lights for the holidays.

They hadn't spent a lot of time planning their wedding since they'd only invited family, but Delia was new to having so many siblings-in-law and she wanted to entertain them well. Do things right. Make sure they had fun.

"We'll visit with them soon enough." Jager's blue gaze was for her alone.

And from the heated flame in their depths, she knew he wasn't thinking about family.

"Then I guess I'll follow your lead, husband." She set her bouquet aside as the chamber orchestra began the opening strains of their wedding song.

"I wouldn't steer you wrong," he assured her, nibbling at her neck as they turned together on the small parquet floor. "I taught you to ice skate after all."

It was such a happy memory. And they had so many more left to make together.

"I trust you." She followed his steps, letting him guide her as they twirled past a waiter bringing in the wedding cake, which consisted of layers and layers of red velvet iced in white. She didn't need to see the cake to know the bride-and-groom topper danced inside a snow globe. She'd adored the magical romance of the pretty decoration, so fitting for how she'd fallen in love.

"Should we make New York a yearly trip at Christmastime?" Jager asked, and she guessed his thoughts were following the same line as hers. "We'll have to introduce our child to his or her great grandfather nex year."

She couldn't wait for her second ultrasound appoint ment two days from now, before they flew back to Mar tinique. It was too soon to determine gender, of course but she wanted to see their baby.

"I'll be surprised if Malcolm waits that long for a meeting." She'd had fun visiting with the older man in their two trips to the McNeill mansion since that dubi ous first meeting. He had been overjoyed at the news of the marriage, all the more so since he'd been afraid he'd driven a wedge between Delia and Jager.

"He is a family man, through and through," Jager admitted. He and Damon had agreed that they would try salvaging a relationship with this branch of the family.

Gabe, with his own child to consider, had been game all along. He was already in discussions with his half brothers about taking over some of the Caribbean prop erties.

"How do you think your brothers will fare with the marriage maneuvers?" She was worried about Damon

He had stayed in New York to attend the wedding but there was a deep sadness in his eyes even at happy times.

"They'll set the old man straight," Jager said with certainty as the closing bars of their song filled the room. "Malcolm McNeill might be growing on me as a person, and as a grandfather. But that doesn't mean he controls us."

Delia glided to a stop, peering over at the patriarch surrounded by grandsons who obviously adored him Even Damon sat close by, listening intently to some thing Malcolm had to say.

It warmed her heart. But then, everything about this day did.

"I love you so much, Jager." Happy tears welled up, as they had all week, and she knew it didn't have anything to do with pregnancy hormones.

Jager kissed her, giving her a moment to compose herself. A moment to savor how perfect and special this day was.

"I love you, Delia." His words wrapped around her as surely as his arms. "More than I can ever say."

* * * * *

MILLS & BOON®

Desire™

PASSIONATE AND DRAMATIC LOVE STORIES

YOU LOVE ROMANCE?

WE LOVE ROMANCE!

For exclusive extracts, competitions and special offers, find us online:

- **f** facebook.com/millsandboon
- **🐦** @MillsandBoon
- **📷** @MillsandBoonUK

Visit millsandboon.co.uk